A Court of Wolves and Witches

Rockwell Pack, Book One

Rose Gravestone

To both my insomnia and the nightmares that inevitably come when I do sleep, I couldn't have done this without you—at least you're good for something.

To my family, especially my maternal family, who have never been anything but incredibly supportive: you'll never read this book if I have anything to say about it, but you're in my thoughts and thanks all the same.

Author's Note

Hello lovely readers and welcome to A Court of Wolves and Witches.

This is my first published book, so most of you won't know that I will be writing dark romance. The extent of the darkness in the romance will vary from book to book and series to series—this one is rather dark. It contains violence and gore, dubious sexual situations, a morally grey hero willing to do whatever it takes to keep his mate, including manipulating her, and a mythical mate-bond that makes saying no rather difficult for the heroine, even when she's thinking it. The heroine, who's by no means a pushover, will fight the anti-hero tooth and nail for her freedom.

This is the first book in a duet that will kickstart the Rockwell Pack series. It ends on a cliffhanger, and the story between the main characters will be concluded in the next book.

Contents

Prologue

Camden Kent

I stare silently at the Rockwell Pack's witch doctor as he sits across from me at a large wooden desk. We're in the room he uses for his practices and studies, an eccentric space full of books stacked haphazardly on bookshelves with hundreds of herbs and ingredients bursting from every visible surface.

The room always has a lingering scent of sage, as Claude cleanses his space after every ritual, but today there's also the fresh scent of jasmine to accompany it. Jasmine, which will be used in a mixture for a ritual to help locate my soulmate.

"You know the dangers that are associated with such a ritual, Camden." Claude's tone is harsh, and if it were anyone else who spoke to me that way, they might be jailed before their next breath, but Claude is an exception. He goes on, "Good things come to those who wait, and the fates will punish those who don't. I don't want to see you suffer more than you already have...lose more than you already have."

I know he's right, as all shifters are taught that trying to tamper with the timeline on which we'll find our better half will merely tempt the gods to make our lives difficult in turn. Nevertheless, I'm not afforded luxuries such as time. I have not only a kingdom but an empire to run; an empire that's under mounting threats from enemies.

"Almost every shifter finds their soulmate by the time they're thirty, before they hit their prime of power and virility," I point out. "I'm four years past that deadline, and my patience is running thin, old man."

As Alpha, it's past time for me to have my Alpha female. And as a man responsible for several continents worth of shifters, sitting on a throne of absolute power that's currently being threatened, I can wait no longer.

Claude's deeply tanned face is set in a mask of concern that emphasizes the wrinkles on his forehead as he regards me. "The gods will put your mate in your path when the time is right. Don't tempt their wrath, Camden. It *never* goes well."

"The vampires are assimilating their numbers on Earth." My tone is mild. "Their nature is as dominant as ours; they will do their best to replace us in this realm's power structure. I need to be at full strength when they attack."

I have no option but to be ready for the upcoming battles that grow nearer with each day. Full strength means having fused my half of the soul with the woman who holds the other; without it, I can't properly protect my kind.

Claude shakes his head, tying his shoulder-length silver hair back with a ribbon, before fixing me with a hard stare. "This is not how shifters behave, *especially* wolves. We do not cut corners; that is the way humans brought about their own end. They became reliant on technology which turned them passive. You should take caution from the lesson they proved to be."

"Their reliance on said technology made our invasion from Myth-icacia shockingly simple," I say, referencing our home realm. "It's almost fortunate that many of their gadgets let off that pesky high-frequency noise that hurt our ears and prompted us to be rid of them. One strong electromagnetic pulse toppled their technology. After that, human societies tumbled with remarkable ease."

Most humans fell right alongside them. Without the benefit of planes, cars, phones, and other devices, we didn't even have to go to war with them—they died out on their own.

Humans are different from mythics; for one, they have no magical blood running through their veins, making them highly fallible and easy to kill. For another, the Earth realm is not home to any native magical beings. Nature itself on Earth is alight with magic, but there have been no offspring of said magic here for centuries—the last recorded earthly witch was a monarch in the late 1700s, whose magic died with her bloodline long ago.

Since humans never sensed the magic they were gifted through nature, they tore down much of it—most of their natural resources, in fact—to suit their own selfish needs.

Claude releases a sullen sigh. "Listen to this old man, for I have wisdom imparted by age. I was there when your grandfather invaded this planet nearly two centuries ago; I *opened the portal* that led to it. I watched the feline and dragon shifters trickle in after us, observed as the sirens, witches, fey, and most recently vampires followed from our native Mythicacia, in search of better lands. I helped your grandfather establish shifters as the most dominant figure through our hierarchy and watched the human population wane as a result of the changes he imposed."

"Do you have a point?" I cut in.

Claude goes on as if I hadn't spoken. "Not once did your grandfather attempt to take the easy route. He put in the hard work it took to get us shifters and *all* mythics where they are today, on a planet lush with resources absent in our homes. If he'd cut corners, he'd have been unable to build the shifter empire of Acuria—an empire that has a grip on this entire planet, with shifter packs scattered across every continent."

Not only did my grandfather build this empire but he brought with it the hierarchal structure from our home realm—a pyramid structure, where stronger packs sit higher in rank, and weaker packs sit at the bottom. The strong protect the weak, and the Rockwell Pack, of which I'm Alpha, rules over all of them. So, when the time comes for war, I will be the commanding Alpha—the monarch all shifters will look to for guidance, advice, and protection. For that, I need to be prepared.

"I'm not cutting corners, I'm using the tools at my disposal to do what needs to be done, just like my grandfather did," I growl.

I've been raised on stories of the great conquests of my grandfather, and at this point, I've grown tired of hearing about his superiority. He never faced a war with a species as powerful as vampires; his job was one of cleansing and rebuilding this world, not protecting it from forces that threaten to bring about our end.

"I swore to your mother, gods rest her soul, that I'd guide and protect you on the day of your birth," Claude tells me. "Your father's deterioration in recent years from the severing of their mate bond, combined with your obstinance, have indeed made it difficult for me to stand by my vow. Still, it is my duty to tell you that I cannot condone this ritual. You are my king, so if you order me to, I will perform it, but I advise *strongly* against it."

Claude is the royal family's official witch doctor, one of few wolves in existence who's able to wield magic. He's walked the realms for a long time—longer than any other living shifter, to my knowledge—an added benefit of his dualistic nature as a hybrid, a cross between a witch and shifter wolf. While I usually hold his advice in high regard, the simple fact of the matter is I need my mate.

"I don't have another choice," I say, growing irritated with his protests. "I might be capable of ruling alone, but I cannot lead our people into battle alone. I *need* my mate, whoever she may be. Even if she is human, she will complete me in a way the packs around the globe require from their leader."

Beyond the resources, shifters draw to Earth was that many had found their soulmates in humans upon entry to this realm. It's exceedingly rare for soulmates to be members of other mythic species, but for some reason, people of Earth have indeed made many soulmates for various mythic species. Regardless of whether a shifter's mate is human or another shifter, a fully fused soul often doubles and sometimes triples the power that mythics have before being bound.

After a long moment of watching me, gauging my sincerity, Claude gives me a single resigned nod. "Very well. Let's begin."

He's already ruled out my mate being from my home realm via an earlier ritual, which indicates that whoever my Alpha female may be, she lives on Earth, and is quite possibly a human.

My eyes wander around the extensive map laid on the surface of the table between me and Claude, taking in all the many pack territories as well as human villages. When shifters first invaded, we were horrified at the monstrous structures humans had built and the technology they'd developed. Now, there are villages and towns for humans, and territories for packs—where far more eco-friendly cities reside.

Claude grinds various herbs in his mortar with a sturdy pestle, quietly chanting words under his breath. I've witnessed him perform many rituals—most for healing—but the magic he wields never fails to intrigue me. Primarily because shifter witch doctors are in very short supply, *especially* ones as powerful as him.

He sets the mortar on the wooden desk, hovers his hands over it, closes his eyes, and continues chanting. After a moment, the herbs float from the mortar, forming a cloud of sorts, and begin traveling over the map. A niggling sense of anticipation and excitement unfurls within me.

The cloud of herb debris stops its travel over the map, and after hovering for a moment, drops. I stand from my seat and lean over the table to see where the mixture indicates I'll find my mate.

"Aesara," I murmur. A small, rural human village in the mid-west of the former North American continent, renamed Acuria upon the mythic invasion. It's merely a day's ride from Kinrith, the Rockwell Pack's capital, where my family's seat of power resides.

If I recall correctly, the village of Aesara is known for its bursting trade market that caters to other human villages within a hundred-mile radius despite being rather small and sparsely populated.

The complication of having a human mate mainly lies in the delicacy of their composition. I don't care on a personal level that she's human; if she was gifted to me by the gods then that's good enough for me, but the fact that humans are so breakable by nature is cause for concern. Fortunately, once the bond is formed and strong enough—with the aid of a mark and consummation—she'll gain some of my speed, power, and accelerated healing. That, mixed with my watchful eye, will ensure her safety for as long as we live.

A small smile curls my lips—a rare occurrence really. "*There* you are."

Chapter One

Sierra West

The feeling of a sudden weight jumping onto my chest yanks me out of my fitful sleep. My eyes pop open and I find myself staring into my younger sister's smiling golden eyes.

Leisel throws her arms around me in a hug, kisses my cheek, and chirps, "Good morning!"

Despite the fatigue still weighing on me, I can't help but return her smile. The nine-year-old is always bursting with energy and wakes me almost every morning like this. I wrap my arms around her and hug her in turn, also lightly kissing her cheek.

"Morning, trouble," I murmur, pushing myself upright.

Chip, the small chipmunk Leisel saved from a ferret in the forest years ago, is sitting on her shoulder as usual. The two have been inseparable since Leisel found him, and anywhere she goes, he goes. I give his soft fur a gentle stroke in greeting before stretching my arms over my head and wincing at the crick in my neck.

"Have you already washed up?" I ask Leisel, setting her on the mattress next to me. Leisel is fourteen years my junior, and in the absence of our parents, I've raised her as my own daughter more than as a sister.

It was my mother's last wish, right before she passed away giving birth to Leisel. If mythics hadn't invaded the Earth and destroyed most of our technology and way of life, Mom could've gotten proper medical treatment to keep her alive. Unfortunately, such things haven't been available to humans for more than two centuries. Now, there are only stories and rumors about how advanced our world used to be.

"Yep," she responds. "Chip has too."

I nod, suppressing a yawn, and slowly stand from my dingy bed. "Give me a few minutes to do the same, and I'll get started on breakfast," I tell her.

With a brilliant smile, she tosses her long strawberry-blonde hair over her shoulder and happily skips out of the room.

In a world of darkness, Leisel has always been a bright ray of sunlight. That's likely why all the villagers in Aesara adore her—despite the difficult, unyielding times we live in, she's always a bubbly presence.

I take a quick shower, trying to conserve water as much as possible. The bits of technology mythics have allowed us to retain are minimal; primarily electricity, just enough to power running water, stoves, and lights. Everything else, items that didn't suit their needs, was destroyed.

In the beginning, there were massive rebellions against this. Humans were rightfully angry that *our* world was being invaded, *our* technology destroyed, *our* lives upended. Those rebellions were quelled swiftly by shifters, who were the first mythics to invade. It was easy to see that they outclassed us in just about every way and that we didn't stand a chance.

Now we scrape by however possible. Some are more fortunate than others; those who have learned to make the best of what they can. But no human is truly *fortunate* these days. The gilded ages of human monarchies and people living in extravagance are now only stories in old books.

After brushing my teeth with an herbal paste bought in the village market, I get dressed in worn-down, somewhat tattered clothing. Then, winding my red hair into a bun, I head through a small hallway into the kitchen and living area.

The cabin we inherited from our parents is modest, a one-story home with a living room and kitchen combined into one space, two bedrooms, one bathroom, and a spare room that I use to paint whenever I can find the time. Our home is on the very edge of our village, Aesara, and sits on a few acres of rich farmland, with a small stable that's home to two horses. It's bordered by a vast forest that makes excellent ground for hunting. Thanks to my mother and father, we have everything we need to sustain ourselves—an abundance of fruits, vegetables, and grains I grow and harvest each year to sell or trade in the market of Aesara.

Although my father died when I was thirteen, days before my mother found out she was pregnant, he'd already taught me everything I needed to know about hunting and harvesting. Both are gifts that have allowed me to provide as comfortable a life as possible for Leisel.

Leisel's already sitting at our small circular wooden dining table, leafing through a book. Another thing we inherited from our parents was a small, albeit rich in literature, collection of books. My father was an avid Shakespeare reader, my mother loved all classics, and after their deaths, Leisel and I were left with about a hundred books of our own that are stacked around the house. That's a far greater sum than can be found even in our village's old bookshop.

"What are you reading?" I ask her, walking over to the stove to start on breakfast. Oatmeal for Leisel and fresh fruit plucked off our land for me as always, and a handful of grains for Chip.

"The Pearl," Leisel responds absently.

I smile. "Ah, Steinbeck. Wonderful author. Tell me about what you've read so far."

Education is in very scarce supply these days, and the majority of schooling is done from home. Along with a rich book collection, my mother left several textbooks for me—on topics ranging from math to languages to science and even farming techniques. She taught me various subjects from the time I can remember until her death. From there, I used what I'd learned to teach both myself and later Leisel.

I listen as Leisel gives me a synopsis of what she's read so far, nodding along while preparing our breakfast. By the time I set our bowls on the table, she's moved on from talking to me and is back to reading while absently petting Chip.

I drop a handful of nuts onto the wooden surface of the table by Leisel's bowl for Chip as well as a strawberry, and he quickly runs down Leisel's arm to get to his breakfast.

As we eat, I say, "I'm going to muck out the stables after breakfast—I expect you to have finished with your history lesson once I'm back, and we'll go over it." Leisel, like I was, is an incredibly advanced student—we're already going over ninth-grade textbook material, years ahead of her educational age range.

"History is so boring," she mutters with a pout.

I chuckle. "I didn't like it much, either, but it's important nonetheless. We'll have lunch, and after that, I'll be in the forest for an hour or two emptying out traps and hunting, during which time you'll have your English lesson. Once we've gone over that, if you're up to it, I think you're ready for the next chapter in our spell book."

That offer *really* gets Leisel's attention, and her eyes widen with excitement. "The one about wards?"

Along with our collection of classic literature and textbooks, my mother left behind a few ancient books, of which there are a very limited number of copies in the world. Books of witchcraft—books that were passed through the generations of my mother's bloodline.

"Yes," I tell Leisel, scooping up a bit of oatmeal along with a strawberry on my wooden spoon. Once I've chewed and swallowed the bite I say, "The chapter also goes over beseeching favor of the gods."

As far as everyone is concerned, there are no longer such things as earthly witches, *human* witches. They simply don't exist in the eyes of those on Earth. The population of both humans and mythics are blissfully unaware that there are still a number of human witches left, such as me and Leisel.

I was taught from birth to hide my magical blood because if anyone found out about it, I'd either be lusted after due to my powers or killed by those who fear such power. Another reason I'm grateful for living a distance away from the village is that Leisel and I can practice what little witchcraft I've learned without worrying about a nosy neighbor catching wind of our activities.

I only have one discernable magical power, but it's a rare one that my mother told me hadn't surfaced in thousands of years. Leisel only has one as well; the power to heal. Despite her young age, she's already remarkably capable and powerful. I suspect the reason Chip has lived for four years is because of his constant contact with Leisel. Her powers have expanded his lifespan, possibly indefinitely. My power, however, is geared much more to harm than help—hence why I'm particularly careful with it.

Leisel bounces up and down in her seat. "Can we start with that instead of history?"

I laugh. "You know the drill, sweet girl. First the boring, then the fun. After we're done with your studies and my work for the day we'll be heading into the town to trade and buy some food and supplies."

Her eyes brighten even more at that. Although I believe Leisel enjoys the little slice of paradise we live on, she's an incredibly social person and also loves spending time around other people. I try to take her into town at least a few times a week—sometimes simply to walk around and marvel at the bustling market Aesara is home to.

"Can we have beef stew for dinner?" she asks.

I smile, knowing it's her favorite dish. All of the recipes I know, I learned from my mother, who was a spectacular cook. She was a spectacular *everything*, a true role model. "Absolutely. Now finish up, I need to get going."

Chapter Two

Several hours later, once I've taken care of our stables, rubbed down the horses, fed Leisel lunch, gone over her lessons, and gone for a relatively bountiful hunt, we make our way into town.

I ride on the back of my gleaming-black stallion, Shadow, with a cart pulling behind us that contains fruits, vegetables, grains, and meats—rabbit and buck primarily—all separated in brown sacks. Leisel rides beside me on Duchess, a beautiful mare with a rich dark brown coat, who adores Leisel as much as Leisel adores her.

Chip is happily munching on a hazelnut, perched contentedly on Leisel's shoulder, enjoying the afternoon sun. Leisel refuses to go anywhere without him, so he's used to our regular visits into the village.

Aesara, as always, is bustling with trade. A market is set up in the large town square, with dozens of wooden vendor stalls for selling a variety of items lined up in rows. Bright clothes are on display along with other textiles, as well as knickknacks, tools, and foods of just about every kind. The smell of grilling meat wafts around, mixed with aromatic spices. Chatter fills the entire space as sellers and buyers negotiate, bargain, and haggle their way through sales.

As always, my first stop is the butcher's shop—a stone establishment on the very edge of the market. I dismount my stallion, help Leisel off her mare, and tie the reins of both horses to a post within reach of water buckets. Then, grabbing the quarry I've collected over the last few days, I lug the sack into the bright interior of the shop. Leisel hovers near our horses outside, since she doesn't much like the smell or energy of the shop. As a natural-born healer, I doubt she'll ever be capable of inflicting any harm, even when hunting is necessary for our survival.

The butcher, a seasoned man I've known since birth who was close friends with my parents, smiles as I walk in. He's a giant of a man with nut-brown skin and warm chocolate-colored eyes.

"Afternoon, Sierra," he greets, setting down his gleaming sharp knife and washing his hands in a small sink. "What do you have for me today?"

"Hello, Parker," I approach the display cabinet that separates us and hand him my sack. "The usual. Rabbit and buck, both skinned and partially cut up."

The plump man nods contentedly, unloading my haul onto a clean wooden board and sorting through the cuts of meat. "Excellent haul," he comments. "You know, you're getting quite handy with cutting up your catches. I could use an extra set of hands around here."

I laugh. Parker's been trying to get me to work for him for years—and I would if I didn't have a small farm to run on my own and a child to raise on top of it. Some days I'm truly shocked that I manage everything, and thank the gods for giving me a strong, healthy, and capable body. Without it, Leisel and I would've starved long ago.

"I already bring you meat several times a week, Parker. I'm afraid that's all I can manage with Leisel and the farm."

He glances up, brown eyes meeting mine. "Your parents would've been very proud of you."

I swallow around the clog of emotion that forms in my throat and blink a few times before looking away. I miss my parents every single day, pray to the gods for their souls each night, and despise mythics for being the reason for their downfall.

Papa's illness could've gotten treatment if hospitals and medications were still available to humans, and Mom wouldn't have bled out on her birthing table, leaving a frantic fourteen-year-old me to take care of an infant.

After a moment, when I know my voice won't crack, I murmur, "Thank you." Then, to lighten the subject, "I heard Wesley turned fifteen last week."

Parker nods. "Yep, and my boy's strong as an ox. He helps out here on occasion, but not nearly as much as I wish he did. He's out in the woods hunting now, otherwise he'd be around to entertain Leisel." Done sorting through what I've brought him, he says, "This'll fetch you a hundred silver coins. Sound fair?"

I nod. "Sure does."

One of the greatest reasons I value Parker is that he gives fair prices for my hauls, and never tries to swindle me. Money is in relatively scarce supply for humans these days, and I work overtime to ensure Leisel and I have enough to stay afloat—and some extra to save in case things ever go wrong.

"I'll throw in half a pound of beef, assuming Leisel will be wantin' your ma's famous stew?"

That brings a smile to my lips. After years of trading, not to mention having been friends with our parents and acquainted with Leisel and me since birth, Parker has come to know us quite well. "That'd be much appreciated, thanks."

He puts together a package of beef for me while we chat a little more about menial things, then hands me the brown package wrapped with a string and a small bag of coins for my haul. "My wife should already have your order ready at the bakery. You take care, now."

Leisel accompanies me as we walk around the market, selling our produce and grains to a vendor I'm familiar with, before buying groceries. I pick up a few new pencils and notebooks for her schooling and a mixture of herbs for myself that nobody would ever assume have magical uses. Then, impulsively, I buy a few new paints as well. It's markedly rare for me to have spare time during the day to paint—but I can normally squeeze in an hour once Leisel's gone to sleep.

My mother taught me to paint—it was her favorite thing to do, and she was a truly incredible artist. I'm nowhere near as good as she was, but painting always both relaxes and invigorates me. On occasion, I sell my paintings to the market in town. Despite the difficult times we live in, humans haven't yet stopped appreciating the beauty of art.

Our last stop, and Leisel's favorite, is the bakery. The owner is a grandmotherly woman married to Parker, with graying hair always up in a bun and a caretaker disposition. Mariketa hurries from around her counter to Leisel and me as soon as we step in, sweeping Leisel into a hug that nearly crushes poor Chip. She gives me a friendly pat on the back before looking me up and down and exclaiming, "By gods, girl, you're skin and bones! Come, let's get you sorted."

I'm at her shop three times a week, always requesting the same order, so she already has a basket prepared for me. Leisel's eyes brighten when Mariketa slips a few of her famous cookies into the basket, before taking only half the money I extend to her.

When I open my mouth to protest, she says, "Hush, child. I know runnin' a farm ain't cheap." Then, to Leisel, "Share those cookies with your sister, you hear? A strong gust of wind could blow both of you over."

Leisel giggles and thanks Mariketa, who then offers Chip a small chunk of bread which the little chipmunk happily accepts and immediately tucks away into the pouch of his cheek.

"Oh, before you go, make sure to lock your doors tight tonight. Word has it the Rockwell Pack will be passin' through to sniff out mates," she warns us.

The Rockwell Pack is the most powerful pack of shifters—and they reign over all other shifters on Earth, as well as most mythics. It's because of their imposed laws and cultures that humans were forced to live under such tumultuous conditions.

Many humans do, indeed, have reason to be worried—few have any interest in joining with those who upended our entire world. I've never batted an eye at packs passing through, however. From all the material I've read—and I have read plenty on mythics, everything I could get my hands on—those monsters are always either soulmates to one of their own species or humans. Leisel and I don't fall under either category—although our magic is Earth-bound, it makes us a slightly different species than humans. Therefore, we're nice and safe from the horrors that await humans when they're soulmates to a mythic.

Those horrors are *vast*. If you're a mate to a mythic, you're *forced* in close proximity to them. *Forced* to allow them to ravage your neck with a mark, forced to have sex with the beasts, and in the cases of females, forced to carry their offspring.

By my estimations, that's a fate worse than death. It's my deepest hope and wish that a plague targeting mythics alone sweeps through Earth, forcing them back to the realms they invaded from to leave humans in peace.

"Like they already do every year?" I question, raising an eyebrow.

Mariketa wrinkles her nose. "Not quite, child. The Alpha's family will be comin' through these parts too. Apparently, the Alpha and Beta are gettin' antsy about wantin' to find the other half of their souls." She shakes her head. "If Prometheus has any favor left for humans, those wretched men will both die alone.

"They deserve nothing less," I respond, my voice hardening. "Unfortunately, it seems the patron god of humans turned his back on us long ago, so I doubt we'll get any protection from him. We're on our own."

"Only thing worse that a shifter rogue is a shifter on the hunt for a mate, *especially* wolves," Mariketa says solemnly,

"At least you know what to expect from rogues: bloodlust and insanity. Shifters looking for mates, however, are completely unpredictable and have a habit of breaking down doors during their searches. I'll be sure to close mine extra tight."

Leisel takes my hand, giving it a tentative squeeze, and offers me a smile. I shake my head slightly, clearing the darkness of my thoughts, and smile back, before taking her home.

Chapter Three

Later that evening, once Leisel's tucked into her bed after having eaten twice her weight in beef stew, I ask her, "What story will it be tonight?"

A nightly tradition of ours is me reading to her. Most often she requests Shakespeare—just last night we finished Romeo and Juliet. Despite being relatively young, she has a surprising adoration of Shakespeare's works, tragedies and all. I suspect it's something she got from our father, gods rest his soul. He was a true lover of the classics and could quote most of Shakespeare's works by memory alone.

"Hamlet," she immediately requests. I long ago got over the worry that reading such tragic, sometimes gory plays would affect her bubbly disposition—*nothing* can affect it.

I nod, briefly leave her room to retrieve the worn old copy, and then make myself comfortable in a chair beside her bed before starting to read.

Chip's already sound asleep next to Leisel's head on her pillow, and it takes only twenty minutes for her to join him in dreamland. Once I'm sure she's in a deep sleep I stand, set down the book, and turn out the lights before leaving and quietly closing her door behind me.

Then, blowing out a deep breath, I get to work bolstering the protective wards I carved into every corner of the cabin years ago with the help of my mother. Pricking my finger with a sharp knife, I go to each symbol—a small conglomerate of squiggles, barely visible—and use a smidgen of my blood to power them up.

All witches have magical blood—even my mother, who never manifested any powers. The stronger the magic in your blood, the more effective it is in rituals and practices. Even though I have every confidence that the Rockwell Pack will see no reason to disgrace my home with their presence, it never hurts to have an extra boost of protection.

The symbols themselves, in essence, beseech the gods for favor and to protect the occupants of this residence. Adding my blood to them on occasion strengthens them. Although the wards aren't actually capable of keeping people out—I don't have access to spell work that powerful—at minimum they bring a bit of luck to my life.

Afterwards, I pour myself a small glass of wine—a delicacy I can only get my hands on maybe once every few months—and head to the spare room at the rear of the cabin, flicking on the lights. It's a modest studio of sorts. There's a rickety old desk set up in front of the window with a few palettes, an assortment of ancient brushes in a wooden cup, and a colorful array of paints in glass jars, along with smaller containers of pigments. On the edge of the desk stands a large tub of linseed oil.

In the center of the room is an easel, with my half-finished painting of a startlingly bright moon and sky full of stars above a forest propped on it. On the walls hang other paintings I've completed, and several of my mother's as well.

I head over to the table, set down my wine, and get to work mixing a few greens on a palette before moving in front of the easel and getting to work. The sky is almost done—it's the forest that needs the most work. I lose myself in the shades of the colors and the strokes of the brushes on the canvas.

Despite trying not to recall the past, I can't help but remember how many nights I watched my mother paint in this exact spot. My father would sometimes pull up a chair, and the three of us would discuss anything and everything. Then, when Papa passed away, it was just me and Mom here—but somehow, she never allowed me to be melancholy. Even though she was a single mother to a teenager with a baby on the way, her spirits were always high.

It's been many years since my parents passed, but I still feel their presence so acutely they might as well be here. I feel them every day while doing the things they taught me—caring for horses, farming, hunting, painting, teaching Leisel—and it never fails to make me miss them.

Truly, having Leisel in my life was the only thing that kept me going after Mom's death. I *had* to be capable for her, *had* to learn how to provide for both of us. There was no other option since I absolutely refused to lose yet another family member. If it had been just me, alone, I doubt I would've forced myself to become an adult and work as hard as I have.

It's just as I've finished my wine, and head to the kitchen to wash the glass in the sink that I feel a prickle of awareness race up my spine. That in itself makes me freeze because the only time I feel such a thing is when danger's approaching.

My entire body tenses when three thunderous booming knocks sound on the front door. They're so loud and aggressive that I fear the wood just might splinter.

Mariketa warned me that the Alpha's family would be passing through Aesara tonight to scent out mates, but there's no possible way for either Leisel or me to be a mate to a shifter, since we're not quite human. At least, there's never been a recorded case of an earthly witch being the other half to any type of mythic.

Then again, the number of earthly witches in existence can be counted on one hand. Could Leisel or I possibly be the other half to a shifter? *Just because it's never happened before doesn't mean it's impossible.*

I give my head a shake. My fear is probably a needless one—the knocks could've come from any one of the villagers.

At this time of night? With the sort of force that rattled the entire house?

Trying to ignore the small warning voice in the back of my head, I pick up a knife from the knife block in the kitchen, slide it into my back pocket, and slowly walk towards the door. Three more knocks resound, nearly blowing the door off its hinges, and making me wince.

Swallowing as I approach it, I tentatively call out, "Who is it?"

A female voice answers from the other side. "By decree of the Rockwell Pack, entrance into this home is demanded."

The fact that the voice is female doesn't calm the panic her words ignite. Shifters travel in groups; just because a female is knocking on the door, doesn't mean there aren't males around her. One of which could potentially upend my entire life.

Oh gods, Leisel. If my worst fear is true, and I'm the unlucky mate of a mutt, I don't know what would happen to my little sister. I'd have to be dragged out of this home kicking and screaming to abandon her, but the fact of the matter is that she very well might end up alone.

I frantically think through options when it comes to her. Just about every villager adores her, so I have no doubt someone would be willing to take her in, in the event of my absence. Mariketa would surely do so happily, but even the thought of separating from her makes me nauseous. Although Leisel is technically a sister, I've raised her as my own from birth. Sheltered, nurtured, and cared for her. I can't imagine having distance between us.

"If this door isn't opened within thirty seconds, it will be broken down," warns whoever's on the other side of the door.

A wave of disgust towards mythics—shifters in specific—washes over me, and the anger gives me the necessary gumption to unlock and swing open the entrance to my home.

As soon as I do, a wave of cold fresh fear washes over me. The woman banging on the door, as I suspected, isn't alone. She's accompanied by three men, all of whom watch me with expressions of partial curiosity, partial irritation—likely at how long it took me to follow an order. I very much doubt any shifter is accustomed to not being instantly obeyed by humans.

The woman takes my measure with sharp eyes, her brows furrowed as she looks me over. She looks to be in her late twenties, but that's no real indicator of her age. Once mythics reach mid-twenties, their aging slows to a crawl. She could be half a century old despite her somewhat youthful features. Her eyes are a deep amber, and she has shoulder-length blonde hair. She's two or so inches taller than me, standing at around five-six.

One of the men with her steps forward, drawing my attention to him. The breath catches in my throat as we make eye contact. His eyes are a peculiar silvery blue—a color that I know is unique to Alphas. He's tremendously tall, towering well over a foot above me. He has short, light-brown hair that's wind-tousled, and his body consists of pure powerful muscle, visible underneath his simple white shirt and dark pants. His feet are encased in riding boots, made of what appears to be fine leather.

Forcing aside the urge to step back and slam the door in his face out of fear, I keep my tone as bored as possible. "May I inquire as to why four shifters are gathered on my porch?"

The Alpha seems amused by my words, and one corner of his full lips ticks up. That small gesture sends a flare of lust so strong through me that my knees almost buckle as heat pools low in my stomach, the sensation completely foreign and entirely unwelcome.

Fucking. Shit. That's the sort of reaction I've read and heard mates have towards each other; soul-rending lust. *Shit, shit, SHIT!*

How could the fates be so cruel towards me? I've led a good life. I try to do well by others. What could I have *possibly* done to deserve this?

"Tell me your name," the Alpha demands.

The order angers me immensely because he has absolutely no right to demand *anything* from me. It's because of his species that both my parents are dead, and humans are back to living in the Middle Ages. Even being in his presence is sickening.

Thankfully, the lust clears up with my thoughts.

I stare at the Alpha as he stares at me, growing more disgusted by the second at the sight of him. Instead of answering him—as I'm sure everyone always jumps to do—I say flatly, "You haven't answered my question."

He appears momentarily shocked at my nerve, but it is quickly replaced by intense scrutiny. "I think you've guessed the answer to that. Unless, of course, you're a simpleton."

Battling with the urge to take my knife out of my pocket and bury it in his chest, I grit my teeth and glare at him. I'm far too outnumbered for an assassination attempt, and besides, I doubt I'd get very far.

Before I can say anything, another one of the males steps forward. He has an air of authority surrounding him that's similar to the Alpha's, but not quite as powerful. I catalogue him as the potential Beta.

His deep-brown eyes flare along with his nostrils, and then he *pushes past me*, entering my house without a word.

I leap in front of him, all of my protective instincts jumping into overdrive. "Get out of my house," I growl.

His eyes darken with anger as he stares at me. "I know you're merely a human, but even you should know better than to get between a shifter and their mate."

Dear fucking gods, *Leisel*. He can't possibly be talking about anyone else. *How could this be?* Both of us, fated to abhorrent perversions of nature?

"Not another step," I say, my voice bordering on hysterical as I think of my little sister. The fates must truly despise us both to pair me with an Alpha, and a nine-year-old *child* with a Beta.

Because the entire universe seems to despise me, at that moment, I hear Leisel's door opening, followed by her tentative voice behind me. "Sierra?"

Before the Beta can take another step or make another sound, I'm in front of my little sister, shielding her with my body. I feel the anxiety coming off of her as one of her small hands grasps mine.

"This town is not under the jurisdiction of any mythics," I say through clenched teeth as the Alpha also steps into my home uninvited. "You have no right to invade my home. Get out."

The Alpha looks delighted by my spine, disregarding my words altogether. "Sierra," he says, testing my name. I suppress a shiver of pleasure the sound causes to race up my spine. "I'm Alpha Camden Kent."

"And I'm bored," I fire back. "Get. Out."

When neither of them moves, I glance over my shoulder at Leisel. "Go to your room, sweet girl. I'll be there in a few minutes."

Knowing this isn't the time to argue, she promptly rushes back into her room, shutting the door behind her.

I press a hand to my forehead, recent events causing an overwhelming headache. My only potential way out of this situation would be to declare duelum—a law that allows humans the chance to battle their way out of having to mate. When a human declares duelum, they're paired with a member from their mate's pack or clan or coven and the two have a duel. If the human wins, which has only happened a handful of times, they're free. If they lose, which is almost always, they'll be bound to a monster for the rest of their lives.

Leisel, however, is too young to take the path of duelum. According to mythic laws, shifters can't mate with humans under the age of eighteen. So, at least she's somewhat safe for the time being.

I, however, am an entirely different story. If I lose the duel, I belong to the pack. I could win it with ease if I used my powers, but revealing them is not the wise thing to do. If the Alpha finds out that I'm a very rare type of witch, with an even rarer ability, he'll view me as *far* more of an asset than simply being his mate, and then he might never stop searching for a way to keep me.

Trying to shore myself up, I remember the tens of thousands of hours of hard labor I've put into the farm—labor that's given me above-average strength. And then, there are the vague memories of the fighting lessons Dad used to give me. Even if I don't utilize my powers, I have better chances than most humans would in a duel with a shifter.

Hands landing on my arms abruptly draw me out of my thoughts. I jerk back from Camden's grasp and glare at him. "Don't touch me."

His eyebrows hit his hairline with surprise at my aggression, and then he lets out a low, dark chuckle. "My beautiful little mate. Don't make this difficult. I've waited plenty long for you—I'll wait no longer."

Squaring my shoulders, I look him in the eye. "Your people have ruined countless human lives. You've caused more death, pain, and despair than even the worst of our dictators and tyrants did through-out our history. If you think there is *any* chance that I'll ever be a compliant *little mate*, think again. Duelum."

Chapter Four

S hock flares on Camden's features at my rant, followed by a blazing anger. Before I can blink, he has me in the firm, unbreakable
cage of his arms. They wrap around my waist with a steel grip, and the
warmth of his skin against mine draws a gasp from my lips.

Glaring at me, he addresses his Beta. "Wyatt, go check on your
mate."

I try to jerk out of his grasp as Wyatt steps around us, opens the
door to Leisel's bedroom, and steps in.

"Don't touch her!" I shout at him. "She's protected by human laws!
She's nine years underage!"

My words are cut off when Camden fists one hand in my hair, turns
me to face him, and practically crashes his lips down on mine. Trying
to push against him is perfectly futile, and after a moment, my body
inadvertently relaxes in his grip. A strange tingle travels through my
chest, and after a moment I realize that the sensation is the mythical
bond that connects all mates flaring to life. The tingle turns into a
heat that bathes my body, traveling through me and focusing on my
extremities, making me sag against Camden as pleasure fires up every
nerve-ending within me. Although I know in my right mind that I
despise Camden on principle, I can't seem to communicate the fact
to my body, which is completely pliable within his arms. My lips part

at the firm probing of his tongue, and I'm helpless against him as he indulges in a thorough taste of my mouth.

I don't know how long it is until Camden finally pulls back, but at the same time, Leisel's shrill words cut through the air. "Don't touch me!"

I renew my struggles against Camden, struggling against the bond between us, which I can somehow feel is attempting to keep me relaxed. A faux sensation of warmth travels through me, trying to lull me into a state of calm compliance. I fight against it with everything in me, refusing to submit. "I declared duelum," I remind Camden, my voice rising in pitch as fear turns the blood in my veins to ice. "You can't touch me until I win or lose the duel."

Duelum carries with it a list of regulations; right now, they're all I have to protect me and my sister.

He lets out a frustrated breath, untangling his hand from my hair and instead using it to hold me snugly against him. "It figures that I'd get paired with someone as stubborn as I am." Giving his head a shake, he goes on. "You will be in the town square tomorrow at six a.m. for the duel. Afterwards, once you've lost, you and your sister will accompany me back to Kinrith. Am I clear?"

Grimly, I respond, "I have no intention of losing, but even if I do, you can't take Leisel. She's too young."

He scoffs. "You intend to leave her here alone? I see no parents in this home, and I'd guess she can't be older than ten. Who will take care of her?"

The acute pang of pain that sends through my chest is enough to nearly double me over. If I lose the fight, the fact of the matter is that I *will* have to separate from Leisel. Although it'll feel like a knife to my heart, she'd be safer here under the care of Mariketa than amongst shifters. A mate being underage may mean nothing to shifters, but I will *not* allow Leisel to be ravaged by their depraved ways. It's also why I need to get to Leisel *now.*

Wyatt emerges from Leisel's room with a look of absolute shock on his features. I notice that his neck and cheek are bleeding from what appear to be shallow bite marks made by a small animal and that almost makes me smile.

Chip's as fierce a protector as I am. Any time Leisel clearly dislikes someone—which is a rarity—her trusty chipmunk will attack full force, switching from a subdued pet to a rabid creature in the span of a second. It'd appear that Wyatt got an unpleasant lesson in keeping his hands away from where they're not wanted. The idea that he might've touched her chills my very bones though. Did he attempt to kiss her like Camden kissed me?

Camden releases me so abruptly that I stumble back. "Two pack members will be guarding this house," he tells me. "Don't try to run. They will escort you to the town square in the morning. I suggest you mentally prepare for your upcoming move, and prepare your sister, as well."

With those words, he grabs Wyatt by the arm, drags him out of the house, and slams the door behind them. I rush forward to bolt and lock it before sprinting to Leisel's room.

She throws herself at me as soon as I cross the threshold, hugging me as if I'm a lifeline. Her tears soak the material of my shirt, and her quiet sobs send pain radiating through my chest.

I gather her into my arms, barely noticing that Chip leaps onto my shoulder to avoid being crushed, and silently carry her to bed.

Taking a seat on the mattress and setting her down on my lap, I stroke my hands through her hair in what I hope is a calming gesture, even though I'm still beyond wound up from Camden's forced kiss, my upcoming duel, and the fact that my life just got upended.

"Shh, sweet girl," I soothe.

Leisel's likely terrified after having shifters in the house—one of which apparently attempted to touch her. I can only pray that it wasn't as inappropriate as Camden was with me.

I'm on the verge of bursting into tears—which would be the first time I've cried since my mother's death—but manage to hold back. I quietly rock her back and forth until her sobs turn into occasional hiccups, and she settles down slightly.

"Don't leave me," she begs, pulling back and staring at me with watery golden eyes. Evidently, she heard Camden's threats. I wish I'd made use of the knife still resting in my back pocket, after all.

"I'm not going anywhere, Leisel," I quietly vow. I will win the duel tomorrow because there is no other option. Leaving Leisel would tear me in two, even if I knew she was in good hands.

She doesn't look entirely convinced, and I suspect she's a hair-breadth away from bursting back into tears. I look over her face and body, gratified that no bruises are forming on her flesh, making it clear that Wyatt never got around to putting his hands on her. Shifters are famous for forgetting their own strength and oftentimes injure humans with a mere touch.

"How about a warm glass of milk with honey?" I ask her, pushing a few wet strands of strawberry blonde hair off her face and tucking them behind her cheek. That's a comfort drink of sorts for her and never fails to calm her.

Sniffling, she nods, and gingerly climbs off my lap. Chip leaps off of his perch from my shoulder onto hers, curling against the side of her neck. I think the little guy senses her need for comfort as much as I do.

"What happened while I was gone, sweet girl?" I ask her, leading her into the kitchen and watching as she sulks onto one of the chairs at the dining table, eyes following me as I fire up the stove, pour some milk and honey into a saucepan, and leave it to warm.

"He tried to hug me," she murmurs.

My eyes flutter closed briefly with relief. Although I don't want mutts anywhere near Leisel, it's preferable that Wyatt merely tried to hug her to a number of more inappropriate things he could've attempted.

I give her a conspiratorial smile, wanting to lighten her mood. "And I'm sure Chip kicked his butt for the effort, didn't he?"

Wanly, a half-smile flits across her lips. It's quickly replaced by a frown. "Promise me you won't leave," she whispers.

Holding her gaze, I say solemnly, "I'll never leave you, my love. Ever. Sisters stick together and protect each other, yes?"

She watches me, gauging my sincerity for a moment before nodding. "Yes."

I blink several times, pushing aside the swell of emotion that rises at the prospect of separating from Leisel. We haven't been apart for more than a few hours from the moment she was born. Turning back to the saucepan and grabbing a spoon to stir the milk and honey together, I try to gather my thoughts. Unfortunately, all that results in is a fast-forward reel of memories with my little sister.

I didn't have time to grieve my mother's death because I had a wailing infant to look after. An infant that I had no idea how to care for. I remember walking from the birthing establishment in town into Aesara's market with a tiny Leisel bundled in a blanket in my arms and tears streaming down my cheeks and asking Mariketa—who I already knew well—what to do. Horrified at my predicament, Mariketa ushered me to my cabin with Parker, bringing an excess of supplies needed to care for an infant left over from the birth of their son.

For several days, Mariketa lived here with me, teaching me how to care for Leisel. Parker would drop by with Wesley periodically. After three days, although I was still bursting into tears randomly, sick with grief, I had a good idea of how to look after a baby. Mariketa gave me a woven basket that doubled as a portable cradle. So, while struggling to keep the farm running—still working the land, hunting, and caring for the horses—Leisel would always be within arm's reach.

She was a relatively subdued and quiet baby but was incredibly attuned to my emotions even then. When I was sad, she started crying. When I was having better days, she'd be smiling. She grew so quickly, and before I knew it, she was a toddler—still glued to my side at all times, running around me while I worked.

The first time I left her alone in the house for a few hours was when she was five. I knew she didn't enjoy hunts—it'd make her sad to see any sort of life taken—so I'd snuck out early in the morning to get my business done. When I came back she was sitting on my bed, clutching my pillow, and sobbing. When I'd asked her what was wrong she said she thought I'd left her. My heart broke in two, and I made a point to tell her any time I planned to leave her for even an hour or so from then on.

Beyond being my last living relative, Leisel was...everything to me. She still is and always will be.

Which is why I *have* to win the duel tomorrow. I can't leave her. I would never put her in the precarious position of living amongst shifters—but I also refuse to separate from her.

I turn off the stove, pour her milk into a mug, and set it in front of her before taking a seat across the table from her. "Drink up, sweet girl," I tell her. "Tomorrow I'll put an end to this craziness. Neither of us is going anywhere, and we won't be mates to anyone, you hear me?"

She gives me a single nod. "I hear you."

Chapter Five

I don't sleep that night. I can't—I'm too wound up to do anything but think and train. For hours, I run through every fighting move I learned from my father, almost breaking the meager furniture around my house in my crazed enthusiasm.

By the time the moon is starting to set, as evidenced by peeks I take through the curtains drawn over my windows, I've concluded that, although I'm confident I'd hand most humans their ass, my odds against a shifter are not good. Which means I'll need to fight dirty.

I know there aren't any weapons allowed—which is ridiculous, since shifters have sharp claws that come out on command, and I'm sure whoever my opponent is will be happy to use them. I'll have to use my brain as much as my body during the duel and think several steps ahead to have even the tiniest chance of success.

In an attempt to get myself into a strategic mindset, I pull out my father's chess set. We used to play the game several times a week, and he taught me many tactics to win. The primary one being to think at *least* five steps ahead, though ideally eight. For hours, I play against myself, imagining each piece on the chessboard to be a fighting strategy or person and setting them against each other.

Then, as the first rays of light start to peek through the curtains, I sit on the floor in front of the worn old sofa in my living area and pray.

Praying isn't an abnormality for me—I pray to the gods almost nightly, asking for health for both Leisel and me, and praying that my parents' souls are resting in peace. This morning, however, my prayer is different. More ritualistic. It's a prayer directly to the goddess of magic, Hecate.

All mythic species have a specific god they pray to, the same god that's said to have created them. For shifters, it's the moon goddess Selene. For vampires, it's the war god Ares. For sirens, Poseidon. For demons, Hades. For witches, Hecate.

Although my magic is from the earth, it's magic nonetheless—which gives me a direct line of sorts to the goddess of all witches. Possibly more so than witches from other realms, since there are many of them and so few earthly witches. My mother once told me to only pray to Hecate when truly necessary because she will always hear me, but she wouldn't be pleased with unnecessary disturbances.

The last time I prayed to her directly was when Leisel got pneumonia at five years old. I was watching the life slowly seep out of my sister, listening to her wheezing breaths and horrible coughs, horrified at the possibility of losing her. I begged the patron goddess of witches to heal her, to let her live. The following day, Leisel was cured, as if she was never ailed in the first place. That was a miracle in itself since she'd been at death's door mere hours before. The following week she developed her first—and so far only—power: healing.

The power became apparent when Leisel had accompanied me on a horseback ride through the forest—not a hunt—and had seen a baby chipmunk being ravaged by a ferret. She leaped off of Duchess, scared the ferret away, and took the bloodied, barely breathing chipmunk in her hands. She held him to her chest, and I remember seeing a faint golden glow emanating from her hands. When the chipmunk was visible again, he was completely healed. Leisel proclaimed that she was keeping him and named him Chip.

Since then, she healed Shadow when he broke his leg during a hunt and healed me multiple times when I would hurt myself working the farm or out in the forest.

I don't expect my prayer to Hecate to result in another miracle—but I hope to get some guidance. Something that will help me in my upcoming fight.

My mother taught me the way to activate my connection to Hecate before a prayer; to shed a drop of my blood and use my magic. So, I prick my index finger with a sewing needle, and let loose the power I've spent countless hours learning to control.

Holding the palm of my unbloodied hand to the ceiling, I let out a deep breath, and summon a small bit of fire.

From my understanding, having the ability to summon and wield fire isn't uncommon among witches. What makes *my* fire such an anomaly—a dangerous anomaly—is that the flame I summon isn't red and orange; it's gold and black. It's a flame that destroys anything it comes into contact with—incinerating objects with a mere lick.

The ability first manifested when I was eight and demolished an oak tree by accident. I'd broken my leg while in the forest with my father, and the acute pain somehow tore my power out of me. Both my father and I had been terrified because it was merely a spark of the golden-black flame that turned a century-old oak into ash. For years, I struggled to learn how to control the black fire, because it would burst forward whenever I was angry or injured. I was twelve by the time I truly mastered being able to summon and control it at will.

Since then, I've had no reason to use it, outside of the last time I prayed to Hecate. Even still, the flame manifests in the palm of my hand with ease, as enchanting and dark as I remember it being. It's black at the core, gray at the edges, with a gold shroud dancing across each flicker of fire.

"Hecate," I murmur, keeping my voice quiet because I know how good shifter hearing is, and close my eyes. "I call upon you for guidance. In a mere few hours, I'll be dueling with a shifter—someone who's no doubt far stronger and faster than me. I fear for not only my own well-being but the well-being of Leisel. I cannot use my magic during the fight because I do not seek to expose myself. If there's any assistance you could give, it would be met with my eternal gratitude."

Opening my eyes, I clench my fist, extinguishing the fire, and hope to gods a miracle will occur that gives me a much-needed advantage.

***

At six a.m., I stand in the center of the town square—empty of the vendors that normally set up later in the morning. A crowd of both shifters and my fellow villagers is gathered. Evidently, word of the Alpha discovering his mate spread like wildfire because at least fifty people are standing about.

Leisel and I rode in a mere few minutes ago, accompanied by two pack members who were guarding us in wolf form through the night. They stayed far enough behind so as not to spook the horses, but both my sister and I noticed them. I'd mulled over the idea of leaving Leisel in the cabin—but I feared that would result in her getting snatched up by shifters while I wasn't there to protect her.

After tying up the horses to their usual post, I walk straight to Mariketa and Parker, both of whom are gathered with the human portion of the crowd, and ask them to keep an eye on Leisel while I'm occupied trying to win against impossible odds.

Now, I stand silently by them, eyeing the group of shifters across the stone-paved town square from us. Camden and Wyatt are conversing with eight of their packmates, as well as watching Leisel and me from the corner of their eyes.

Almost all of the shifters are male, the only female being the one who nearly knocked down my door last night. I imagine I'll be paired with her, even though she's taller than me, and most likely a lot more competent with fighting. She's the closest thing to an *even match* that's currently available.

Parker brings me out of my thoughts when he puts a hand on my shoulder. "Your father once told me something that's stuck with me, even decades later," he quietly tells me.

That instantly snags my attention, and I turn to face him. I know that Parker was friends with Dad—they grew up in the same village, and even before doing business together, they were almost like brothers for how close they were.

"What was that?" I ask him.

Parker gazes meaningfully at me. "That morale is the most important aspect of any battle. If you go in with a losing mindset, you'll lose. If you go in with a winning mindset, you'll prevail." His voice lowers to a whisper. "You know where the trachea is on the neck, yes?"

I nod.

"A blow to the trachea will hurt and slow down even a shifter. Let your opponent tire themselves out and wait for an opening. Once you see it, give a punch to the trachea full force. That'll give you enough time to get an arm around their neck, even though they'll heal far faster than humans. Then you grip their neck with everything in you, and hold on like your life depends on it because it damn well does."

I look at Parker in an entirely new light, because he sounds like he's speaking from experience. All my life, I've known him as the cheerful village butcher, married to the even more cheerful village baker, but right now, I'm not staring at the man I sell meat to several times a week while chatting. I'm staring at a warrior.

I blink slowly. "It almost sounds like you've fought shifters before, Parker."

A small, slightly sad smile flits over his lips. "You're not the only one who's had to declare duelum, Sierra." His hand drops from my shoulder. "Remember what I've told you."

Camden steps forward from his crowd of shifters and addresses me directly, his voice echoing around the town square. "You will be dueling with Aspen," he says, motioning to the blonde female. "The rules are simple. No weapons allowed. It is a fight until you yield or lose consciousness. Afterwards, you *will* accompany me to Kinrith, whether in chains or by your own free will."

His assumption that I'll yield or pass out isn't lost on me—he's not even slightly worried for Aspen and has every confidence she'll win. He clearly doesn't think I stand a chance. That sparks an anger in me that I vehemently push aside because being emotional will only hinder me.

I walk into the middle of the town square, halfway between the humans and shifters. Aspen follows suit, looking me up and down with a predator's eyes.

"I advise you to yield now," she tells me. "I have no wish to harm my future queen."

She sounds surprisingly sincere on the latter, but that only makes me more determined to prove to the shifters here that I'm not quite the helpless human they assume me to be.

"Thank you for the consideration," I respond mildly, "but I'd really rather die than have any relations with mythics."

Chapter Six

Aspen's eyes flare with anger at my gall, and her nails transform into claws. I don't bother pointing out that they're weapons—my words would be overlooked or altogether ignored. Before I can blink, she strikes out with her right hand, claws aimed for my torso.

I intercept the strike with my forearm, but her strength still outmatches mine, so instead of her claws tearing the flesh of my stomach, they sink into my left thigh. They're sharp enough to slice through my skin like butter, and a hiss escapes me at the stabbing pain that spreads through my entire leg like sharp needles tearing through skin.

I retaliate with a swift strike to her solar plexus that sends her stumbling back two steps, and she looks positively shocked at my strength, looking from the spot where I hit her to my hand with widened eyes.

Twelve hours of daily manual labor has its perks.

Then, the strangest thing happens. Time seems to slow down to a crawl, and all of my surroundings dim. My initial assumption that blood loss is already affecting me clears when I see Aspen launch at me *in slow motion.*

My movements, however, aren't slowed like hers. I sidestep her as she comes careening towards me and deliver a swift kick to the back of her knee that sends her sprawling to the ground.

I glance around me to see if time outside of her has also somehow been altered to a slow pace and am shocked to see that it has. Mariketa is whispering something to Leisel, her lips moving at the speed of molasses. Leisel's blink looks like it takes several seconds.

That's when I realize that Hecate must have heard my prayer and has responded in turn.

When I prayed to her for Leisel's healing, it shortly unlocked a hidden power within my sister. When I prayed to her earlier for help, it looks like she chose to grant it. I don't think this is a new power—I don't *feel* any magic pushing out from myself—which makes me think that Hecate herself is the one slowing time right now. If that is the case, I can't fathom why, but this is a much-needed advantage.

My frozen shock ends up costing me because a blow to my spine sends me tumbling onto the uneven stone ground. Despite the pain now shooting through my back, when I flip over to face Aspen, her movements are still unusually slow, giving me time to roll out from beneath her and jump to my feet before she can crush my ribs with her foot.

The blood from the wound in my thigh is leaking out at an alarming pace; Aspen likely hit a vein, but not an artery, thankfully, or the blood would be spurting.

Knowing that fatigue will soon start weighing on me, and the pain in both my back and thigh will grow as battle adrenaline subsides, I recall Parker's advice. I close the distance between Aspen and I in one swift step and aim a punch directly to her trachea in the center of her neck, putting all of my force behind it. Her startled gasp is a choked inhalation, and her hands move to instinctively clutch her neck. Before they can, I aim a brutal kick to her uninjured knee, forcing it backward at an impossible angle, and catch her by the hair as she begins to fall. I leap behind her to wrap an arm around her neck, and with that, time returns to a normal pace. Knowing that her accelerated healing will give her strength any moment, I cut off her air supply entirely.

"Yield," I demand.

She doesn't. One of her hands flies to my arm, claws digging in and trying to pry it off, but her other hand slams down into the knee of my already injured leg, those claws slicing into the tendons surrounding my kneecap.

I gasp in pain which is unlike anything I've ever felt—sharp, stabbing, and draining. My knee buckles, forcing me to use my good leg to support my body weight as I let out a muffled cry of agony, blink multiple times as my vision wavers and starts to swim, but don't loosen my grip.

Hold on like your life depends on it because it damn well does, Parker told me. I heed his words carefully and tighten my arm to the point that I know it's starting to crush her windpipe.

Her claws fall from my knee as her body slackens in my hold. For all their strengths, not even shifters can survive without air.

Alarmingly, I feel my darkest power beginning to rise inside me. The black flame that lives within me and can manifest on my command is starting to slink closer to the surface, drawn by my pain and distress, just like it was on the day it first came out.

Trying to force it down while fighting the urge to pass out and keeping a grip on Aspen is the single most difficult thing I've ever done. My entire body aches, stabs, and burns. The fear coursing through my veins is near incapacitating, and what I wish for is a warm bed to crawl into so I can sleep away this damn nightmare. Instead of letting that slow me, I tighten my arm around Aspen's neck *even more*, ready for this to be over.

After what feels like an eternity, Aspen uses a sluggish hand to tap my thigh twice, the universal sign for yielding.

Gratefully, I release her, before falling to the stone ground, my injuries getting the best of me. The impact of my battered body meeting the ground sends a wave of pain so acute through me that my vision briefly blackens.

When the momentary darkness recedes, I'm horrified to see a black flame dancing in one of my palms. What's even more horrifying is that I'm not the only one who sees it.

Everyone in the town square does.

With the last of my strength, I clench my palm into a fist, putting out the small flickering fire. That final wave of pain must've sent my powers into a protective frenzy, pulling them forward without my permission.

The humans look from me to each other and back again with shock. They know I'm not a mythic—mythics have a very distinctive energy about them that even humans can sense. It doesn't take the villagers gathered more than a second to put two and two together—though I'm not a mythic, they saw my magic, which means my power stems from the earth.

To my profound relief, after a few beats of silence, many of them break into cheers. I watch through blurry vision as Parker lifts Leisel and swings her around in a triumphant circle, while Mariketa claps with delight.

I don't miss that several stragglers *don't* seem joyful at my win—they're too busy staring at me with a new distrust laced with disgust. Most of my fellow villagers, however, seem pleased.

My many years of living among these people, trading, and helping out the less fortunate have paid off. Even with the torturous aches, throbs, and stabbing sensations all over my body, I feel a small smile pull at my lips.

I won the duel. I'm free from the pack. Despite villagers now knowing that I'm not quite human, *they're still celebrating my win.* The exile and cruelty I was taught to expect should anyone discover my powers is mostly absent. I do notice the group of villagers who abstained from cheering gather together and begin to murmur amongst themselves, casting distasteful looks in my direction. The majority of the gathered crowd, however, is unexpectedly supportive.

Leisel breaks away from Parker and runs up to kneel beside me. Chip drops from her shoulder and onto my neck at her sudden moves, chattering with irritation. When she puts her hands on my chest, I know she intends to heal me. I can't let that happen—I don't want her powers to be revealed in the same breath as mine.

"Leisel, *no*—"

Before I can get the words out, a golden glow starts to emanate beneath her palms, and a pleasant warmth is ignited in my chest. That warmth rushes to my thigh, knee, arm, and back, her magic traveling right to each injury and healing them at a remarkable speed. I watch as the slashed-up skin beneath the torn material of my pants starts to knit together, and the unbearable pain in my body ebbs before disappearing entirely. The blur in my vision also recedes, leaving me clear-sighted once more.

My eyes flutter closed with both relief at the absence of pain and fear of what's to come.

Technically, by mythic laws, I'm free. I won the duel fair and square. I didn't use magic during it, though unbeknownst to anyone else, the goddess of witches seemingly decided to give me an edge. My flame only sparked after Aspen had yielded, so that can't be called cheating.

The problem is that now more than ever, Camden will desire me. Before, I was a mere human, my only worth being the fact that I'd strengthen him through the mate bond. Now, I'll be of far more interest because I have magic coursing through my veins. I have actual, tangible value that far supersedes what the wolves could've imagined. I'm ready to *crucify* myself for the exposure—being released by the pack will now be that much more difficult.

Leisel will have a similar problem, as well. In her frantic fear for me, she outed herself. I can't find it in me to be upset with her, however. As soon as the glow from her hands disappears, I take her into my arms and hug her.

I do not doubt that Camden will attempt to appeal my win in the high shifter court, which oversees all shifters—even him. The court is the top dog of the top dogs—literally. That appeal better amount to nothing because *I won*.

The Rockwell Pack can't take Leisel, either, since she's too young. I have no doubt they'll try to come for her once she's of age, but I intend to spend the next eight years training her to win her duel since I'm positive she'll declare duelum when the time comes.

For the moment, we're both as safe as possible. The elation that thought sends through me is vast. "Thank you, sweet girl," I murmur into her hair, kissing the crown of her head. She hugs me back with all the strength in her body.

Both Mariketa and Parker approach us. I let Leisel go, hand her Chip, and rise to my feet, ignoring the wave of fatigue that rolls over me. Although I'm healed, I still lost a good amount of blood—only rest will return me to full strength.

Mariketa, without prompting, folds me into a hug. "You should've told us, child," she says, pulling back. I see a flicker of hurt in her eyes—Mariketa's known me since I was born and has seen me through difficult times, so it's fair she'd expect me to be open with her.

I look to my feet, knowing she's referring to my magic. "My mother told me to always keep it a secret," I explain, looking back to her warm eyes. "She thought people would turn on me."

Mariketa scoffs lightly. "Tsk. We hate mythics, but you ain't a mythic."

Parker interjects, "So what does your little flame do?"

I feel my mood darken. "Nothing good."

He accepts that with a nod, then looks at Leisel. "Never would've guessed you were a healer. I suppose I should've since your little rat has lived so long."

Leisel wrinkles her nose in an adorable gesture. "He's a chipmunk."

Parker waves a hand at that. "Same difference."

I glance over Parker's shoulder to where the shifters are gathered. Camden looks absolutely furious and appears to be scolding Aspen. Her eyes are downturned and her cheeks are red with embarrassment. Wyatt looks as angry as Camden, pacing back and forth. The rest of the shifters look simultaneously shocked, impressed, and pissed.

I take Leisel's hand in mine, sensing her anxiety as she watches the shifters alongside me. "Let's go home," I say, brushing my free hand through her hair.

For the moment, we're both free of the Rockwell Pack, though the future is still uncertain.

Chapter Seven

Although I'm bone tired, I don't rest when I get home. I can't afford to let my guard down while the Rockwell Pack is still near. I warm up leftover stew for myself and Leisel, since neither of us ate breakfast, and go over a math lesson with her while we eat.

I won't allow shifters to upend our day-to-day lives—both of us will go about business as usual.

For an unusual change of pace, Chip spends the meal on my shoulder. He's always been as comfortable with me as he is with Leisel and never seems to mind when I hold or pet him. I think he recognizes me as her provider and protector, and that formed an accord between us, even though he's relatively antisocial with most others. That is, unless they're offering him food. Maybe, similarly to how he curled up against Leisel's neck last night, perceiving her need for comfort, he's now perceiving my need for comfort, and responding accordingly.

I feed him bites of the bread I bought from Mariketa yesterday, as well as a few pieces of lettuce I harvested from the farm earlier in the week. He accepts all the offerings contentedly, grooming himself in between stuffing his little cheeks.

Leisel watches me with a penetrating gaze throughout our meal. She's always been intuitive—alarmingly so—and easily senses how wound-up I am.

As I'm washing our dishes, Chip having departed to his normal perch on Leisel's shoulder, she says, "You're my hero, Sierra."

That stops me short, and the bowl I'm washing clatters into the sink. I turn to face her, feeling my heart swell in my chest. "What do you mean, sweet girl?"

She lifts one shoulder. "We've been going over archetypes in English. A hero always overcomes impossible odds and comes out on top. A hero protects everyone around them at all costs. A hero is noble, caring, and courageous. You're all of those things.

"I saw how much you were hurt in the fight, but you kept pushing through, and ended up beating a shifter. A *shifter* who's way stronger and faster than you." Her voice quiets. "And I know you didn't beat her for yourself. You beat her for me."

Gods, for a nine-year-old, Leisel has a remarkably advanced mind and vocabulary. She's mature far beyond her years. It probably comes from the rigorous studies I put her through as well as her love for reading classics.

I say the only thing I can think of, meeting her honesty with some of my own. "You have no idea what that means to me, Leisel. No idea how much *you* mean to me. If not for you—" My voice cuts off with a crack, and I inhale a deep breath to steady myself before continuing. "If not for you, I'd be a different person. I'd never have learned to be a hero. You came to me in the darkest time in my life and brought beautiful sunlight to overshadow the endless haze I lived in."

Her eyes well with tears again as she runs up to me and hugs me tightly. "I love you," she says, her voice wobbly.

I kneel to hug her back, resting my chin on her shoulder. "I love you too, sweet girl. I'll always protect you. Always." After a moment, I say, "Thank you for healing me earlier. I doubt I'd be awake if you hadn't."

"I'll always protect you too," she murmurs.

I let go of her and walk over to the window in front of the kitchen sink—the view outside concealed by the drawn curtain. All the curtains around my cabin have been drawn since the Rockwell Pack came banging on my door last night; I don't want them to have any peeks into my life. Not even through the windows.

I lift the edge of the curtain a touch, just enough to glimpse the fields that lay beyond the cabin. I don't spot any wolves, but I know the pack wouldn't leave me unguarded despite my freedom from them, so I suspect their presence nonetheless. I let the curtain drop, inhale a deep breath, and turn back towards the cabin.

Even though I try to stay optimistic, I can't help but suspect that my business with the Rockwell Pack has not yet concluded. Not after what's been revealed.

Chapter Eight

Camden

The few members of the Rockwell Pack who traveled with me have set up in a spacious building a few miles away from Aesara where shifters stay when they're traveling through. It's on the edge of the forest, giving our wolves ample space to run about—a necessity for our more primal halves.

I received word that more members are on their way, wanting to offer their support in the face of the difficulties I'm currently up against.

Those difficulties are *vast*.

I sit at the head of the large chestnut table in the dining room, watching my brother pace back and forth over the stone floor in front of a fireplace on one side of the room. The rest of our packmates are littered throughout the large home—a few in the dining room with me, chatting with each other, and more occupying the many other rooms.

Both Wyatt and I had the fortune to find our mates in Aesara—but that fortune soured rather quickly. Wyatt's mate, Leisel, is too young to be taken, as per the laws my father enacted during his reign to give the remaining humans an illusion of protection and power. My mate, though she's old enough to be taken by my pack, despises me with every fiber of her being and actually managed to *win a duel* to stay away from me.

I glimpsed her hatred each time she looked at me. Her tempting lips curl ever so slightly in disgust, and her eyes glitter with malice. It's hatred that seems to extend to all shifters, and I'd wager all mythics as well.

I expected complications with having a human mate. There have only been a handful of cases where humans were accepting of mating with mythics from the start, and I can't entirely blame them. This world was theirs before we made it ours, and the changes we imposed caused much damage and discontent to their ways of life. Not to mention the fact that all but a few hundred thousand humans were killed off without the aid of technology they'd come to rely on, along with their silly attempts to fight off mythics.

I never expected the complications to be a soul-deep hatred from Sierra, however. I assumed there would be fear that my mate would need to be coaxed past—even a strong dislike. But Sierra doesn't fear me whatsoever, nor does she *just* dislike me. If I'm reading her correctly, she simply wishes to see me suffer and most likely drop dead.

Wyatt casts a glance at me as he paces. "Our mates are earthly witches. Leisel's an even more powerful healer than Claude, and she's a child. Your mate *has the Black Flame*. We need them, for more than just the strength to be gained through bonds; the pack will need their powers."

I nod. "Quite so."

I only got a small glimpse of the fire Sierra manifested—but that fire was *golden and black*. If the lore surrounding that particular variation of magical fire is anything to go off of, black flames destroy anything they come into contact with. That ability will be *incredibly* useful in the war that's brewing.

I recall overhearing the plump man Sierra was speaking with after the duel ask her what her fire did. I looked at her just in time to see her eyes darken, and hear her solemn response, "*Nothing good.*"

As for Leisel, the healing capabilities I saw her display are remarkable. If she's already able to heal extensive wounds within the span of a few seconds, it stands to reason that she'll be able to do a great deal more in the future.

"We can't leave without them," Wyatt says, running an agitated hand through his dirty blond hair. "I *refuse* to leave without Leisel, and I doubt you'll leave without Sierra."

If Sierra lost her duel, I'd have no problem tying her up, throwing her over my shoulder, and forcing her to come home with me. Once there, I'd have plenty of time and space to build a relationship with her—to attempt to bypass her innate hatred of mythics and of me. It's impossible to do that at present, though, because she won her duel.

I must admit, watching how soundly Sierra beat Aspen both angered and impressed me. It should have been impossible that a mere human—even if she's an earthly witch—could beat one of the warriors who always travels with me for protection, yet Sierra didn't use any magic during the fight—just blurring speed, and unbelievably accurate strategies. She seemed to know the few weaknesses shifters have and capitalized on them brilliantly.

I respond to Wyatt, "Legally, I have no power to take her with me; Sierra won."

Which means I'll need to get clever with how I go about this. I could appeal to the shifter high court, as I know and work closely with all the counselors seated on it, but that would be a lengthy legal process requiring time I don't have.

"There has to be some loophole we can use," Wyatt rumbles, rubbing his temples with his index finger and thumb. "If we don't have our mates, the pack will end up crumbling. *We'll* end up crumbling."

He's right. Aside from the fact that I need to be bonded before facing war with the vampires, I now understand that Sierra will prove quite a dangerous distraction until we've completed our bond—or at least reinforced it with a mark and consummation. A bond can take a long time to reach completion as it requires a couple to achieve a certain level of openness and emotional intimacy, but once the bond is sealed with a mark and consummated with sex, it's mostly formed and highly functional. Until those two cornerstones are reached, though, it seems the bond will only torture me with mental images of Sierra, memories of her taste and scent, serving as the most alluring distraction.

The few times we've been in proximity, she held my attention so soundly that I struggled to form coherent thoughts. When we're apart, I can't think of anything but her. Last night I tossed and turned in bed, unable to fall asleep, our kiss playing on repeat in my mind, experiencing a growing desperation to kiss her everywhere. I know that's the bond at work, but it's also the fact that she's so singularly unique and captivating.

Everything about her is enthralling to me. Her flaming long red hair, her remarkably unique golden eyes, the light dusting of cinnamon freckles on her nose and cheeks. Her lithe, toned body that gives me an erection the likes of which I've never felt in my thirty-four years of life.

I've known her for less than twenty-four hours, and I'm already a man obsessed. I want to know everything there is to know about her. I want to fucking consume her—body, mind, heart, and soul. I'm already addicted, and an Alpha with an addiction is a very dangerous thing, especially when it's for someone who'll go to the grave with resistance.

It doesn't help that my inner wolf is pushing me to seek her out, to fuck her in any and every way possible. To hear her compelling, lilting voice without the coating of anger it's carried the few times she's addressed me.

I glance up as Aspen strolls into the room. Her embarrassment of losing a fight to a human is still vast, and she apologized to me profusely after the duel, begrudgingly admitting that she's barely seen any warriors of my pack move with the speed that Sierra did. I gave her a stern scolding before instructing her to venture into Aesara to gather all the information she could on Sierra and Leisel as penance—a task achievable with enough gold coins.

She approaches me, eyes downcast, and motions with a hand towards a seat to the left of me requesting permission.

"You may sit," I allow. Once she has, I ask, "What have you gathered?"

She clears her throat, still not meeting my eyes. Although both she and her wolf are particularly dominant, it's difficult for anyone to hold my gaze—being an Alpha compels submission in almost all those around me. The fact that Sierra stared into my eyes without flinching is a testament to her strength of soul.

Within packs of any shifters, there are two primary categories; those with a dominant inner animal, and those with a submissive one. Alpha's have to be the most dominant of all, or they risk being overthrown by other pack members.

"Your mate's full name is Sierra West. She's twenty-three years old, and Leisel is nine," Aspen tells me.

Wyatt perks up at the mention of his mate, pausing in his pacing to listen to Aspen. The rest of the shifters present also stop their conversations, curious to hear about their future queen and princess.

"Go on," I encourage.

Aspen clears her throat. "Sierra's father died from cancer when she was thirteen. Her mother shortly found out she was pregnant, and then died giving birth to Leisel when she hemorrhaged on the birthing bed. There are no accounts of any magical blood in her family—it's an incredibly well-kept secret."

My eyes flutter closed. It's little wonder that Sierra can't stand me—she lost both her parents because humans are no longer afforded the medical attention they once had direct access to. In a roundabout way, they died because of mythics.

"By most accounts, Sierra's relatively solitary, oftentimes keeping to herself while working on her farm. She does, however, trade in the village multiple times a week—anything from meats she gathers on hunts, to produce and grains she harvests from her farm. On occasion, she'll sell paintings she makes as well. Every Sunday she visits the struggling families in Aesara, bringing whatever food she can spare for the children."

My chest warms. Aspen's words tell me that my mate has a considerable soft side hidden under her armor. Perhaps I can coax that softness out and use it to my advantage.

"All the villagers seem to like her well enough—and they all positively adore Leisel. Sierra raised Leisel as her own daughter and has seemingly dedicated her life to providing for her sister."

My assumption that Leisel and she are *very* close was spot on which means Leisel is the only leverage I have on Sierra.

"How did the villagers respond to seeing their magic?" I ask Aspen.

With any luck, that'll have turned some of them against her, leaving her in need of a safe haven which I'd be most happy to provide.

Aspen replies, "Mostly positive, but there's a group that's not happy with finding out that two magical beings, mythics or not, have lived right under their noses for decades."

History shows that mobs don't take long to spread hatred; if there's already a group of individuals that have turned on Sierra and Leisel, they might grow in numbers and pose a threat. That's something I might be able to use to my advantage, as well as it serving as an additional reason for wanting to get Sierra away from here, where there might soon be danger to her afoot.

"You're dismissed," I tell Aspen.

With a bow of her head, she scurries off. Wyatt takes her place, clenching his hands into fists.

I watch the fireplace thoughtfully. "Leisel didn't declare duelum," I say, thinking out loud.

"She's not old enough to," Wyatt responds, brows furrowing as he watches me. As both my brother and Beta, we grew up quite close, and he often helps me strategize during tumultuous times, especially since our father abdicated the throne to live out the rest of his life in solitude.

"Very true," I allow, "but technically, she is a member of the Rockwell Pack by association. The laws state that humans under the age of eighteen can't be marked or officially mated, but if I recall correctly, nowhere is it stated that mates can't still be brought to pack territory."

Wyatt's eyes spark with interest as he listens. "In other words, I have jurisdiction to take her to Kinrith with me."

I incline my head. "And anywhere Leisel goes, Sierra will undoubtedly follow."

It's an underhanded plan—a dirty one without a doubt—but I have no compunction about playing dirty to get Sierra.

I knew from the first five seconds in her presence that she's not a person who'd ever submit to anyone, let alone me. I doubt even physical punishments could bend her will—not that I intend to hurt her. The longer we spend in proximity, the stronger our bond innately becomes, even without her bearing my mark or consummation. That means that soon enough, her pain will trickle over to my body through the bond; even if I wanted to hurt her, which I don't, it wouldn't be in my best interest to do so.

The only real thing I can use against her is her love for her sister, and I intend to use it as much as is necessary.

Sierra will come to accept me—few can resist the pull of the bond for long. In time, she might even come to love me. How much I crave that truly startles me.

I glance at one of my packmates, Oscar, and motion him over with a hand. The tall, burly blond is our pack scribe—when letters or documents need to be created and sent about, he's the one who writes them.

"Put together a formal invitation for Sierra and Leisel to join us for dinner tonight," I instruct him. Then I stand and walk to the kitchen, instructing my chefs to replicate the normal dinner spread Wyatt and I are offered each night.

Beyond wanting to feed my mate a hearty meal—foods not afforded to mere humans—I'm curious to see how she'll interact with the pack. Curious to see just how deep her hostility towards us runs—if there are any chinks in her armor I can press on. At the end of the evening, I'll inform her that Leisel will be taken to Kinrith in the morning and prepare for the fight of a lifetime she'll no doubt put up.

Chapter Nine

Sierra

For the rest of the day, I'm so wound up and on such high alert that I get my daily tasks done in a fraction of the time. That leaves room for me to focus on my painting for a few hours—a novelty I usually only experience late at night.

At six that evening, three knocks sound on my front door. This time they're not booming or invasive—they sound as though a human made them.

Assuming that Mariketa's dropping by, which isn't entirely un-common, I wipe my paint-stained hands on a rag, walk through the house, and open the door without much forethought.

The pleasant mood that was built in me throughout the last several hours as I painted and spent time with Leisel dissipates. The man standing in my doorway is very clearly a mythic—a shifter from the Rockwell Pack, no doubt.

I feel my jaw clench as I regard him. He's dressed in semi-casual clothing—as the rest of the pack members have been the few times I've glimpsed them—simple beige trousers and a blue shirt with buttons running down the front. I'm sure shifters all dress much differently when they're in their home territories, likely draping themselves in regal, expensive clothes, the prices of which could feed a human family for a month.

Having no interest in conversing with a shifter—neither Leisel nor I owe them anything—I slam the door in his face.

Or try to. He stops it with a big hand braced in the center of the wood.

"Get off my property," I say between gritted teeth.

He doesn't appear angry at my hostility, which is somewhat of a surprise, since shifters are known for short tempers and low tolerance of humans. Then I recall Aspen's words; *I have no wish to harm my future queen.* At the time, I was too distracted by the upcoming duel to focus much on them. Now, I recognize the undercurrent of what she said—a loyalty of sorts.

Even though I have no intention of accepting Camden, it looks like being his mate automatically puts me at the top of their hierarchy—right next to him. Which means that the pack members just might automatically afford me some measure of respect.

I don't like getting things automatically. I prefer earning what I have. I work my ass off to earn a livable, somewhat comfortable life for Leisel and me. I've worked for hundreds of hours to hone my painting abilities over the years, making myself a decent artist and enabling me to sell some pieces for extra cash when they're completed. I bend over *backward* to make nice with all the villagers to ensure a safe and pleasant environment for Leisel to grow up in.

I haven't earned, nor do I want respect or loyalty from any mythics—certainly not from shifters and especially not The Rockwell Pack. Being the soulmate to Camden Kent is the epitome of a joke from the fates, not something I want to dwell on.

The shifter polluting my porch hands an envelope to me, wearing a smile. "The King Alpha and Prince Beta request the presence of their mates at dinner in two hours. It'd be an honor if you would dine with the pack."

I don't take it and instead let out a snort. "I'd rather starve, thanks for the offer." My words aren't even a lie—I'd rather go hungry than sit amongst the creatures that have ruined humanity with their presence on our planet. Besides, I'm more than capable of making dinner for Leisel and me.

His smile falters slightly. "I'm not sure you have a choice."

A cold niggle of fear moves through my chest. "I'm not sure I give a shit. I won my duel. Leisel's underage. Neither of us has an obligation to be near you."

He clears his throat, shifting his weight. "From my understanding, if you don't come willingly, you'll be forced to attend." Then, pasting on his bright smile again, "The warriors guarding your house will escort you. I look forward to seeing you there." With that, he thrusts the envelope into my hands and walks off my porch—his stride the same confident and self-assured one I presume all mythics have.

I close the door and resist the urge to bang my head against it. The fact of the matter is that shifters can easily force Leisel and me to join them. I'd rather avoid stressing Leisel out even more than she recently has been. Although dinner with shifters will be an overload of anxiety for both of us, it would be better to go without chains.

If the mutts have any expectation of me acting pleasant, cordial, or even putting effort into my appearance, they're in for a rude awakening. Even if I wanted to dress up for dinner—which I don't because I have no intention of giving the impression I care what they think about me—I'd have nothing suitable to wear. I only have clothes designated for hunting, farming, mucking out the stables, going into the village, and sleeping.

Walking over to the dinner table with resignation, I tear open the envelope—uncaring that some smudges of paint end up on the expensive-looking paper—and read over the letter.

It's the same thing the shifter just told me, the only difference being it's printed in pretty formal script.

"Leisel," I call out, knowing she's in her room reading and playing with Chip. She appears in the doorway, looking me up and down with her eyebrows raised in question. I give her a grim smile. "Get dressed, sweet girl. We're dining with mutts tonight."

***

Leisel's hand trembles in mine as I help her off Duchess. Two shifters who were sent to "escort" us—in other words, to ensure we attended—dismount their horses ten feet away.

We stand in front of the mansion where shifters rest when traveling through Aesara—a gothic-looking structure, four stories high, as imposing as it is beautiful. It's comprised entirely of old stone and has an eerie way of holding one's attention.

I assume that the shifters want to impress us—as evidenced by the deferential treatment we received from our escorts, the polite way they greeted us, and the small talk they attempted to make. Small talk that was met with one-word answers and then silence. I have no interest in speaking with the creatures that have forced humans to the bottom of the proverbial food chain.

Leisel and I are both dressed in the clothes we wear when going into town—worn-down pants and a shirt that's a few washes away from falling apart for me, and a newer version of a similar getup for Leisel. Since she's still growing, her clothes are newer and in a better state than mine—I buy her new outfits several times a year, whereas the last time I bought myself clothes was when I was eighteen and stopped growing.

One of our escorts, the same man who extended the command for us to join the pack for dinner, walks up to Leisel and me before gesturing towards the open wooden door of the mansion with a smile. "Please, follow me."

I glance at Leisel who's staring at the mansion with wary eyes. I can practically feel her urge to run home and have dinner just the two of us, as always, and it breaks my heart that I can't accommodate that. This situation makes me feel like I've failed in my role as her protector.

Even Chip, curled up on her shoulder, looks slightly unnerved, his small nose sniffing the air for signs of danger.

I reluctantly follow the shifter inside with Leisel in tow, hating everything about our current predicament. Hating that I can't refuse, even though I won my duel, and therefore have no legal ties to the Rockwell Pack.

The interior of the mansion is also made of stone, lit by dim lamps etched into the walls, with candles providing additional light to the entrance hall.

"You okay?" I murmur to Leisel, peering down at her.

Her big golden eyes turn to me, and she slowly shakes her head. I know the shifters in front of us and behind us can hear me, but they thankfully don't interfere in the conversation.

"I'll be right by your side," I quietly vow. "We'll leave as soon as we can, alright?"

Her voice trembles when she responds, "Okay. I trust you."

Our quiet exchange is abruptly cut off as we come to a stop in front of a floor-to-ceiling set of double doors, both of which are open to reveal a formal dining room.

A long gray polished-stone table takes up the majority of the space, with at least thirty shifters seated at it, talking animatedly with each other. I assume that more pack members arrived today since there weren't nearly as many shifters present at the duel. As soon as my eyes find the elaborate spread of food on the table, rows of overflowing dishes and bowls covering the entire length, my stomach begins to churn with nausea.

As beautiful as the setup is, it's built on the pain, death, and humiliation of countless human lives. This entire mansion screams of blood money and it makes me sick. The dinner spread alone could feed my entire village for a week—instead, it's being wasted on the invaders who took our planet from us.

The entire table falls silent, and I suddenly find myself the center of attention under thirty scrutinizing stares. Although a few shifters flick Leisel glances of interest, their primary focus seems to be me. I can't help the self-consciousness that ignites inside of me, making my cheeks and neck heat. Unfortunately, being a redhead, blushes are impossible to hide.

I lift my chin and run a gaze that I know is brimming with disdain over every person seated at the table before my eyes land on Camden who's seated at the head. Wyatt is seated to the left of him, and the seat beside Wyatt is vacant, as is the one to the right of Camden.

The Alpha offers me a charming smile that drips with charisma, displaying pearly-white teeth.

He motions to the seat beside him. "Sierra, Leisel," he purrs, "I'm so glad you accepted my invitation—"

"We weren't given a choice," I interject.

He's not put off, and his smile doesn't waver in the slightest. "Join us."

The only way out is through. My father would always tell me that when I was a child. He'd reiterate again and again that whatever obstacle I was facing *was* the solution—that avoiding difficulties was pointless, whereas overcoming them head-on was the true objective.

Outside of the loss of my parents, this is one of the most difficult obstacles I've ever faced, a dinner with a room full of shifters.

Knowing that my options are limited, I slowly walk to where Camden is sitting.

Once I'm next to the vacant seat to his right, I ask Leisel, "Would you prefer to sit with me or by the Beta?"

I don't use beta as an honorific title—I use it to avoid personifying Wyatt, which he catches onto.

With a bristle, he says, "My name is Wyatt."

I don't look away from my sister when I respond. "Which is irrelevant to me, but thank you for the information."

To my surprise, a few laughs sound in the room, and I see Camden's lips tilt up at the corners. Wyatt, however, glowers at me, clearly not finding my comment amusing. He'll soon come to understand that I could not give less of a shit what shifters think or don't think about me.

Leisel, with mirth dancing in her eyes, says, "With you."

I nod, sink into the seat, and then perch her on my lap. I sift my fingers through her hair, ignoring the shifters surrounding us.

After a moment of tense silence, Camden tells the pack members, "You may begin."

With that, everyone begins loading food onto their plates and filling silver goblets with assorted drinks. Chatter starts up again, and Camden takes the liberty of sliding an extra plate for Leisel beside mine and loading both dishes with exotic-looking foods; spiced grilled meats and fishes, roasted vegetables, and colorful side dishes I've never seen before.

I don't have any intention of partaking in the offered meal. Even accepting food from Camden could send a signal of acceptance, and that's the *last* thing I want. I intend to whip up a proper family meal once Leisel and I are back home, not indulge the Rockwell Pack.

Camden blatantly stares at me, even as he begins to eat. The rest of his pack members are slightly more subtle now—merely sneaking glances out of the corners of their eyes rather than facing me head-on the way their Alpha currently is.

I stiffen when he leans towards me over the arm of his chair, and turn to pin him with a stony stare.

He gives me a long, slow perusal with his eyes, making me feel naked and exposed despite being fully clothed. His eyes blaze with lust as he takes in every inch of my body, his gaze turning smoldering. Just like that, warmth ignites in my belly, causing my cheeks to heat even further.

The mate bond is clearly doing its work. I know from my reading that the more time I spend around Camden, the firmer grip the metaphysical bond between us will get on me, and the more I'll be attracted to him. The thought of something invisible controlling me makes me clench my teeth so hard that my jaw starts to ache.

With a mere look, he's inspiring more lust in me than I've *ever* felt—aside from when he kissed me last night. To be fair, I can't exactly pretend to have ever felt lust before, so the mere sensation of being sexually attracted to another being is jarring. There have been a few boys in the village that have caught my eye over the years, granted, but I was too busy raising a child to do anything other than flash a smile.

"You *really* don't like me, do you?" Camden questions, sounding amused at the prospect.

I sniff. "I'm not a fan of rhetorical questions."

He rubs a hand over his stubbled jaw, and I suspect he's hiding a smile. "Okay," he drawls. "What *are* you a fan of?"

His already deep voice drops an octave, gaining a smoky edge that sends heat whipping through me. I know he's doing this on purpose—trying to exploit the innate physical attraction between us.

So, I say the one thing that I know will stop this conversation from becoming inappropriate—because he's projecting an untamed need that makes me beyond uncomfortable, mainly because of how deeply it's affecting me. "Humans. Human men, specifically."

His gaze turns from smoldering to deeply irritated in a flash. His hands clench and his eyes burn a brighter silver-blue. Somehow, I can tell that his wolf is slinking closer to the surface.

The reading I've done on shifters has taught me that they have a dualism to their souls—that their inner animals are separate yet attached entities. If I'm not mistaken, a shifter and their inner animal are often on par with each other, but they both have their own personalities. The animals have a primal way of thinking—I'm willing to bet that Camden's wolf simply doesn't understand why I'm being resistant, which angers the animal within. I doubt the wolf is able to grasp the nuances of the situation—in his eyes, I belong to him, and he wants to claim that belonging. I'm sure Camden thinks similarly, though he's capable of assessing the intricacies of our circumstances. It almost makes me want to smile that neither the man nor his wolf are getting what they want, something that's likely a new experience for both of them.

"A word of advice, Sierra," Camden rumbles. "Tread very, *very* carefully when talking about other men."

I cock my head to the side. "Why? You have no right to control me—*I won my duel*. I don't owe you or your fellow shifters anything. I don't belong to you."

I realize that the table has once again fallen silent, everyone watching my exchange with their Alpha, riveted.

A growl sounds low in Camden's throat. "Incorrect. You're the other half of my soul—you belong to me in every goddamn way, whether you like it or not."

My temper—something I normally have solid control over—snaps.

"If you think a royal meal will change my hatred of you, think again." I motion to the table in disgust. "Ask yourself this: why *wouldn't* I prefer humans over you? mythics—shifters specifically—forced humans to go back to a miserable way of living. You stole our resources. Destroyed our technology because it didn't suit your needs or whims. You caused billions of deaths. You consistently *steal* the lives of your mates, giving them no option but to submit to your disgusting ways. Standing with you is akin to accepting the horrors you have put us through, and I will *never* accept that. Likewise, I will never accept *you*."

Disbelief, anger, and fury flicker over Camden's face. I enjoy every one of the emotions, because I want to see him suffer as he has made humans suffer, and I'm now in the prime position to incite that torment within him.

"We've been laden with the consequences of your rule for over a century. We've had to fight for survival on a planet *that was ours to begin with*. We've bled because you didn't care enough to protect us. You've all but destroyed the human race, and yet you seek my allegiance?"

With a mask of determination on his features, Camden tells me in a quiet yet steely voice, "But you're not human either, are you, Sierra?"

I really wish I hadn't let the secret of my magic slip.

"My kind was on this planet *long* before yours," I shoot back. "Those with earthly magic, along with humans, have rights to Earth. Whereas you have nothing but a long history of causing pain and death to those weaker than you." I inhale and exhale deeply, willing myself to gain some calm. I whisper in Leisel's ear, "Ready to go, sweet girl?"

She's stiff on my lap, but when she looks at me, there isn't a hint of fear in her eyes. No, there's an anger that almost matches mine. My impassioned rant seems to have riled her up—which wasn't my intention. Leisel is kind, sweet, and the very definition of wholesome. I have no right to corrupt that with my anger. She nods, the motion jerky with rage.

"If you stand up from my table right now, you'll pay the price," Camden says, every syllable dripping with danger.

Ignoring his threat, I help Leisel up and then stand. Locking eyes with my so-called mate, I declare, "You have no jurisdiction over either of us. Leisel is too young to be mated, and I won my duel. I have no interest in dining with you or spending a moment in your company. So, I'll kindly ask you to stay out of my life."

Before I can blink, Camden's on his feet and has a hand wrapped around my arm. His stern unyielding expression—as well as his blurring speed—startles me, but I don't let that show. Instead, I try to jerk out of his hold. Unfortunately, that achieves nothing because his strength undoubtedly exceeds mine.

He addresses the pack though his eyes never leave me. "Please, continue with your meal. I need to have a word with our future queen." Then ever so briefly glancing at Wyatt, "Watch your mate in my absence."

Those words feel like a bucket of cold water thrown on my anger, replacing it with a soul-deep fear. I instinctively reach out for Leisel's hand, but Camden's already dragging me away, his stride none too gentle.

"Stop!" I demand. "You can't take me away from her!" I do my absolute best to escape his grip, but my efforts are perfectly futile. Within seconds, he has me out of the dining room and continues forcibly pulling me away from the one person in my life I truly care about.

"Fucking *stop! You can't do this!*" I practically shriek, feeling tears start to well in my eyes at the thought of little Leisel left in a room of wolves.

I can't stop Wyatt from doing anything, since *I'm not there to protect her.*

When I stumble and almost fall flat on the ground, Camden sweeps me up into his arms, holding me tight against the muscled expanse of his body. The close contact incites a new, stronger lust within me, but my fear for Leisel overshadows it, and I try to wriggle out of his hold.

"Don't fight me," he bites out. "Not fucking now. You have no goddamn idea how close I am to sinking my teeth into your neck and permanently marking you as mine."

Chapter Ten

That stuns me into both stillness and silence. I go tense in his arms, my thoughts running a mile a minute worrying over Leisel. If he marks me, it'll be a step towards cementing the bond between us. A bond that will permanently bind me to him in an irrevocable way.

I clearly won't be able to escape Camden using brute force, but if I give him some obedience, there's a chance it'll calm him, and I'll return to Leisel sooner.

Despite my worst fears, I doubt he'll want to separate us for long—he *has* to be smart enough to know that'll only increase my hatred of him.

"Take me back to my sister, *please*," I beg, absolutely despising myself for how quickly my strength crumbles when I'm worried for Leisel.

"I will," Camden says through gritted teeth, opening the door to a room and stepping inside before shutting it behind him.

I tense even more to see that we're in a bedroom. There's a large four-poster bed situated against the far wall and a fireplace across from it. At the corner is a desk with a few papers and pens strewn around it.

My breaths turn shallow as Camden sets me on my feet in front of the door and pins me against it. His hands land on my arms, securing them at my sides, and leans his full weight against me, effectively trapping me.

"Let's get one thing clear, Sierra." The possessive way he says my name sends a shiver of exhilaration through me, followed by a healthy dose of disgust with my body for reacting to him in such a way.

"You *are* my mate. You were *made* for me, as I was for you. I *will* have you, in every way I can. I'm not an average shifter who's bound by laws of duelum—I'm the Alpha of the most powerful pack in this realm and ruler over *all* packs of all shifters. If you think winning the duel will truly allow you to escape from me, *think again.*"

I open my mouth to refute his words, but he cuts me off by crushing his lips to mine. Although my mind continues formulating reason after reason why I truly despise him, my body melts against him—forced to do so by the bond. After a mere few seconds, I'm sagging in his arms, and his hands turn from restraining to supporting. Slowly, all reasonable thought begins to escape me until all I can think about are his soft, full lips against mine, his tongue exploring and tasting me, and the length of his hard, powerful body pressed against mine. He's bigger than me in every way, and that only makes him more attractive. My nipples pebble inside my bra, and I feel liquid heat pooling in my core.

I have to wonder if he brushes his teeth with pheromones because his kiss literally makes me feel drugged, dizzy, and giddy.

His hands travel down to my ass, squeezing and molding the flesh, and he groans into my mouth. Pulling his lips away from mine, he presses his nose into the hair cascading down my neck, and inhales deeply. A low sound of pleasure rumbles up from him.

"Never forget that I'm a wolf, Sierra," he growls. "That means when you try to dominate me, my instinct is to force you to submit."

That dampens the arousal scorching through me instantly and I stiffen again. "Are you saying you're going to beat me if I don't act the part of a perfect mate?"

He removes one hand from my ass, fists it in my hair, and pulls my head back, forcing me to stare into his eyes. "I don't want a perfect mate. I want you, but if you run from me in any way—whether that be physically or by trying to keep me at a distance—I *will* punish this perfect ass of yours."

Anger gives me a rush of adrenaline, and I find the inner strength to shove at him again. "Don't you fucking *dare*."

In a move that's so fast it leaves me dizzy, especially since I'm still unstable with the aftereffects of his kiss, he spins me around and pins my front to the door.

Guessing his intention, I struggle with all my might, kicking and thrashing and trying to get away from him. I curse Camden both in English and in Latin—a language my mother taught me so that I could read ancient books on witchcraft—which makes him let out a puff of amused laughter. He remains in position easily, barely seeming to notice the effort that leaves me panting angrily.

When I've tired myself out and my struggles have turned from vehement to pathetic, he pins both of my wrists above my head with one hand and brings his big hand crashing down on my ass, creating a stinging sensation that spreads over my cheek. I jump and gasp, which makes him release a dark chuckle as he rains down a series of sharp slaps on my ass and the top of my thighs, so hard that I feel the burn even through the thick material of my pants.

The worst part isn't the pain. It's the fact that him...*spanking* me only serves to turn me on more.

"Stop! Enough!" I exclaim when the blows harden until I *really* start to feel them.

"This is how shifters deal with defiant mates," he tells me, his voice having turned slightly breathless. He stops the spanking but leaves his hand resting on my ass.

"I'm never going to be submissive!" I snap back.

His tone gentles. "I know that, Sierra. I don't expect you to be submissive to anyone."

That gives me pause. "You won't demand my submission?" I ask.

"No, I won't, but I *will* demand your acceptance." His palm starts to rub over my stinging flesh soothingly, and I can almost feel the mate bond getting to work to alleviate the pain—turning it into pure unadulterated pleasure. I think I hear him mutter, *and submission in bed*, but hope to the gods I'm hallucinating from whatever drug his mouth is laced with.

"I'll never accept you," I hiss.

His response is a pleased rumbly laugh. "Then why is the sweet scent of your arousal wafting around my room?"

Oh, shit. Shifters have an enhanced sense of smell—*of course* he can smell just how turned on I got by the spanking he just gave me.

"Because the goddamn mate bond is warping my thoughts. Trust me on this, Camden, I'll never feel anything but disdain for you, no matter how strong the bond gets. And if my body responds to you, it's not because of me, it's because one of the gods decided to play a cosmic fucking joke by pairing us!"

He spins me back around so that I'm facing him again, wrapping his arms around me to hold me still, and I see how intently he's staring at my lips.

"Such dirty words out of such a sweet mouth," he murmurs, look-ing entranced.

"You bring out the worst in me," I shoot back.

His grin is molten and absolutely wicked. "You're so godsdamned sexy when you talk back to me."

"And you should really come with a warning label: biggest idiotic incompetent asshole alive."

His eyes travel over my lips and settle on my neck. "You have no idea how much I want to make you mine."

My fists clench. His teeth are not getting anywhere near my neck. "Try it and I'll educate you on what your testicles taste like."

Gaze half-lidded, his smile widens. "You're stunning when you threaten me with bodily harm."

"You won't be sporting that smug grin when I mutilate you."

He licks his lips. "If you had any idea of the things I want—and *will*—do to you..."

"I'd kill you in your sleep," I finish for him.

"If anyone else said that to me, they'd be dead before they could draw their next breath," he points out, his tone turning stony.

I wait for the innate fear all humans have of mythics to hit me, but it doesn't come. For a moment, that puzzles me, until I come to a realization. The mate bond is already corrupting me—making me feel safe in Camden's presence despite the blatant danger he poses to both me and the one other person I truly love in this world.

I say slowly, "You won't kill me." It feels like the words are pulled out of me by an unseen force—as if the bond demands a verbal acknowledgment of what I somehow know to be true.

"I won't," Camden agrees softly. "But there are many ways to punish you, Sierra, and not all of them even involve pain."

I try to jerk away from him, incensed at the threat, but he doesn't allow it. His arms tighten until I can barely twitch.

He rumbles, "I don't want to punish you—at least, not in ways you won't love." The sexual innuendo in his tone sends a shiver through me. "But if you force my hand, I will."

"If you try *anything*, I will castrate you—"

He cuts off my words with a hard, chaste kiss. "Listen to me very carefully," he says once he pulls back. "I don't expect total obedience. I don't *want* total obedience—it would bore me since that's all I get from those around me—but I think it pertinent to give you a few guidelines on what will get you punished."

"You act as if I'll agree to go anywhere with you," I interrupt. "The likelihood of that is somewhere south of zero."

He lets out a hard breath of frustration. He thinks quietly for a moment before seeming to settle on a decision. "Leisel is a member of the Rockwell Pack by association. I am her Alpha. If I issue a command for her to be taken to Kinrith, that command will be followed through. The laws won't protect her from that."

The last time I felt the sort of fear that wholly encompasses me in this moment was when Leisel was dying from pneumonia. It feels like a casing of ice settling over every inch of me, making me shiver down to my very bones.

"Y-you can't," I whisper, my voice breaking from the onslaught of sheer terror I'm experiencing at the thought of this mutt taking my sister. "She's underage—"

"Which means she can't be marked or mated," he interrupts. "That law will be respected, but I'm still her Alpha. Tomorrow she will be moved to Kinrith."

That's when I see it. Camden's checkmate. He's seen how much I love Leisel. He knows that I'm her protector in every way. He also knows that I won't *ever* leave her—especially not if she'll be dragged to live amongst shifters. I'd die before leaving her to bear that burden on her own.

Camden knows I'll follow her to the ends of the Earth and he's using that against me. By moving her to Kinrith, he's ensuring I move with her.

"You *motherfucker!*" I yell at the top of my lungs, renewing my struggle with such vehemence that Camden actually stumbles a step back. I slap him across the cheek with all my strength, so hard that his lip splits and a trail of blood drips from it before the cut quickly heals.

Then I do something I never thought I would; I call forward my flame with lethal intent. I'll kill Camden before I let him have my little sister.

This time, my black fire doesn't just ignite in my palm—it covers the entirety of my hand, as well as some of my arm.

Anger fueling me, I strike Camden again, fully expecting him to turn to ashes on the spot and not caring that I'll be killing my so-called soulmate. Not caring that I'm about to take a life because all that matters is protecting Leisel from his kind.

Shock flares on Camden's features as I slap him with my flame-covered hand, but nothing happens. He doesn't disintegrate. Not even a scorch mark is left on his cheek. *The fire doesn't affect him at all.* He must have immunity to my abilities—evidently, a side-effect of the bond. The fire on my hand dissipates.

Camden's blue eyes burn brighter as they lock with mine, and I instinctively stiffen. Being given that raging stare from a being who's an apex predator in every way makes me freeze. He sucks in a deep breath as if trying to calm himself, and when he speaks, his tone is cold and flat. "Did you think that would kill me?" He gives his head a single mechanical shake. "Mates can't kill each other, Sierra, but attempting that is something that will earn you a heavy punishment."

Chapter Eleven

Camden seizes my arms and pulls me to the bed, tossing me face-down on it. When I try to scramble upright, he presses a hand to my spine and holds me down, not seeming put off in the least by my struggles. I'm sure, in his mind, I went way too far with my attempt to kill him. In reality, he's simply yet to realize that I will do anything to protect my sister. He holds me down for several minutes, and I get the sense that he's trying to calm himself—but that doesn't stop me from continuing to try to escape.

Finally, he speaks, the words chillingly cold. "You were afraid for your sister," he says, as if to himself. "Likely assumed she'd come to harm while under my care. That made you lash out, which is understandable, but trying to kill me is still *not fucking acceptable.*" After another pause, he continues. "I'm going to stripe your ass with my belt—perhaps that will act as a deterrent for any future foolish endeavors."

Stripe my ass with his belt? I don't think the bond could turn that level of pain into pleasure. The spanking before was a mere warning; this will be an example of what Camden's going to do if I cross him so severely in the future.

"Wait," I rasp. "I'm sorry—"

"Oh, you will be," he says darkly. "I'll make sure you're sorry enough to never repeat an assassination attempt. The more you struggle, the harder I'll go on you, so it's in your best interest to stay still."

I fall motionless at once because I fully believe he'll deliver on any threat he makes right now. Although I was acting rashly out of fear and anger, I *did* just attempt to murder him. To him, not punishing me for that would be a concession of weakness—something I doubt he or his wolf would permit.

Camden still keeps a cautioning hand on my back, but I hear him take off the belt with the other. "You get to keep your pants on this time, but if you ever do something that suicidal again, I'll whip your naked ass until you bleed."

With that, he lets the belt swing. I hear the telling displacement of air before a stripe of pure, torturous fire ignites my ass from the impact. I can't help it—I cry out. My entire body jerks involuntarily. Camden isn't going to take it easy on me.

"Stay. Still," he warns, before hitting me again and again, not deterred by my yelps and eventual screams when the pain simply becomes too much.

He hits me ten times in total, the blows so shockingly aggressive I'm surprised he didn't snap my tailbone. The agony is scalding, burning, and unbearable. My entire ass is on fire, and the slightest twitch only amplifies the pain.

When he's done, I shut my eyes against the tears of pain threatening, forcing them back. I won't give him the satisfaction of seeing me cry. I simply lie motionless on the soft bedding, trying to regulate my breathing.

Camden lets out what sounds like a breath of relief. "Don't make me do that again."

When his hand moves from my spine up to my face, in an attempt to brush the strands of hair covering my face aside, I snap, "Don't you *dare* touch me, you piece of shit!"

I sit up on my haunches and face him, wishing that he wasn't immune to my power but knowing better than to try to hit him with my flame again.

He stands fully upright, crosses his arms, and gazes down at me. It looks like it takes every ounce of his willpower to remain still. "Go home. Pack your necessities and Leisel's as well. Tomorrow morning I'll be taking you to Kinrith." His tone gentles slightly when he sees traitorous tears welling in my eyes. "It won't be so horrible, Sierra. Don't try to kill me, and I won't belt you again—that's a punishment that'll only be administered in extreme circumstances."

I don't say anything because as soon as I open my mouth, I know I'll cry. Not from the pain though—it's already subsiding, and I have a pretty high tolerance. I suspect that though I'm not a healer, the magic within me does make me heal faster than humans. No, I'll cry because Camden is quite literally ruining my life, and worse, Leisel's.

"You'll want for nothing," he tells me softly. "Anything you could possibly wish for will be yours."

After that, I hear his unspoken words: *Anything but your freedom.*

***

The ride home is unbearable. Every jostle on Shadow reignites stinging pain on my backside. I keep my winces to a minimum because I don't want to frighten Leisel even more than she was being confined in a room with shifters for upwards of twenty minutes.

When I walked back to the dining room, I refused to hang my head like a disciplined mate would. My chin was in the air, my eyes disdainful as I took in the curious shifters. My posture was straight as if every step wasn't painful. I got the sense that Camden somehow *liked* that about me. When he bid Leisel and me farewell—in the smuggest way possible, of course—I'd seen a glint of pride in his eyes.

Well, fuck that and fuck him. If the bond was a physical thing, I'd light it on fire and watch gleefully as the connection between us was destroyed. Unfortunately, it's magical and impervious to tampering.

I haven't yet broken the news to Leisel that we're going to have to go live with shifters because I don't know how to. I promised her I'd protect her. I vowed it. And yet, my protection hasn't proven to amount to anything when it comes to shifters. I've never felt so powerless, furious, or ashamed.

We're both quiet until we get into our home. Then, without speaking, I get to work on our dinner. I'm in the middle of putting together sandwiches when I feel two small arms close around my waist from behind.

"Are you okay?" Leisel asks in a tentative voice.

I blink several times, looking at the ceiling and trying to control the tears that seem determined to escape.

Once I'm confident I'll be able to keep a handle on my emotions, I turn, crouch, and wrap my arms around my little sister. Even after what I know was a terrifying experience—being alone with a room full of shifters—Leisel's worried about *me*. She's so kind, gentle, and caring. How will she survive if we live among mongrels?

"I'm okay, sweet girl," I tell her, pressing a kiss to her temple. "I just got some tough news from Camden." I pause, choosing my words carefully. "He's issued an order for us to go back to the wolves' capital, Kinrith, with him. It's non-negotiable and utterly unavoidable. I—I'm so sorry, Leisel. I did my best to free us."

She pulls back to consider me, her expression unusually somber. Chip makes a chattering noise that sounds almost consoling from her shoulder.

"Everything's going to be different now, isn't it?"

I open and close my mouth several times. "Yes." Then, trying to focus on something remotely positive I add, "But we'll be living with much better accommodations. In something resembling a palace, I think, similar to fairytales." *Except in fairytales, the Princess isn't soulmate to the villain.*

"I don't want a fairytale," Leisel says, her golden eyes wide and frightened. "Not if it means being with...*them.*"

Having nothing else to offer, I repeat, "I'm so sorry."

"Will we be safe there?" she asks.

I consider the question before responding. On a physical level, I think so, because from my understanding mates have a primal drive to protect each other at all costs. Wolves *especially* turn protective with human mates, since they're so much more fragile than fellow shifters, even when receiving strength from the bond post-consummation. Granted, Leisel and I aren't exactly human, but we're still more physically fragile than mythics.

On an emotional level, however, is an entirely different story. My intuition's telling me that upcoming events will put me under more stress than I can imagine. I'm determined not to allow the stress to spill over to the young healer in my arms.

"As safe as we can hope to be," I tell her. "I'm not a fan of shifters...but being mated to such powerful ones will give us more protection than we have here." As much as I wish my fire had burned Camden right into a grave... "Wyatt would give his life to protect you." If for no other reason than the bond will drive him to do so.

Leisel blinks slowly. "Will Camden protect you?"

I swallow because he'll be the biggest danger to me possible. While Leisel's young, and will therefore be treated according to her age, I'm an adult, and I'll be punished for my indiscretions as an adult—as Camden demonstrated tonight.

Not wanting to worry Leisel with details, I say, "Yes."

Leisel's hands tighten around me, and then still for a moment. "You're hurt," she somehow realizes and pulls back to look me over. *She can sense pain too? Not just see it?* A powerful healer indeed.

"I'm alright, my love."

"Where are you hurt?" she demands.

Knowing that she won't let this go, I murmur, "I think I might have twisted my ankle earlier. I'll be fine by morning."

It's not a lie—I *did* awkwardly roll my ankle when Camden was pulling me out of the dining room, but that pain's been overshadowed by adrenaline born of fear, as well as the pain from the belting.

I feel a warmth spark in my waist and know it comes from Leisel. Before I can protest, it travels to my ass, healing the raw flesh, and then shoots down to my ankle. Within seconds, I no longer feel even a twinge of discomfort anywhere on my body.

Seeing her power at work makes my thoughts flick back to the duel earlier today. More specifically, the fact that time somehow slowed down to my benefit. That wasn't a power stemming from me; I know that for sure, which meant it was most likely somehow a result of divine intervention. I prayed to Hecate and she responded. The question is, *why?* Why would the goddess of witches do that? Initially, I thought it might be to help release me from the Rockwell Pack, but that clearly isn't the case as Camden still found out about Leisel's and my powers. A divine being such as the goddess of magic must've known that would happen.

Perhaps she wanted to spare me pain or perhaps it could've been her intent for my powers to eventually be revealed, though that doesn't explain her aid. Whatever the case is, it seems I'll never know, and

I certainly don't intend to tell anyone just what occurred. After all, magical aid—whether stemming from me or not—would be classed as breaking the laws of duelum and would give Camden further grounds to take me with him.

I release a sigh and give my sister a squeeze. "Thank you, Leisel. Now let me finish making the sandwiches. We'll pack in the morning, and then we travel to the capital of mutts."

Chapter Twelve

Camden

"How'd your *talk* with Sierra go?" Wyatt asks me in a teasing voice, swirling amber liquor in a tumbler.

We're enjoying a nightcap in his room, sitting in front of a crackling fireplace. After seeing Sierra and Leisel off, I decided to join him for a drink—clearly a strategic error on my part, since he's taking the opportunity to rib me.

"As well as expected. She didn't like it when I informed her she'd be joining us when we return to Kinrith tomorrow." An understatement, considering how the time ended. "How'd trying not to scare her sister in Sierra's absence go?"

Wyatt's amused expression sours instantaneously. I don't revel in the change—probably because I understand the discomfort that comes with being rejected by one's mate. Fortunately, my brother does have it easier, since Leisel's so young; his regard for her is currently brotherly and pure. It'll change to romantic only once she's of a mature age. So, he's not a sexual mess like I am.

"She stared at her fucking pet the entire time, pretending no one else was in the room. I never thought a Twolf could be jealous of a goddamn chipmunk. Clearly, Sierra's only fed Leisel negative information about us. Lies, probably."

My expression hardens. His words are an offhanded insult of sorts to my mate, which is unacceptable to me. My wolf doesn't like it either and directs a snarl at Wyatt. *I* might take issue with the views of my mate, but I won't allow others to disrespect her.

"Tread carefully," I tell him quietly. "Sierra is to be your queen. Humans often villainize mythics—they have no reason to see us as anything *but* monsters."

That fact has never bothered me until now because humans were frankly beneath my notice. Now that I have a mate who, though not entirely human, grew up among them, I'm being lent an unpleasant new perspective.

My father was merely a boy when my grandfather first invaded this realm. Grandfather didn't actively kill any humans *himself,* but in the absence of the technology they so heavily relied on, humans started dropping like flies. It really was a case of survival of the fittest—the strong bloodlines prevailed, the weak fell.

I don't entirely agree with his decision, but I can understand it. He'd been disgusted by just how much of this world had been destroyed by its inhabitants—repulsed by how much greed had impacted this realm. To him, the logical solution was to allow the weak and greedy to die out. There were a few groups of individuals who actively hunted humans, mostly rogues, but for the most part, natural selection took its course.

Even if I did wish to change his actions, I can't. What's done is done, and my penance for not making changes during my rule is experiencing my mate's anger.

It took me off-guard, however, that Sierra was so angry she actually tried to kill me. There's no other explanation for using such a destructive power against me. I can see that worry over her sister pushed her to act rashly and even sympathize with the sentiment. If anyone threatened Wyatt's life, they'd be dead before they could second-guess doing so.

As unfortunate as it might be, I was left with little choice but to punish her in a way that will serve as a hard deterrent from her ever trying such a thing again. While shifters are animalistic when it comes to sex, *especially* with mates—biting, scratching, leaving marks for all to see—a belt wasn't fun and games. Although I believe it worked, and Sierra won't try such a thing again, it certainly didn't help change her view of me. Instead, she now has more reason than ever to view me as the villain.

Fuck.

I gulp down the whiskey in my cup and run a hand through my hair, wondering if I'll experience the harmony of matehood. Perhaps Claude was right; I should've waited for the gods to put her in my path, though I don't see how that would've changed any outcome. Whether our meeting was by accident or construct, she'd have despised me.

Wyatt watches me before quietly conceding, "You're right. I guess it's our job to shift our mates' views from openly hostile to something better."

"Indeed," I respond gruffly. "How are preparations for our newest members going?"

Wyatt snorts. "Speedily. Everyone in the castle is working around the clock. By the time we arrive, everything for the Queen and Princess will be ready. Are we riding all the way to Kinrith in one day, or will we make camp somewhere overnight?"

"We'll make camp. Sierra and Leisel don't have our strength or stamina; traveling will tire them. Have lady's maids been assigned?"

Wyatt nods. "Yes. Greta will be Leisel's—she does well with young ones. Cara will be Sierra's."

"Where are their rooms located?"

"The two attached rooms in the East Wing. Both wardrobes are already being assembled and will be prepared by the time we arrive."

I nod in satisfaction. Then, recalling what Aspen told me about Sierra's painting hobby I say, "Get a painter's studio set up in the castle. Have it filled with any and everything an artist would need."

"It'll be done," Wyatt responds easily. "You think that'll earn you points with your mate?"

Recalling the hatred-filled glare Sierra gave me before leaving, I grimace. "No time soon. But hopefully it'll afford her some comfort while she adjusts."

***

The following morning, Sierra pulls the door to her small cabin open before I have the chance to knock, clearly having expected me.

She's dressed in similar clothing to what she wore last night—extremely worn-down shirt and pants, both articles looking like they might fall apart any minute. Somehow, Sierra manages to make the tattered clothes look sinful, her curves filling them out beautifully. Still, I look forward to seeing her in more expensive clothing—materials I expect will hug her body as if they were made for her. In many cases, they will be.

With her expression set in a look of disgust, one I'm starting to get accustomed to, she gives me a once-over. She glances behind me and sees a group of my pack mates gathered on the horses we'll be using to travel. Wyatt stands by two mares that I intend to offer to Sierra and Leisel for the journey.

"Good morning," I say to my lovely, pissed-off-looking mate. "Did you rest well?"

"Yes," she clips.

It's obviously a lie—there are dark circles under her eyes that indicate she hasn't slept in several nights. Now that I think about it, it's a solid possibility that she *hasn't* slept since meeting me—probably wanting to stay alert to protect herself and Leisel.

My wolf, who pestered me to seek out Sierra from the moment we parted, lays down with a whine, upset that we've caused our mate distress.

He was in complete agreement with me last night on punishing Sierra, furious that she struck out at us with lethal intent. He wasn't, however, happy to see her go—wanted to soothe her, at the very least, before parting ways.

Unfortunately, I don't see my presence being soothing to my mate any time soon. The dilemma between knowing that Sierra will need her space and wanting to constantly have her around me will certainly play on my self-control. Self-control that has been trained into me from a young age and has never faltered—until I met my mate.

"I need to saddle and prepare our horses," Sierra tells me. "It'll take twenty minutes."

She calls over her shoulder, "Leisel, it's time to go, sweet girl."

Within moments Leisel appears at Sierra's side and stares right into my eyes with an anger that belies her small size. I'm mildly surprised that she's able to hold eye-contact with me, but I shouldn't be. Whatever bloodline these sisters come from, it's remarkably powerful. If they were shifters, they'd both undoubtedly be dominant enough to be Alphas.

"I have horses you're welcome to ride," I offer.

Sierra wrinkles her nose at the thought. "No, thank you, we'll take ours. I assume there'll be a place for them in whatever stable you use at Kinrith?"

I incline my head. "The Alpha's stable is on the same land as my home, a fifteen-minute walk from the house. The stable hands are all very good at what they do—your horses will be well taken care of."

My mate snorts. "Nobody touches our horses but Leisel or me. I was there through their births, when they were broken in, and have been taking care of them singlehandedly for a decade." She pauses, looking surprised at how much she's divulged. The bond's coercing her into revealing more about herself which satisfies me, though I doubt it brings her the same satisfaction.

"I want to know more about that," I tell her.

She gives me a look of such contempt it almost makes me wince, bringing a growl of displeasure from my wolf.

"I bet you would," she says, and walks away, hand in hand with Leisel.

I lean against the wooden logs making up the exterior of the cabin, watching as the sisters traverse through a field of crops, and go right into a small, red-painted stable. Then, once they're out of sight, I wander into the house.

My objective is simple; learn more about my mate. The more I know her, the more I'll know what to do to get in her good graces.

I glance around the main area, marveling at the cleanliness of the space. My eyes flit briefly over the row of books stacked strategically in each corner of the room, as well as a collection on top of the fireplace mantle. On a worn sofa are two small bags that I have no doubt carry Sierra and Leisel's meager belongings. On the kitchen counter, I see a note lying on top of a white letter titled *Deeds to the Land and Cabin.*

I glance over the note with interest.

Mariketa,

I thank you, from the bottom of my heart, for the many ways you have helped Leisel and I over the years. I can't describe how fundamental your teachings were when Leisel was an infant, or how much it meant to know I had someone to turn to.

It's with my deepest regret that I must leave Aesara, on orders from Camden Kent. He found a technicality that puts Leisel under his pack's reign, and where she goes, I go.

I've signed over the deed to this land to you and Parker. The cabin, fields, and stables are yours to do with as you please—whether that be to use the land or sell it.

I'll never forget the days you spent here, teaching me to care for Leisel when she was born. I'll never forget your generosity or kindness during the most difficult times in my life. I'll forever treasure everything you taught me.

I hope I can use any influence I gain to return resources to humans—especially considering they were ours to begin with. I envision myself walking through Aesara one day, not greeted by poverty and difficulty, but instead by a booming, progressive town filled with opportunity.

Please give Wesley a hug for me and thank him for all the time he's spent with Leisel. She adores him and will miss him dearly, as will I.

With my deepest appreciation,

Sierra West.

I set down the letter, wishing there was more information and more specifics on Sierra's life. It's obvious she faced difficulty from a very young age, difficulty that grew as she did. She's learned to be so independent that I'm not sure she knows how to let someone else care for her, which will be another hurdle in our relationship. Those seem to be piling up.

I peek into the two bedrooms, not finding much of interest, but am frozen in astonishment when I step into the last room at the back of the cabin.

It's covered in paintings—*beautiful* masterful paintings that depict everything from landscapes to nature to inanimate objects. On an easel in the center of the room is a stunning painting of a luminous moon hanging over an intricately detailed forest. The midnight sky is covered in stars so picturesque they might as well be diamonds, and the forest is remarkably realistic and intricately detailed, looking like it's straight out of a fairytale.

I'm not much of an art-lover—I respect people who create art but rarely have time to appreciate it. This painting, however, is so vivid and encompassing that it *demands* my attention.

"What are you doing in here?" Sierra's voice snaps from behind me. I spin around, knowing that I've been caught, but not ashamed of that whatsoever.

Sierra stands in the doorway, her face red with indignation, arms crossed over her chest. I see movement from behind her, and guess that Leisel's in the cabin, likely gathering last-minute items.

"Admiring your work," I respond honestly, glancing back at the painting again. "You're remarkably talented."

"My work isn't yours to admire," she says through gritted teeth. "You have no right to be in here."

It's clear to see I struck a sore spot by invading her painting room—likely because artists often feel sentimental about their creations. The painter my family commissions for royal portraits tends to go off on prolonged rants if we move or even breathe too much during sittings.

"I have every right to be in here," I respond calmly. "We're mates. What's yours is mine, and vice-versa."

Her golden eyes blaze with anger. "Get. Out."

Knowing I've pushed as far as I can for the moment, I stride past her. "We're ready to leave when you are. The journey is long, and I'd like to make camp before sundown."

With that, I leave the cabin, letting out a sigh of frustration, knowing that tearing down Sierra's fury at my mere existence will be no easy task.

Chapter Thirteen

Sierra

By the time we make camp that evening, Leisel is so exhausted I fear she might fall off of Duchess. The night is chilly, so after helping her off her horse and tying their reigns to a tree I bundle her in a blanket I packed.

The pack members riding with us have given us space while we've journeyed through the day—whether that be on orders from their Alpha or not wanting to tempt my anger, which is so prevalent it's palpable, I'm not sure.

I'm as tired as Leisel, if not more, considering I haven't slept the last two nights, but I don't let myself rest. While the shifters begin setting up tents and unpacking the food they brought, I set about starting a fire to keep Leisel and me warm.

It isn't difficult—we stopped in a clearing in the midst of a heavily wooded area, so I assemble some sticks and logs from the forest floor as well as dead leaves, set them up in a teepee structure within a ring of rocks, and strike flint and steel a few times before the leaves catch fire. The flame quickly spreads to the rest of the sticks. After a minute, as the fire begins to grow and heat up, I add some thicker pieces of wood, and then sit down next to Leisel, huddling close to keep her warm.

We only stopped once during the day for a brief lunch break, during which Leisel and I ate sandwiches I'd packed for the journey, while the others ate whatever they'd brought with them. Still, I'm absolutely starving, since trotting and cantering for an entire day is an exhaustive task.

"I'll be right back," I tell Leisel.

I stand, walk over to Shadow, pluck the picnic basket of food I brought off his back, and take it back to her.

I break off a big chunk of a loaf of bread and hand it to her, before setting the pot of stew I brought on top of the fire to warm.

Leisel breaks off a smaller hunk of the bread and offers it to Chip, who's sleeping in the folds of her shirt. He instantly wakes up, rubs his little cheek against her fingers in an affectionate gesture, and starts gobbling down the bread.

While I'm stirring the stew, Leisel quietly asks, "Can you read to me?"

I smile at her and pull Hamlet out of the picnic basket. I brought several books with me, including the old books on witchcraft passed down from my mother, wanting to ensure that my nightly ritual of reading to Leisel won't die despite the humongous changes in our lives. At some point, I'll have to ask Camden for access to a library, but I intend to put that off as long as possible.

As I'm turning to the page I left off on last night, I hear shuffling footsteps approaching that make me tense. Looking up, I see that Camden and Wyatt are crossing from a group of tents over to Leisel and me.

"There'll be a warm tent set up for you two," Camden says simply, seating himself on the forest ground not far from me.

Not wanting to accept anything from him, but also not wanting Leisel to freeze tonight, I simply say, "Thank you."

Wyatt plops down not far from Leisel and gives her a fond look that makes her scoot closer to me. I wrap my arm around her shoulder, pulling her into my side.

When neither brother makes a move, I ask, "Is that all?"

I want them to move along so that Leisel and I can eat in relative peace, and I can read to her without disruption. That desire comes to an abrupt halt when Aspen also approaches, sitting across the fire from me. She's followed by several other pack members until there are at least ten people crowded around.

Aspen, examining the fire, asks me politely, "Do you have experience camping?"

"I have experience being impoverished and having to work with nature," I respond bluntly.

Leisel looks around the gathered group with a surprising amount of contempt for such a young, innocent girl, and that sends pride soaring through me. Pride and hope that she'll be able to survive Kinrith despite her kind predisposition—though I've already found out that her kindness doesn't extend to shifters.

Once the stew's steaming hot, I serve two portions in wooden bowls, handing one to Leisel.

Then I ask the shifters, "Don't you all have a dinner to be preparing? Or things to be doing?"

That disperses the crowd quickly enough, but Camden and Wyatt stay, much to my annoyance.

"You know you'll have to spend time with them," Camden drawls. "As their queen and Alpha female, regular interaction is required."

I snort. "I won my duel, Camden. I'm not obligated to do anything you tell me—I'm not a pack member."

Camden clicks his tongue. "Be that as it may, the high court will decide whether or not your duel truly releases you."

I look at him sharply. "I won. The laws on that are sacrosanct."

He nods casually. "In many cases, amongst normal shifters, yes. However, I'm not a normal shifter—I'm an Alpha of a very powerful pack. Without you, I'll lose strength, and then the pack will lose strength, which might lead to the entire power structure amongst shifters crumbling. If you take the case to them, I'd wager the counselors making up the high court will overturn your win in favor of ensuring the shifter population doesn't suffer."

I let out a laugh. It's an empty, mirthless laugh that conveys without words just how furious I am, just how completely unfair this entire situation is.

I say in a controlled tone, "Considering the vast corruption amongst shifters, I wouldn't be surprised if you manage to put yourself above laws that you're responsible for enforcing on others."

"Which is not the mark of a good leader," Leisel pitches in between bites of her stew.

I plant a kiss on the crown of her head, wishing she didn't have to be stuck in the middle of my conflict with Camden.

"The more agreeable you are, the easier this will go," Camden says, his temper rising. "I have no wish to fight with you. I don't think I'm being unreasonable."

"If you expect compliance from me, you'll be sorely disappointed," I shoot back. "And you are absolutely being unreasonable. You pulled the rug out from under my carefully constructed life, disregarded the laws that protect me, used my love for my sister against me, and expect me to accept you? Are you blind to how warped that is?"

Camden's eyes darken. "No, I'm not blind to how unorthodox our situation is, but if nothing else, this should teach you that I'll do *anything* to have you. There's no line I won't cross, no boundary that'll keep you away from me."

I snort. "So I have no free will? What you say goes?"

"No," Camden snaps. "You'll have more power than anyone in this realm—the same amount I have. You'll be a *queen*."

"I don't want to be a queen," I respond, working to keep my tone even. "I'm not interested in power. I'm not interested in the world of mythics or shifters. I had a good life before you came along and ruined it."

"A good life?" he scoffs. "You labored like a dog. Pinched every penny. Overworked yourself to the extreme, all while raising a child. You call that a good life?"

I'm surprised by how much he already seems to know about me, but I shouldn't be. Being who he is, Camden can probably get information on anyone and everyone. What surprises me more is that he isn't *entirely* wrong; my life was difficult and laborious, but that didn't bother me because it was fulfilling.

"I was happy," I tell him. "I was content in my routine. If you think I'll be either of those things at your side, you're delusional."

Camden seems to wrestle with himself for several minutes, stirring in a tense silence. Finally, he says, "You'll change your mind. You'll come to know me, and then you'll feel differently."

I tilt my head. "What's it like living in dreamland? Because in the real world, your words sound ridiculous and more than a little fucking pathetic." I normally don't swear in front of Leisel, but I can't help myself.

Instead of getting angry and storming off like I'd hoped, his lips quirk with amusement. "Sassy, witty, and foul-mouthed. You're my perfect woman."

I resist the urge to drop my head in my hands and groan. Instead, I reply, "If you insist on staying here, please don't make me suffer through talking to you. It's the least you can do."

Camden lets out a deep sigh, seals his lips, and finally stands. He walks off, with Wyatt standing to follow behind him after casting one last look at Leisel.

Chapter Fourteen

Later that evening, once Leisel's sound asleep in our tent, I creep out of it and sit in front, keeping a watchful eye out. Although I'm so exhausted I think I might drop, I force myself to stay lucid in case any threats come around. With the anxiety that's been my constant companion, my vigilance is beginning to border on paranoia. Everything looks like a threat; the dark trees, the tents scattered about the clearing, even the embers of guttering fires.

Picking up a rock lying near the tent, I withdraw the pocketknife I inherited from my father from my pants and start sharpening it in a ploy to keep myself busy and calm my racing thoughts. The sound of metal sliding against rock is surprisingly soothing, and it offers the feeling that I'm in control of at least *one* aspect of my life; how sharp I make this blade.

The gentle night breeze stirs my hair, tickling the back of my neck. Aside from the faint echoes of leaves rustling on their branches and the occasional call of an owl, the night is as silent as it is dark. It's as if the entire forest knows it's playing host to predators, and the nocturnal creatures have decided to hide away—even the insects. The only light comes from the faint beams of the moon, overshadowed by the occasional cloud.

"I hope you're not intending to use that on me," a highly irritating familiar voice calls out.

I look up to see Camden standing outside of his tent—maybe twenty-five feet away from mine—hands in his pockets, his posture as regal as always. His shoulders are squared, his dark hair is wind-tousled, and he appears ready to go to battle. Which, considering our recent interactions, may well be the case.

"Not unless you give me a reason to," I inform, and then focus back on sharpening.

When Camden closes the distance between us and takes a seat on the ground across from me, I let out a sigh of pure exhaustion. "Shouldn't you be asleep?"

"I could say the same to you," he responds, a note of concern creeping into his tone. "When was the last time you slept?"

Who is he to worry over my sleep schedule when it's his fault it's been so disrupted as of late? "Last night."

"Don't lie," he warns, then repeats, "When was the last time you slept?"

I give him a sharp look. "None of your business."

In truth, I haven't slept since I met Camden. I couldn't afford to let my guard down in case anything went wrong and either Leisel or I were put in danger. It's a miracle I managed to ride all day. It's even more of a miracle that I didn't fall asleep while reading to Leisel twenty minutes ago. Then again, considering the frazzled state of my mind and growing paranoia... maybe it's less a miracle and more an indicator of stress.

Camden's lips thin. "You need to rest or your body will suffer and eventually shut down on you."

"Probably," I agree. "I also need to keep myself and my sister safe, which takes precedence."

Camden cocks his head. "Why would you need to stay up to protect Leisel? You're both under the direct protection of my pack, which is no small thing. You're as safe as you can possibly be."

When we first met, he offhandedly referred to me as a simpleton. Now, it's my turn to wonder if *he* isn't the fool in this scenario. "If you think being under the protection of your pack makes me feel safe, think again. You're the greatest danger to us possible."

Camden looks genuinely confused at my words, cocking his head to the side. "How do you figure that? You're my mate; I'd give my life to protect you without thinking twice."

His words sound surprisingly sincere, and what I've read on matehood supports them, but that doesn't make me feel safe in his presence. It doesn't erase that, thus far, I haven't exactly received the kindest treatment; not that I've treated any mythic I've come by kindly either.

"You'll also whip me with a belt until I'm screaming and kiss me without my consent. I can take that—Leisel couldn't."

Camden thinks for a moment, and then his head jerks back and his expression morphs into disgust. "Do you think Wyatt would try to touch Leisel inappropriately? Is that what this is about?"

"Absolutely," I respond honestly. "You had no compunctions doing it, so it stands to reason he'd be the same way."

"Sierra, any affection he has towards her right now is brotherly or paternal," he says, his tone seething with conviction. "Shifters aren't fucking perverts. It's only once she's older and matures that his feelings will shift towards romantic territory."

I study his face. His expression is genuine and his words sound sincere. Unfortunately, that doesn't make me believe him. Even if it did, I'd still stay awake to protect Leisel for the simple fact that, no matter how tired I am, I'm too anxious to rest.

"I hope you take offense to this: I don't believe you. Notice how you glossed over my mention of the whipping and non-consensual touch."

He lets out a growl of frustration. "You took action with intent to *kill* me. I had to ensure you wouldn't do so again. On top of that, if we're going with blatant honesty here, it's impossible to ask a shifter to keep their hands away from their mate. Touching you is a compulsion for me; it's physically painful not to."

I smile at the thought of that. "Then I guess you'll get a good education of what it's like to not have everything you want and to feel pain at the mercy of others."

Camden's eyes darken at that. "Don't pretend to know anything about me, Sierra. I've felt pain at the mercy of the fates many times, and I've lost things very dear to me."

For the briefest moment, his words cause a flicker of interest, because there's an edge of pain to them I'd yet to hear from this Alpha. Then I recall the many horrors his kind has inflicted upon the native residents of Earth and find I don't particularly care if the King has experienced some hardship.

"So has everyone," I say dismissively.

Camden leaps to his feet, runs a hand through his hair, and starts pacing back and forth. I watch him cautiously, continuing to sharpen my blade. The *sshrk* of sharp steel against stone fills the silence, along with the sounds of Camden's footsteps crunching over dead leaves and stray twigs.

"Why are you being so difficult?" Camden demands.

I toss back, "Because you wreaked havoc on my life without a thought as to how it would affect me, and more importantly, my sister."

"I'm offering you a new life; a *better* life."

He says that as if it makes a bit of difference. "One that I'm not interested in."

He glares at me for several moments, looking a mixture of stumped and frustrated. Then, with a growl, he stalks off into the tree line, apparently having decided to leave me alone for the time being.

I peek into my tent briefly, ensuring Leisel didn't wake up at the sounds of our argument. She's sleeping peacefully in a pile of blankets—several of which a pack member provided and I begrudgingly accepted. Chip is likewise in dreamland, snuggled into Leisel's long hair.

I close the tent's flap and resume my post in front of it. Tiredness does weigh heavily on me, but anxiety keeps my thoughts racing and my heart pounding, preventing me from dozing off.

Several minutes later, I startle as I spot a magnificent black wolf break through the tree line. His fur is so dark I wouldn't have noticed him if I hadn't been on high alert, and he appears to be twice the size of normal wolves that I've crossed paths with on hunts. As he trots closer, I see he's holding a mouthful of clothes—the same clothes that Camden was wearing, which makes me relax minutely because it tells me this is Camden's wolf, his more primal half.

The wolf's eyes, the same silver-blue as Camden's, lock onto me as he slows his pace to a hesitant walk, as if not wanting to frighten me. He comes to a stop in front of Camden's tent, releasing the clothes from his mouth to allow them to fall on the forest ground with a light thump, and simply stares at me.

Strangely, I don't find myself wanting to scramble away from the wolf. Maybe it's because I know he's more elemental in his thinking and is unable to whip me with a belt if I piss him off. Maybe it's because I'm innately drawn to magical things, a perk of my heritage.

Maybe it's the undying curiosity that's always lived within me. Maybe it's the fact that I'm too exhausted to kick up a fuss.

Whatever the reason, I don't move or run. Instead, I tip my chin at the beautiful beast, eyeing him warily. "Hello, wolf."

He takes my greeting as an invitation to move a few steps closer, stopping a mere five feet in front of me. He lets out a snort that might be a greeting.

The wolf looks me over with sharp, alarmingly intelligent eyes. Then, shockingly, he lets out a whine. Not a bark or growl or any other noise of demand, but rather one of discomfort and longing. Several beats of silence pass before he whines again, shifting forward without taking another step.

It seems almost as though he's asking *permission* to come closer, which is a tad astonishing considering the forceful personality of his human counterpart.

"You want me to sit with me? Is that why you're whining?" I question hesitantly, confounded by this situation. Is it possible the wolf is more gentle than the man?

He paws the ground in front of him and lets out a chuff, which I translate into a yes.

I tilt my head to the side, considering. "If I say no, would you leave me in peace?"

Another, longer whine, but he doesn't make a move to step forward, which makes me far more agreeable. I'm inclined to like the beast, and my curiosity is slowly unfurling.

"Come on, then," I offer, patting the ground beside me. "I suppose you can stand guard with me."

He slowly pads over to me, as if not trying to frighten me, and then lies down right next to me, blue eyes staring at me expectantly. His tail begins to wag lightly as we watch each other.

I let out a small puff of laughter, set aside my knife and rock, and tentatively reach out to stroke his fur. It's softer than it looks; luxurious and silky smooth. He leans into my touch at once, eyes fluttering closed and a low rumble of pleasure escaping him that emboldens me. When I scratch behind one of his ears, he scoots closer, then lays his big head onto my lap, right over my legs.

"You're not so bad," I murmur, continuing to pet him. The contact sparks a warmth within me, followed by the strangest sensation of safety.

Eventually, the wolf falls asleep with his head resting on my legs, his breathing turning deeper and slower and his body relaxing. I don't get the urge to move or get away from him, so I simply remain where I am, hand resting on his head.

"If only your human would be as sweet as you, we might not have such substantial problems," I whisper.

***

The next day, around noon, we make it to Kinrith.

Camden's wolf woke up with the first rays of dawn and trotted back into his tent. He emerged a few minutes later, in human form and fully dressed, just as the rest of the pack members also began to rise. He bid me a polite good morning and asked me if I got any sleep. I bid him a less polite good morning and disregarded the question.

Neither of us mentioned my meeting his wolf. I think Camden knew that commentary would quickly sour the experience. I also think he suspects that I'm fonder of his wolf than I am of him—which, to my surprise, is true.

Still, the fact that I feel a stronger connection to his animal half doesn't mean I'll ever fully *accept* either the wolf or the man. I'm simply more comfortable with the beast, mainly because he proved to be kinder than Camden.

Leisel's eyes are wide as we ride into the citadel. I'm sure mine are too because Kinrith is an entirely different world than what Leisel and I have experienced.

Beautifully carved horse-drawn carriages ride on the smooth paved roads—something I suspect the elite make use of when not going to more rural destinations. Shifters roam along sidewalks with purposeful strides. I notice that some of them have slitted eyes, like a cat's, which tips me off that there are feline shifters intermingling with the wolves.

The buildings on each street vary vastly in height and architecture. Some are one or two stories tall, others so tall they disappear into the clouds. They're all made of either brick or wood, shiny and polished and expensive in appearance.

I don't spend long reveling in my surroundings before anger quickly sets in; mythics stole places and things like these from humans.

Many pedestrians freeze as Camden passes, bowing their heads in respect. Unsurprisingly, everyone recognizes him, and everyone seems to be both admiring and wary of him. The stares cast at him range from reverence to fear and Camden seems to eat the attention up, nodding and waving at selective passersby.

He steers his stallion to the side until he's riding right next to me. As he does so, more curious gazes are drawn towards me and the people begin murmuring amongst each other speculatively.

"We altered as much technology to suit our needs as we could," he tells me. "A lot of that fell to my father. Many things were salvageable once we tweaked them to no longer admit high-frequency noises, which caused us quite the headache."

I fix him with a glare. "Bragging about the technology you stole from my people isn't going to go over well."

His lips thin and his look turns piercing. "As Queen, you'll have the chance to help your people but only if you take your rightful place by my side."

Yet another checkmate from Camden—and an opportunity that he *knows* I won't be able to pass up. By making acceptance of him necessary to help those victimized and outcast by mythics, he's ensuring I won't be able to leave him. I'll give the Alpha this; he's clever.

I know he's not giving me the opportunity out of the kindness of his heart—instead, he's using my morality against me. In this moment, I make a silent vow to myself.

One of these days, I'm going to destroy Camden. I don't know when, and I don't know how, but where there's a will, there's a way. I'll need to wait for the *exact* right moment to act. I'll need to scrounge up every bit of patience and self-control possible to keep myself in check before the time comes.

When the perfect opportunity presents itself, I'll strike Camden where it hurts most. I'll make him as weak and helpless as his kind has made humans. I'll happily serve long-awaited and much-deserved justice.

Instead of saying that, I produce an entirely insincere smile. "How magnanimous of you, Camden, but be careful when you try to manipulate me because two can play that game."

Chapter Fifteen

T he royal castle is like nothing I could've pictured or imagined—it's a towering palace that looks like it came right off the pages of a fairytale.

It's about half an hour's ride from Kinrith's citadel and has what looks like hundreds of acres of lush land bursting with flowers and rich greenery surrounding it, as well as an extensive forest beyond it.

The palace itself has a gothic twist, made of old-looking materials. Gray bricks of varying dark shades make up the exterior, with both stone and wooden doors serving as entrances around the base. There are nine spires so high that it's difficult to see the very tops of them, and the structure itself looks like it spans several acres of land on its own. Sunlight glints off stained glass windows with beautiful swirling designs, reflecting onto the paved stone courtyard.

I stare at the structure with open-mouthed awe as I dismount Shadow and then help Leisel off of Duchess. We've stopped in the courtyard in front of the palatial home to monarchs and Alphas, and I get the feeling that I could spend a year exploring the castle, yet fail to discover each room, corner, and crevice; it's gigantic.

"Wow," Leisel whispers, grasping my hand with hers. "You were right, it really is like a fairytale."

In her free hand, Chip is curled up and sleeping, his little body rising and falling with each breath. It seems the journey tired him out as much as it did us.

Camden walks over to me, seemingly enjoying my wide-eyed intrigue. Servants are already making their way out of the palace, greeting him and Wyatt formally by their titles—either Alpha, Beta, Your Majesty, or Your Royal Highness—but Camden merely nods at them in greeting.

"It's beautiful, isn't it?" he questions, also gazing at his home. "My grandfather built it when he first came to this realm."

His grandfather also extinguished most human life on Earth, but I'm too busy drinking in every detail of the palace to respond.

"There are stables on the southwest side of the property," Camden says, motioning for one of the servants to come over to us. "Reynold can get your horses situated for you."

I'm inclined to do the task myself, but when I see Leisel's eyes drooping with exhaustion, I decide to merely check on our horses later. If I left to take them, she'd insist on coming with me, and right now what she really needs is rest. I wouldn't be surprised if she sleeps for the next day straight—it's been a taxing few days, physically and emotionally.

"Fine," I respond.

Reynold, a young boy who looks no older than a teenager, approaches with a bright smile, taking Shadow's reins from me and Duchess' from Leisel. "Welcome home," he greets.

My mood sours instantly. This is not, nor will it ever be my home. I'll always be an outsider here—no matter how immersed Camden forces me to be with shifters and with his life. I'll never truly feel settled or calm—I'll always be on guard, ready to fend off potential threats.

When Reynold sees my expression of extreme displeasure, he quickly clears out with the horses, leading them down a stone walkway that winds through manicured lawns and gardens.

"You and Leisel will be staying in the East Wing of the castle," Camden says. "I'll show you the way. You're welcome to explore, if you'd like, or settle in and get rested. Wardrobes have already been assembled for both of you, as you'll find in your closets. Dinner's at eight—a servant will come show you the way to the dining hall."

I look down at Leisel, who's starting to sway slightly from how tired she is. "I'm not sure we'll be awake to attend dinner," I admit, looking back at Camden.

I'm not sure what dinners here are like, but if the mannerisms of the servants and castle alone are anything to go by, they'll be formal, tiring events with too many people and too much food, most of which will go to waste.

Camden's eyes narrow. "It can't be later than one right now. That means you can get around seven hours of sleep, which should be sufficient."

He probably thinks I'm trying to make an excuse to get out of spending time with him. Admittedly, it certainly is a plan of mine—but not the reason I want to skip tonight's meal. Right now, I'm genuinely worried for the welfare of my sister, and in no mood to cart her around.

"If she's awake, we'll attend dinner. If not, we won't," I say with absolute finality.

I don't care about Camden's position as Alpha—there's simply no way I'll ever bow to his whim. I'm sensing that he wants to be the main figure in my life, wants to occupy my every thought and action—the way it's said to be between mates—but that'll simply never happen.

Leisel's been the primary figure in my life for nine years, and that won't change now that I have a mutt trying to attach himself to my side.

Camden's lips thin and his eyes flare with irritation, an instinctual reaction to disobedience—something he doesn't have much experience with, I'm sure. Well, I'm more than happy to introduce him to what it's like to *not* get what he wants when he wants it.

Wyatt walks up beside Camden and rests a calming hand on his arm. "Cam," he says softly. "Look at Leisel—she's half asleep. Humans can't keep up with our stamina."

Camden turns an irritated glare to Wyatt. "They're not humans."

I debate whether or not to point out my displeasure at being spoken of in the third person but am too curious to watch the power exchange between the Alpha and Beta brothers to intervene. If there's discord among them, that's an advantage I intend to press on. Considering how abruptly I was taken from my life and brought here, I think I'll be happy to sew strife wherever I can in turn.

"They're not mythics either," Wyatt points out. "They need rest and rehabilitation after taxing events. Let them rest."

After a moment, Camden turns back to me, his irritation having visibly dimmed. "Do you intend to sleep?" he questions.

I'm curious as to why that matters, considering the monumental amount of stress he's happy to heap on me. "Yes," I lie.

His brows draw together. "Was that a lie?"

That gives me pause and brings a new question to my mind; whether or not he can sense if I'm lying through the bond that connects us.

"I don't know, was it?"

Camden studies me in silence for several moments, and I gain confidence that he doesn't know through the mate bond whether or not I'm lying—he's simply using deductive reasoning to draw conclusions. I haven't slept since I met him, so it's more than likely I won't sleep now.

I know that, eventually, fatigue will overwhelm me to the point where I'll pass out, but hopefully that time is later rather than sooner. I'll think about the repercussions when I face them. For now, I have a different set of priorities, all of them surrounding the safety and well-being of my sister. I can't see to those if I'm asleep.

Instead of responding, Camden turns towards the castle and starts walking. "Follow me."

"Do you need me to carry you?" I ask Leisel, worried that she'll topple over at any second.

She wearily shakes her head, pushing a few stray strands of hair out of her face and tucking them behind her ear before taking my hand. I nod, plant a quick kiss on the crown of her head, and then follow Camden as he walks into the castle.

Wyatt walks alongside his brother, and I study him as he moves. He appears to be more level-headed than Camden, though I've seen snippets of his temper as well. The two seem reasonably close as siblings, which makes sense since they likely grew up being groomed to take over Alpha and Beta positions. Beyond that, they were prepared for duties that reach far beyond those of a mere Alpha or Beta because they aren't just responsible for overseeing a single pack; they're responsible for overseeing *all* of them.

Wyatt hasn't particularly pressured Leisel—not like Camden's pressured me. Maybe it's because he's worried about frightening her, maybe it's because he understands the concept of his mate needing space. More likely, however, their mate bond hasn't yet begun to develop, since Leisel's far from maturity.

When Camden said Wyatt views Leisel more as a sister, and his feelings will only change when she comes of age, I sense that he was telling the truth. That only affords me a small measure of comfort, however, since I believe Wyatt will eventually push to spend one-on-one time with my little sister, which is not something I'll be accepting of.

Inside the castle, servants bustling about their daily tasks all greet the four of us warmly and formally. It's obvious Camden spread word of me and Leisel as soon as he found us because it seems everyone already knows us by name and title. *Queen and Princess, Alpha female and Beta female, Your Majesty and Your Royal Highness.* The shifter's version of nobility. It serves as an irritant that I've gone from an impoverished human-adjacent to *royalty* simply by rights of being fated to the Alpha and King. Twenty-three years of having very little has suddenly morphed into deference and splendor I wouldn't have ever dreamed of.

I walk hand in hand with Leisel through a grand stone foyer, past so many rooms I lose count, and up several flights of stairs. When we pass a room decorated with paintings and statues, I pause, drawn to it. At the far end of the room, visible from the entrance, is a beautiful marble statue depicting a young woman with an outstretched hand. In her palm rests a brilliant blue stone so dazzling I can't seem to look away from it. I'm more enchanted than I've ever been. I can't seem to pry my eyes away from the gemstone specifically—it fascinates me in a way I've never experienced. I've never seen jewels up close, only in pictures, and the way the light glints off of it, bathing the stone flooring in brilliant shades of blue enthralls me.

Camden's hand landing on my arm is what finally manages to tear me away, as I step back to evade his touch.

He glances from me to the gem with a small smile on his lips. "It appears that a witch's acquisitiveness extends to those with earthly powers," he murmurs as if making an observation to himself.

At my puzzled look, he elaborates. "Witches of other realms are known for being inexplicably drawn to precious objects—gold, jewels, anything shiny that has great value. Gifts as well. It's a common practice among their soulmates to use gifts as a wooing tactic." His gaze wanders to the statue. "Perhaps that's why you're so drawn to art—it was the most precious thing surrounding you as you grew up."

I'm startled that he noticed such a thing about me, but then I consider his comment about gifts.

Although it lowers my self-respect considerably, there's something...compelling about being given something by another person. Not in a quid pro quo situation—where a mutually beneficial exchange takes place—but when someone puts enough forethought to devote resources and effort into giving a gift. Especially a meaningful gift—something invariably expensive, or simply priceless, such as beautiful or timeless art.

Considering that I'm not someone who could ever be bought, Camden must be right: I share that strange trait with the witches from other realms. I can't help but wonder what other quirks I share with them, ones I know nothing about because my information on them has been extremely limited.

The thought of sharing anything with mythics churns my stomach, but witches don't deserve my hostility. They don't actively humiliate and demote humans to the bottom of their food chain—that's primarily done by shifters. On the contrary, I've heard accounts of witches going to human villages and offering their help.

They've even visited Aesara a few times to my knowledge, and each time I hid away on my farm with Leisel for fear of discovery. From what I've heard, they're more prone to frequenting other human villages to offer aid and healing—though perhaps that's due to Aesara being surrounded by shifter territories. Witches are known for having solitary covens that don't ally with other mythics—from what I've read, mythic species are not known to cross lines or intermingle with each other often.

It's no wonder Camden's so set on having Leisel and me under his thumb; we're a very useful novelty. I have the feeling that getting out from under it will be no easy task.

Chapter Sixteen

The rooms Leisel and I are given are luxurious, elaborate, and regal. They're both the size of my entire cabin, with bathrooms half as big, and closets already bursting with garments.

They're also connected by a wooden door, so I can go to and from her room at my leisure, without having to step foot out in the hall. It also means I can keep a close eye on her, as I'm accustomed to doing.

My room is decorated in cream, gold, and teal tones. The walls are made of cream-colored polished stone with teal spiral patterns. There's a five-piece golden furniture set in front of a cream-tiled fireplace that is bigger than I am. In one corner of the room is an empty bookshelf built into the wall. The four-poster bed looks like it could comfortably fit five people, and has teal sheets and coverlets. On either side of the bed is a golden nightstand, each sporting a beige lamp. The closet is bigger than my old bedroom and Leisel's put together. It has a full-length mirror, and each side is decorated with cream shelves, as well as row upon row of clothes.

The bathroom has a golden bathtub that can easily fit eight people, a two-sink counter with toothbrushes, paste, and fragrant soaps already provided, a grand tiled shower with a stone bench built into the wall, and three showerheads.

The lavishness sickens me. The ornate decorations and expensive furniture alone must've cost a fortune—not to mention all the clothing in the closet, and other things I've been provided with.

It's all blood money.

Part of me wants to rifle through the closet to settle my curiosity, which just reaffirms that I probably do share an acquisitiveness with witches. That part of me also marvels at the entirety of my living quarters. The rest of me, however, is nothing less than appalled. The richness, the wealth, the vastness...all of it serves as a reminder of the poverty I grew up in, because mythics—especially shifters—took all the wealth and beauty for themselves.

Leisel's room is similar to mine, except slightly more feminine and suited to a young girl, with tones of pink and gold. I watched as she explored with wide eyes filled with excitement, curiosity, and trepidation earlier, her hair flying behind her as she scurried around it, examining each table, lamp, and furniture item with intense interest.

When Camden escorted us here, telling us to press a button on our bedside tables if we needed servants for whatever reason, Leisel looked both awed and intimidated by her new enormous room. While I unpacked our meager belongings, she busied herself exploring both rooms. Though I know she's not the happiest with our current situation, I also understand there's an element of child-like wonder for her in such a beautiful new place. That, or her acquisitiveness is also coming into play.

Now, as she bathes, I sit on my bed, pondering how much my life has changed in a matter of days. The door connecting our rooms is open, so I can hear the faint sound of running water from Leisel's bathroom and keep an eye out.

I want to be within shouting distance of her at all times, in case Wyatt makes a surprise appearance or something else goes awry. I've observed he seems very inclined to spend time with her, but Leisel does not seem to share the sentiment.

It's not quite that she's frightened of him, as I initially assumed. There is a fear factor between her and shifters, but I suspect it's more Leisel's anger that steers my sister away from her so-called mate. Leisel knows our mother and father are dead—I never hid or sugarcoated that fact, but it's only been in recent years while she observed other children with their parents in Aesara, that the true magnitude of what she's missing has hit her. She also knows the specific medical complications our parents died from and is naturally furious with mythics for taking *our* technology away from us and effectively depriving us of our parents.

Hence, she has no interest in Wyatt. Or any other shifters, for that matter. In fact, she seems to hold a great deal of anger towards them. I don't know how to feel about that.

A certain amount of guilt assuages me because Leisel is too young and too *pure* to be living with such anger in her. It'll taint her view of the world. On the other hand, that anger might very well keep her alive and sane with the events to come.

The water running in her bathroom shuts off. A few minutes later, she pads into my room, covered only with a towel, and blinks at me. "Is it bad to put on the clothes in my closet?"

I expel a deep breath. "Of course not, sweet girl. We might as well take advantage of what we're offered. No sense in cutting off your nose to spite your face."

While here, I hope to ensure that such luxuries will once again be afforded to humans. Although I can't stand Camden, it'd be a betrayal to humankind not to take advantage of the opportunity he's given me; the opportunity for change. I understand that it'll take quite some time to achieve my goal, and there will likely be many steps I must take before even amassing enough influence to make real changes, but I'm willing to do what it takes.

Leisel nods solemnly and makes her way back into her room, emerging soon after dressed in new pants and a white sweater, made of expensive soft-looking material, both of which probably cost more than what I make every harvest.

"I'm going to go wash up," I tell her. "If anything goes wrong—if anyone knocks on your door, call for me, and I'll be right there."

She nods, kisses me on the cheek, and then heads over to my bookshelf—which is now stocked with a dozen novels and several textbooks. I leave her to read and make quick work of washing myself.

Much to my dismay, I appreciate the steaming hot water and the expensive products I've been provided with. It's so rare for me to truly feel *clean*, since the water pressure in my cabin was a joke, and my soap and shampoo were both dismal and mostly useless. The cleanest I felt was when bathing in the river a short hike away from our cabin, as the rushing water was able to wash away the dirt and grime built up from life on a farm.

When I reemerge from the shower, intending to head into my closet and throw on clothes, I glimpse Leisel curled up on her bed, fast asleep, with Chip snoozing next to her. After hastily pulling on clothes—flexible loose pants and a shirt made of material so soft it feels like a cloud against my skin—I pull the bed covers over Leisel and leave her to rest. Poor thing is so exhausted she doesn't stir at all.

The stone making up the palace gives both of our rooms a natural chill, so I start fires in both her fireplace and mine. Then, sitting on the soft sofa in front of my fireplace, I think. I spend hours contemplating everything, absently fiddling with my hair.

My instinctual inclination to get away from Camden at all costs is overshadowed by his cunningness. By making my acceptance of him necessary to give me the power to facilitate change for humans, he's metaphorically chaining me to his side. In addition, the point he made about the high courts most likely ruling in his favor just to keep the peace seems true, though it's frustrating to no end.

Although I hate to admit it, the position he's offering—no, *coercing*—me into is rather enticing. In addition to the chance to help humans, I also have the chance to learn as I never have before. I'd assume the castle has a library somewhere, which probably houses extensive literature about all the mythic species, and if I'm lucky, witches. Hopefully I can read about them and learn more about those like me.

If I share acquisitiveness with witches, we may share several other traits as well. There's a chance I can read up on magic—learn spells I've never fathomed, spells that just might help my current situation.

Perhaps there's even a spell out there with the potential to dull the pull I feel to Camden or numb the mate bond between us entirely. Doubtful but possible.

After a few hours of mulling over the new life Leisel and I have been thrust into, and trying to plan out contingencies for when things inevitably go wrong, I start to feel hot, despite the fire not entirely staving off the chill in the room. When I stand, intending to walk over to the window beside my bed and throw it open for some fresh air, I'm alarmed that I'm suddenly seeing double.

I sink back into the sofa, rub my eyes and my temples, and try again. This time my vision's normal, but I still feel too warm, even once I've managed to throw the beautifully molded window open. Ignoring that, I take a seat on the edge of my bed, and once again get lost in my thoughts.

Leisel wakes up shortly afterward, quietly moving about her room, most likely exploring further. It's not too much later when a booming knock sounds on my door—no doubt one of the servants ready to escort Leisel and me to dinner. Glancing at the clock propped on the mantle above the fireplace, I see that it's nearly eight. Night has fallen outside, and I've been so lost in thought I hadn't even noticed.

Unfortunately, when I open the door, I find Camden standing there. He's dressed very differently than how I've seen him so far, sporting a navy blue button-down shirt that looks to be made of fine silk, a black suit jacket, and black slacks.

He glances at my clothes, glances at the room behind me, and then looks into my eyes. "Are you and your sister ready for dinner?"

I open my mouth to utter a snarky *yes* but find it a struggle to make my lips form words. Random black spots appear in my vision. Frowning, I blink several times and attempt to speak again.

That's the last thing I recall before the ground tilts beneath me, and darkness swallows me whole.

Chapter Seventeen

Camden

Sierra lays on her bed, appearing angelic in her sleep, while Claude assesses her. Being a talented witch doctor with a specialty in the healing arts, he should be able to diagnose exactly what made Sierra suddenly lose consciousness. He knows if he doesn't, I'll be extremely displeased. Despite our long-standing relationship and him being the closest person to me outside of Wyatt, he knows it's not wise to earn my displeasure.

If I hadn't caught Sierra, she would've taken a nasty fall to the stone floor. As soon as she'd opened the door, I noticed the slight paleness in her features despite the flush in her cheeks, but it didn't alarm me as much as it should've. My anxiety rose as her lips moved lethargically and soundlessly. She'd blinked several times with a dazed look and then tipped over.

Leisel, ever the healer, ran in as I was frantically trying to speak to Sierra and get her to at least open her eyes. She healed Sierra from whatever was afflicting her instantly, but Sierra's yet to wake up. Now, Leisel sits next to her sister on the bed, watching Claude with sharp eyes as he examines his future queen.

I stand at the foot of the bed, arms crossed over my chest, ready to fend off any possible threat to my mate—even though I don't know what the threat is.

"Was her skin feverish when you healed her?" Claude asks Leisel, peering at her with interest.

I'm sure it's exciting for him to have full-blooded witches, especially *earthly* witches around him, but so far he's curbed that excitement. I do suspect he'll take it upon himself to teach Sierra and Leisel his craft—help them navigate their powers and learn the higher arts of magic. At least, those that he's familiar with. Claude doesn't have the extensive powers of a pure-blood witch, but he has enough magic to hold his own. In addition to his healing capabilities, he occasionally gets random glimpses into the future—only small snippets though that usually aren't enough to serve as reliable indicators of what's to come.

"It was hot when I touched it," Leisel responds.

Claude nods slowly. "Wyatt told me a little bit about your healing abilities. From what he's observed, when you heal, any area of injury glows a golden color. Is that correct?"

Leisel nods solemnly.

"Where on Sierra's body was there a glow when you healed her just now?" Claude questions.

Leisel answers instantly, "Her chest, her head, and her neck."

Claude proceeds to ask her a series of mundane questions about Sierra—from her daily activities to her food intake to her predisposition towards illnesses.

"Has she been sleeping well recently?" Claude asks.

Leisel bites her lower lip, casting me a brief, displeased glance. "No. I don't think she's slept since he showed up," she replies, pointing towards me with a small hand.

I've suspected as much, but there isn't anything I could do about that. Ordering my mate to sleep would've likely had the exact opposite effect, so I left the topic alone aside from polite questions. Clearly, I should've been more concerned with it.

Claude winces. "That's three sleepless nights if I'm not mistaken." He looks at me. "Are the rumors that Sierra had a taxing duel with Aspen correct?"

I give a single tense nod. "Is lack of sleep enough to make her fall ill?"

Claude lets out a heavy sigh. "That, combined with high levels of stress from shifters appearing in her life, would easily compromise a human's immune system. Add in that she's a witch, and..."

"And?" I prompt.

Another sigh. "And it's a wonder she didn't faint sooner. Those with magical blood are strong of body and soul—able to tolerate pain and hardship well—but their greatest vulnerability is emotion. Stress and anxiety often have physical effects on witches, especially young ones."

I think back to the immense stress Sierra's been under since meeting me and feel shame. I had no idea that anxiety prompted by meeting me and a change of scene would affect her well-being since I'm not very well-versed on witches. I also didn't take her lack of sleep as seriously as I should have—shifters can go up to a week without sleep before succumbing to it, but humans are quite different. Sierra and Leisel are both a blend of human and witch—their bodies are vulnerable, but their magic makes for shared traits with witches of other realms.

"What can be done?" I ask Claude.

"Let the Alpha female sleep," he responds. "Ensure she eats enough. Allow her to adjust; if you smother her with new tasks and responsibilities, she'll certainly lose sleep over it, and gain a substantial amount of emotional turmoil. Then she'll find herself bedridden again."

He gives me a meaningful glance that, coming from anyone else, would be unacceptable. Claude, however, has earned leeway with the many ways he's helped me over the years. After my father's abdication a decade ago, I came to be quite reliant on him for advice.

With that, he walks out of the room, closing the door behind him.

I lock eyes with Leisel, who's staring at me like I'm an enemy combatant who infiltrated her camp. It doesn't cease to amaze me how easily she and Sierra hold my gaze. As though I'm not an Alpha whose very presence is frightening to grown hardened shifters. She shifts her body to face me fully, and I get the sense that she's trying to be intimidating—trying to protect Sierra from me. Which is more amusing than irritating, given her size.

"She needs to rest," Leisel snaps, her words harsh and clipped.

I let my gaze travel over Sierra—taking in every detail of her existence. I love looking at her most of the time, but seeing her so...*vulnerable* rankles me. I'm accustomed to seeing her hold her own against me and refuse to back down even when fighting back tears, so her current fragility is disconcerting.

"She appears to be resting just fine," I point out, not appreciating Leisel's subtle hint for me to leave.

I understand it—in her eyes, I'm quite literally the big bad wolf. The enemy. A direct threat to a woman who single-handedly raised her.

"She's in this bed because of you!" Leisel exclaims. "The least you can do is back off! You've already hurt both of us enough!"

I see her eyes starting to shine with tears which tugs on my heart, as do her words, because I know they're true. Sierra is bedridden because of me and me alone. That knowledge kills me. If I thought it would help, I would wrap Sierra in my arms and hold her close, protecting her from anything and everything. Unfortunately, it currently appears that I'm the biggest threat.

I murmur a curse and start pacing the length of the room, ignoring Leisel watching me quietly.

I'd come up to retrieve the sisters for dinner on impulse after receiving extremely unpleasant news on the movement of the primary vampire clan, one of the groups within their species, that threatens my kingdom. My first reaction was to seek out my mate, and the comfort she provides with her mere presence, even when that presence is edged with palpable hostility.

The very last thing I need right now is to be facing off with my Sierra, the one person who can potentially take out dozens of vampires with the lick of her flame.

It's obvious to me why the gods paired Sierra and me; together, we'll make an unstoppable team. I have substantial strength and battle stamina to back me, along with a track record as one of the best warriors to live in some time, and she can incinerate anything with her powers. Once she's trained, it's possible that she could demolish the entire hoard of vampires threatening us without needing to touch them.

Her viewing me as the enemy complicates our situation.

"I know you don't like me, Leisel—"

"You don't know," she interrupts, shaking her head slowly. "You can't possibly get how the sight of you disgusts me."

Through the wave of irritation her words bring, I also feel a flash of admiration. Leisel's remarkably intelligent and well-spoken for such a young tiny thing. That can only be attributed to Sierra's teachings.

"I don't want to be your enemy," I tell her sincerely. "I want us to be on the same side."

Leisel gives a snort that reminds me very much of Sierra.

I fall still when Sierra stirs. She shifts restlessly on the bed, her hands moving over the teal silk covers, as if in search of something. I can't help the brief hope that washes over me; the hope that Sierra's somehow reaching for me. That our bond is subconsciously pushing her to seek me out.

That hope is squashed when she speaks a mumbled slurred word. "...Leisel?"

Leisel, whose attention turned to Sierra when she first began shifting, reaches for Sierra's hand and clasps it in her small ones. Sierra visibly settles at the touch, obviously only having clawed her way out of her slumber to ensure Leisel's presence.

Leisel's chipmunk, who I've heard her refer to as Chip, leaps onto Sierra's chest and curls up on her as if offering comfort.

I let out a long, measured breath. "When she wakes up, I'd like to know immediately," I tell Leisel, trying to word my request gently. "You're welcome to stay with her while she rests—food will be brought up. I'll pop in every few hours. Outside of that, you shouldn't be disturbed."

With that, I force myself to walk out of the room—which is easily one of my most difficult undertakings yet, since leaving my mate while she's vulnerable feels like my own personal version of the underworld's worst bowel.

***

It takes forty hours for Sierra to wake up. Forty hours in which I find it exceedingly difficult to function. Leisel, unsurprisingly, stays by Sierra's side the entire time. The little healer sits next to her all day, reading or thinking, and sleeps beside her as well. I have no doubt she's simply mimicking the behavior Sierra has displayed towards her—unfailing loyalty.

I check on them over a dozen times, disregarding Leisel's irritation and demands for me to leave Sierra be while she rests. Little does the young witch know, that what I'm doing is the bare minimum contact that I *need* to stay sane.

When Wyatt informs me that a servant, delivering food for Leisel, found Sierra awake, I push aside my instinctual urge to go to her and visually confirm she's alright. Instead, I bury myself in work, trying to drown out my need to see her because I doubt that *she* wants to see *me*.

That comes to an abrupt halt when Wyatt strolls back into my office a few hours later, saying, "Thought you should know; Sierra's down at the stables, taking care of her horses."

My head snaps up from the map I'm pouring over—which has known locations of militant groups of vampires pinned down—and hope to gods I've heard my brother wrong. "What?"

I can see Wyatt's amusement from the twinkle in his eyes, the bastard. "After eating, she had one of the servants show her to the stables. Now she and Leisel are running their horses in a round pen—something about giving them necessary exercise, from what was passed on to me by a stable hand."

I exhale an irritated breath. "She's supposed to be *resting*. Does she *want* to fall ill again?"

My instant urge is to track her down and demand she stay within the castle and take it easy on herself, but she'd likely do the exact opposite just to spite me.

Wyatt looks at the bookshelf behind me, his expression thoughtful. "Honestly, Cam, I'm pretty sure that is her version of rest—or, at the very least, something that calms her."

Infuriated that my mate is tiring herself after only just having woken up from a deep sleep caused by exhaustion, I snap, "Working with horses is not resting! We *pay* people to do that for us!"

Wyatt, who's normally the less level-headed out of us, gazes at me steadily. "What do you think her daily tasks were back in Aesara?"

I pause to think. Running a farm single-handedly couldn't have been easy for Sierra, and I highly doubt she allowed Leisel to do much work. The list of what she was forced to do every day is doubtlessly extensive. For one, she had a sister to raise and teach on her own. From the textbooks I've glimpsed, as well as Leisel's eloquence and vocabulary, I'd guess at least a few hours were dedicated to just her sister's studies. On top of that, she had to keep the horses' stables clean and the horses fed and exercised. She also had to keep her lands up to par—from the little I know of smaller shifter villages that supply grain and produce, that involves planting, turning over soil, fertilizing, and harvesting. Then there's the hunting and trading several times a week in Aesara's market. I also have no doubt there was constant maintenance around her land that she had to do.

So, put in perspective, merely spending a bit of time with her horses probably *is* Sierra's version of rest. It still boils my blood that she's up and about so soon after being passed out for nearly two days.

I push away from my desk, stand, and stalk past Wyatt on my way out of the room.

"Going somewhere?" he asks sarcastically.

I spare him a brief glance. "To ensure my mate's okay."

Chapter Eighteen

Sierra

It's as I'm brushing down Shadow after his run in the round pen, side by side with Leisel who's tending to Duchess, that I *feel* Camden's aura creeping up behind me. That in itself scares the shit out of me. I've been conscious of Camden's presence every time we're in a room together, but I've never quite *felt* it this way before. There's a slight tingling in my chest, as well as the primal knowledge that he's near.

Setting aside the brush I was using on Shadow, I turn around. Sure enough, there stands the Alpha in all his glory. He's a few feet away from the entrance of the stable, and the halo of sunlight surrounding him makes him look like a dark angel. He's in a dressed-down getup of loose dark trousers and a crisp white button-up.

I woke up only a few hours ago, after the strangest and longest slumber of my life. I'd obviously underestimated the consequences of my skewed sleeping schedule—something I'll try to keep more consistent moving forward.

"Hello," I greet Camden.

Leisel throws a glance over her shoulder, gives Camden a distasteful up-and-down, wrinkles her nose, and returns her attention to Duchess. *Dismissed.* I never knew my sister was capable of such sass. I think it might run in the bloodline.

"How are you feeling?" Camden questions without preamble.

I don't say *like shit*, even though it's true. Though I slept for an obscene amount of time, the weight of worrying about...well, everything, makes me feel like I'm a hundred years old. My body is stiff and sore, and my mind is a muddled mess.

"Well enough," I tell Camden.

A muscle in Camden's cheek ticks, betraying his irritation. I find myself loving how easy it is to get a reaction from him. I also find that tick in his cheek enticing, and I have to subdue the urge to reach out and stroke it with my finger. Which means that though I've been asleep for nearly two days, the bond hasn't been sleeping with me. It's progressing.

I need to prioritize reading up on the bond more; what little I've been able to get my hands on about it living in Aesara clearly isn't enough to understand the full strength of it or its development. I know that the bond activates the moment two fated soulmates meet, and strengthens consistently thereafter, but I need more specifics if I'm going to be prepared to handle the force of it.

"You look better," Camden comments.

"I no longer look like death incarnate," I correct.

The corner of his lips ticks up. He takes a few steps forward, leaning against the stable door. "You could never look like death incarnate. You're too beautiful." He pauses, looking surprised with himself. As though he was trying to keep a leash on himself but the compliment just slipped out.

Leisel snorts quietly, and Camden shoots her a look of exasperated amusement. He doesn't chastise her for disrespect like I assume he would most others, considering his position as Alpha.

"Is there a reason you're here?" I ask, brushing off my dusty hands on my pants.

He pauses long enough to make me think he might not have come here for any particular objective. Leisel told me he'd been in and out of my room every few hours, day and night, checking on me like clockwork.

He clears his throat. "Yes. If you're feeling up to it, I'd like you two to join me for dinner in a few hours."

I feel my brows draw together. If dinner's a big event with many people, I don't know that I'll be able to tolerate it well. For the last nine years, my tolerance for people other than Leisel was minimal—I could handle them long enough to trade in Aesara's market a few times a week. The rare exceptions to that were Mariketa and Parker, mostly because they saved me many times over the years without even knowing it. I'm still not feeling my best, so the prospect of being around several people in a confined space isn't appealing.

"It'll be a small affair," Camden quickly assures me, as though he's reading my thoughts. "Just you, Leisel, me, and Wyatt."

I glance at Leisel, who's likely been going crazy cooped up in a room with me. She practically jumped for joy when I offered to go spend time with our horses after waking up.

It'll be good for her to get out—and I've sensed that her fear has lowered while I've been out. She doesn't trust the shifters, but she doesn't believe they'll harm her. I don't believe they will, either, though that doesn't set me at ease.

"I'll send your lady's maids up to help you prepare," Camden says.

My head jerks back. "Lady's maids?"

I feel both repulsed, because I have no need to be waited on, and at the same time slightly curious. How are these women treated? What exactly do they do?

My acquisitiveness is at play once again, nudging me to enjoy the luxury I'm being offered. With it comes a wave of guilt, because the luxury I'm curious about is absent in the lives of humans. They deserve such things too. I might not be able to get humans the equality and opportunities they deserve overnight, but if I'm to truly stay here as Camden's mate and the de facto queen, I believe I'll be able to extend aid to the less fortunate eventually. It'll take planning and great tact, but if I'm very clever and proactive, I might actually be able to effect positive change.

In order to achieve all this, the shifter population must respect me for my human side, not merely my magical one. That'll innately boost the value of humans in their society.

The plan I've formulated since waking is simple, really. I do what I've always done; work hard and be seen as working hard, not just by royalty and nobility but by everyone.

I'll learn diplomacy—or try to apply what I've read about diplomacy over the years. Let Camden include me in his world; impress those in his world in whatever intellectual way possible. Be seen as someone who's both a hard worker in the physical sense and someone who's intelligent and helpful. In short, I'll make mythics see humans as people of worth. I may not be *entirely* human, but I'm much closer to human than mythics are, and I was raised as a human so I understand them.

It's quite a large responsibility to take on, winning over shifters and working on human rights. I'll also need to research witchcraft to better Leisel and me. Still, someone has to put in the work, and I'm perfectly set up for the task.

The biggest complication is my mate, who'll demand my time, attention, body, mind, heart, and soul. He'll also want to fuck my brains out if the way he's staring at me is any indication.

"Yes, lady's maids," Camden replies. "They'll be sent up to introduce themselves and help you dress at seven. They'll always be around your wing of the castle, so if you ever need anything, they'll be happy to help."

Unsure of how to react to such deferential treatment, I simply say, "Thanks."

Then, when an awkward silence begins to stretch between us, I look to Leisel. "You done, sweet girl?"

She turns her attention to me and gives a brilliant smile. "Yep." Her eyes slide to Camden, and her smile disappears. She regards him with a stoic expression that's at odds with her young age. "Do you have a library in the castle?"

He looks shocked that she's addressing him. I'm surprised, too, though I shouldn't be. I'd intended to ask Camden for access to more reading materials at some point soon, but Leisel beat me to it.

"Of course," he replies. "It's rather extensive. You're welcome to explore it tonight or tomorrow—Wyatt can show you after dinner."

Recognizing his sly attempt to get Leisel to spend time with Wyatt, I interject, "That's alright, thanks. I'm sure we'll find the way."

I get the sense that Camden is trying not to roll his eyes. He clenches and unclenches his fists, and says, "You know, Sierra, you can't keep Leisel and Wyatt separate. They're mates—distance isn't an option."

"Explain the mechanics of the mate bond then." The words escape my lips before I can think them through.

Perhaps I won't need to do copious reading to discover more about the mate bond; I could get my information straight from a shifter who I assume grew up learning about it and understanding it, simply by watching those around him with mates. I don't know that he'd have gleaned anything from his parents, as the stories of them say that the shifter queen died long ago when Camden was still a child.

Camden looks pleased that I'm actually holding a conversation with him before suspicion shadows his expression. His brows furrow, as though he's had a thought he *really* doesn't like. He watches me from under lowered brows for a moment, assessing me. Then, a sly gleam enters his eyes, preceding his next words. "I'd love to tell you all about it. Walk with me and I will."

I shift closer to Shadow who lets out a soft snort before gently butting my arm with his head. I stroke his forehead, enjoying the feeling of his thick short fur beneath my fingers.

I'm not in any way partial to spending more time with Camden; my awareness of him is already intensifying, which leads me to believe my draw to him will soon strengthen. That means I won't be able to trust myself around him for long. If a tick in his cheek and close proximity is enough to get me hot and bothered, I don't want to know what bodily reactions being alone with him would create.

"Can't. I'm busy," I respond airily.

"After dinner, perhaps?" he offers. "We can chaperone Leisel and my brother to the library."

I tilt my head to the side. "The fact that you think chaperones are necessary is deeply concerning. Do you not trust your Beta?"

Camden's lips thin. "I'd have thought that would put your mind at ease."

I think for a breath. "Are you going to force Leisel to spend time with your brother?"

"I'll strongly encourage it. They're mates, Sierra. With Leisel's age, Wyatt will have an intense drive to protect and support her."

"I hope you understand I'll strongly *dis*courage their time together." Mostly because the only person I truly trust around Leisel is myself, and I can't stand the thought of there being a figure in her life that might draw her away from me.

Camden's gaze flares with both irritation and bemusement, and he gives his head a slight shake. "I'll see you at dinner." It's a promise that holds a note of warning.

***

At seven on the dot, a knock sounds on my door, followed by one on Leisel's. Since the joining door between our rooms is open, I see Leisel tense up from where she's lying on the floor in front of her fireplace with a book on her chest, reading. Chip is curled up on her stomach, dozing. Leisel sits up abruptly, catching Chip as he nearly tumbles off her body.

She looks to me for direction.

"Go ahead and answer it, my love," I tell her. "I'll be right here." Since we're expecting visitors, I'm not terribly worried.

Keeping an eye on her, I walk over to the door of my room and open it, revealing a woman who looks like she's in her mid-thirties wearing a bright smile. She has black hair pulled up into an elegant bun, warm hazel eyes, and smooth walnut skin. She wears a modest knee-length black dress, with a white apron draped over it. Her hands are folded in front of her, and she looks...eager to please, for lack of a better term.

"Hello," she greets, looking like she might start vibrating with excitement. "My name is Cara. I'm sure the King Alpha has told you I've been assigned as your personal lady's maid. Anything you need, I'm here to help with. I'm so pleased to be able to serve our future queen. It's a pleasure to meet you, Your Majesty."

I give her a slow up-and-down, deciding whether she's one of the people I dislike on sight—like just about every other shifter I've encountered. After a moment, I battle down the part of me that has a disdain for all mythics because Cara genuinely looks eager to help. I don't want to repay kindness with cruelty.

Besides, my intention is to be diplomatic and open, not to give shifters reason to view me as a bitch. I need to make nice with as many of them as possible. Not including Camden or Wyatt, because I simply can't conjure up any goodwill towards them, but I can try with others.

"Please, call me Sierra," I say. "It's nice to meet you. To be transparent, I have no idea what customs are in the shifter world, so it's a relief to have someone to ask and talk to."

Cara practically beams. "I'll be happy to answer any questions and explain anything. For now, I was told to prepare you for dinner. Is that alright?"

I nod, just as another woman appears in the doorway joining Leisel's room to mine, sporting a bright smile and an outfit identical to Cara's. Leisel slips by her through the doorway and comes to stand near me as I look her lady's maid up and down.

She appears to be somewhere in her sixties—though she might be centuries old for all I know—and instantly reminds me of Mariketa. Like Aesara's town baker, I sense that Leisel's lady's maid is very grandmotherly and a caretaker by nature. The nurturing energy emanating from her calms me, as does the fond look in her eyes every time she glances at Leisel. Hopefully she'll be a good fit for my little sister.

"Your Majesty," she greets.

I barely hold back a grimace. "I'm not one for titles. Call me Sierra, please."

She inclines her head. "My name is Greta. I've been assigned to the Princess and future Beta female—"

"My name is Leisel," my sister interjects, her brows drawn together.

Greta smiles warmly at Leisel. "Alright. Shall we get you cleaned up and dressed for dinner?"

Leisel, again, looks to me for direction. I run my hand through her hair. "Go ahead," I say softly.

Quietly, Leisel asks, "Can we trust them?"

Dear gods. A mere few days in Kinrith, and she's already becoming jaded and untrusting. Though that soothes me because there are likely people out there who will try to take advantage of her, it also worries me. Leisel's just too young to be so wary.

"I think so," I murmur, knowing that despite my soft volume, both Cara and Greta can probably hear us perfectly, courtesy of their enhanced shifter hearing. "Listen to your gut, sweet girl. A witch's intuition never leads her awry." That's a valuable lesson I learned from my mother.

Although intuition is a tricky tool that can often be elusive, there are times when I simply *know* something in my bones. When Leisel caught pneumonia at five years old, I knew that if I didn't get her help, she wouldn't survive it. Likewise, when my mother went into labor, I had a soul-renting feeling that she wouldn't come out of it.

Leisel nods, turning to give Greta an assessing look. Then she smiles. Greta takes that as her opportunity to usher Leisel back into her room and walks right into her closet.

I look back to Cara. "Where should we start?"

"With clothes," she says at once. "Tonight's dinner will be a small affair, but I'd still recommend you wear a dress. I'll help you style your hair if you'll allow me." She pauses, looking at my face. "Normally I'd recommend a light layer of makeup, but I don't see the need here. You're a natural beauty."

I blink. "Um. Thanks."

Cara smiles indulgently. "I'm sensing you're not used to compliments, are you?"

I shake my head. "Not particularly."

She nods as though she understands perfectly. "Well, be prepared for that to change. I have a feeling you'll get a *lot* of compliments, especially from males." Her smile widens. "It'll drive your mate insane. I must admit, it'll be interesting to watch our Alpha deal with it. He's so stoic most of the time—" She cuts off with an embarrassed laugh. "Please excuse me. Sometimes I speak before thinking."

I wave a hand at that. "We have that in common. What were you saying?"

She briefly glances at the grandfather clock in the room. "Can we talk while I prepare you? I'd hate to make you late for your first official meal here."

I nod and follow her into my closet where she surveys the collection of clothing with pursed lips, looking between me and the impressive number of dresses. I accept her suggestion of a simple yet elegant forest-green dress, swiftly changing into it. The dress is quite beautiful; it's made of sheer lace sewn over silk. The top half molds to my upper body, showcasing only a hint of my cleavage with a modest neckline held up by silk straps. The lace extends from the straps to cover my shoulders, creating a stark contrast between my pale skin peeking through the green woven threads. The skirt flares out, where the lace is studded with small white jewels, and stops about an inch above my knees. The material is foreign and luxurious, yet surprisingly comfortable and breathable. When I catch a glimpse of myself in the mirror, I can't hold back a small gasp; I can't remember the last time I enjoyed the sight of my reflection.

After sitting me down in front of the sink in the bathroom, Cara begins to brush my hair while telling me bits and pieces about Camden, all of which intrigue me.

"He couldn't have been older than nine when his mother died," she says, weaving several intricate braids into my hair. "It hit him hard. Overnight, he went from a playful child to a serious solemn boy." Her voice quiets. "He grew up too fast, after that. Greta was his caretaker—she saw first-hand how he changed."

Seems like Camden and I do have something in common after all. We both had to become adults far too quickly. I recall his words to me in the forest, *I've lost things very dear to me.* Despite myself, I feel a twinge of empathy for him, but the feeling doesn't last long. Regardless of my distaste for him, losing a parent as a child is something that fundamentally changes a person, which I know all too well.

"What about his father?" I question.

Cara's bright smile falters for a moment. "The Dowager King abdicated his title and duties in the years after losing his mate. He passed on the responsibilities and crown to Camden. A wise choice for a wise monarch."

Her answer is somewhat evasive which strikes me as intentional. She doesn't tell me exactly why the previous king abdicated, only that he did. I want to push for more of an explanation, but I'd rather not risk Cara shutting down, so I resolve to find out more details on my own. Part of me also wants to point out the amount of suffering the *wise monarch* caused, but I keep a lid on my anger, instead focusing on Cara's words and learning as much as I can about the life I'll now be living.

I sift through the many questions that have been floating through my head, wanting to take the opportunity to get some of them answered from a source I don't despise. Thinking about the various titles

I've been called by, I ask Cara, "Shifters have been calling me Alpha female, Queen, future queen, and Greta just referred to me as Your Majesty. How does the rank and title system work? What does it all mean exactly?"

Cara's smile returns. "Alpha female is technical terminology for anyone fated to an Alpha, or a female with an inner animal dominant enough to be Alpha. About forty percent of packs worldwide are headed by Alpha females. In terms of Queen and future queen, you're currently queen-to-be; once you consummate your bond with Camden, you'll hold the official position of queen and there'll be an official coronation. In the meantime, you'll likely be referred to as Queen because there's no doubt you soon will be one. For titles, the Queen and King are referred to as Your Majesty, while the Prince and Princess are Your Royal Highness."

I'm not sure how I feel about all of these formalities, but I remind myself this is a conversation for me to get some questions answered, not to pass judgment on answers. I can do that later.

"What do you mean by dominant inner animal?" I ask. "I've read that shifters can be dominant or submissive, but I don't know much beyond that."

Cara replies, "Dominant versus submissive refers to the power and strength of one's animal and human, which is really up to the fates. The more dominant shifters are often in pack leadership or part of warrior ranks, while those with submissive animal counterparts are more commonly seen in positions of service. For example, I'm a submissive shifter—a certified people-pleaser—which is why I enjoy my job so much. Greta, on the other hand, is dominant, which comes in handy when keeping rowdy royal children in line."

I hang onto each of her words with growing fascination, surprised to find that the complexity of a shifter's nature is actually very interesting to me. "Can dominant shifters be mates to submissive ones?" I ask curiously. "It seems like that dynamic could be inherently unstable."

Cara's eyes twinkle. "Yes, submissive shifters can be mated to dominant ones. Greta and I are an excellent example of that. Her strong, outspoken presence is actually a great aid to my natural shyness. We complete each other in many ways."

Oh. I hadn't gotten the sense from either of them that they were intimate, let alone mated, so that takes me a bit by surprise. What's also surprising is the significant age difference between them, though I imagine age gaps can't be terribly uncommon in shifter culture.

"I'm sorry," I say a bit awkwardly. "I didn't know."

Cara laughs. "It's no trouble really. We don't exactly advertise our status while working, but any shifter can tell just by scent."

"How so?"

"When fated mates complete the bond, their scents mix. Marks also contribute before the bond is complete, as they embed a shifter's scent permanently in their mate's skin."

Each piece of information she feeds me only deepens my appetite for more. I have to hope I'm not irritating her too much with my prodding.

Seeing an opportunity to learn more about the bond, I question, "Exactly how do bonds work? Are they fully complete through mark and consummation?"

Cara shakes her head. "Marking and physical consummation are two integral and significant steps to completing a bond, but they alone can't fully complete a bond. For a mating bond to fully take hold there needs to be emotional, physical, and soul intimacy between a couple. Only marked and consummated, the bond is mostly formed; in cases where shifters are mated to humans, the acts together strengthen the bond to the extent that the human would receive some of the shifter's strength and accelerated healing, but to have it fully functional, two beings need to become one."

Interesting. I'd always assumed that the bite and the sex were what constituted a fully formed mate bond; I didn't know it was more complex. That's something I'll need to think on. "One more question, if I haven't annoyed you too much," I say.

Cara's smile reappears in full-force. "It's not annoying, Your Maj—Sierra. It's rather endearing you wish to learn more. Please, go ahead."

I nod pensively, then blurt the question I've been wondering for my entire life because no books I could get my hands on covered such topics. "Why did mythics leave their realm? Is anyone still residing in your home realm? Do you ever intend to return?"

Cara pauses for a long moment, her fingers stilling in my hair. Finally, she says, "The mythics who came to Earth were drawn here by the abundant natural resources, some of which were absent in our home realm, as well as the magic of the nature itself. As for our home realm, Mythicacia, our kind still reside there with their own hierarchies and power structures, though they mirror ones on Earth and are loyal to the leaders on Earth. In terms of return...few mythics who walk this world and experience its beauty and abundance *want* to return."

She finishes styling my hair as I fall silent, digesting all the information she's given me. I never truly thought mythics wished to return to their own realms, after all, they've stayed here for over two centuries, but I had the faintest hope someday they'd get sick of this world and leave. Perhaps not a hope, but a dream—the possibility of a distant future in which the planet returns to humans.

Then again, there's no point in denying that humans didn't exactly treat this planet well; they drove it to the very brink of collapse, and as much as I hate to admit it, the shifter invasion is what saved it. They destroyed humans but saved and restored nature.

Removing her hands from my hair, Cara asks, "What do you think?"

I meet my eyes in the mirror before taking in the intricate layers of braids weaved into my hair. The plaits are small and delicate, forming a knot at the back of my head that flows down with the rest of my hair, the majority of which was left untouched. The irritating fly-away strands that always get stuck on my forehead are pulled back into the braids, and the style, along with the dress, makes me appear regal in a way I never could've imagined.

"It looks beautiful," I respond, snapping out of my dismal thoughts with amazement. Cara couldn't have been working on me for more than twenty minutes, yet she managed to create a genuine work of art.

Cara beams. "I'm glad you like it! Dinner's in about fifteen minutes—I can show you the way when you're ready. Do you need anything else in the meantime?"

I shake my head, still trying to wrap my mind around having someone whose job is to serve me. For someone who's only been able to rely on herself for the better part of a decade, the very concept of a person existing to aid me is jarring.

"In that case, I'll be right outside. Greta just finished up with Leisel, so we'll wait for you in the hall—come on out when you're ready."

I walk her to the door of my room, thanking her again before shutting it behind her. Leisel wanders into my room then, looking nothing short of adorable in a blue sundress and matching sandals. Her hair was left untouched, flowing down her back in its usual beautiful waves.

"Chip's sleepy, so I left him in bed to rest." She bites her bottom lip. "Is it bad that I like Greta?" Leisel asks.

My heart sinks. "No, sweet girl. A person's value is based on their soul—not the species they were born into."

I worry that my innate prejudice against the beings who destroyed my family has stained Leisel, which I don't want. I'll need to get over my prejudice if I'm going to get any good work done—I'm going to have to listen to my own words. My mother's words really. She hated mythics on principle, but even so would always tell me to judge a person on their soul and not anything else.

Getting to know shifters intimately, as I just did Cara, might not make that as much of a herculean task as I'd previously assumed. They have more humanity in them than I expected.

I'm relieved when Leisel nods in understanding, taking me at my word.

She gives me a long look over, taking in my hair and dress, and then says, "You look like a princess."

My heart warms, and I smile at her, taking her hand in mine. "No, *you* look like a princess. Now, let's go eat. Then we can find that library Camden mentioned. Sound good?"

Leisel nods. "Sounds good."

Chapter Nineteen

Greta takes the liberty of escorting Leisel and me to dinner. It's on the ground floor of the castle, in a room that looks more like a work of art than a place to use for meals. Every room in the castle—that I've seen so far—is a work of art. From the masterful paintings and colorful tapestries that decorate the walls, to the sculptures situated strategically, to the chandeliers and beautiful light fixtures. The dining hall is no exception.

The flooring is made of cream-colored marble and the walls are white stone. Along the walls are a collection of paintings depicting landscapes and solemn-looking rulers sitting with their families. In each corner of the room, there are statues of what appear to be gods atop marble plinths. The ceiling is high and vaulted, with a magnificent crystal chandelier that's holding up *floating orbs of light*. Those orbs combined with the crystals hanging beneath them cast a kaleidoscope of colors across the room.

Camden sits at the head of a long table made of dark wood, situated in the center of the room, with Wyatt seated to his left. The room seems disproportionately large with only them, Leisel, and me inside, as does the spread of foreign-looking foods on the table that makes my mouth water. It's been days since I've had anything substantial to eat, so even the sight and smell of such an elaborate meal has me drawn to it like a bee to sweet nectar.

Camden stands from his seat as Leisel and I appear in the stone arch entrance to the room, as does Wyatt. Camden looks me up and down with heated eyes, before offering me a sinfully attractive smile. The curl of his lips is somehow carnal and seductive, yet at the same time subdued. Like a wolf who's choosing to be polite rather than pouncing on its prey. Dangerous, taut, ready to spring into action.

"Good evening," he greets as I lead Leisel to the table. There are two seats with white and crystal-studded plates; one to the right of Camden, the other next to Wyatt.

"Evening," I respond, settling Leisel in the seat beside mine. I then reach across the table to drag the placemat next to Wyatt in front of her, prompting him to let out a sigh. Dishware clatters with my abrupt gesture, and a crystal glass nearly tips over, making a clattering noise that echoes around the room.

"You look stunning," Camden offers.

I don't return the compliment, though he looks incredibly appealing in a charcoal-gray suit that perfectly molds to his body, managing to look elegant while drawing attention to his muscular frame. At the neck of his white shirt is a silk blue knot, matching the color of his eyes.

I take a seat next to Camden, lean back in the chair, and gaze at him steadily. He stares back at me, eyes running all over my face.

Softly, he says, "Let's begin."

I turn my attention to Leisel. "What looks good?"

She looks at each dish laid out in front of us, brows furrowed, probably because she's unfamiliar with almost all of them. As she points to several different plates and bowls, I load measured portions of food onto her plate for her. By the time I'm done, it's practically overflowing. I know Leisel probably won't finish even a third of the food in front of her, but I can see the interest shining in her eyes as she looks over her selections.

Only once I've made sure she is satisfied with the contents of her plate do I load my own as an afterthought, barely paying it any attention. I feel Camden's gaze on me as I move, staring at me as though my very existence enthralls him. As soon as I've finished serving myself, Camden picks up his silverware and cuts into a piece of grilled meat to begin the meal.

Seeing Leisel look at her plate with trepidation, probably overwhelmed at so many options, I encourage, "Go ahead, sweet girl."

She picks up her fork and knife, gingerly cutting into her food. As soon as she puts the first bite in her mouth, her eyes widen, and she begins tucking into her choices with a renewed vigor, seeming to love each new thing she tries.

I likewise begin eating, nearly groaning as flavor bursts on my tongue. The spices seasoning each dish are exotic and delectable. Every bite I take is delicious, and I can almost feel myself regaining the strength I lost in the last two days while I was sleeping. I only had a bowl of soup when I woke up, feeling too queasy from my long sleep for more, but now I'm practically ravenous.

Camden pours red wine into my wineglass. "Try it. It goes well with the meat."

Though my initial urge is to ignore his suggestion merely to be contrary, my curiosity gets the better of me. I reach for the wineglass, bringing it to my nose and inhaling notes of dark cherry and spice, before taking a small sip. As much as I dislike the fact, Camden's right; it goes excellently with the food. It's the best wine I've ever tasted—oaky, earthy, and spiced, neither too dry nor too rich. Of course, the only wine I've had before was the cheap kind I could afford in Aesara's market.

"Good?" Camden asks.

I begrudgingly incline my head before returning to my meal. A tense silence descends on the four of us as we eat. I can tell Camden wants to speak, evidenced by his body language, but for some reason he refrains, opting for openly watching me. Wyatt vacillates between taking peeks at Leisel and focusing on his food.

After several moments, Wyatt addresses Leisel. "My brother told me you were asking about our library. Is that so?

Leisel glances at me for direction. I briefly fight an inner war, wondering if I should discourage her from speaking with Wyatt or encourage her. On one hand, I dislike Wyatt on principle; both because he's a mythic and because my protective instincts towards Leisel innately demand that I have disdain for any of her suitors. Though I believe Camden was being honest when he said any affection Wyatt has for Leisel is currently brotherly or paternal, that of a protector and supporter, it'll change to romantic in just a few short years, and that doesn't sit well with me.

On the other hand, if Leisel and I are to stay here—build a life here—Leisel will need more than just me guiding her since I know little of this world. She needs someone more versed in mythics who will answer her questions, work in her best interest, and above all, protect her. I believe Wyatt would do any and all of those things.

I incline my head with approval, smiling at her, silently wondering how I'm going to keep myself sane in this new life we've been thrust into.

Leisel turns back to Wyatt, and says, "Yes."

Wyatt gives her an easy smile, taking a sip of his drink. I can sense an undercurrent of pleasure from him; pleasure that she's finally speaking to him.

"I'd be happy to show you once we're done," he tells her, before locking eyes with me. "You're welcome to accompany us as well."

I blink. "Was there ever any question that I'd be chaperoning?"

Surprising me, Wyatt laughs. I expected him to be irritated with my intervention—as he's seemed so far when I've interfered in his dialogue with Leisel—instead, he seems to accept it easily. Maybe giving him some leeway *is* in my best interest. After all, if I'm to make any substantial changes, I'll need both the Alpha and Beta behind me. Camden's support will likely hinge on my acceptance of him, on how many proverbial bones I'm capable of throwing him. Wyatt, on the other hand, will be a bit trickier, especially since I haven't made my distaste for him a secret.

Out of the corner of my eye, I see a brief flash of movement come from nowhere that makes me stiffen. Then, abruptly, a newcomer comes into view at the end of the dining room table, appearing out of nowhere. He's tall, though not as tall as Camden and Wyatt. His body is heavily muscled. His skin is fair to the point of paleness. And his eyes...*fuck me*, his eyes are blood red.

From what I've read, I know I'm facing a vampire—only they have red irises. And this one somehow managed to teleport into the castle and is taking the measure of everyone seated at the table, malice practically radiating from him.

Camden and Wyatt leap to their feet immediately. I stand, too, ready to jump into action to make sure Leisel's safe. I grasp her wrist with my hand, pulling her from her seat and drawing her to me.

"Stop right there," Camden commands, voice resounding with authority as he stares at the newcomer. His face hardens as he looks over the vampire with lethal intent. "Kyron," he practically spits out.

The vampire's gaze settles on Camden. "Alpha," he says mockingly, making the word sound like a curse. "How's Daddy dearest? Has he gotten over the loss of his mate yet?"

Two things click in my mind. First, Camden and Kyron obviously have history. Second, that history may consist of Kyron having something to do with the death of Camden's mother—something I suspect from the mocking way he asked after her.

Camden's nails lengthen into sharp, lethal-looking claws. "He'll be far better now that her death will be avenged."

Kyron shakes his head, wagging his finger that's tipped with a black claw at Camden like one would at a silly toddler. Then his gaze turns to me. "I heard you and your brother had found your Fated Ones. Camden, I daresay I just might envy you. This one's *beautiful.*"

The lustful glint in Kyron's eyes angers me as much as it makes me uneasy. My heart pounds in my chest, my arms break out with goosebumps, and my thoughts are all geared toward protecting Leisel.

"But then, I also heard they're humans, so my jealousy doesn't extend too far," Kyron goes on.

From my understanding, news that Leisel and I aren't quite human has already circulated amongst shifters. However, it clearly hasn't yet reached the vampire's ears—possibly because most species avoid them like the plague they're said to be.

"It was a mistake to appear here," Camden growls. "One you won't get a chance to repeat."

In this moment, Camden is every inch the Alpha his people revere him as. Danger radiates off of him, and his sheer authority is palpable. I almost look forward to watching him take down Kyron, though I'm not sure how he will. Kyron's sudden appearance indicates an ability to teleport. *How does the royal family not have precautions against this?*

"Oh, I'm not staying," Kyron says easily, flicking his eyes around the room. "I just wished to stop by and pick something up."

"What?" Wyatt practically barks.

The vampire's eyes run over each of us briefly before settling on Leisel. "Leverage."

My breath escapes me in a gasp as Kyron vanishes, reappears in front of Leisel, wraps his arm around her, and teleports back to the other side of the room, making her disappear from my grasp. Leisel struggles against him, wriggling in his grip but to no avail. She cries out my name, and everything within me demands action as my heart shrivels with fear. It feels like ice is injected into my veins as I watch the only person I care about in this world trapped in the arms of a monster.

Wyatt roars, "Let her go!"

We both start for Kyron at the same time, which prompts the vampire to hold one of his sharp black claws up to her delicate neck. "Steady," he says. "Move and she dies." With a happy sigh he adds, "Gods, killing humans makes for such good sport."

I freeze in place barely noticing that Wyatt also stops moving, taking Kyron's threat as seriously as I do. Panic overwhelms me, making my breathing turn shallow. Leisel's the only family I have left; I can't lose her. I wouldn't survive it. She is everything good in this world—without her, all the light in my life will disappear. I won't *want* to go on. From the moment of her birth, I've been her protector, I've raised her as my daughter. She's *everything* to me.

On the heels of my soul-deep fear comes a burst of anger so acute it makes my vision go red. The vampire is threatening my sister. *My sister.*

I want him dead. I want to wipe him from his miserable existence—I want to *destroy* him for endangering the most precious person in the world to me.

His eyes locked with mine and a cruel smile curves Kyron's thin lips as he looks me up and down with a lascivious glint in his eyes.

"The future queen of the mutts," he says, drawing his gaze leisurely over my body. "You'll be a lovely asset to us."

That's when I realize that, though Kyron is holding Leisel, she's not his real target. His real target is me. He probably grabbed her first in a ploy to make me complacent; to make me desperate to do anything, as long as it keeps Leisel safe. It wouldn't have been difficult to discern that she's my sister whom I love dearly; something he could've gathered just from how I reached for her immediately in response to his appearance. As to *why* he'd go through the effort of taking her first, I can only assume he's enjoying playing with his food.

"She won't be *shit* to you," Camden growls.

"Shut the fuck up!" I snap at him, not wanting any distractions. To the vampire, I say, "You're right—I'm far more valuable than the girl. Take me instead of her."

Kyron tilts his head, his smile widening. "A martyr," he says, sounding delighted. "How exciting. I accept your deal, little human. Walk over to me, and you have my word I'll release the girl."

"Sierra, don't you *dare*," Camden snaps, reaching for me with an outstretched hand. I evade him with ease, disregarding him entirely as I take slow measured steps towards Kyron. Camden doesn't advance any further, likely because he believes that Kyron will rip Leisel's throat out if anyone makes a wrong move, in which case I *will* find a way to kill everyone in this room. My sanity very much hinges on Leisel's vitality.

I don't trust Kyron's word on letting Leisel go, but at least I'll be able to shield her if I'm close. The need to kill him burns as hotly as the fire that lives within me—nobody who threatens Leisel can be allowed to live.

"Anything you want is yours for the taking," Camden says to the vampire, a note of desperation in his voice. I can *feel* that he'll do anything to protect me—something that only pisses me off at the moment because I can't have any distractions while I end the vampire who had the fucking *gall* to target my sister. "Just leave my mate be."

"I want her," the vampire drawls, nodding to me. "The Queen. I'll leave you in peace today, if you give her to me."

"Over my dead fucking body," Camden snarls.

I step farther away from his reach, ignoring him altogether, crossing slowly over to the vampire, ignoring the threats and warnings Camden throws at me to stay in place. I will give up my life before endangering Leisel, but I have no intention of letting the vampire live long enough to take me anywhere.

I cross to him in several steps. He eyes my body with obvious appreciation, before offering me a magnanimous smile as he releases Leisel with a small push.

"Go to Wyatt," I command her. I may not trust the Beta in general, but I do trust him to keep her safe—he'll be compelled to by the bond between them.

Leisel, knowing better than to argue, complies, just as the vampire bands an arm around my waist and pulls my back flush to his front, holding me so tightly I know his hand will leave a substantial bruise.

"I'm going to enjoy fucking your woman," he tells Camden. "And if you try to inhibit my kind in any way, know that she will die."

Done with this shit, I say quietly, "Oh, you silly creature." I put one of my hands on top of his arm that holds me in place. "If you think you're taking me with you, think again."

The vampire has the nerve to chuckle, enraging me even further. "What are you going to do, little human? You deign to overpower me?"

"Overpower?" I echo softly. "Of course not. You hurt Leisel. That means you can't be allowed to live."

I draw forward the flame within me until it's just shy of coming out—resting right beneath the surface of my skin, its power causing pinpricks of anticipation to break out all along my body.

"I have a word of advice for you, vampire," I say, keeping my tone mild. "Though it won't be very useful, since your clock's just about run out. Before trying to take a hostage, *make sure you know their species.*"

I've never taken a life before, but the need to kill the vampire is so overpowering that I can think of nothing else. Before Kyron can respond, teleport me away, or even twitch a muscle, I let loose my black flame. Both my hands light up instantly, covered in a magnificent gold and black fire. It crackles and pops and hisses aggressively, attacking the vampire with a vehemence that startles me. The fire shoots from my hand to his arms, rapidly spreading to his chest, and then to the rest of him. I step out of his grasp with ease as he recoils, hissing.

He barely has a chance to yell before the flame kills him. No, not kills, *consumes.* It covers every inch of his skin, and within two seconds, he's gone—nothing left in his place. Not even ashes. That's what makes my golden-and-black fire so dangerous; it doesn't just burn, it annihilates, rarely leaving anything behind to prove it was ever there. That's why I worked so hard in my youth to learn how to control it—it's possibly the most dangerous magical power in existence. Really, it's more of a curse.

My hand is still alight with the flickering dancing fire. I suck in a deep breath, withdrawing my magic, watching as the flame slowly winks out, disappearing back into me.

Leisel promptly runs up to me, jumping into my arms. I hold her tightly to me, closing my eyes and kissing the crown of her head repeatedly, still shaking from the fear of nearly losing her. Though my flame is no longer covering my skin, it's still just below the surface. My riling emotions make it difficult to contain.

I set Leisel on her feet, sink the floor in front of her, and look her over, grasping her shoulders with unsteady hands. "Are you alright?" I ask her in a shaky voice.

There's a red imprint of a hand on her arm and a pink scratch on her neck left by the vampire, but other than that, she appears unharmed.

She nods, throwing her arms around me again. Her small frame trembles from fear, and that alone tugs at my heart.

I hate that she had to watch me kill. What really frightens me, however, is the fact that killing the vampire seemed like the most logical thing in the world. He was threatening the only person I have any regard for, so the fact that he had to die was no more than a mathematical equation in my mind.

"Sierra," Camden says softly, "that was...remarkable."

"That was survival," I respond, trying to calm myself, lest my flame appear unsummoned.

"Are you okay?" Wyatt asks Leisel. She glances at him over her shoulder, nods, and then returns her face to the crook of my neck.

I hold her close, breathing in her scent, assuring myself that she's *alive* and safe in my arms. Assuring myself that no matter what, I'll always make sure she's protected.

After several minutes, once I've at least somewhat calmed, I release Leisel. She appears to be calming down quicker than I am; she's no longer shaking, trembling, or hyperventilating. Instead, she's looking at me like I'm her savior.

I tuck her hair behind her ear. "Let's get you back to your room, sweet girl."

"Sierra, we need to talk," Camden says, approaching me.

I hold up a hand that stops in his tracks and give him a venomous look as I stand. "Yes, we do."

We need to discuss why in the ever-loving fuck Camden didn't have preternatural security measures in place for instances like this. From what I've read, though teleportation is rare, it's not unheard of, and the *King* of all people should've been prepared.

I believe I recall reading about wards against teleportation in one of the books passed down from my mother, which I intend to carve into the castle walls—even if I have to do it with nothing but my nails. I'll never put Leisel in such a position again, *especially* while she's so young and vulnerable. If I hadn't been here... I can't allow myself to imagine an alternative or my flame just might pop back up. As soon as I get Leisel back to her room, I will search through my books to find the wards. At the very least, our rooms will be shielded before long—the rest of the castle be damned.

Camden's eyebrows raise slightly in surprise at my harsh tone. He quickly schools his expression, and tells me, "I'll come for you in half an hour. We'll speak then."

Chapter Twenty

Camden

As soon as Sierra ushers Leisel out of the room, carrying the child in her arms, I summon Claude, as well as the dozen warriors on security detail tonight into the dining hall. I'm ready to take all their heads for the damn near *catastrophe* that occurred, barely keeping my wolf in check as he howls and growls and wrestles me for dominance. It's a miracle I have the presence of mind to assign stand-ins for the patrol men I've called on—my anger is taking away the majority of my rationality.

The image of Kyron holding Sierra to him, threatening to fuck her and kill her...it's enough to drive me out of my mind with fury—to make my control over my wolf slip, which could be detrimental to everyone around me.

I've never felt so helpless in my life. I wanted to snatch Sierra and protect her from all danger, but Leisel's life was in jeopardy—I couldn't take the risk of losing Rockwell's future Beta female. I also knew that any sudden moves could set Kyron off, making him react dangerously.

Inhaling deep breaths, reaching for a calm that evades me, I look over the thirteen men lined up against the wall of the dining hall, all of whom watch me with expectation, though none of them meet my eyes.

Wyatt is still seated at the table, twirling a steak knife in his hands and silently seething, while I stand in front of the line-up of people, flexing and relaxing my fists.

"You're all likely wondering why you were summoned," I say, unable to keep the sheer fury out of my voice.

The warriors cast nervous glances at each other but remain silent. As of now, the only people who know of the vampire appearing are Wyatt, Sierra, Leisel, and me.

"Fifteen minutes ago, a vampire teleported onto the premises. Into the very room we are standing in. He threatened the lives of both the Princess and the Queen."

That sends a stir through the gathered men, all of them bristling, preparing to launch into action. Unfortunately, at this moment, no action *can* be taken. The one person who could've given information—though likely only after an extended bout of torture—was killed by my mate.

The sight was enthralling. Sierra's irises began to swirl with gold, brightening until they were impossible not to stare at. The unnerving calm she displayed while in a critical situation, as well as how she got herself free, was stunning beyond compare. The way her fire roared, raged, and consumed Kyron confirmed that the ledgers were not misrepresenting the danger and sheer power that a black flame offers. It was both worrisome because Sierra could destroy the whole castle without blinking, and encouraging because she's more than capable of protecting herself and others.

Unknowingly, she also displayed all of the most important qualities of an Alpha female. I could see that she was willing to sacrifice her life for Leisel, as true leaders are driven to do for their people. She also stayed collected in the face of a serious threat and proved that she is more than strong enough to be a queen. It wouldn't surprise me if Sierra will turn out to be the strongest queen this realm has seen yet. Perhaps even stronger than my mother, whose life was taken by a vampire.

Claude, face pale and concern etched into every line of his face, asks, "What happened?"

I know there's pride in my voice when I say, "Sierra neutralized the threat using her fire, killing Kyron faster than I could blink."

"Kyron?" Claude repeats. "Of the royal family?"

I nod, knowing that his death will bring a whole slew of new problems, though it was inevitable considering he had the gall to invade my home.

Similarly to how shifters have a royal family that presides over all packs within the mythic species of shifters, vampires also have a royal family that presides over all clans that make up the vampire species. Kyron was the youngest member of the royal bloodline, with three older brothers—one of whom currently sits on the throne. Kyron's death will prompt the royal family to speed up their plans of attack. They'll take this as a declaration of war, using it to rile all vampires to fight against shifters.

Vampires don't need much riling in the first place, as they're natural enemies of shifters, but I'm now looking at mere weeks before battles begin, rather than the months I previously might've had.

"First of all, I'd be interested to know how Kyron managed to get into the castle," I snap. Turning to Claude, I demand, "Don't we have security to protect from magical intrusions?"

"We do," Claude responds. "Or, at least, we did. The boundary of the castle grounds is protected with magic that keeps out anyone not explicitly brought or invited in. About twenty minutes ago, I felt the magic fading and went out to investigate. It would appear that Kyron had an accomplice with him, a young vampire who also has magic—a hybrid of some sort, I'd wager, which is a rare specimen amongst their kind. I attempted to detain him, but he fought, and I was ultimately forced to kill him."

I clench my jaw. I should have been told the moment it happened so I could've had some forewarning. I could've done *something* rather than stand numbly in place like an idiot while Sierra and Leisel's lives were threatened.

Claude must read my thoughts in my expression because he says, "There was no time to tell you. As soon as I disposed of the young vampire, I received your summons here—I was already on my way to speak with you."

I glance at the dozen warriors. "Where were all of you when this happened? Ignoring your duties?"

Claude interjects calmly, "They were all at their posts. The vampire was a mile off property beyond their reach. The only reason I found him was I could sense his magic."

Frustrated that there's not anyone left for me to interrogate, I ask Claude, "Was the other vamp of any importance?"

Claude shakes his head. "Not that I could tell. His clothes were plain, and he didn't wear any royal or noble seals."

"What are you planning to do to prevent something like this from happening again?" I demand.

Claude shifts his weight slightly, eyes drifting behind me as he thinks. Finally, he offers, "I can reinforce the barrier, but it will inevitably fall if someone whose magic is stronger than mine attacks it, like the vampire hybrid. I barely managed to kill him in the fight, and mostly by luck."

Hit with a thought, I ask, "Would Sierra's magic hold against others?"

A small smile spreads on the witch doctor's lips. "Oh, yes," he drawls. "I've never met anyone with magic as powerful as hers. I could feel it radiating from her, even when she was unconscious. She's singular, and it's safe to assume her blood carries great magic with it."

That doesn't entirely surprise me. Though it takes someone who has magic to sense magic in another, it isn't difficult to discern how powerful Sierra is merely from her presence—the force of which is never anything less than overwhelming.

If a barrier means protecting herself and her sister, I'm confident Sierra would agree to help. However, I also suspect she'll assume that I'm using her for her power—that she only has value to me because of her magic. That couldn't be further from the truth. I desire Sierra for far more than her magic; I desire her for her nature and soul, which is where her true beauty lies.

Her body is stunning, without a doubt, but some of the most beautiful people I've known were also the cruelest. She is far from cruel—at her very core, Sierra is *good*. That's what truly attracts someone like me to her, a man who has many sins staining him. That, her fiery personality, and the fact that she's a natural protector.

"I'll speak with her about that," I tell Claude. Then to the warriors, "Schedules will be changing. I want two dozen pack warriors on shift at a time, and you will be expected to patrol areas outside of the boundary. Two miles to start with, including the forest. For now, return to your posts; expect further orders within the hour."

Watching as the warriors file out in a hurry, I fold my arms over my chest and look to Wyatt. He has a haunted expression on his face, which I understand all too well. He came as close to losing his mate tonight as I did; I'm surprised he's sitting quietly rather than throwing things across the room. I'm equally surprised that I got through the conversation without tearing someone's throat out.

Meeting my eyes, he grates, "I almost lost Leisel. I've known her for such a small amount of time—all of which she's spent disliking and distrusting me—and she was almost *gone*."

I know the depth of anguish he feels; the same anguish I felt when Kyron was holding Sierra just before she destroyed him. My heart stuttered and my very being felt like it was shriveling. I couldn't imagine *not* having her, though I'm yet to *truly* have her. The fear I felt still lingers within me, though on a much smaller scale.

"Be grateful to Sierra," I tell Wyatt, knowing that he doesn't particularly like her, primarily because she tries to keep him away from his mate, though I don't believe he truly *dis*likes her either. They just don't know each other yet.

Wyatt nods. "I am. She displayed a great deal of power today, Brother. Power is what we respect. Once news of this spreads, Sierra will be even more accepted by the Rockwell Pack, as well as shifters everywhere."

He's right. Though Sierra will be accepted by shifters simply because she's my mate, this situation will draw shifters to her as a person, not simply her title. She eliminated a threat that's been terrorizing us for quite some time.

Kyron was known for invading rural shifter towns to rape and pillage and persecute the citizens—he'd often lead a battalion of men with the sole purpose of killing as many shifters as possible. Though the vampire hoards reside on a different continent than us, they periodically teleport groups over to cause mayhem and remind shifters that they're never entirely safe. Many people have tried to kill him. All of them have lost their lives until Sierra took him down with what seemed like relative ease.

She'll be vital in the coming war *if* she decides to fight for us. Which is a very big if. Commanding her to do so wouldn't yield any results, she needs to *want* to help, and I don't know why she would ever want to aid us. *Unless, of course, there was a direct benefit to her...*such as the safety of her sister.

"I'll set about rebuilding a boundary," Claude says, walking towards the entry to the room. "You'll get progress reports regularly, though it should be done by dawn. If Sierra agrees to help ward, everyone on the royal territories could rest easily."

Knowing that this will be a grueling, taxing ritual, I grit, "Thank you, Claude. I'll work on Sierra."

As Claude strides out, Wyatt says, "I heard a bit of advice from a mated shifter male once, on how to deal with his female when she was rightfully angry."

I turn to look at him, equal parts exhausted from the evening and intrigued. "What would that have been?"

Anything that could help cool Sierra's malice towards me would be most welcome.

Wyatt smiles, and from that smile alone, I know whatever he suggests isn't going to be enjoyable for me.

"Provoke her," he says simply. "Get her angry enough that she explodes. Then listen to everything she says while her words aren't being carefully thought out. *That's* where you'll get true information. That might help you get insight as to what steps you need to take with her."

"Provoke her?" I echo incredulously. "Anger her? Wyatt, I do not need to give my female yet *another* reason to hate me."

"But you do need to know more about her if you want to get anywhere," Wyatt points out. "This is the fastest way."

Although everything within me rebels against causing Sierra upset, I have to admit that Wyatt has a point. Sierra has a quick mind and it's easy to see she thinks through everything she says before she speaks. Her words are always measured, as is her demeanor—her only obvious grievance is that she has a grudge against all mythics. It would be prudent to learn more about her. I know that her parents died due to lack of medical care among other tidbits I learned from Aspen back in Aesara but not much beyond that.

"This might get me killed," I admit, "but I see your point."

Wyatt smiles, appearing reluctantly entertained despite the taxing evening. "You're impervious to her magic, are you not? The bond should protect you from it."

Recalling the time she slapped me with her flame-covered hand, I nod. The fire felt faintly warm when it touched me, but in no way harmful. I believe it's fair to assume that I'm as impervious to it as she is.

"Nevertheless, good luck," Wyatt says. "I have a feeling you're going to need it."

By all the gods, I know he's right.

Chapter Twenty-One

Camden

Half an hour later, I'm knocking firmly on the door to Sierra's suite. I hear footsteps approaching before the door opens to reveal my fiery mate. She's holding an ancient-looking book in her hand with a cracked tattered leather binding, and her expression is one part focus, one part anger, and one part exhaustion.

Before I can speak, she sets the book on a side table in her room, and says, "I just got done warding Leisel's and my rooms against intruders, so it's time for us to chat."

It shouldn't surprise me that Sierra's already taken action, but it does. It's been less than an hour since she killed the vampire, but she didn't take any time to calm herself down—the color is high in her cheeks, her eyes are sparkling with malice, and she looks ready to incinerate the next person who even mildly irritates her.

Unfortunately, that person will be me. Despite my reservations about angering an exceptionally powerful witch, I can feel that my mate's soul is heavy and burdened—I sensed that the moment I met her. *One of the reasons we're a perfect match.* We're both damaged, we both have our own set of demons. Maybe if I can draw hers to the surface, I'll find that they match mine in their own twisted way.

"Thank you," I say.

She blinks, as if surprised at my words. That makes me pause to think.

I've yet to show Sierra—verbally or otherwise—just how much she means to me. I've given her little reason to see that she is the most important figure in my life. That's something I'll have to change.

It's been a long time since pretty words were thrown around my family. Almost twenty years. When my mother was alive, she never let any of the Kents forget that she loved us—through word and deed. When she died, that changed. My father turned somber, solemn, stoic, and eventually cruel, which rubbed off on both of his sons. Me more so than Wyatt.

My father. He no longer lives in the castle—he has his own property not far away—but I'll need to send word of what happened here soon. His health has been declining quickly as of late and I haven't wanted to bother him, but he deserves to know when something happens of the magnitude of what occurred during dinner tonight.

Suspiciously, Sierra says, "You're welcome. Leisel just fell asleep, so we can't talk here—I won't risk waking her after the night she's had."

My heart warms. Sierra will be a wonderful mother—she already is. She treats her younger sister like one would a daughter, which stands to reason considering she raised Leisel.

Though I don't see us having children anytime soon, it will happen eventually, and when it does, I know I'll never need to worry about their safety—Sierra will protect them as fiercely as she does Leisel. Even so, I'll be just as protective, and I can already see just how much

I'll adore any of our offspring. Whether they be earthly witchlings or shifter wolf pups.

"Let's go to the sitting parlor on the second floor," I offer. "It has a fully stocked bar, and you look like you could use a drink."

She looks at me warily for a beat, before letting out a soft puff of laughter, her shoulders slouching. "It's that obvious?"

She sounds incredibly...tired. Exhausted not just in body but in mind. Everything within me demands that I take her into my arms and soothe her, but I resist the urge, clenching my fists to keep myself from reaching for her. "Follow me."

"One moment," she mutters.

She pulls a knife out of her pocket—the same one I recall her sharpening when we were camping for the night while en route to the Kinrith—and flicks open the blade before I can blink.

Is she going to try to stab me? The last time she hurt me with lethal intent, I delivered a punishment that I have no wish to repeat. I tense, preparing to defend myself and disarm her, but find doing so unnecessary when she pricks her thumb with the blade.

I know enough about magic to understand that magical blood bolsters spells exponentially, especially if it's powerful—and Sierra's blood is *very* powerful. Claude echoed my suspicion earlier. Nevertheless, seeing her blood drawn makes my wolf slink closer to the surface. He despises the scent of it and the fact that she's injured—no matter how small that injury might be or the fact that it's self-inflicted in service of magical protection.

She walks up to Leisel's door and uses her bloodied finger to draw a small symbol at the base of it, repeating the same gesture on hers. Then she pockets her blade and straightens.

I grit my teeth against the questions wanting to spill forth, knowing that she won't be keen to give me answers. Also knowing that my real objective—no matter how much I may not like it—is to piss her off enough to make her control slip. Something that may well be detrimental.

We walk through the halls and down sets of stairs in silence. As soon as I lead her into the sitting parlor—one of many in the castle, but my personal favorite—she pauses for a moment to examine it. Her eyes run over the polished wooden walls adorned with paintings of past royal families. She takes in a bookshelf in the corner of the room before her gaze rises to the orbs of brightness hovering by the ceiling and casting light about the room. It lowers to examine the ornate marble-carved fireplace with a settee before it and finally flicks over to the carved stone bar in the far corner of the room. I watch as her eyes take on a glimmer of curiosity with each new item she examines and follow the path of her gaze with my own, feeling like I'm seeing everything through new eyes.

Sierra's inquisitiveness and interest in things that are menial and commonplace to me serves to incite my own curiosity, giving me the chance to look upon my surroundings with a new perspective.

Once she's done thoroughly cataloguing the room, she rounds on me. "How did the vampire get in tonight? Why weren't there preternatural security measures in place to prevent something like this?"

I close the door behind me and calmly walk over to the bar in the corner. Selecting a bottle of wine and another of aged whiskey, I tell her, "There were. Kyron had an accomplice—a vampire hybrid with magic. The accomplice took down the barrier surrounding the castle, which kept out intruders and allowed Kyron to teleport inside."

She doesn't pause before questioning, "Was Kyron a hybrid too? Is that how he could teleport?"

I shake my head, grabbing a corkscrew from the counter and getting to work opening the bottle of wine. "No. Members of certain species, even those who don't inherently have magic, occasionally develop a single magical power—a twist of fate, so to speak. Kyron was one of those individuals. He was also the youngest member of the vampire's royal and ruling family, so his death will not go unnoticed or unavenged."

Sierra pauses as she takes in the new information, turning her gaze to the fireplace with a contemplative expression. That contemplation quickly gives way to a solemnness edged with disgust as she looks back at me. "Leisel told me about the witch doctor who examined me when I passed out. Is he the one who put up the barrier?"

Walking over to the sofa in front of the grand fireplace, I set both our drinks on the table in front of it before motioning for her to join me. As expected, she doesn't, so I remain standing. "Yes," I respond.

"So, his magic is weak to have been overpowered by another," she concludes.

"Not weak," I correct, "but not as powerful as yours."

Sierra lets out a bitter laugh. "And I suppose you expect me to put up a new barrier that'll hold against powerful intruders?" She adds with a mutter, "Using me for all my worth, typical of your kind."

Seeing my chance, I demand, "Why is it you seem to despise all mythics?"

She looks at me like I'm slow, eyebrows furrowed. "Are you kidding me?"

"No. I want to know why you look like you'd happily kill me every time we're in the same room together. I want to know why you fight against us being mates so vehemently."

Sierra blinks slowly, her cheeks starting to heat. "You ask as if I haven't already told you. Do you not remember or do you just not care? Please tell me you're not so stupid that you can't figure out why I have a distinct distaste for all mythics, especially shifters. Tell me you're not that blind to what your kind has done to this world."

"We cleansed it of pollution and the many plagues humans brought to it," I point out, which is an entirely true statement. In the two centuries since shifters have overtaken the Earth, it's gone from a planet on the brink of collapse to a beautiful world, lush with greenery, nature, and the magic that stems from nature.

Her fists clench. "You fucking *ruined* it!"

I'm almost certain Sierra wants to take that knife out of her pocket and chop me into pieces, but I press on. If getting her mad is the only way to get her to talk, I'll do it. I've already proven I'm not above playing dirty to get what I want. "Go on," I encourage, my tone intentionally condescending—even though condescension is the last thing I feel right now—as I stalk closer to her.

In reality, I understand her frustration and anger. I want to help her work towards her goals, whatever they might be. I wish for us to be on the same team, but I can't do that if she blocks me out at every turn.

"I'm not having this conversation," she snaps. "Get out of my face—I'm sure you have plenty of Alpha duties to be going about. I'll help ward the castle tomorrow—"

"No," I interject. "You were on quite the roll as to why you hate shifters—don't let me stop you." Her eyes start to shine, and it feels like someone's twisting a blade in my chest, but I persevere. "Tell the truth, Sierra. Exactly why do I get the sense you want to see all of us dead?"

My taunt works. Her face and neck flush a deep red with anger, and she loses the tight control she always keeps on herself. "Because I wouldn't have had to become an adult at fourteen if it wasn't for you stuck-up piles of goat-shit invading!" she shouts. "Because I would've still had a family! You might know a thing or two about responsibilities, but you know *nothing* of having to work around the clock just to stay afloat." For a change of beat, she steps into my personal space, hands twitching like she wants to wrap them around my throat. "You don't know what it's like to get up at the crack of dawn every morning to run a damn farm. You don't know exactly what goes into it—at least ten fucking hours of hard labor every single day. You don't know what it's like mucking out horse stalls, plowing, planting, harvesting the land, hunting for meat, and raising a *baby* on top of it.

"I was fourteen when my mother died—bleeding out from birthing little Leisel because there were no damn doctors to help her. I didn't have any time to grieve her death—instead, *I* became the mother. *I* became the provider. *I* became the man of the house when my biggest worry should've been studies and boys!" She pauses, flushed and breathing hard. Then, she walks away from me, prowling to the other side of the room. "Scratch that, I grew up when my father died because I couldn't bear to have my pregnant mother miscarrying due to overworking herself." A tear rolls down her cheek, and she swipes at it angrily. "The day I first held Leisel in my arms, the day I lost my mother, I was *fourteen*. I'd just gotten my period." Her voice is wobbly now—heart-wrenchingly vulnerable. For a moment, she looks the same way I suspect she did the day she lost her mother—like a lost afraid girl. Her eyes are wide, her lips are trembling, and her chin is wobbling. It's only through sheer power of will that I force myself to stay in place instead of going to her to try to comfort her. Protecting her from everything—even her own inner difficulties and turmoil, which I know she won't let me do any time soon.

In a small voice, she continues, looking at the floor. "I wanted to die, that day. In the few minutes between my mother breathing her last breath and a nurse handing me Leisel, I saw no reason for living." I'm quite sure that, at this point, our bond is the only thing keeping her talking; subconsciously pushing her to open up because it knows I'll do my very best to be there for her. I can only hope she'll let me. "In that moment, I forgot about everything—the farm, my new-born sister, and my parents' wish for me to have a fruitful life. I wanted to go to the river in the forest behind my home and allow myself to drown." A sad smile touches her lips, and I know she's currently lost to the memories of that day. "Like Ophelia in Hamlet, who succumbed to her difficulties. That idea was fascinatingly symbolic and so incredibly enticing."

Her eyes harden with determination, her posture straightens, and I get the sense that she's moved on from that dark memory. It relieves me on a fundamental level because I'm a hairbreadth away from disregarding common sense, crossing the distance between us, and kissing her pain away.

"I think the nurse washing and bundling Leisel in blankets could see that I was on the precipice of giving up entirely. One second I was staring at my mother's corpse, and the next second the nurse handed me my sister, asking what her name was for the birth certificate. I looked at Leisel—her infant self as tiny and vulnerable as I felt—and saw a reason to live. She'd been crying, but as soon as her golden eyes met mine, she quieted. Then, after less than a heartbeat of studying me, she smiled. I saw my future in that smile. I saw her growing up under my care, on the farm. I saw thousands of her smiles at different stages in our lives. I saw myself wiping her tears and holding her when she was upset. I saw myself annihilating anyone or anything that *dared* upset her. And I knew then I'd do anything—*anything*—to keep her safe and happy. So, I survived for her. After a few months, I began living again. The most precious gift I've ever received was her existence because it point-blank *saved* me. And tonight, the last living member of my family was put in jeopardy *because of your kind!*" She wraps her arms around her waist, shrinking into herself. "I couldn't survive if she was gone. I wouldn't want to. And it's because of *your* presence in my life that a vampire held up a black fucking claw to her neck. So excuse me for detesting the very sight of you, Camden, but surely you'll understand why there's a surplus of bad blood between your kind and mine.

"Any duties I carry out or help I lend will always be in the interest of humans and my little sister, *not* in you. I will *never* accept you. I will *never* care for you. The only reason I'll tolerate you is for the sake of others."

I let out a deep breath, stunned into silence. I knew Sierra had by no means led an easy life, but I didn't know the depth of her turmoil before. Now, I'm at a complete loss for how to approach her or how to overcome the barriers between us, especially since she doesn't want them overcome. In fact, she'll be actively working *against* my efforts.

Sierra walks to the table with our drinks, gulps down her wine, and then looks me right in the eyes. Calmly, she says, "The next time you provoke me, I will begin burning things down. This beautiful castle of yours will only take a few licks of my flame to disappear. Tread very carefully, Alpha. Fate might have played a cosmic trick by pairing us, but I only adhere to the wishes of myself and my sister."

With that, she sets down her glass. "I'll speak with your witch doctor in the morning and set about making a sturdy barrier tomorrow. If you could stay the fuck out of my way while I work to protect Leisel, it'd be much appreciated. I warn you now that my mood is foul, and whenever that happens, things tend to burn."

I narrow my eyes. At this point, there's only one play I can make; one guaranteed sensation I can spark within Sierra. *Arousal.*

Before she can walk away, I snake my arm around her waist, pull her against me, and slant my lips over hers.

Chapter Twenty-Two

Sierra

I thought I'd felt lust for Camden before—thought I already knew what it was like to be eaten up by desire for him, but now, as his lips crash down on mine, I understand that I knew nothing of how intense the pleasure could be.

Maybe it's because the bond is progressing. Or it could be the fact that I'm exhausted, homesick, and utterly terrified that I won't be able to protect Leisel in this strange land surrounded by people I don't know or trust. Whatever the reason, his consuming kiss doesn't just send lust scorching through me, it somehow manages to comfort me.

I've felt so incredibly alone even in the short time I've been conscious in Kinrith. Although I've always enjoyed my privacy, I was still social regularly in Aesara, and I never realized just how much I took for granted the lighthearted interactions I had with fellow villagers until I lost the opportunity. I never felt as utterly alone as I did tonight while tucking Leisel into bed and scrambling together ideas to keep both of us safe.

Camden's possessive, *consuming* kiss wipes the loneliness away. It wipes the fear away. It disperses my rage and anger at him, along with all the turmoil floating around within me, and replaces it with an arousal so captivating it leaves my head spinning.

His lips devour mine with an intensity that would scare me if I didn't crave it so much. His tongue clashes with mine, his teeth nip at my lip, and his hands hold me so tightly against him I can't move an inch—all I can do is feel. Feel the comfort. Feel the burning desire he's instigating within me, which I know deep down he'll satisfy by the end of tonight.

My body goes entirely pliant against him; my hands clutch his shoulders for purchase as I hold on for the ride, unable to do anything but accept the forceful, dominating kiss that has no business riling me the way it does.

Camden abruptly swings me up into his arms, keeping his lips pressed firmly against mine. His hands grip my ass, and my legs instinctually wrap around his waist. I clutch onto him for dear life and accept his toe-curling kiss. My nipples harden into tight points, sensitive even against the soft material of my bra. Heat pools in my core, and I feel my panties growing damp. I wrap my arms around his shoulders and kiss him back just as aggressively as he's kissing me.

He starts walking us somewhere and I feel soft cushions against my back as he lowers me onto the couch, before climbing atop me. In the brief moment that his lips are separated from mine, rational thought returns.

No, this is wrong. This is all sorts of wrong. I shouldn't be accepting this from the person who has put me in such extreme distress that I spent days unconscious in the first place. I should be hitting Camden and fighting him, not welcoming his touch docilely.

I press my palms against his chest, stopping him and attempting to scramble back. His hands clamp on my hips, his facial features twist into a snarl, and his eyes turn a startlingly bright icy blue.

I know that the human half of shifters can be as primal and instinct-driven as their inner animals, especially when it comes to something like sex. What I realize too late is that wolves love the challenge, love the hunt and chase. My simple act of trying to hold Camden at a distance just kicked his dominating instincts into overdrive.

I can somehow feel—probably through our bond—that this Alpha *wants* me to fight him. He wants me to push him away and run, only so that he can have the elation of chasing me down and claiming me as his prize.

Logically, I know I should stop squirming. Challenging Camden in any way right now won't bode well for me. However, the logical part of my brain shuts down at the feral look in his eyes, and all I can think is that I need to get away from him before he loses all control.

When I try to scramble back again, one of his hands grasps the bare skin of my throat; I go limp as that simple touch seems to invade my very soul, forcing me to not only accept his touch but revel in it. His hold isn't hard enough to cut off my air, but it isn't soft either. He's telling me without words that he has all the control in this situation, and there is nothing I can do about that fact.

Why is the thought of that causing wetness to gather between my thighs?

When he leans down to nuzzle the side of my neck before sucking on my pulse, I let out a whimper that embarrasses me. The feel of his hot tongue on my throat is so insanely good that my eyes briefly roll to the back of my head. Tingles travel throughout my body, focusing on my core and making my body hum without my permission.

"That's it," he whispers against my skin. "Relax for me."

Hearing him say that pisses me off. I don't want to relax for him. I don't want to feel aroused for him. I don't want to find strange comfort in his touch. I can't seem to control my body when he touches me, which is *infuriating*. I shove at his chest with all the strength in my body, and actually somehow manage to force this man who is twice my size to slightly lose his balance, giving me the chance to leap off the couch.

Exhilaration surges through me, but it doesn't last. Before I can take even one step toward the exit, Camden grabs me by the waist again and pulls me back down on the couch. This time, he straddles me so that his entire weight is resting on my hips, holding me in place, and his hands shift to pin mine over my head.

"Stop struggling," he grits out, sounding like the words pain him. "It'll only excite me more."

I open my mouth to yell at him; he takes the opportunity to claim my lips yet again, thrusting his tongue into my mouth. This time, the kiss is nothing short of violent. I bite his tongue to attempt to get him to back off, he responds by biting my lip so hard the metallic taste of blood flavors the kiss.

My anger heightens, putting a much-needed damper on my arousal. Camden growls, feeling the change. Shifting my wrists into one of his hands, he uses the other to slip under the neckline of my shirt and beneath my bra, cupping my breast. Though I'm still seething mad in my mind, my body isn't on board with my emotions—my back arches up into his hand. He brushes his thumb over my nipple, back and forth, again and again. Each brush sends a violent jolt of pleasure through my system, and I can feel my panties growing *soaked.*

He pulls away from my mouth, releases my wrists, uses both hands to tear the soft shirt I changed into after the dinner disaster right off of me, and then slides his hands under my back to unclip and discard my bra with an expertise that hints to plenty of experience. Before I can make a protest of any kind, both of his hands cup my breasts.

"My gods, you're perfection embodied," he whispers, sounding awed. He stares at my bared breasts with hunger and reverence warring for supremacy in his gaze.

In spite of myself, his words warm some long-dead part of me. The young part of me that used to adore receiving praise—reveled in it. Of course, this is a very different kind of praise than what I was accustomed to in my youth, but it serves to send warmth through my chest.

He pinches both of my nipples softly, releasing a low noise of satisfaction when I arch into his hands with an unwilling moan. I open my mouth to tell him to stop, but I can't physically get the words past my lips. It's like the bond is prohibiting me from rejecting him again—it craves his touch so much that it's barring me from refusing.

He leans down and licks along the swell of my breasts before sinking his teeth into the soft flesh right above one of my nipples. My yelp of pain turns into a moan when he swipes his tongue over the bite, soothing it.

"You have no idea how impossible it's been to keep from marking up every inch of you," he rumbles. "I'm driven to leave bruises and bites all over you; to warn everyone else away from what's mine. Since you're not ready to wear my mark on your neck yet, I'll make do by marking you elsewhere."

His words are a straight-up threat—he's telling me that he's driven to *hurt* me to stake his claim. I can't manage to muster any fear over that though, because the bite he left on my breast turned me on even more than his scorching kiss did; the pain somehow heightened my pleasure.

I moan yet again when he pulls one of my nipples into his mouth and laves his tongue over it before sucking so hard his cheeks hollow. With a whimper, I bury my hands in his hair, unable to stop myself from clutching him closer to me, chasing the insane pleasure his touch offers. He pulls back only long enough to say, "So. Fucking. Perfect," before switching to my other nipple.

Realizing that I'm helpless to stop this, and that deep down I don't truly want to, I relax entirely. Camden, feeling the tension seep out of me, releases a pleased growl that makes my thighs clench. Of course, he notices. He releases my nipple and studies my facial expression closely, carefully. "You like it when I growl?"

It takes all my effort to hold back from nodding frantically. That would be entirely pathetic. When I stay still, Camden leans forward until his mouth is right by my ear and lets out another chest-deep growl that I can feel against my skin. Somehow, that alone makes me moan in pleasure.

Holy shit. How is that so hot? Why does that send my libido even further into overdrive?

Pulling back again, he says with amusement, "Look at you rubbing your thighs together, chasing your pleasure."

Realizing that I *am* rubbing my thighs together, my core seeking friction, I freeze guiltily. *What is wrong with me?*

Camden tsks, shifting his body lower. "Don't be ashamed, Sierra. Never with me." He slowly spreads my legs and settles between them; I watch, wide-eyed and totally enthralled. Once again, his words seem to reach a deep part of me—the part that does feel shame in seeking pleasure from him because he's the enemy. With a few simple words, he manages to subdue that part.

Just how strong is our bond for him to affect me so deeply?

He hooks his thumbs into the waistband of my loose sleeping pants and panties simultaneously, then pulls both down my legs and throws them somewhere to the side.

Panic sparks within me. What is he going to do? Is he trying to lead up to sex? *I'm not ready for that. Yet.* I sit up, ready to push him away—he flattens his hand on my stomach and pushes me back down on the soft cushions.

As though reading my mind, Camden assures me, "I'm not going to fuck you, but I will taste you." When I bite down on my lip, confused about my feelings and unsure what he's planning on doing, he presses, "This is a lifelong fantasy of mine, Sierra. Don't deny me your pussy now."

I murmur, "What do you mean?"

To say I'm not versed in sexual matters is an understatement. I'd never even kissed anyone before Camden. I understand the anatomy of sex—one of my textbooks explained it quite clearly—but that's about it. Realizing my naivety makes me flush further in embarrassment.

Camden's eyes soften, as though I've charmed him. "You don't even know about oral pleasure, do you?"

Oral pleasure? As in—

"Oh dear gods," I cry out when Camden's tongue darts out to lick along my slit. It's hot, wet, and feels like sheer heaven against my most sensitive flesh.

Amusement and desire saturating his voice, Camden says, "This is what I mean when I say oral pleasure."

I arch and grip the silky tresses of his hair when his tongue circles my clit, letting out a loud moan of pure abandon. How can anything feel this good? This level of pleasure, the feeling of connection, shouldn't be possible. It frightens me. A knot of tension forms low in my belly, winding tighter and tighter as he lavishes attention on my pussy.

That fear dissipates when Camden's tongue plunges inside me, the rapture so intense that my vision blurs. His hand on my stomach flexes. He growls against my dripping flesh, "You taste like my new favorite dessert. I'm already addicted."

Then his mouth is back on me as if starved. I don't recognize the noises I make as my own—a symphony of moans, groans, and whimpers. I can feel Camden's pleasure from the act of giving me pleasure, which excites me even further.

He pulls away from my pussy, and my whimper turns in a squeal when he bites down on the sensitive flesh of my inner thigh, sucking the skin hard to leave a mark. When he said he wanted to mark me, he wasn't kidding; I can feel his drive to stake his claim in every way possible. Pulling his mouth away from my thigh, his eyes meet mine as he slides one thick finger inside me. There's no resistance—I'm drenched from his ministrations. Embarrassment heats my cheeks and neck. How can I be so turned on by this? By him?

Camden curves his finger inside of me, causing my mouth to fall open on a gasp as he hits a spot that makes the coil in my stomach tighten even more. This shouldn't be happening. I shouldn't be accepting pleasure or comfort from the enemy—from the reason my parents are dead.

That thought puts a much-needed damper on my arousal. By being with Camden, I'm betraying my parents' memory. They'd be rolling over in their graves if they could see me now.

I open my mouth to demand he stop, but again, can't get the damn words past my lips. The bond is demanding that I accept this as my due—it won't allow anything else.

Camden sinks his teeth into my other thigh. This time, the bite is harder—sharp and stinging, as if he's punishing me. "Get out of your head," he growls. "Stop thinking. Stop fighting. You can go back to hating me tomorrow. For now, let yourself enjoy this."

He adds another finger inside me, and I can feel my inner walls spasming and quivering around the intrusion. It's a stretch, but the pain doesn't bother me like I thought it would. Then, Camden pulls my clit between his lips and sucks. That throws me right over the edge, plummeting to the most intense pleasure I've ever felt in my life. I don't just orgasm, I detonate. My whole body feels like it goes up in flames as I arch my back, toes curling and hands moving to clutch Camden's hair. I shamelessly grind against his mouth, too far gone to question my actions. As I ride out the wave of unbelievable pleasure, I feel a tug on my chest—my bond with Camden—somehow...grow in intensity. Does intimacy strengthen mate bonds?

I expect Camden to back off now that I've come, but he doesn't. He licks up my orgasm and then sets in once again, not giving my body reprieve from his dangerous mouth.

"W-wait," I murmur, still trembling with aftershocks. His tongue swirls around my clit before joining his fingers inside me, and then moving back up again. My skin feels hot and flushed, tingling every-where. "Camden, I'm too sensitive."

He pulls back only long enough to say, "I'm not done yet. You taste too good for me to stop, so there's no point in trying to make me."

His mouth goes back to me, tongue licking along my slit. His fingers move to pinch my clit as he thrusts his tongue inside of me, drawing another loud moan from me. When I try to close my legs, too over-sensitized, Camden grips my thighs and forces them to spread wider. The pleasure he's giving me is too much, but it's also so good that part of me doesn't want him to stop. When I explode once more, Camden backs off—but not before cleaning every last drop of my orgasm with his tongue. He climbs back over me and seals his lips over mine, thrusting his tongue inside my mouth.

"Do you like the way you taste?" he asks, pulling back, his eyes blazing. "I'm already addicted. I'll need my next fix soon."

Panting, utterly exhausted from the events of the night and the two momentous orgasms Camden wrenched from me, I let my head fall back on the cushion as my eyes flutter closed. I can deal with the repercussions of what happened tomorrow—for now, a deep slumber pulls me into its dark embrace.

Chapter Twenty-Three

I awaken sometime later to the sensation of fingers gently sifting through my hair. I'm not entirely unused to Leisel waking me up by playing with my hair when she has one of her less hyper days and decides not to wake me up by treating me like a bed of bouncy moss, but the warm, strong body behind mine that exudes raw masculine power is most certainly not the one that belongs to my little sister.

All at once, the events of the previous evening flash through my mind. Kyron threatening Leisel, me readily slaughtering Kyron in turn, warding my room and Leisel's, and then... *oh fuck, Camden.* I let him do things to me I'd never even imagined, and in the moment, I loved every second.

So *this* is what the aftereffects of true idiocy feel like. A conglomeration of shame, guilt, embarrassment, and total bafflement at my own stupidity. *Is this really who I am?* Someone who will cave under stress and pressure? All it took was a few kisses, and I was like clay in Camden's hands. I was reduced to a moldable, pliable toy with no will of my own, only the will of the bond.

No. *No.* This is not who I'm going to be—someone weak enough to succumb to the pressure of a mythical bond that I can't even *see* along with a handsome face. That's not who my parents raised; that's not who the hardships of my life have created.

For better or for worse, I've been thrust into a position I didn't ask for nor desire, but my options are to lament it and live in misery or take advantage of the power of my new rank and actually make relevant changes—start fixing what Camden's ancestors broke. Falling into his arms is *not* part of the plan.

Even if those arms are extraordinarily warm, strong, soothing, and inviting, lulling me into a false sense of safety and security. Irritation fueling me, I wriggle out of Camden's hold and get to my feet, looking around the floor for my discarded clothing from last night.

"If you're looking for your clothes, I've hidden them to ensure you don't get to run away first thing in the morning," Camden's voice calls from behind, thick with sleep.

Unbelievable. Knowing what he knows about me so far—mainly, that my primary policy for dealing with him is to *not*—he preempted my early morning escape by taking away something I'd need to *make* that escape. I look around the elaborate room, filled with antique furniture, spending a moment deciding whether or not I want to search out my clothes on my own and ignore the large male presence behind me.

Peeking over my shoulder and seeing Camden's eyes glued to my bare ass, I decide that no, I won't be able to bear the weight of his gaze. Dejectedly, I sink back onto the very edge of the couch, crossing my arms over my chest to give myself some semblance of modesty.

"That's not very dignified. Aren't rulers supposed to be dignified?" I say sharply.

Camden lets out a light puff of laughter, pushing himself into a sitting position and letting his eyes rove over me. "Don't mix up human monarchies with mythic ones; we're very different, starting with our senses of dignity. Shifters are half-animal—nudity is commonplace for us. There is nothing undignified about the naked form, whether it's human or wolf. Shame over nudity is a failing specific to this realm, and why I knew hiding your clothes would be enough to keep you here with me."

"Thanks for the lesson on shifter modesty," I respond dryly. "Can we get on to whatever I need to do to get my clothes back? I'm *not* walking back to my room naked."

"Quite so," Camden agrees with a nod. "The thought of others seeing you naked bothers me enough to want to rip throats out, which I've heard is common amongst mates, but I rather enjoy the sight, so I'm in no rush."

"I am," I shoot back, tilting my head towards the grandfather clock stationed by the closed door to the room. "It's almost six, which means Leisel's about to wake up, if she hasn't already. I won't subject her to waking up just to find me gone—she wouldn't cope well with it."

Camden's features soften ever so slightly as if he appreciates the maternal side of me, which makes me frown. If he's thinking something along the lines of our future children, he has another thing coming; I have no intention of bringing *his* children into the world, *ever.*

"Very well then. If you agree to join me for a private breakfast and spend the morning with me, I'll give your clothes back now," he offers.

My frown morphs into a scowl. "And abandon Leisel? Absolutely not—"

"Greta is more than capable of caring for Leisel for a morning, raising royal children is her specialty."

I raise an eyebrow. "You think I feel comfortable leaving Leisel alone while another vampire could teleport in and snatch her at any moment? My room might be warded, but the rest of the castle isn't, and my sister is a notorious explorer. Besides, I thought I was scheduled to spend the first half of the day fixing your fuckup in security?"

Camden clenches his jaw, irritation marring his chiseled features. "You know, not everything has to be a battle, Sierra. We just shared an intimate night. That's a step forward, so can we avoid taking two steps back? Instead of shutting me down entirely, perhaps you can offer an alternative to breakfast."

Is he serious? With everything that's going on, especially the situation with Kyron last night, his focus is on us spending time together?

"Perhaps the highest thing on *your* agenda is our mating situation, but my priorities are different," I snap.

That really is one of the fundamental barriers between us—the complete differences in our priorities. His priorities are based on his society, culture, and the role he was raised in; namely to protect his people, rule his kingdom, and claim his mate. My priorities are to avoid getting locked into a lifelong attachment with him while making life better for *my* people, humans. I might not be entirely a human, but my kind shared the Earth right alongside them for thousands of years before *his* kind came in and all but destroyed us.

While our priorities are so opposed, there is no way for us to lead a compatible life together. The fact that we might be somewhat compatible sexually—as evidenced last night—is an entirely different story, and one I don't intend to think on for long.

"Don't be naïve, Sierra. Our mating is the priority of everyone in this castle, and every one of my subjects. The sooner we complete our bond, the sooner there will be the prospect of heirs on the horizon, which will offer long-term security and stability to the crown that is currently absent. Beyond that, I'll be stronger and more capable of protecting my people—and they'll have *you*. Stories will soon make rounds of what happened at dinner last night; you'll be viewed as a blessing to our people and a curse to our enemies. *Us together* is in the interest of this very planet you're so attached to."

The truth of his words strikes fear into my very soul because they force me to realize just how right he is. From the perspective of his people, I am a necessary piece to make the monarchy, and the stability it offers to all shifters on Earth, work. In fact, I have the power to help them thrive and overcome their barriers due to my magical affinities.

The problem is, I have no interest in helping them—in fact, if I didn't see a potential solution to human suffering here, I'd be actively working to collapse the shifter power structure and incite chaos in the name of revenge.

I suck in a slow breath, deciding to go with bluntness. "I don't like you, Camden. I find the very idea of you reprehensible. I understand that you expect me to bend to your culture and ideals—to settle into a completely new life that's been forced onto me without argument, but that's not going to happen. Just because I had a moment of weakness last night doesn't mean that I've docilely accepted my fate. I have no intention of ever being *intimate* with you again. No matter how many times you coerce me into spending time with you, it won't change my dead parents and the history of blood between our people."

Camden's silent for a moment, searching my features. Then, he says lowly, "You haven't experienced the strength of the bond, Sierra. You don't comprehend the depths of the connections between us. Over time, that'll change. It'll grow within you. Slowly, at first, but surely. And with each *intimate night* we spend together—and I assure you, there will be more—it'll strengthen a notch. Eventually, you'll come to view me as I view you. You'll come to want me as much as I want you. It'll take time and effort, both of which I'm happy to put in, and it won't be simple, *especially* at the beginning, but the end result will be worth all the chases, arguments, and battles."

I feel my palms heat at his words, a sign that my fire's rising within me. One of his revelations stands out to me as the warning it is; that the more we're...*intimate*, probably in the sexual sense, the stronger the bond gets. The fact that I feel a flutter of warmth in my chest—which I somehow know is Camden's amusement at my fight—is only a testament to his words.

Oh, *fuck* this. As soon as I ward this godsforsaken property, I'm going to read every book ever written on the shifter mate bond and figure out how to better navigate it. Maybe there are even darker arts that would allow me to do damage to *his* end of it, though that vindictiveness won't put me in a favorable position to make cultural changes in his society, which I'll need to insert myself into for the sake of my people.

The complications of royal life.

"So, anything sexual equates to the strengthening of the bond, huh? Thanks for that little tidbit. I'll be sure to keep that in mind and stay as far away from you as possible in this monstrosity of a palace."

His smile seems more wolf than man—not in that he's shifting or looks lupine whatsoever, but in that he's more so baring his teeth with victory than actually smiling with any semblance of warmth. "Then you'll be trapped in this room with me until you feel differently because the door is locked, I have the only key, and only I know where your clothes are."

I slam my fist against the couch. "*Damn* you, Kent. Fine. Dinner this evening, and then we can chaperone my sister and your brother on a little trip to your library. Happy? Satisfied?"

"Only if dinner is a private occasion. If you think you'll get out of spending at least *some* time alone with me, you're very wrong. However, if it'll make you feel more comfortable, I'll agree not to touch you without your explicit permission. It won't be easy since I'd much prefer to eat *you* for dinner, but I'll hold back. You have my word. Acceptable terms?"

I stare at him for several moments, trying to gauge the sincerity of his offer. Nothing about his expression or tone indicates deceit, but Camden is a king and has been for some time—surely he'd have learned to lie believably in his many years at court.

"Considering you've locked me naked in a room with you, I'm not sure how much value your word has here," I say speculatively.

Camden throws his head back and roars with laughter, startling me. The sound is so carefree, amused, and mirthful, I'm taken off guard. I wouldn't have expected him to be able to laugh so... freely, and with his whole body.

"When you say it that way, you make me sound like a monster," he says after he's calmed, eyes shining with amusement.

"You *are* a monster," I grit out emphatically.

"Perhaps, but I'm *your* monster now. Just as you're *my* earthling witch. Now, agree to the deal and go wake your sister and get on with your day. I guarantee you won't get a better one."

"Fine," I grit. "Now where the *fuck* are my clothes?"

Chapter Twenty-Four

My morning is spent tending to Leisel—who, surprisingly, was kept occupied just fine by Greta in my absence. I'm starting to realize that Greta's accustomed to playing nanny to any children in the palace, and Leisel seems to like her. While I'm hesitant to trust anyone other than myself with my sister, I understand that I can't supervise Leisel around the clock and get work done, so I need to somehow ensure Greta's loyalty lies with me. If I can trust that she's *my* ally above Camden's—quite the difficult undertaking considering the difference in our very species—I can breathe easy leaving Leisel with her.

In Aesara, Mariketa and Parker were my go-to for when I needed to leave Leisel somewhere for a few hours while running errands. In Kinrith, I have no one, and that'll quickly become problematic.

So, I decide to take the familial approach—try to bring Greta into the fold, so to speak. I ask if she wouldn't mind joining me for tea in my room while Leisel does her morning lessons, and she hesitantly agrees, muttering about breaking etiquette.

In one of the corners of my bedroom, a servant brings in a rolling teacart upon my request—I pay attention as Greta undertakes an elaborate ritual of picking out a selection of tea leaves from the offered dish, enclosing them in an oval porous metal device, and pouring hot water over it into a beautifully painted, rose-patterned teacup. I follow her motions in making myself a cup, much less gracefully than her, but functionally nonetheless.

"I assume there's a reason you extended an invitation to join you, Your Majesty," Greta murmurs, taking a sip from her steaming cup. "How may I be of service?"

Her posture is stiff, shoulders tense, neck corded, hands tightly folded over her lap, and her eyes are narrowed in speculation. She may have taken a liking to Leisel, but Greta is quite obviously not yet sure of me. If I seek to recruit her to *my* team, I need to solidify my intentions in her eyes. She may view me as an ignorant human for all I know; I need her to view me as an aspiring hardworking queen—which I fully intend to be.

I offer her a shy smile. "If you'll forgive my boldness, Greta, in the last days I've found myself utterly lost in the ways of the palace—I feel as though my head's spinning from the drastic changes in both scenery and custom. One thing I have managed to observe is that you seem to be very seasoned and versed in palace life and are something of an expert in guiding young royals. While I am by no means a child in need of round-the-clock care, I know very little of royal etiquette as I never received appropriate education, and you strike me as the best person to ask for a few pointers on how to conduct myself properly."

I see Greta soften slightly at my words, relaxing in her seat and taking another sip of her tea. "Well, I can imagine such abrupt changes would be difficult for anyone—young or old—to get accustomed to. That you can recognize your difficulties and ask for aid is a credit to you. I will not lie to you, Your Majesty, there is much you need to learn, but in the short time I've had to observe you...you do have an innate grace with which you walk, speak, and generally act that I think will serve you well. If it would please you, I'd like to offer thrice-weekly lessons where we may go over some finer points of royal etiquette. It would also serve the young Princess well for you to learn, as she looks to you for many of her own mannerisms."

I cast a glance towards Leisel's room, glimpsing her hunched over the study table that's been brought in for her with a notebook and textbook open side by side in front of her. She scribbles away furiously at the notebook, her face a mask of concentration.

Looking back to Greta, I decide a touch of vulnerability might endear her to me further.

"I've raised her since she was born," I say nostalgically. "Until now, we've only ever had each other. Life has taught me to be jaded and untrusting; these days, I often find myself fearing how that reflects on Leisel. I've done everything in my power to give her a proper childhood filled with happiness and laughter—now, living in a foreign palace within a confusing culture, I don't know how to keep her from growing up before it's time. Already, she's wise beyond her years."

"Indeed," Greta agrees, nodding. "With a keen appreciation for learning. I've raised half a dozen royal children in my time, and never have I encountered a mind quite so inquisitive."

I smile warmly. "She's remarkable, isn't she? Her thirst for knowledge alone is singular."

Greta gives me a curious look. "It is. Rumors have circulated that both new additions to the royal family are singular. I don't wish to overstep, Your Majesty, but if you'd allow me..."

"Please, speak freely, Greta. It is my hope we will become friends."

She smiles ever so slightly, nodding again. "It's been said that your mother died while giving birth to the young Princess, your father having died not long before that."

"Both true," I confirm sagely.

Greta bringing this up reminds me quite clearly that we're innately on opposite sides of a blood feud, and I have to take a moment to compose myself and remind myself that I need to let go of my grudge against *all* shifters if I have a hope of surviving here. I don't see anything wrong with hating some of them, especially when they're assholes, but Greta isn't being cruel or controlling or anything but helpful. From what I've seen so far, she's great with Leisel, which gives me hope.

"You were left to care for a farm and an infant at the age of fourteen?" Greta asks, disbelieving.

I merely nod in affirmation, not caring to delve into the unpleasant memories.

"All on your own?" she presses, looking increasingly surprised. "I thought the rumors were exaggerated in your favor."

I shake my head with a sardonic smile. "No, the rumors haven't been exaggerated. I had a few friends in Aesara, but on the farm, it was just Leisel and me. I always made do."

There's a weighted pause in which Greta seems to be searching for the right words. To pass the time, she carefully refolds the napkin on her lap and adjusts the teaspoon beside her cup. "How?" she finally asks. "How did you manage it when you were still, by all intents and purposes, a child yourself?"

I lift one shoulder, finally taking a sip of my richly steeped tea. "Honestly? I didn't have another choice. There was no option *but* to figure out a way to keep the farm running and take care of Leisel. I couldn't fail her or leave her on her own, so I did what I had to for her. If it wasn't for her, I can say quite confidently I wouldn't be sitting here today."

Greta gives me a prolonged once over, her sharp eyes seeming to crawl over every inch of me as though she's trying to see into my very soul. When she finally meets my eyes, she holds my gaze for several long moments before speaking. "Well, I am very glad that you *are* sitting here today, Your Majesty. And if you'd forgive my forwardness, you've done a terrific job with Leisel. I'm honored to serve you both."

I *feel* the shift in her demeanor, feel the beginnings of fondness for me begin to take seed within Greta. I even sense the slightest shift in her loyalty; not as though she's turning her back on Camden, but more so that she now feels loyal to me as well. Although it's not my end goal, it's a start.

Score one for the witches.

Chapter Twenty-Five

I end up spending the entire day with Claude, getting to know the castle's live-in witch doctor. Apparently, a hybrid of his brand is in short supply these days. As an offspring of a strangely chosen fated match between a male wolf shifter and female witch-wolf hybrid, Claude made it clear that he understood a thing or two about odd and seemingly conflicting pairings as soon as I met him while we walked to the perimeter of the castle's lands.

While he was teaching me warding sigils of a much higher caliber than those I've learned from my books, he offered to give me a few pieces of advice learned from his parents, and I declined as diplomatically and politely as I could because I currently have *zero* interest in getting along with Camden. I'm pissed off by his manipulation last night and this morning, so I'll gladly leave him miserable for life. I had ranted to him about how much I despise shifters and gave him all the reasons why, and his response was to kiss me in places I had never dreamed of, thereby strengthening our bond. I'd admire that level of cunning if I wasn't so vexed.

After I learned how to create the necessary wards from Claude—an intricate conglomerate of sigils to be placed around the premise of the castle grounds and activated with various spells—it takes the better part of an hour for me to create and activate the first sequence of sigils. The incantations are in Latin, which Claude was surprised to learn I'm already fluent in. That doesn't make the spell work any easier; the only thing I've ever been able to do with my magic—other than summon a very destructive fire that I much prefer to keep locked up—is some minor mending, warding, and odd-out spells taken from the text of ancient books. Suddenly, I'm practicing the highest forms of magic with none of the necessary education, and doing so *successfully*, albeit with a great deal of effort.

It takes hundreds of individual sigils to create a wide enough shield to protect the vast land the castle and other royal buildings sit on, and each sigil requires an extensive magical ritual, as well as my blood. The symbols themselves need to be drawn in my blood, activated with a spell, put into the proper place in accordance with the other sigils using yet *another* spell, and then reinforced with a final incantation.

By the time I'm putting the final ward in place, night has fallen over the castle grounds. Claude has decided that standing is overrated and is sitting on a nearby log with a small fire he created crackling in front of him, and I'm pretty sure I've lost at least a third of my blood in the last hours.

"His majesty will not be pleased when he sees you," Claude says, though his voice is resigned.

He's spent half the day trying to get me to slow down, with very little success on his end. Evidently, Claude is worried that Camden will rip out his throat if I return to the castle in a worse state than I was when I left. Several hours ago, he insisted we stop for the day so I could rest; I asked him if he believed the vampires were spending their time resting after losing one of their royal family members. The arguments stopped after that.

"Aren't there some rules of etiquette that say you shouldn't speak to someone of my station with such insolence?" I respond mildly.

Claude lets out a soft snort. "If there's anything today has taught me, it is that you, child, could not care less about royal etiquette."

Considering I spent our first hour of casting cursing a blue streak every time I made a mistake, I can't really blame his assumption. I don't bother telling him not to call me child; compared to Claude's many centuries of life, I'm essentially still an embryo to him.

"Quite the contrary. In fact, I spent the morning convincing Leisel's nanny to give me etiquette lessons—*fuck*."

My hands, shaky from the amount of blood I've doled out, falter in the intricate tactile gestures that go in tandem with the incantation required to transfer the sigil from its place on my arm and to the air, where it will complete the net of warding that'll keep the castle safe from any and all types of intrusion. The other sigils I've created thus far are visible, glowing a faint white, and suspended in a large, interconnected web of glowing white threads made of pure protective magic.

"What were you saying about etiquette lessons?" Claude asks dryly.

I flex my hands, shaking out my fingers as quickly as possible. If I don't move the sigil from my skin to the net before the blood dries, I'll have to redo it, as the ritual requires fresh blood.

"If you were powerful enough to cast an effective warding, we wouldn't be here," I snap, before cringing at my own words. They're unnecessarily cruel. The castle has obviously stood for quite some time with Claude's protection; it isn't his fault that the opposition's heating up.

I turn to look at Claude, ready to apologize, but pause when I see his expression isn't angry or pained; it's thoughtful.

"You're right," he agrees, surprising me. "Perhaps that's why Camden found you when he did, just in time for an attack that could've ended in several royal deaths. Fate does like her tricks."

I frown, sensing something more to what he's saying. "What do you mean?"

Claude's gaze falls to the flames. "In shifter culture, it's bad form to use magic to find one's mate. Doing so is considered a snub to the gods—as if we don't trust that events will unfold as they're intended to. Many believe it brings bad fortune. A few days before he found you, Camden requested I perform a ritual to locate his fated mate; my compliance was reluctant at best because I've seen the fates punish shifters for impatience. Instead, your arrival—though by no means simple—has already proved a blessing."

"To you," I say under my breath, because being here has by no means been a blessing to me. I miss Aesara desperately, miss having a simpler life free of the many current complications. I had my fair share of difficulties, but they were difficulties I knew how to handle.

"In time I think you'll find it's a blessing to you as well," Claude replies, apparently having heard me.

"Perhaps," I murmur doubtfully.

"Finish up so we can head back," Claude says. "Camden will already have my head in a basket for commandeering your entire day. I won't dare make you late for dinner."

Noticing that my blood's gone dry on my arm, I sigh, reach for the knife resting in my pocket, and cut into my palm again. I let out a small hiss at the pain of renewing the wound I've been using as my blood source all day before using it to retrace the sigil on my arm, which is barely visible with the firelight.

Then, holding my hands out in front of me, I begin speaking in Latin while going through various tactile gestures. The sigil starts to glow red before peeling off my arm, delicately floating through the air, and finding its home in the center of several other sigils. The strands of the glowing white net that connect the other sigils reach for the new sigil, twining around it and turning its red glow to white, mirroring the others.

"You might want to shield your eyes for this part," Claude says, just as a ripple travels through the entire net that encapsulates the palace grounds, stretching far out of sight.

The ripple stills just as the white glow brightens until it turns positively *blinding*, making me shut my eyes and turn away with a grimace. A moment later, the glow subsides, and I turn back to see that the net has turned into a solid single shield rather than a web, and all the sigils have fused into it. After a moment the shield's glow disappears, turning invisible, but I can still feel a strong hum of power radiating from it.

"The brighter it glows, the more powerful it is," Claude says faintly. "In all my years I've never seen a shield create such an explosion of light. Not here, and not in any of the realms I've visited."

His voice sounds more shocked than praising, so I turn to look at him apprehensively. He's staring at me with wide eyes and raised brows, the wrinkles on his forehead deepened under the weight of his surprise.

"That's a good thing, right?" I ask slowly. When he doesn't respond, instead continuing to stare at me, I press, "Did I do it correctly? Is it good enough? Am *I* good enough?"

I'm not quite sure why I ask the last question, considering I shouldn't care less about Claude's opinion, but despite being above him on the power spectrum, he's half a millennium of knowledge, wisdom, and *experience* ahead of me—which is as valuable as raw magical ability. He's the only other witch-adjacent being in this castle and possibly in this city, so he's probably who I'll be turning to for all things magical.

Claude lets out a soft puff of laughter. "To tell you the truth of it, child, you are remarkable."

"Fucking *gods*, I just nearly went *blind*," a voice calls out to my far left, in the direction of the castle. I swivel my head, barely able to make out the silhouette of someone walking in our direction through the darkness of night. Although I can't see who it is, I quickly place the voice as belonging to Wyatt.

"And here comes another foul-mouthed royal," Claude comments wryly. "I expect the two of you should get along famously."

"Considering he intends to claim my sister in a matter of years, not to mention his species and position, there is no reality in which we will *ever* get along," I say quietly so only Claude can hear,

Claude stands abruptly and walks to me, clasping my arm tightly. "You should," he says seriously. He snaps his fingers together with his free hand, and a small shockwave of power flows out from him, making me tense. When I look around, my eyes land on the fire, and I'm shocked to see its flames appear frozen in time, not fluctuating or flickering in the least.

I turn to Claude, wide-eyed. Before I can ask for an explanation, he says curtly, "That time-freezing spell buys us a few minutes of guaranteed privacy. I'm going to give you advice, and you are going to listen for the good of yourself and your sister. Are we in accord?"

Shocked at his sudden bluntness, I can't do anything other than nod mutely.

His grip on my arm tightens. "It's time for you to open your eyes, Sierra, because you're in shark-infested waters, and if you want to survive, you don't stand a chance of doing it alone. You need connections in high places. Connections that you *already* have the sort of access to that others would *kill* for. Besides being a prime candidate to protect the young Princess from any harm that might befall her, Wyatt could be your best ally. He loves his brother, but he doesn't agree with some of the segregation shifters impose between species—he thinks that cultural restrictions and prejudices are the reason we're at war with the vampires in the first place."

Claude releases my arm as though I've burned him, and proceeds to walk around me in a circle, appraising me with a newly critical eye. "You're young. You're sharp as a tack. You're powerful beyond comprehension. If you should wish to, Sierra, you could change the world—not just for humans, but for *everyone*—and destiny has given you the perfect way to do it. Yet you spend time wallowing in resentment and anger because Camden's grandfather did things that resulted in a chain of events that ended with the death of your parents. Have you considered that Camden himself is not at fault? He's done nothing to earn your wrath other than try to keep a kingdom running under enormous pressure. I've gathered you fault him for the injustices humans experience, yes?"

I nod tersely, unsure how to respond to this version of Claude. So far today he's been fairly quiet and task-oriented, and now I'm getting the sense that he presented himself that way so he could have an opportunity to study me without my being on guard. *Clever.*

"Have you stopped for a moment to think on the possibility that Camden quite simply does not have *time* to focus on anything outside his own kingdom? Shifters are by no means easy to rule—they're mercurial, prone to violence, and only bow down to the strongest and most dominant of all. There are packs scattered across three separate continents, packs made up of three factions of shifters—wolves, felines, and *dragons*—which makes keeping them all in line a logistical nightmare. In the little time Camden isn't traveling between packs on royal business, he is attending to the countless other duties that befall a king. Finding you has set him weeks behind in work, and yet he carves out time for you in a full schedule. You can't stomach the thought of him yet—I see it will take time to change that. In the interim, get to know his brother. You may find the two of you have much in common and could accomplish a great deal together. Get yourself an ally, Sierra, or you'll sink."

He snaps his fingers again, and I feel whatever power he let out recede back into him as time around us resumes. The fire once again crackles and pops, and Wyatt steadily treks closer until he's visible within the light of the flames. All the while I'm mulling over Claude's words, deciding how much merit they have.

He's right that Camden himself hasn't actively inflicted harm on humanity, but he has passively turned a blind eye, or so I assumed. The fact of the matter might well be that he didn't have time to turn an eye on them at all—I learned from my lady's maid that he never really got a childhood; he's been wrapped up in serious royal duties from a young age. A youth in which he *lost his mother,* something we have in common. Still, even though I might've unfairly assigned the blame for human suffering to him, he's caused *me* plenty of suffering that's reaped resentment.

Wyatt, however, hasn't. My interactions with him can be summed up to my trying to keep him away from Leisel—I haven't bothered to get to know *him* as an individual, mostly because I assumed there's absolutely nothing we have in common, but that might not be true.

"Cam was getting ready to send out a search party for you two since you've been out here over ten hours; I offered to come instead," Wyatt says, stopping beside the fire and looking between Claude and me. "Judging from the flash that nearly cost me my eyes, I assume the new shield is functional?"

"*Very,*" Claude responds. "I'd even go as far as to say it's impenetrable. No living being could make it past the barrier and into the castle unless they were invited. Usually, anyone who tries to penetrate such shields would run into it face-first and get sent back a few steps, but I think with this one...contact with the shield alone could kill enemies."

I nod in approval, pleased at the protection that now surrounds Leisel, while Wyatt whistles. "*Nice.* That'll come in handy. Sierra, you're scheduled for dinner with my brother in fifteen minutes, and the walk back takes about twenty, so you should probably go straight to his wing once we're back. I'm here to walk you."

Lovely.

Chapter Twenty-Six

I eye Wyatt, thinking over Claude's words. I *can't* stomach the thought of Camden yet—especially while I'm freshly mortified from last night and aching to spend the rest of my life avoiding him, but Wyatt is a different story. My hostility towards him is more on principle than anything else.

What's an icebreaker that might work with Camden's little brother?

After several moments of sifting through possible conversation openers, I ask, "Do you read?"

Wyatt looks mildly surprised at the question. "Sure. I had a lot of alone time growing up, and I spent a decent amount of it in the palace library."

I don't entirely believe him, but he seems sincere. He's simply never struck me as an intellectual, but that could be because I never bothered to look closer.

"Earthly literature or books native to your realms?" I ask.

"I grew up in this realm, so I made a point to read the books native to it," he responds. "Classical literature making up the body of what I perused."

I arch an eyebrow at him. "Shakespeare?"

"Of course," he returns.

That I can work with. "Favorite play?"

"Hamlet. Or King Lear."

I nod slowly. "To be or not to be, that is the question…"

Wyatt grins, taking the bait. "Whether 'tis nobler of the mind to suffer the slings and arrows of outrageous fortune—"

"—Or to take arms against the sea of troubles, and by opposing, end them," I cut him off, finishing a verse from Hamlet's most famous soliloquy. If Wyatt were bullshitting me, he wouldn't be able to quote it from memory alone. "You just might be okay, little Kent."

Wyatt barks out a laugh. "Glad you think so. Let's get back before my brother sends in the cavalry."

Claude gives me a nod of approval as Wyatt and I start in the direction of the castle together. It's dark out, so our guiding light is made up of the moon, shining brightly in the center of the sky, accompanied by countless glittering stars.

We're traversing a cobblestone path through several gardens when Wyatt asks, "Pride and Prejudice or Persuasion?"

I feel a smile tug at my lips as I keep pace with him. "Persuasion all the way. Jane Austen's masterpiece. The story arc is *way* better. War and Peace or Anna Karenina?"

Wyatt laughs again, this time genuinely. "Trying to trip me up with Slavic authors? War and Peace, arguably Tolstoy's masterpiece."

I fall silent for several moments as we walk, trying to figure out the best way to bring up what Claude told me earlier—that Wyatt disagrees with cultural and interspecies discrimination within his kingdom. While he hasn't at any point struck me as a philosopher who spends his time contemplating international and socioeconomic problems, Claude succeeded in opening my eyes to the fact that without allies, I'm fucked, and Wyatt is currently my most viable prospective ally.

Claude also shut me down faster than I could blink when I hinted at searching for literature that might affect the mythical mate bond. I hadn't specified that I wanted to negatively affect the bond, but mentioning my curiosity about what could impact it must have been enough to raise the witch doctor's hackles because he told me in no uncertain terms that literature on witchcraft powerful enough to affect a bond between mates is forbidden and unavailable.

So, for now, I need to do my best to deal with Camden and see if I can find another member of the royal family I can tolerate a little more. If I can build anything resembling a friendship with Wyatt and determine that he is not a threat to my sister, maybe I'd be able to breathe slightly easier.

Worrying for Leisel requires the majority of my time and attention here, even more so than back in Aesara. The only reason I've handled my all-day separation from her so well is I'd discussed her hourly schedule with Greta, giving it my stamp of approval.

If I could have the confidence that Wyatt was a decent enough person to no longer lose my head over the prospect of him in a room with my sister, I might actually end up with a very strong friend in the palace. Camden told me not long ago that what Wyatt feels towards Leisel right now is more fraternal or paternal than anything—the bond between them won't manifest as anything beyond a strong protective instinct in Wyatt, one that drives him to keep Leisel safe, until she's matured. If that's the case, a good relationship with Wyatt could buy me at least half a decade of not worrying quite so much over my sister.

While the mama bear instinct within me is always quick to push me to disregard any possibility of Leisel ever having a love life, let alone being a fated mate with a fucking *wolf shifter*, I'm not in a position where I can be ruled by my base instincts, because I alone am not capable of protecting Leisel *here*. This is a palace, city, and society that I know very little about, which means protecting not only myself but another person will be close to impossible unless I have the help of someone who *does* know it. If I can form a reliable connection with Wyatt, I'd get my first real foothold in the palace, along with a substantial amount of peace of mind—at least for the immediate future.

"Whatever you're thinking, spit it out," Wyatt says. "I don't do well with awkward silences, and you strike me as too direct to beat around the bush."

I cast him a brief glance as we trek through meticulously trimmed and beautiful gardens, boasting more varieties of plants and flowers than I've ever seen, all bursting with vibrant colors lit by moonbeams.

"Why do you think we're at war with the vampires?" I ask.

Wyatt's steps falter ever so slightly, and he gives me a look with raised eyebrows. "Claude's been whispering in your ear, huh? Are you truly interested in knowing or is this a poor attempt at small talk?"

I feel my eyebrows furrow. "I don't think discussing a war that could destroy my home planet is small talk. At the very least we'd be discussing political theory and speculation of mass destruction—that's quite a stretch from talking about the weather or the most recent harvest."

Wyatt lets out a laugh, lighthearted and entertained. "Fair enough. How familiar are you with the history of this realm, of its continents and kingdoms?"

I shrug. "I read anything I had access to my whole life. Most of the time that ended up being old history textbooks or biographies. I don't have any formal education, but I've tried to not be completely ignorant about the world I live in."

Wyatt gives me a nod. "Good. Then you'll know that just about every war ever fought on this planet has been a result of when one group of people decided they were superior to another, for whatever reason. Whether it was because of the gods they worshipped, rulers they obeyed, or regions they lived in, that's been the moral of every war. You'll also notice a pattern in history is that wars always grow markedly worse after borders are closed and any dialogue between opposing monarchies or governments is ended."

I nod. "Yes, that's all true."

"And yet," Wyatt says, "the very first act of my grandfather upon his initial invasion was to declare shifters superior to *all* other species, not just humans, and try to create a societal hierarchy that left shifters at the top while crushing any other mythics that would also inevitably invade beneath us. That didn't bother the sirens, as they were interested in the oceans, or the witches and faye, as they're elusive and like to keep to themselves, but the vampires are a notoriously prideful and aggressive species, just like shifters.

"When the vampires made their way onto Earth, my father was reigning monarch and Alpha, and he refused to reach out to them and create a dialogue that could give way to any semblance of peace. We could've invited them to create societies that could coexist with ours; instead, we acted with a supremacy mindset that isolated the vampires, leaving them on undesirable land with no prospect of connections that could help them flourish here. So, of course, the vampires have spent their entire time on Earth amassing numbers and preparing for war and conquest—we haven't given them another choice. Not all vampires are these bloodthirsty, horrendous creatures mythology paints them as—not all of them are like that bastard Kyron—but we are giving them every reason to lean into their deadly archetypes."

I take several beats of silence once Wyatt's done talking, mulling over everything he's said. I can't say I disagree—this is clearly a topic that he's spent a significant amount of time contemplating. He also seems to genuinely care about the sociopolitical state of this planet, which is more than I've observed of Camden.

Camden cares about shifters and only shifters, while Wyatt has a broader view of the world, which I can appreciate. A broader view isn't going to cut it if I'll be allowing Wyatt to step into Leisel's life, however.

I point out calmly, "Interesting that while referencing human history you neglect to mention humans."

Wyatt volleys back, "Because you've been trying to wipe each other out for thousands of years—there's plenty of written text to support that. It's only recently that new species of beings made their homes here—"

"And since that has happened, you'll notice that the human population has dropped by something like *eight billion humans*," I interrupt, growing irritated.

Wyatt holds his hands up in a placating gesture. "I'm not denying that the invasion of mythics is the worst thing to ever happen to the human population, but let's not forget that this planet was on the precipice of the sort of war that would have destroyed it. The day we invaded was the same day one of the most progressive governments of the time was gearing up to launch a nuclear weapon to the other side of the world. Had that weapon gone off, it would have prompted several other nukes to be launched. Then there would have been nothing left on this planet to guide us here—all of the plant, animal, *and human* life would've been wiped out."

Wyatt's right, which *infuriates me*. All historical accounts agree on one thing; the day mythics actually made their way onto Earth could've otherwise been a doomsday. It was in the middle of the third and last World War, one that almost ended all life on Earth permanently. Threats of nuclear bombings had been made from all sides of the conflict, and the civilians of the world spent several months holding their breath, wondering each morning if that day would finally mark the start of the nuclear holocaust.

Instead of nukes going off on every continent, turning Earth into a wasteland, we received the invasion of mythics.

Much of the outcome for humans was the same as it would've been otherwise; most of the humans are dead. The only standing difference between what inevitably would have been and what is, is that the Earth is now lush with nature and greenery and wildlife that humans almost wiped out entirely.

I will never forgive mythics for the part they played in the mass deaths of humans, but I'll also never forgive humans for almost destroying the planet they were gifted. My magic is a product of the very thing they almost annihilated for their own selfish ends and desires.

Is that the moral of the story? Everywhere I look, every species I consider, is awful in its own way? Humans are the very embodiment of self-serving, having almost been the reason for their own destruction. Shifters only care about the pack and hierarchy. Witches and faye care about nature and their own covens and clans. Vampires care about killing anyone who isn't one of them, evidently because shifters haven't left them much of another choice.

"Maybe that's just the nature of being alive," I murmur dejectedly. "One person's prosperity has always come at the cost of another's from the beginning of time. That was the case with the nomads and all the civilizations that followed. One kingdom would flourish by destroying another. One government would become stronger by bombing its opposition, often killing far too many innocents in the process. And later on, after the invasion, species of mythics could prosper and live, only at the cost of human death and suffering."

"I don't think life is quite so nihilistic," Wyatt volleys back easily, bumping my shoulder with his. "If it was, things like fate and destiny wouldn't exist. Yes, in the grand scheme of things, we're all insignificant ants, but we don't live in the grand scheme of things—we live for finite periods, and what we do has the potential to affect *many* lives that'll follow ours."

The light of the castle illuminates our surroundings the closer we get to it, and I notice many floating orbs of light scattered about. They're beautiful, and I realize now that they're probably a courtesy of one of Claude's spells.

"I guess we'll have to wait and see what fate and destiny have in store for us," I say as we cross the courtyard and step through the entrance of the palace.

"I think it's pretty clear that, whatever the endgame with us is, our actions are going to inevitably impact a *lot* of people. That's our burden."

The rest of the walk is in comfortable silence as Wyatt guides me through many halls, passageways, and staircases on our way to his brother's personal wing. Once we're in front of a large twin-arched double door, Wyatt says, "I'll see you later when we take your sister to the library. Maybe she can grill me on my knowledge of books too."

With a half-smile, he strolls away, and I nervously finger the hem of my shirt as I face the entrance to Camden's wing. Before I can knock to announce my presence, the door slides open, revealing my treacherous mate.

Chapter Twenty-Seven

I expect Camden to look his best for our dinner tonight, to try to tempt me. What I don't expect is for him to be so successful. The moment I see him, I have to stop my jaw from dropping. He's always well dressed, whether he's in simple clothes or a suit, but I've never found my eyes glued to his corded biceps and broad shoulders, visible beneath the well-tailored fabric of his dress shirt. Or the way his forearms, thick and veiny, are exposed by the rolled-up sleeves of said shirt. Or the way his eyes are locked on me with a singular intensity that makes me feel like a deer faced down with a hunter's crossbow.

I'm filthy from spending the entire day shedding blood, sweat, and tears to ward the entire castle grounds, which are *very* expansive. If I gave a shit what Camden thought of me, I might feel embarrassed at my appearance—my shirt and pants covered in grass, dirt, and blood. As it is, I only feel resentful of the Alpha for fucking me over last night, *literally*.

"You look like you've had quite the day," he remarks calmly, stepping aside and motioning for me to enter the room with an arm.

"You have a very large estate, and seeing as Leisel is quite the explorer, I wanted to ward as much of it as possible," I respond, tentatively stepping into the room and looking around.

I'm in what appears to be a living room—decorated in royal blues and silvers, it has a high ceiling with gorgeous glass prisms serving as lightbulbs that bathe the entire room in light, wooden flooring, and a beautiful fireplace with a silver-encrusted carved mantel. In front of the fireplace is a large blue sofa, and across the room, a square table large enough to seat four people is set with dishes, silverware, glasses, and an array of delicious looking foods.

Leading me over to the table with a hand hovering above the small of my back, Camden asks, "How did it go? Were the wards successfully placed?"

I nod. "Yes. The crown's entire land is safe, and Claude suspects anyone who tries to cross the wards without invitation or with ill intent will perish."

Camden smiles at me, looking genuinely proud and pleased. "I know everyone will sleep easier knowing they're protected by one of the strongest witches of our times. Thank you, Sierra."

This is the second time he's thanked me for something in twenty-four hours, and I don't know how to respond to a display of common decency from him. Generally, from what I've seen, he has very little. While my observations of Camden thus far have been clouded by a deep personal disdain towards his existence, it is evident that he was raised in a very particular way that didn't teach him the value of commonplace manners, such as everyday politeness.

While I can understand that, as a king and Alpha, Camden's not in a position in this world to indulge in niceties, I also dislike feeling like I'm a puppet on strings, and Camden has a keen way of making those around him feel like objects. Things to be used to achieve a desired outcome. My usefulness to him is as his mate; as the only person who can sire heirs to him, strengthen him, and complete his soul. I'm his path to success, prosperity, and happiness, whereas he is the person who's turned my life upside down without a single care as to how it'd affect me.

Since I've already said much of that aloud, I settle on an awkward, "You're welcome."

Camden inclines his head. "I know I don't thank you enough, or show you that you matter to me beyond just being my mate. I want to be very clear that I like you for you, with or without the bond that connects us."

I can't help the irritation that curls in my stomach. While Camden's words are nice, his actions do not support them. He might say he likes me regardless of us being mates, but none of what he's done thus far has demonstrated that. He's ripped me out of my home and village only to throw me into a society that I neither know nor understand. He hasn't shown any particular amount of compassion—only ambition to get what he wants, which is currently me.

For a reason that's absolutely beyond me, I find myself saying, "Sorry, Camden, but your words mean shit to me."

Camden's eyes flicker between irritation and confusion for several moments before hardening with resolve. He gives me a single nod. "That's fair. Actions speak louder than words. Follow me."

Abruptly, he turns and walks to the other side of the room. Not the exit leading back to the hall, but deeper into his personal chambers. He pauses at the door, looking at me expectantly.

Torn between genuine curiosity and a whole lot of well-placed distrust, I cast one last glance at the admittedly inviting-looking dinner spread before taking several uncertain steps toward Camden.

With one hand on the golden door handle, he holds his free hand out to me with a conspiratorial smile that is at once boyishly charming and unsettling. Unsettling, because Camden's smiles usually range from regal to condescending—rarely is there anything boyish about him; he's clearly *all* man.

"Trust me?" he asks.

The earnestness in his tone makes me close my lips around the *fuck no* that was ready to fly out. Before this moment, I've never seen or heard earnestness from Camden. He's too busy with his station and duties to lower himself to the rest of us mortals. More than anything, it's curiosity that directs me to incline my head in agreement and hesitantly slip my hand into his.

His grip is warm, strong, and sends an entirely foreign rush of sensations through me. Previously, whenever I had skin-to-skin contact with Camden, I was able to mostly ignore any feelings of sparks or pleasure that the bond ignited within me—my hatred of him overshadowed them. Now, however, the sensation the bond creates is decidedly more subdued—as though it's no longer a physical jar to my entire system—yet strong enough that I can't ignore it. The strange feeling of safety I've only felt flickers of previously is now much more intense. The bond between us really did strengthen overnight in ways I couldn't have fathomed, because there is *nothing* safe about this man, especially when it comes to me.

I try to yank my hand from his, ready to veto wherever he's taking me so we can eat our dinner in uncomfortable silence. Camden, however, doesn't allow it; he merely tightens his grip so I can't escape, opens the door, and leads me into a hallway with dark polished wooden walls and flooring. I startle when I glimpse the art hanging on the walls; two of the paintings displayed are *mine*—ones I left behind in Aesara when Leisel and I had to move.

One painting is of a jewel-studded fruit bowl filled with rotting fruits that are crawling with maggots—a social commentary on wealth I don't think Camden picked up on, otherwise he wouldn't be displaying it. Another is a bright painting of a river near the farm where I used to take Leisel every weekend. Looking at it causes a feeling of nostalgia to sweep over me; it reminds me of simpler times.

Before I can ask Camden why the paintings I deliberately kept away from him are now gracing the walls of his personal chambers, he stops in front of a door and pulls a key out of his pocket, unlocking it. He pushes it open and when I glimpse what fills the room, my heart stutters before tripling in speed with excitement. Camden doesn't protest when I pull my hand from his and rush into the room.

It's every painter's dream studio combined into one. The far side of the room is comprised of windows, showing a gorgeous view of the moon and countless stars lighting up the royal grounds. During the daytime, the light that filters in would be *perfect* for painting and sketching.

On the other three walls of the large room are easels, canvasses, pigments, paints, brushes, and just about every tool a painter could need. The items are the best quality I've ever seen, and the whole room might as well be straight out of a fairytale.

I walk up to the wall of glass facing the castle grounds, dazed.

Camden says from behind me, "I first ordered construction on this room when I saw your paintings in Aesara. You're remarkably talented. It took some time to complete, but I had the builders consult with artists and architects on what would best suit a painter's needs." When I don't respond, too awe-struck to string together a sentence, I hear his footsteps carry him across the polished wooden flooring closer to me. He goes on, "The space is yours. You can come here whenever you like."

"Don't think I don't notice you deliberately had a studio constructed in *your* wing instead of mine," I murmur. The only reason I don't resent that right now is because I'm still taking in the fact that Camden went through what sounds like a good deal of effort to create a space solely for me.

A soft breath of laughter tickles the back of my neck as he stops behind me, sweeping my hair over my shoulder. I remind him, "You promised you wouldn't touch me without permission."

He lets out a grunt of displeasure but drops his hands and moves to stand beside me. "Apologies. It's challenging to be so close to you yet unable to touch you. As for your art studio's placement...well, you can't blame a tiger for its stripes. I saw an opportunity to have you in my personal space and I took it. I like having you near me, Sierra; you center me. But I won't disturb you when you're working. I don't know much about art, but I know very well from royal commissions just how temperamental artists can be. Your painting time is your own."

I swallow past the knot in my throat, unsure what to say or do. Camden's never been so blatantly kind to me, and although the placement of my studio is expectedly manipulative, this is an act of kindness. My painting hobby has no measurable benefit to him; the only reason he'd go through this effort is for my happiness and comfort.

The last time anyone went out of their way for my happiness and comfort was when my parents were still alive. Since then, it's been me looking out for Leisel's and my best interests, with minimal outside help. To have someone else go through so much effort on my behalf is such a foreign sensation I've forgotten how to respond to it.

I remember the way my parents loved each other, eternally and endlessly. They would've done anything for each other. They survived many hardships together, always forging on despite impossible odds. My father doted on my mother as much as he was able—he'd pick her wildflowers every other day so our kitchen and living room were always bursting with colorful bouquets. He'd buy her art supplies from the village when harvest was plentiful and we had some extra money, brought her mugs of tea and coffee when she was painting, and showered her with love. Despite being dirt poor, our quality of life was as rich as it got, and that was because of the strong bond my parents shared.

Camden hasn't completed any herculean tasks for me, but he did go out of his way to do something that would make me happy. That's not something I expected of him, and because I didn't expect it, I have no defense formulated, so the gesture batters at the resistance I've naturally accumulated against Camden rather effectively.

Camden holds out his hand, the key to the room resting in his palm. "It's yours. I hope you use it as often as you like; it's here for you. Now, let's get you fed, and you can tell me about your adventures with Claude and Wyatt."

Chapter Twenty-Eight

D inner ends up being a subtle affair, with no fights or tantrums to punctuate it. In fact, I'm surprised to find I don't exactly *mind* spending time in Camden's vicinity, which bothers me on merit. While his gesture of creating a studio space and filling it with supplies for me is surprisingly touching, it doesn't erase the animosity that's built between us up until now. I won't soon forget the first night I dined with him, which ended in me getting my ass whipped until I wanted to cry. I also won't forget that—aside from the blood vendetta that separates us—so far, I haven't seen all that much to like in Camden. If I were a shifter, it might be different, but his sole focus is on his kingdom and kin—from an outsider's perspective, that isn't a particularly attractive trait.

We spend an hour or so dining together, with only the occasional small talk to fill the silence. Camden watches me the entire time, every predatory inch of the Alpha wolf on display. Maybe it's because I've gotten used to him blatantly staring at me when we're in a space together, but at this point, it doesn't bother me like it did at first. What does bother me is the effect his gaze has on me; previously, him looking at me could make my hair stand on end in discomfort—I could always circumvent my attraction to him with anger. Now, though, his gaze causes my nipples to harden beneath my bra, and an uncomfortable warmth to take up residence low in my belly.

The fact that being in proximity to him is enough to get me aroused, despite the fact that all we're doing is eating, is immensely frustrating. The lack of control over my own body and its responses isn't something I've ever had to grapple with before, and having to deal with it now is another reason I don't wish to spend all that much time with Camden. If I can't control my body's responses, that goes to show that it won't be long until I'm not entirely in control of my actions either. The bond is a very powerful mythical connection, and one of its greatest assets is lust; as of now, I worry that I won't be able to fight my lust for Camden forever.

Once we're done eating, Camden asks, "Now, was sharing a meal with me really so terrible that I'll need to continue coercing your compliance?"

I finish the dregs of the wine in my glass before responding, "If you keep saying shit like that, yes."

If he hadn't opened his mouth and ruined the calm, however—or even stated his question in a slightly less asshole-ish way—I would've said no, my compliance needn't be coerced. If I need to sit through eating with Camden every once in a while, I think I can manage that; especially if he continues to keep to his word of not touching me without my express verbal permission. I can tell it isn't easy for him, considering the heat of his gaze, but he keeps himself restrained, which I appreciate.

"I'll rephrase. Would you grace me with the pleasure of your company again tomorrow?"

I roll my bottom lip between my teeth, considering. Saying yes feels like forfeiting, but saying no would only be inviting a challenge that I ultimately can't win. And after Camden's gesture tonight, I'm feeling ambivalent towards him more than anything, especially with Claude's words from earlier still floating around in my mind. I can't say I like Camden, but I can't say I entirely *dis*like him either anymore. He has qualities that I find admirable, it's mainly circumstances that make us such a strange pairing. If I were born a shifter, I think we'd actually get along quite well. As I was born an Earth witch, however, it'll take a lot of effort from both of us to make any progress, and I'm not sure how much effort I'm ready to dedicate to the cause yet.

Still, for the sake of avoiding arguments, I respond, "Sure."

Camden blinks at me in surprise. "That was easier than I thought it would be. I didn't even have to bribe you to get you to agree." He tilts his head to the side, concern creeping into his gaze as he looks me up and down, nostrils flaring. "Are you feeling well?"

Gods, are we really so bad that he assumes I'm sick if I agree to spend time with him? I guess, considering the track record of catastrophes occurring almost every time we're in a room together, his reaction is appropriate. It also emphasizes the oddity of this entire situation.

"I'm not feeling like fighting a losing battle tonight," I clarify.

That seems to displease him. Camden's eyebrows draw together as he swirls the wine in his glass, taking his eyes off me for the first time since we sat down together. He stares at the rich crimson liquid for several seconds before swallowing what's left in the glass, setting it down on the table with a distinct clank, and rising as he holds out his hand to me.

I stare at it for a beat before deciding to go with the flow and placing my hand in his, allowing him to pull me to my feet. All in all, he's behaved himself tonight, and it wouldn't be smart to repay decency with rudeness. This is, in fact, perhaps the most decent and non-hostile interaction I've had with Camden to date, which makes me slightly more amenable. Also, there's no denying his studio gift bought him some leeway.

Leading me to the couch in front of the fireplace, Camden says, "I know I'm not your favorite person to spend time with, and I hope that will change. In the interim, I recall you being more relaxed around my wolf, and he has been pushing *relentlessly* to get some one-on-one time with you for several days. Before we go to the library, would you spend a few minutes with him?"

"You say 'him,'" I observe, "as if you're separate entities. Is that how shifters view their animal counterparts? As separate?"

Camden shakes his head. "Not at all. We share our soul with our wolves, or whatever animal resides within us—that's as entwined as two beings can get. But while we are one, we are also two sides of the same coin: two faces representing the same soul. So, for the sake of that distinction, it's easier to refer to our animals as separate." He pauses for a moment before continuing, "You're unusually curious today."

Instead of saying the first thing that pops into my mind—*you can't beat an enemy you don't know*—I say with a placid smile, "I'll spend some time with your wolf. He has a stronger grasp on the concept of consent."

A half smile curls Camden's lips. "Not quite; if you tried to run, he'd tackle you. But he is also very fond of you and craves your affection. The human part of me was raised to forgo such luxuries; animals are far more elemental in their sentiments."

I nod at the glimpse of insight, feeling more and more curious. Maybe it's the magical part of me, or maybe it's that I've always had a curious mind, but listening to Camden speak on his relationship with his wolf—explaining the ways they differ and how that correlates to a separate yet entwined nature—is fascinating to me.

My eyebrows lift in surprise when he shrugs off his dinner jacket and his fingers move to unbutton his shirt. Apparently, he's not going to change somewhere else and come back in wolf form; in fact, I suspect he wants me to watch him undress, probably to tempt me. I spin around to face the fireplace so quickly that it makes me dizzy, and Camden's low chuckle taunts me.

I'm not mentally prepared to see Camden naked after we shared a not-disastrous evening together. I know what we did last night strengthened our bond—tonight has been proof of that—and I don't want to find out just how much by inviting temptation. So, I stare into the guttering embers of the fireplace until I hear a soft whine behind me that most definitely could not be made by a human.

I turn back around, coming face to face with Camden's better half. The last time I saw the wolf, it was dark and we were camping in the middle of a forest, so I didn't get a proper look at him. Now, in the well-lit palace, I see that *magnificent* is not a strong enough word to describe this beast. He's twice the size of a normal wolf, covered in jet-black silky fur. His ears, tipped with a softer shade of gray fur, are perked in my direction. His eyes, icy and bright, are locked on me with all the intensity of a wolf but none of the danger. Despite everything about this creature's appearance advertising *danger*, I get the strange sense that his energy towards me is more along the lines of an *overgrown teddy bear*.

As if to punctuate that thought, he lays down on the floor, rolls onto his back, presenting his gray furry belly, and cranes his head to look at me with pleading puppy-dog eyes. I feel a puff of astonished laughter escape me at the fact that this Alpha of Alphas, King of Kings wolf is begging me for a belly rub, complete with one long ongoing whine for attention.

The wolf's tail starts to thump against the floor as I walk over and plop down beside him, resting my back against the base of the couch and leaning over to pet him.

"And your human half wonders why I prefer you over him," I murmur. After a moment of the gigantic wolf—that really looks more like a grizzly bear from size alone—enjoying a belly scratch while panting happily, he flips over and scoots closer to me, resting his massive head on my leg. When I don't immediately return to petting him, he whines and nestles closer to me.

"So, you might wait to initiate contact, but once you get an inch you take a mile, hmm?" I coo, scratching behind his ears. Seeing the dualism of the shifter soul up close really is intriguing.

The wolf lets out a soft bark of agreement, draping one of his paws over my leg. We sit in comfortable silence for ten or fifteen minutes, the wolf progressively cuddling closer as I pet him and murmur to him, until he's draped halfway across my lap, making a noise that's suspiciously close to a purr for a canine.

A flurry of soft knocks at the door announces a new arrival; from the speed and strength of the sounds, I already know it's Leisel knocking. Greta probably took her up here since we haven't left for the library yet. The wolf's head lifts from my lap as he looks in the direction of the door, inhales deeply through his nostrils—probably scenting for danger—and then scoots off me with a chuff of irritation.

The wolf picks up Camden's clothes with his sharp teeth and trots out of the room, through the doorway leading deeper into his chambers. Apparently, the wolf even has a deeper sense of modesty than the man. When the knocks come once again, I stand and walk over to the door, not keen on keeping my sister waiting.

It wasn't uncommon for Leisel and me to spend part of our days separate, especially when it was harvest time—I worked eighteen-hour days in the fields while she remained inside with her studies. Still, being separated from her all day in a foreign place isn't easy.

When I swing open the door, it reveals Leisel wearing an adorable pink dress, and Greta standing behind her, watching Leisel fondly. My sister leaps into my arms, knocking the wind out of me, and immediately starts to chatter away in my ear about everything and nothing.

I set her on her feet but keep a hold of her hand as she tells me about her day, learning how royal dinners work from Greta, and anything else that springs to her mind. Seeing my sister's habit of talking endlessly return is a consolation because thus far, she's been quiet and withdrawn—especially with what just recently happened with Kyron. I know it rattled her more than appearances show, but seeing my sister's resilience serves as a small reminder that at least I've done *one* thing in this life right: raising her.

When Camden emerges from his personal chambers, in human form and dressed, I ask my sister, "Ready to go see the biggest library in existence?"

Her eyes widen with joy as she bounces on her toes, vibrating with excitement. "Let's go!"

Chapter Twenty-Nine

I 've never actually been in a library before; the closest we had to such a thing in my village was a very old bookstore that sold ancient copies of classic texts, and whatever else it could manage to get its hands on; mostly biographies of one form or another. The shop was small but it was my haven in the village. It had less than a hundred books, mostly one copy of each, and functioned more as a library than a store; villagers would pay the shopkeeper to borrow books for a certain amount of time or pay triple the amount to purchase. Everything I've read that wasn't passed down from my parents, I got in that tiny shop—four dusty walls with rows upon rows of books.

The library in the castle is not merely four walls with a scant collection of books. The entrance is grand arched double doors, which I pass through hand-in-hand with Leisel, leading into an absolute paradise for any book lover.

The first room is gigantic, with a high vaulted ceiling, chandeliers holding orbs of light on spindles, and torches hung on stone walls that give the space a feeling that it's halfway between a fairytale and a gothic nightmare. The room has a circular structure, and the walls are made up entirely of bookshelves that span from the floor to the domed ceiling. In addition to the walls, there are bookshelves *everywhere,* with swirly wooden carvings adorning them. The initial space after the entrance offers a view of row after row of bookshelves—dozens upon dozens of them—a maze that any bookworm would gladly get lost in.

In the center of the entrance area is a spiral staircase that leads to the second floor, which is a landing that wraps around the room in a porch-like fashion, visible from the ground floor. To the left of the entrance is what looks like a reading area, set up with sofas, chaise lounges, and stuffed chairs all arranged in front of a magnificent stone fireplace. I'm drawn to the fireplace like a moth to flame by the otherworldly carvings adorning the mantle and exterior. Upon closer look, I realize it's depicting a portion of Greek mythology; the myth of Prometheus stealing fire and giving it to mortals. Though, at this point, there's little point in thinking of it as mythology, as the arrival of mythics proved that many *myths* were anything but, and the Greek pantheon is the real pantheon.

"Woah," Leisel says beside me in a wondrous whisper, snapping me out of my amazement-induced stupor and drawing my focus back to her.

I look down at her with a fond smile. She's still glued to my side and holding my hand tightly, but her attention is entirely consumed with our surroundings. Her golden eyes are wide as she looks from the fireplace to the couches to the bookshelves to the chandeliers and back around again, as if she can't figure out where to focus her attention first.

I give her hand a little squeeze and offer her a smile when she looks up at me, still wide-eyed and stunned with amazement. She whispers to me, "Am I dreaming?"

I can't help the chuckle that escapes me as I bend down and press a kiss to her cheek, stroking my hand through her long strawberry locks. "No, sweet girl. It's real. Where do you want to explore first?"

Greta and Camden are still lingering at the entrance of the room, apparently having decided to give Leisel and me a moment to take in the astounding luxury and sheer wealth of knowledge surrounding us by ourselves. I appreciate it; the royal library is overwhelming to say the least. Like Leisel, I don't know where to look first or start first.

"I was thinking the fairytale section would be a good starting point," Wyatt calls from the doorway.

I glance over my shoulder, seeing that he's arrived and is giving Camden a slap on the back in greeting. I watch as the two brothers exchange a look that appears to be filled with hidden meaning. I wonder what information they're transmitting without needing to use words. They both look serious, so I assume it's important, and since they aren't using words, it's also safe to assume whatever matter they're silently discussing is private.

I know firsthand how powerful the bond between siblings can be, although I'm also aware that Leisel and I are a particularly special case. She might be my sister by blood, but I raised her as if she were my daughter, and I know that's left us freakishly close—we can have entire conversations with nothing more than an exchange of eye contact, but I usually don't communicate with her silently unless I feel like I'm in hostile territory that I don't trust.

Seeing Camden and Wyatt's exchange momentarily makes me wonder if they don't still view Leisel and me as potentially hostile or untrustworthy. Are we still on opposite sides of the proverbial battle-field? Do I still need to keep them as the enemy in my consideration?

I haven't exactly moved them from enemies all the way to friends in my mind, but I'm making a point to try to view them in a more neutral light. If anything, I'd say earlier tonight I developed what could be the start of a connection that might grow into friendship with Wyatt—I certainly have a newfound respect for his world opinions and intellect—*and* I managed not to harm, threaten, or even insult Camden during dinner. That makes tonight a reliable success in my book.

Does Camden not feel the same way? Do I still need to watch my back around him as much as I needed to from day one?

That bit of doubt surprises me because it's accompanied by a pang of pain, as if some part of me can't stand the thought of Camden thinking less of me. I frown and absently rub a hand over my chest at the almost obscene realization that the thought of Camden having any negative sentiments or mistrust towards me is enough to create a physical reaction. The pain is barely noticeable—more so a suggestion of pain than the real thing—but it's there, and I don't like the fact that seeing him exchange a look with his brother caused uncertainty that translated into negative physical sensation strong enough to border on pain. That means our bond has progressed even more than I realized.

What's even more worrying is the sudden urge I have to seek comfort and reassurance from Camden, as if the bond is pushing me to seek solace with him rather than accept the uncertainty that a simple look exchanged between him and his brother can now spark. As if Camden knows, he turns away from Wyatt, and his burning gaze finds mine. He offers me a small smile and the incline of his head, and at that easy gesture, the doubt inside me instantly settles.

Indignant to my newfound reactions towards the most menial things, I turn my full attention back to my sister. I can unpack the rest of the bullshit later.

"You want to go to the fairytale section?" I ask, already suspecting her answer.

As expected, she firmly shakes her head. I blink as Chip suddenly emerges from one of the folds in her dress—he was probably sleeping in a hidden pocket—climbs his way up the silk pink material covering my sister, and settles himself on her shoulder, rubbing his cheek against her neck in greeting.

Leisel giggles and picks him up in her free hand, asking her chipmunk, "When did we outgrow fairytales?"

Chip makes a chattering noise, and my sister nods along in agreement. "See? We were over them *years* ago."

Wyatt closes the distance between us with a few smooth strides, and I watch my sister's reaction carefully. I'm not as adamantly opposed to Wyatt's presence in her life as I would've been even this morning—my conversation with him earlier calmed me because it demonstrated he has a brain as well as a royal title. From what I managed to read of him, I also believe he's someone who values integrity and decency; both things I can respect even if I don't innately love his presence in Leisel's life.

Leisel looks to me as Wyatt approaches, and the understanding dawns on me that she'll continue taking her cues from me for as long as I continue to guide her. I can sense that her approval of Wyatt hinges on mine—which makes perfect sense considering I've been her sole protector and role model in life, but this also makes me feel guilty. While I believe I did an excellent job modeling the importance of ambition and work ethic, I also fear how much my jadedness has begun to rub off on little Leisel.

Her golden eyes flick between me and Wyatt as he stops in front of us, waiting for my direction before she reacts. From what little I glimpse each time she glances at him out of the corner of her eye, Leisel is innately curious about Wyatt—probably in the same way I'm innately curious about Camden's wolf. Camden, the man, made a shitty enough first impression that I was able to forgo any natural curiosity about him, but his wolf has done nothing to earn my dislike or distrust, and earlier tonight proved beyond a shadow of a doubt that not only am I inherently interested in Camden's wolf, I'm also drawn to it. It strikes me that Leisel might be drawn to Wyatt in the same way and has just been holding her curiosity back because she didn't want to feel like she was going against me.

My heart aches as I give her hand a squeeze and offer her an encouraging smile. Whatever she chooses to do, it's my duty as her guardian and sister to support her. If she's interested in spending time with Wyatt, I wouldn't dare risk harming her by separating them, but the mama bear instinct in me also pushes me to keep them as far apart as possible because I know eventually, Wyatt will try to take Leisel from me.

Wyatt grins at Leisel as she faces him full on. "How about Grimm's Fairytales? Have you gotten over those already?"

My sister's nose wrinkles with confusion as she tilts her head to the side. "Grimm's Fairytales? Are the heroes boring?"

I can practically see Wyatt's excitement at my sister directly addressing him, and for once, I'm not tempted by the immediate urge to shut down any interaction between them and get Leisel away from him. Instead, I'm content to let them be and simply see how things go. Whatever can be said about Wyatt, I see the regard he holds for my sister through the way he watches her. His gaze holds endless affection, a deep curiosity, and I can feel the protectiveness radiating off him. I think he just might make a handy ally in the palace.

"Nope, the heroes are more often anti-heroes, and the villains are the truly interesting ones. Want to check out some of the books?"

Once again, Leisel looks at me before answering, and once again, my heart clenches as I feel like I've failed in some way by holding her back or making her unsure of herself. I give her another smile and nod, even gently pushing her in Wyatt's direction, letting her know I won't protest.

She pulls me down to give me a kiss on the cheek before closing the distance to Wyatt and giving him a very astute up and down. She glances at Chip, who's returned to his comfortable perch on her shoulder. Chip stares at Wyatt for a long moment before letting out a series of noises that sound faintly approving.

Leisel nods, then says to Wyatt, "Okay, show me the Grimm."

When Wyatt offers her his hand, she only stares at it for a beat before taking it and letting him lead her into the maze of bookshelves. Going against every parental instinct I have, I force myself to stay in place as they round a corner and disappear into the shelves. If something goes wrong I'll be by Leisel's side in an instant, and since we're technically still in the same room, I feel it's fair to let her and Wyatt explore for a bit.

Camden murmurs something to Greta, and she bows before turning and disappearing out of the library, apparently intending to leave the royals alone with their fated ones for the evening. I watch as Camden makes his way over to where I still stand in front of the fireplace.

Feeling more than slightly awkward, I say, "Aren't Grimm's Fairytales the original Germanic version of fairytales that the western world later made kid-friendly?"

Camden barks out a laugh. "That's an excellent way of putting it, and yes, that's exactly what Grimm's Fairytales are; the root of most fairytales." With a nod, he goes on, "We have similar issues in my native realm, from what I hear. The old version of literature meant for children is judged as increasingly barbaric and unfit over the years, so we edit old stories to make them more appropriate. As your sister so eloquently put it, that usually means boring heroes."

He gestures between the sofas we're standing in front of and the bookshelves that start up deeper into the room. "Do you want me to show you around the stacks, or would you like a night cap in front of the fireplace?"

I feel a reluctant smile pull on my lips. "If I ever choose to sit in front of a fireplace before exploring a room filled with books, there's probably something medically wrong with me."

Eyes dancing with humor, Camden nods. "Noted, I'll keep that in mind. Let me get you acquainted with the basic layout of the space, then you can choose what to read and where."

I ask curiously, "What will you be doing?"

"My favorite thing," Camden responds without delay. "Watching you."

Chapter Thirty

Camden spends an hour or so leading me through the different sections of the library, watching my wide-eyed wonder with a fond glimmer in his eyes and contently trailing after me as I switch aisles sporadically. Once I've gathered no less than six books—Camden had to remind me that the library is available at any time to prevent me from taking more—we settle on the couch in front of the fireplace.

There, he starts to tell me about the history of the castle. It was commissioned shortly after mythics invaded, upon the shifters establishing themselves as the most dominant group of beings on the entire globe. Camden's grandfather wanted the entire structure to be a tribute to their culture and beliefs, instructing architects to follow suit.

There are nine individual spires; eight are meant to represent the phases of the lunar cycle, and the ninth and tallest central spire is a tribute to the moon goddess Selene. All of the material used for the castle's foundation was imported from their home realm, as was most of the stone used for the rest of the structures because apparently the stone forged in their realm is far sturdier and longer lasting than the materials humans used in their buildings. Of all the natural resources on Earth that drew mythics here, evidently shifters still had to bring some things over from their old homelands.

The longer we talk, the more engaged I feel as I listen and learn. Camden's speaking style is calm, steady, and even a little humorous, throwing jokes in here and there as he explains things to me. After the castle and Kinrith, we get into larger-scale geography, which also starts to tread into infrastructure, economy, and even politics.

He tells me shifters make up the majority of the population of this world and therefore have the largest and most established nations across almost every continent. Shifter culture isn't just comprised of wolf-shifters; there are also packs of feline and even dragon shifters scattered across the globe, though the wolves have command over the entire shifter hierarchy, which Claude hinted at earlier. I also recall seeing some feline shifters on my ride through Kinrith's citadel, evident by their slitted eyes.

"If dragon shifters weren't so antisocial and therefore content to let me take the lead, they'd easily be able to overthrow the rest of the shifter population," Camden tells me with a sardonic smile curling his lips.

"What do dragons look like in their dragon form?" I ask with wonder.

Camden's smile turns indulgent. "They're magnificent. A full-grown dragon can be the size of a small mountain. Their scales serve as the most impenetrable armor. Having them on your side of a battle all but guarantees victory." A frown starts to morph his facial expression. "Unless, of course, you're dealing with magical opponents like witches or faye. Nothing is impervious to powerful magic—not even a dragon's scales."

"Are the witches or faye a potential threat to your kingdom?" I ask.

Camden shakes his head. "Not most of them, no. Witches are very insular, as are sirens and the faye. The only faction that could present a problem is the dark faye—I wouldn't put it past them to ally themselves with the vampires if they're in the mood for battle. Not because their ideologies align but because dark faye are dangerous creatures who feed on chaos."

"What do you mean when you say faction?" I question.

"Breeds within species," Camden responds, "Felines, dragons, and wolves are all factions of shifters. Dark faye, light faye, and noble faye are all factions within the faye species—so on and so forth."

I nod, chewing on my bottom lip while digesting the information he's just bestowed upon me. The world I live in has a wondrous mix of rich cultures all rooted in the gods that served as creators of each species, and before now, I've been too angry at the principle of how this world was built to even admire it. Now, however, I'm finding more and more interest when it comes to widespread interspecies matters. Part of me can't help but feel guilty that, despite my upbringing to rightfully loathe every being that isn't human, here I am actually enjoying spending time with the King of shifters. What does that say about me? That I'm a traitor to my own kind, surely.

Leisel emerges from the stacks of books with Wyatt, who's holding at least ten books in his arms and looking a little befuddled as he follows after my energetic sister. She only has one novel in her arms, which she proudly presents to me with a wide smile. The cover of the tome reads *A Collection of Grimm's Fairytales.*

"I've only read the Hansel and Gretel one so far, and I really like it," Leisel says excitedly, flipping open the book and pointing to a drawing that depicts an old witch boiling a young boy in a pot. I have to stifle a smile that my sister—who comes across as a literal ball of sunshine ninety-nine percent of the time—seems to enjoy the darker nature of fairytales; including one where a boy gets cannibalized by a demented wicked witch.

I reach forward to run my fingers through her hair, before deciding it's been too long since I've cuddled her and pull her onto my lap. Leisel relaxes against me, opening her book over her skirt, and starts on the next chapter, which looks like the original version of Cinderella. It's difficult for me not to be attached to Leisel at just about all times, and I'm starting to get the sense I'll need to enjoy my moments with her when they come the longer I spend in the castle because I'll likely get busier and busier.

I glance at Wyatt, who has deposited his stack of books on the floor and settled into one of the armchairs in front of the fireplace. He meets my eyes with wide ones and says, "Where does she get the energy from?"

I laugh. "No idea, but when she wakes me up at five in the morning, I wish I could borrow some of it."

Camden stands from the sofa and makes his way to the bar set up in the far corner of the room. He pours himself and Wyatt a few fingers of scotch in a beautiful crystal tumbler, and then calls out to me, "Wine?"

"White if you have it," I respond.

I don't know much about wines, but I do like the taste, and I absolutely love the rich history behind wine. It's one of humanity's oldest inventions, passed down from era to era through various regions and trade routes.

Camden returns with a glass of wine for me, hands Wyatt his tumbler, and then settles beside me again, with a single cushion separating us. Leisel spares him a brief glance before returning her attention to the book, gently flipping it to the next page.

Wyatt, staring at her with total fascination, whispers, "Can she even hear us?"

I stifle a laugh. "Not when she's reading. The rest of the world sort of falls away, and she gets into a zone of total focus. Honestly, I think that's something she accidentally picked up from me."

As if to punctuate my point, Leisel flips yet another page, totally oblivious to the conversation going on around her. I hold her a little closer, feeling my heart practically burst with love for this tiny witch that I've been responsible for since I learned the true meaning of responsibility. Leisel is my world—there's no other way to characterize or explain my connection with her.

If I truly start angling to do work that would change the world as mythics know it, it would be with her in mind, *for* her. In fact, that's the only way I could see myself getting over the barrier of being immersed in a world I was raised to hate; I'm only doing it so I can change it for the better for the sake of Leisel. For the sake of all children, really, including Mythic children, who should not live in such a poignantly segregated society.

For half an hour, we talk about light topics related to literature—mostly philosophy—while Leisel quietly reads away on my lap. Eventually, she starts to grow tired, slumping against me and yawning. As if summoned by Leisel's fatigue, Greta enters the library and makes her way over to us.

"Apologies for the interruption, Your Majesty, but it's the Princess's bedtime."

I gently push Leisel off my lap, stand, and take her hand, ready to take her upstairs and put her to bed.

Greta looks horrified by this development, as if a royal putting a child to bed is abominable. "Please, ma'am, I can take her. Enjoy your nightcap."

Hesitant to let someone else put Leisel to bed, but also understanding that she *is* at an age where me tucking her in every night is no longer a necessity, I look at my sister. She smiles and lets go of my hand, walking over to Greta.

"Can you read me a story so I fall asleep?" Leisel asks her, as adorable as ever with her wide glimmering eyes.

Greta visibly softens. "Of course. Come along, now, Leisel."

I watch for any hints of discomfort as they walk out, only relaxing a fraction when I see how easygoing Leisel's demeanor is with Greta. I know I'm as attached to Leisel as she is to me—probably more since she was literally my lifeline at times—but it also might not be a terrible idea to test run how it goes with Greta because from what Camden told me about the rigorous duties that accompany the title of Queen, I'll be swept up in quite a few tasks shortly.

A few days ago, I might've laughed at the idea of integrating into shifter culture; now, I'm truly starting to glimpse the power I could wield. Some of the most powerful figures across human history were women; Jeanne d'Arc, Katherine the Great, Cleopatra, Queen Victoria—all of them were warriors in their own way, and all brought about revolutionary change in their wakes. It means immense hard work and more hours than the day offers, both of which I'm willing to put in if it'll build a better world.

Shifters seem to have a primitive view of diplomacy and foreign relations, probably rooted in the insular nature of packs. They conduct trade with other species on other continents, but they don't actually intermingle very much, which is problem number one. I can testify that the insular nature of my village and life led me to make shifters out to be far more monstrous than they are; fundamentally, they aren't very different from humans as people, which means monstrosity is a decision, not a nature. Camden's wolf certainly looks like a monster, and he spent twenty minutes whining for attention and wagging his tail earlier.

Wyatt stands, stretching his arms above his head. "Well, I'm gonna drop these books off in your wing and head to bed. It's been a long day."

I give him a nod, and Camden murmurs a quiet goodnight.

Once Wyatt's has left, it's just Camden and me in a vast beautiful space empty of other living beings. The environment itself—surrounded by a treasure trove of knowledge and stories—is an aphrodisiac, and with Camden's good behavior tonight, I start to feel myself grow warm in his presence. The sort of warmth that isn't kind or cuddly, but sharp and lustful and *very* difficult to ignore.

"Do you have any idea how much I want to kiss you right now?" Camden asks, his voice so low it's practically a growl.

On cue, the warmth starts to travel to my nether regions, and I practically salivate at the idea of his lips on mine—which is *not* a reaction I would've foreseen. Sure, Camden is an attractive specimen that speaks to just how perfect the male form can be, but I don't have the best record of liking his personality, with tonight being the first exception.

I open my mouth, intending to tell him what a bad idea that is. Instead, what comes out is, "So, why don't you?"

Chapter Thirty-One

I don't mean to lead Camden on. I truly don't. The words I in-tended to fall from my lips were that kissing wouldn't be a good idea, so it's disconcerting that what actually came out was a gods-damned *invitation*. It feels like I have no control over my body or even my *words*, as if the bond between Camden and me is taking the wheel and leaving my free will in the backseat.

I mean, technically, my body *is* interested in Camden. Who am I kidding? It's fucking primed for him as if waiting for him to invade, but my brain is a lot more sensible, and would not give him the go-ahead to touch me unless it served *my* purposes. Regardless of how hot I think Camden is, or how a couple of times tonight I might've even remembered what having his mouth between my legs felt like last night, I *know* engaging sexually with him right now isn't the way to go. If I have a shot of surviving here, let alone making a change, I need to focus on solidifying my position in the palace; not on getting down and dirty with Camden.

"Camden," I start slowly, eyeing him warily, shifting back as he starts leaning towards me with brightening eyes.

He plants a hand on the couch cushion between us and I start to think about how I can knock him off course without creating any blowback. From last night, I remember that Camden very much has an animal's instincts when it comes to something as primal as sex. If I run, it ignites the chase instinct. If I fight, it ignites the subduing and dominating instinct. The only thing I can do here without setting him off is talk. That's proving difficult, though, as his presence is turning so blatantly sexual it's becoming difficult to share a room with him.

"Camden," I repeat when he drags himself closer to me.

"Cam," he says.

I blink. "What?"

"Only my father and other distant family members call me Camden. To those who know me, it's Cam. I want to hear you say it."

Really? That's what he's choosing to focus on? "Okay, *Cam*—"

Before I can continue, one of his hands clutches the back of my neck, and he pulls my mouth right against his, fitting us together. I can't help it; my body melts as soon as his lips touch mine, which is *exactly* what I was afraid of. When it comes to anything sexual with Camden, it feels pointedly like I'm not in control of my body—like the bond between us is driving the show. The worst part is how *good* it feels to not be in control.

Cam's lips are silky soft and deliciously full, moving over mine with a firmness and skill that tells me he knows what he's doing and he's in charge. I have to admit, it feels *damn* good to let him have the control. He bands an arm around my waist and uses it to haul me onto his lap, leaving my legs straddling either side of his on the soft cushion and my arms draped around his shoulders. My entire body feels limp, moldable, and pliable—like it's melted into a puddle of goop Camden can shape however he wants.

Technically, he stuck to his part of the agreement; he didn't touch me like this until I... well, not *asked* him, but more like *taunted* him. So, the person in the wrong here isn't him. I also don't feel like it's me, since I didn't *mean* to say what I did—the bond took control and pushed me.

Now that I'm here, though, with his lips devouring mine and his hands roving over my body with reverence, I can't say I hate it. I can't even say I entirely don't want it; it feels really *really* good. Every time Cam's tongue strokes over mine my toes curl. His greedy and insanely hot hands take handfuls of flesh wherever they can—my breasts, my hips, my ass. I can feel his desperation for me, which makes me feel so powerful and sexy and *desired* that not all of me wants it to stop.

In fact, most of me doesn't. In a warped and twisted way, this is a form of validation for me. I haven't had anyone, other than Leisel, *want* or *need* me—ever. The male beneath me, kissing the breath from my lungs and pawing at me like he can't get enough obviously is *desperate* for me, and while I shouldn't like that, I do. I like being desired on a level so intense it's almost terrifying. That way, there's no doubt the desire is real.

For a moment, I contemplate pushing him away and telling him to stop. Talking him out of it, making it clear that whatever's happening here isn't a good decision. I think if I made a convincing case, it would avoid triggering his hunt-and-subdue instincts, which means I could escape unscathed. But then again...this feels *so good*. His lips on mine and his hands on my body cause a sense of exhilaration and excitement so deep-seated it feels like it takes root in my very soul. Warmth is already pooling in my core, and my body is priming itself for Cam. Pleasure sparks along all of my nerve endings, sending a delicious shiver up my spine.

What's happening now will eventually happen, sooner or later; the only thing I have the power to do is delay the inevitable. At this point, I can see that that won't get me very far. The only real issue I have with what's happening here is the potential aftermath—our bond growing even stronger than it already is. I don't want to give Camden the impression that I'm totally accepting and open for business because I'm *not*. But maybe I could make him agree that this interlude here is just primal fun, blowing off steam, and nothing more.

I manage to tear my mouth away from his to breathe. "Cam, wait."

He doesn't. He kisses a trail across my jaw and down my neck, pausing to suck at my pulse point until I squirm, digging my nails into his shoulders.

He mutters against my flesh, "We had a deal, remember? I didn't touch you until you asked me to. You invited me to. Don't ask me to stop now—I don't know if I can."

Hearing the sincerity in his words makes me consider another aspect I often choose not to; the fact that Cam is, first and foremost, a wolf. Wolves have instincts, and I bet those instincts are seriously amplified when it comes to something as important in their culture as mates. By asking him not to touch me, I'm asking him to forgo basic instinct. He's explained this to me, but I haven't *really* listened.

Previously, I've been stuck in the mindset of me versus him; while I can't say I'm totally out of that mindset, I can see how hindering it is now. Fighting against him is counterproductive; reasoning with him and finding a way where we both win would probably be my best bet here. If his instincts when I run or fight are to hunt and subdue, that means I need to change my approach to get anywhere.

I thread my fingers through his dark, silky hair, using my grip to pull his face up and initiate a kiss. Camden's so shocked he doesn't move, simply going still beneath me with his hands clutching my waist. I've never instigated anything other than conflict between us, so this change of pace is enough to temporarily startle him into stillness. *I can work with that.* As long as the scenario is one where I have at least a *little* control, I can cope with it and work through it.

"Just slow down," I murmur against his lips. Maybe the best approach here is the most obvious one, explaining myself. "When you go too fast, I get scared, and then I fight, and then you overpower—that doesn't do anything for our relationship."

Camden's silent for so long after I speak, I get nervous and start shifting my weight slightly from knee to knee. That has the unintended effect of rubbing the apex of my thighs right against Camden's erection, creating friction that causes a low pulse to start up between my legs and draws a low growl from him.

"If you keep doing that, I'm not going to be able to keep a leash on myself and honor your request," he rumbles.

I go still. His words mean that, at least, he's listening to me. Hopefully, he's leaning towards leashing himself and keeping a lid on his hunger so this doesn't devolve into unhelpful territory. If there's a repeat of what happened last night, I know I'll enjoy it in the moment, but I'll hate both of us afterward. Maybe there's a way out of this that doesn't undo our progress from tonight.

Cam abruptly lets go of my waist, pulls his shirt over his head, and places my palms flat on his hard, muscled, heaving chest. "Touch me."

Okay, then. If what he needs to keep himself in check is some skin-to-skin contact that *doesn't* involve going too far too fast, I can handle that. I spread my fingers on his chest, running my palms over his smooth, hard pecs. If nothing else, his body would make an exquisite subject for painting—he has the most proportional form I've ever seen, with the muscles so well defined it's like he's a study in anatomy. I run my hands up, over his shoulders, sweeping my thumbs over his biceps and triceps before going back to his chest, and down to his abs. *His six-pack is something I could probably do laundry on.*

The longer I touch him, the more Cam relaxes beneath me until his hold on me is loose and his eyelids are starting to droop. I realize with no small sense of wonder the *power* that something as simple as physical touch has over him. This whole time, I've been focused on the perils of contact for *me*, but now I'm realizing an element I hadn't before; shifters are tactile creatures by nature. Physical contact could almost be classed as a basic need for them. A few brushes of my hands along Camden's skin can literally melt him beneath me, switching from hunt mode to laze mode.

I don't think Cam will be able to keep a leash on his sex drive forever—probably not even for much longer—but this might just be a way to buy myself a *little* more time, which is the best thing I can hope for.

Abruptly, he pulls me back into him, crushing my mouth back to his and boldly sinking his tongue inside. When he pulls back, it's to growl in my ear, "Go to bed before I lose control of myself and do something you'll regret in the morning."

Chapter Thirty-Two

Camden

The morning after my trip to the library with Sierra, I awaken in a much brighter mood than I have in...well, ever. Not just because I got to spend several hours with my mate, but because for once, it feels like there was actual progress made between us. Instead of fighting me off and shutting me down at every turn, Sierra seemed far more open to me. I knew that constructing a painting studio for her would intrigue her, but I didn't expect her to be so touched by the gesture.

I also know that I can't take all the credit for her starting to soften, even though she's still mostly closed off—whatever Claude said to her when they warded the castle yesterday seemed to alter her perspective as well. Wyatt mentioned last night that Claude and Sierra spoke at great length during their time together, I intend to seek Claude out so he will tell me exactly what they discussed. If he has an in with her—which would make sense, considering they're both creatures of magic—I will convince him to use that leverage to direct her closer to me.

Everything about Sierra is calming, steadying, and beyond pleasing to me; if I could manage it, I'd have her glued to my side at all hours of the day and night. Last night, when she touched me of her own volition for the first time, it felt like nothing short of a religious epiphany. Her softness pressed against my hardness, her delicate hands roaming my muscles, the steadily deepening interest in her eyes, it was a potent aphrodisiac. When she leaned down to kiss me without having to be coerced...that's probably as close to a divine experience as I'll ever get.

Before getting down to official pack and royal business, I plan to find Claude and interrogate him about Sierra. I open the entrance to my chambers, only to find a startled Sierra standing in the doorway, her hand poised to knock. It looks like she's almost as surprised at her presence here as I am by it—I didn't expect her to seek me out so soon despite the genuine connection I suspect—*hope*—we started building last night.

I can't keep the surprise out of my voice. "What are you doing here?"

She darts a glance around, with an expression of guilt as though she feels she's doing something wrong. Considering her upbringing to hate shifters, she very well might feel she is.

She holds up the key I gave her last night, the one to her painting studio, and says, "I wanted to paint for a few hours while Leisel's doing her morning lessons with her new tutor." A frown furrows her brows, and even *that's* beautiful. "Thank you for getting her the tutor by the way. I also wanted to ask..."

She trails off, shifting uncomfortably foot to foot, cheeks reddening with embarrassment. Has she not caught on yet that she could ask me for just about anything and I'd give it to her? *I suppose not.* Up until last night, our relationship was more combative than anything—I was too focused on doing damage control and preventing her from trying to leave to focus on the upsides of matehood—such as gift-giving. I know witches are particularly inquisitive and prone to shiny, pretty things, and I have every intention of spoiling Sierra, but up until now, I didn't have the opening to do so.

"Anything you want, ask. It's yours," I tell her plainly.

She nods slowly, then says in a rush, "I never got a formal education. I don't feel like I'm fit to lead without it. If you could set me up with a tutor or instructor to go over things I wasn't able to learn from my parents or teach myself with the help of textbooks, I'd appreciate it."

I recognize that her lack of education seems to embarrass her, and that sends my soothing instinct into overdrive. I don't want her to be embarrassed about *anything*. The fact that she—with extremely limited resources—managed to educate herself and her sister to the extent she has is beyond impressive and a testament to her strength of will and value for learning. I want to pull her into my arms, kiss her, and tell her I'd give her my heart on a silver platter if she asked for it.

Instead, I settle for saying, "Of course. I'll set it up. For now, go ahead and paint—tell me if the studio's missing anything and I'll have it brought in." I step aside, motioning for her to enter. "Have you eaten breakfast yet?"

On the same table where we had dinner last night is laid out a breakfast spread. I don't usually have time to eat breakfast, but it's set out for me every day. If I can convince Sierra to join me, though, I'll gladly partake. I don't think she understands what a pleasure it is to just have her in my personal space. My wolf starts pushing to the fore, also wanting to get time with her again. He's absolutely enamored with her after she spent time petting and cooing at him last night, and

I know from here on out he'll be much more persistent in pushing for time with her.

Sierra nods hesitantly. "I did..."

"But?" I offer.

She shifts from foot to foot awkwardly again. "But there wasn't any coffee available, and if I don't get my caffeine fix, I turn into a monster."

"Don't we all?" I say with a chuckle. "You know you could always ask the servants for something additional if everything isn't to your liking."

Sierra lifts one shoulder. "I've never had anyone serve me before, so I feel awkward asking for more. They already laid out such an elaborate spread, most of which will go to waste." She frowns at the latter sentence, obviously unhappy with the thought.

With her upbringing in such a rural, run-down village where the villagers only got to eat what they hunted and harvested each year, I imagine the concept of anything going to waste wouldn't sit well with her. Now that I think about it, I don't know what the servants do with the leftover food—things like that were beneath my notice before Sierra.

Having her around has offered me new perspective after new perspective, and I see more and more just why the gods paired us. We're opposites in many ways, but she sees the world through a different lens than I do, which is invaluable to someone in my position.

"I don't know what happens to the leftovers," I admit, deciding that honesty is best. "There are two orphanages in Kinrith, I'm sure they'd appreciate a food bonus."

Sierra's eyes brighten at that. "Yes, they would. In Aesara, we didn't have an orphanage—we couldn't afford one. Whenever a child was left orphaned, the villagers would meet in a council and decide which couple had the resources to take them in. Then, that couple would be sent leftover foods from markets and shops to help—it was a difficult system since we had little to spare but very effective. Leftovers should never be wasted, not when there are hungry mouths around the continent to feed."

I listen with great interest, as always enjoying the sound of her voice as she speaks and liking even more that she's offering up information without me having to pry it out of her. She looks a little startled at her own talkativeness but quickly recovers when I lead her over to the dining table and pour her a cup of coffee.

"Milk? Sugar? Honey?" I ask her.

"You don't have to serve me," she replies a bit awkwardly.

"No, but I want to," I tell her. "I like doing things for you. It satisfies both me and my wolf, who, by the way, is begging for more time with you."

At that, she smiles a little. "He looks like a grizzly bear but acts like a teddy bear," she says, almost fondly.

It sounds like she just might like him as much as he likes her. Well, not as much—that wouldn't be possible, but I'm confident that at the very least she's curious enough about him and comfortable enough around him to agree to spend more time with him.

"Only with you," I respond. "You should see him in battle, he's fucking vicious. With you, though, all he wants is to be close to you, just like me."

I can tell that my words make her uncomfortable and that I just might be pushing my luck at this point. I wouldn't say I'm on *bad* terms with Sierra after last night, not like I have been before, but I'm not exactly on steady footing with her either. I know I still need to tread carefully. If I let her see the truth of just how much I need her, it'd send her running, and I can't have that.

Sierra hesitates for a moment, then says, "Well, I'm not going to risk spilling coffee in the painting studio, so if he wants to join me for that, I won't oppose. He's kind of adorable."

At that, my wolf lets out a whine and pushes against my skin so hard I almost shift on the spot. That's a rather unusual occurrence; I'm very in tune with my wolf, more so than most shifters, so he usually doesn't surface unless we're both in accord. Around Sierra, though, it seems none of my usual rules apply.

In the end though, I don't care if I'm in wolf or human form—either way, physical contact with her feels spectacular. She's a lot more uncomfortable touching me than she is him, for all the obvious reasons—mainly, I can't seem to keep my desire leashed around her. I can't be touching her and *not* veer in an intimate direction; I want her too much.

Last night was at once bliss and absolute torture. Feeling her soft fingers exploring me, knowing that her interest in me *that* way was there but not being able to act on it...if she hadn't kissed me and then spent twenty minutes on my lap, her delicate hands running over my flesh, I don't think I would've been able to contain myself.

I don't like the lack of self-control I experience around her, but I also know that's exactly what happens with matehood. Instincts take over and wants and desires become insatiable untamed needs.

Before my wolf can force a shift, I retreat to my bedroom, strip down, and give the other half of me control. A flash of pain overcomes me as my vision blurs and dims. Reality fades away as darkness momentarily takes over. When it recedes, my wolf has taken the wheel.

He paws at the ground, stretching and shaking out his fur before trotting back through my chambers and into the main area, where Sierra's seated herself at a table with a mug of coffee. My wolf inhales deeply through his nostrils, picking through her various scents. She smells like a delicious mix of vanilla and jasmine. Beneath that, he senses that she added a splash of milk and two spoons of sugar to the coffee. He stores that information away, wanting to learn as much about her as possible.

She looks over to us upon our entrance, eyes softening visibly at the sight of us in wolf form. My wolf trots up to her and paws at her leg, silently requesting a similar arrangement to last night—where we're both on even ground so he can drape himself over her lap and get covered in her scent.

"Alright, alright," she says with a small laugh, picking up her mug and lowering herself to the ground with her back propped against her chair legs.

I don't love the thought of her sitting on the ground—it's beneath her—but my wolf loves the extra contact and closeness. Like he did last night, he drapes his head over her leg and waits, very impatiently, for her to start petting him.

She doesn't make him wait long, reaching over with her free hand and burying it in his fur, deliberately scratching behind his ear in a way that makes him pant happily. He sits with her, luxuriating in her scent and attention, until she drains the last of her coffee and gives him a small pat along his spine.

"Alright, wolf, it's time for me to go."

He lets out a rumble of irritation at that, not liking the thought of losing the closeness that he revels in. I nudge at him to relent and not push her too hard too fast, and he stands with a chuff, going back to my room, rather unhappily.

When I emerge again in human form, I see that Sierra's already in her painting studio, mixing pigments with a linseed oil base.

I don't think she notices me watching her from the doorway, but then she calls out, "Why are my paintings hanging on your walls?"

"Because they're incredible, and I like having them near me. They're a daily reminder of how talented my mate is," I respond.

Sierra hums but doesn't turn around to face me. I decide I've pushed her enough for today and tell her to stay as long as she likes before leaving my chambers and turning to what's now my second order of business; interrogating Claude.

Chapter Thirty-Three

Sierra

After painting in my brand-new studio for a little while, I decide to track Wyatt down. All morning, I've been thinking about our conversation yesterday, contemplating how we can turn our convictions—that segregation between species is dangerous and destructive—into constructive action.

Conversation is great, but it doesn't fuel change; only decisive moves in the right direction would. If I can work with Wyatt on some sort of foreign policy, that'd cement him as an ally in the palace, one I suspect could bring many benefits. It could also gain me recognition as someone who the shifter population can trust to lead them into the future, which could afford me the power I'd need to eventually shift my focus to humans and humanitarian aid.

I may not have *wanted* my position in the shifter hierarchy, but I have it, and to waste the power I could use to change the world for the better would be idiotic. I have many, *many* valid grievances about my life growing up; if I can do something to make sure no person is ever impoverished and left to fend for themselves like I was, I'd sleep much easier. As of right now, however, helping humans can't be my primary focus, not with war on the horizon. I need to look at the most pressing matters first.

A castle servant gives me directions to the war room, where I'm told Wyatt spends much of his time. The room itself is a marvel—constructed with dark bricks and accented with dark brown wooden tones. It's gigantic, with one huge table taking up the center space. Overhead hangs a brilliant chandelier, and the walls are decorated with art work depicting men and wolves in battle.

Wyatt stands beside the table, leaning over it, appearing deeply concentrated. A map of Earth's continents is painted onto the entire surface, so beautifully colored and intricately detailed I pause for a moment to study the artistry.

The only maps available in my village were old and worn down, most of them dating back to centuries ago when humans held dominance in this world. The map in front of me is so wildly different that I blink several times to take it in. The region that was once North America, Mexico, and the northeast half of Canada is now overtaken by wolf shifters, labeled as the Empire of Acuria. The northwest half of what was formerly Canada belongs to witches, now called Raith. *Fascinating.*

I find Aesara, which is a few hundred miles south of the capital, and my heart pangs at the thought of my home village. At the idea that, while I'm surrounded by wealth, beauty, and luxury, the people who I grew up with and helped me raise Leisel when times were hard are still struggling to put food on the table. I have to do what I can to help them.

Wyatt glances over at me. "Hey. I didn't expect to see you in here today."

I raise my eyebrows, peeling my eyes away from the beautiful map to look at him. "Why's that?"

Wyatt grins. "I thought Cam would keep you busy. Obviously, you managed to escape and then sought me out. Why don't you tell me the reason for that?"

"Foreign relations," I state. "Tell me about them. What are shifters' foreign relations with other species? Who are you on good terms with? Bad terms with? Neutral towards?"

Wyatt arches an eyebrow. "You're curious all of a sudden."

I shake my head. "It's not all of a sudden. Yesterday our discussion brought to light a problem that could seriously inhibit your kind: the lines that distinguish each species rarely being crossed. That will hurtle you into war after war if it continues. Camden is busy with matters pertaining to shifters; if you have time in your schedule, let's start working on foreign policy. Create a path to diplomacy, forge alliances, all of the things that will strengthen your empire even though wolves are too full of themselves to know they need it."

I wince after the last sentence because I didn't mean to be that harsh. I do believe that wolf shifters are particularly elitist, and that blindness will cause them trouble moving forward. If I'm making a home with them—whether by choice or fate—I don't want to be screwed over because of their bad instincts and snobbery. Besides, I'm an *earth witch* in the *shifter palace*. As far as I know, interspecies lines have never been crossed in such a fantastical way.

Wyatt tilts his head to the side, studying me. "What gives you the authority to push for this?"

Is he joking?

I say point-blank, "Being ripped away from my home, life, and village, only to be the first witch to have a position at the top of your hierarchy. And in my new position, seeing that you idiots have been stupid enough to isolate yourself from other mythic species—save for your fellow shifters. I've read about and studied a lot of war and politics that have occurred on this planet, and history tells us that isolation is the first steppingstone to defeat. That's what gives me the fucking authority, Wyatt."

Surprisingly, a grin breaks out on Wyatt's face, and he nods. "Good. That means you're finally ready to get to work. I was wondering how long it'd take before you came back to set up a game plan after our talk yesterday. Lucky for you, I like to be prepared."

He walks to the door of the room and goes into the hall. I watch him exchange a few words with a servant before he comes back in. Meanwhile, I remain standing in place, mildly shocked by Wyatt's ready acceptance to work with me—to the extent that it seems he's put some thought and planning into it.

Wyatt pops his head into the room and says, "I'm going to round up our legal texts pertaining to foreign relations, along with trade agreements and the few other things that bind shifters to others. I'll be back in fifteen; in the meantime, familiarize yourself with the map. Regional territorialism will definitely play into any work we do."

With that, he's gone. I follow his instructions in his absence, walking around the table, trying to memorize as much of the map as I can. On top of it there are also sporadically placed soldier figurines, which I assume connote a military buildup in the respective regions. It doesn't escape my notice that the few territories belonging to vampires—all on undesirable land—are overrun with soldier figurines. There is no doubt that they're preparing for a war.

I recall what Camden told me last night when we were talking in the library; there is a possibility the dark faye might ally themselves with the vampires. In addition to that, there clearly exist vampires with magical abilities—after all, Kyron teleported into the castle on his own—meaning shifters are already in need of magical aid. As far as I know, they have Claude in their magical arsenal who I imagine can't subdue an entire species.

Looking over the territories that the dark faye hold, I come to understand just what a threat that would be. The dark faye have approximately double the numbers of vampires, and the two put together—especially since faye are inherently creatures of magic—could potentially overthrow shifters. If the vampires have the potential for a magical alliance, shifters need to be cemented into one as a deterrent.

The obvious first step would be for shifters to reach out to witches. They share a continent with them, and they now have a direct tie to them through me and Leisel. Granted, earthly witches are different from mythic witches, but everything I've read about witches and heard from my mother before death indicates that they're extremely protective of their own.

When Wyatt comes back into the room, his arms are full of papers, and he's accompanied by two palace servants who are carrying scrolls, tomes, and ledgers. They place all of the items on the table before quietly retreating.

"This is everything shifters have in terms of foreign relations. Read up and then we can get started."

* * *

Six hours later...

"That is *not* how you structure foreign policies and diplomacy!" I snap at Wyatt. "Incentives are not the same things as threats. You don't want to blackmail someone into being your ally, you want them to *want* to be your ally!"

I've managed to go through all of the tenuous agreements shifters hold with other species and factions, and in the midst of trying to figure out steps in the right direction, Wyatt constantly leans towards threatening others into alliances. I understand that there's the shifter sense of dominance coming into play, but honestly, Wyatt should be smarter than to go with the *join us or else* slogan.

"Nobody *wants* to be allied with us!" Wyatt exclaims. "We invaded, took over, and spent the next decades basically ensuring that any other mythic settlers were below us in the power hierarchy. If we want anyone to even come to a negotiating table, it won't be through niceties."

I let out a growl. "Then focus on a common enemy! That's how some of the strongest alliance amongst humans were forged—nations that were in thousand-year wars came together *because they faced a bigger threat*. Besides, you already have something that will bring others to the table! You have a bargaining chip that *will* bring witches to negotiate, if for nothing else than curiosity and their commitment to protecting their own."

That gives Wyatt pause. He's been pushing for our first outreach to the noble faye, who have a chokehold on all of the faye factions. His reasoning is sound; if we get them on their side, it'll be difficult for vampires to get the dark faye on their side. From what I understand, dark faye might be psychotic, but few are stupid enough to go against the royals. While his logic of wanting to go to the faye is sound, it's too big of a step, too fast. Plus, they have nothing tying them to the faye outside of a few trade agreements for materialistic things created on their territories, while they live on the same continent as the witches of the Raith Empire.

"Are you insinuating you'd be willing to use yourself as an incentive to bring witches to the table?" Wyatt asks.

"Obviously," I say. "They're the most attainable potential alliance. Besides, why wouldn't I want to learn my craft from my own kind?"

I understood when I worked with Claude that he has some training in the magical arts, but his magical training primarily still pertains to shifters. Protecting shifters, healing shifters, and so on and so forth. There's only so much I could learn from him. If I want real knowledge of the highest arts, I need to look to the source.

Wyatt nods. "That could work. I'll get the ball rolling to have a liaison reach out and see if we can make the witches interested enough to agree to a meeting. For now, let's write up a proposal that makes it impossible for the witches to decline. Then the real work begins."

Chapter Thirty-Four

As I soon find out, working with Wyatt on foreign policy is the easy part. Camden is the real figure that needs to be convinced, something that Wyatt tells me only after we've drawn up a proposal that condenses our ideas and formulates a plan of action. Wyatt and I spend most of the day and half the evening together working on it, and he also educates me on the generalized structure of shifter politics.

While Camden is literally the top dog of the top dogs—something that I hadn't understood when I first declared duelum, counting on the idea that the shifter high court would protect my win and keep me away from the life I now lead—he also needs to work in tandem with the counselors on the high court.

The counselors who make up the body of the high court can't necessarily *negate* his rulings, but every counselor who has a seat at the high table holds serious power within the shifter packs across the globe, so it's in his interest to work alongside them. That being said, it's also in their interest to work alongside him and cater to him, because an angry Alpha King means a lot of deadly dissent could spark among shifters. At the end of the day, every pack of shifters in every corner of this world answers to and is therefore loyal to Camden.

Wyatt assures me that he can handle the counselors—fifteen in all, one to represent each major pack around the world. He's the in-between man who takes matters from the counselors on the high court to Camden and vice-versa, so he's on good working terms with all of them. While it's Wyatt's job to convince them that foreign policy and diplomacy are shifters' best shot at continued survival, it's *my* job to convince Camden. I have to say, that's not a conversation I'm looking forward to.

I know the proposal for outreach I put together with Wyatt is *damn* good, as I structured it after some of the most effective policies the U.S.A. ever created and enacted before its collapse following the mythic invasion. I also know that telling Camden he needs to play nice with the rest of the world, starting with the witches, is probably going to be a hard sell.

After a fourteen-hour workday that involved several disagreements—which culminated in shouting matches with Wyatt before we finally agreed on a single proposal he could take to the high court and I could take to Cam—I'm ready to tumble into bed and sleep for the next week.

I'm used to physical labor that exhausts my body, but labor of the mind is a different scenario. While I *like* to consider myself a fairly intelligent woman who, despite a lack of formal education, can hold her own, I never expected to be in a position to clock in fourteen hours of thinking, arguing, structuring, writing, and editing on top of editing, all for the sake of bettering shifter kind. The emotional turmoil that creates, on top of the mental exhaustion that comes from having my nose buried in documents for the entire day, makes me seek out my sister before anyone else.

As much as I'm Leisel's rock and her provider, she's also the most stabilizing and calming presence in my life. I enter our living chambers with a swath of papers making up my first ever foreign policy proposal in hand. I set down the leather binder containing the papers I've slaved over all day on the desk in my room before opening the adjoined doorway leading to Leisel's bedroom.

It looks like I came just in time; she's tucked into her bed, looking as adorable as ever surrounded by mountains of silk blankets and pillows. Greta sits on a chair beside her, reading to my sister from the book of Grimm's Fairytales, her nose wrinkled in disapproval.

When they hear me enter the room, Greta looks up from her book in surprise while Leisel sits up in bed, wide-eyed, before starting to excavate herself from the blankets—probably to run to me.

"You don't have to get up, sweet girl," I tell her, walking to her bed and taking a seat on the mattress beside her.

Since it's Leisel's bedtime, I usually wouldn't try to give her any stimulation that'd prevent her from falling asleep—such as seeing me after a day of separation—but, in this scenario, I think I need her presence more than she needs mine. I arrange myself on her bed so that my back's against the headboard and we're sharing the same pillow, cuddled up against each other. Leisel throws her arms around me and hugs me close, either sensing my need for comfort or having missed me because we haven't seen each other since breakfast.

"Is there something I can help you with, ma'am?" Greta asks.

I smile at her and shake my head. "No, but I'll read Leisel's bedtime story to her tonight." When Greta looks like she might argue, I say, "I need some time with my sister. I haven't seen her all day."

Leisel adds, "I want Sierra to read to me," giving Greta her best doe-eyed look that never fails to get her what she wants.

Chip unravels from where he's dozing on a smaller pillow on the other side of Leisel's head, climbs over my sister, and then perches himself on my shoulder, chattering away a greeting in my ear. Then he turns and makes a series of irritated-sounding noises at Greta too, apparently deciding to present a united front along with Leisel and me.

As further enticement to Greta, I say, "I'm sure Cara will be happy to see you a bit earlier tonight. Go home, Greta. We'll see you in the morning."

With a small chuckle, Greta stands and hands me the book of fairytales. "I'd like to see my mate as well. Don't be too long; it's already quite late," she tells me, planting a kiss on Leisel's head. She hesitates before asking me, "Are you aware of the darker stories the young Princess seems to enjoy most? It's concerning to see such a young and bright child gravitate towards the gory and dismal."

I let out a faint snort. "Wait until she asks you to reread the goriest, bloodiest, massacre-heavy parts of Shakespearean literature. Then we can talk concerns." Leisel giggles while Greta trails out of the room, a somewhat perplexed expression on her features, leaving me alone with my sister and her chipmunk.

I tap Leisel's nose. "Has Greta been giving you a hard time over your reading preferences?"

Leisel's nose wrinkles as she nods, snuggling closer to me and laying her head on my chest. "I don't think she likes that I find the normal stories boring. Who wants to read about Prince Charming when you can read about the wicked stepsisters cutting off their toes to fit their feet in a shoe?"

I laugh, flipping open the book to the flagged chapter. Before I start, though, I can't stop myself from asking my sister, "Is it hard for you on days like today? When we spend most of the day apart?"

Leisel contemplates my question for several moments before shaking her head, sending her hair flying across the pillows. "No. I know you're out making the world safer and better, so I don't mind." She gives me a sly smile before saying, "As long as we eat breakfast together or you read me a story before bed, it isn't hard."

I kiss her cheek, feeling my heart swell in my chest as I curve one arm around Leisel, holding her closer and using my free hand to position the book on my lap. "Good. Let's read about the *real* story of Rapunzel..."

Leisel falls asleep halfway through the chapter. I put Chip back on his pillow beside her before giving her one last kiss, flicking off the light, and heading back to my adjoined room where I close the door to hers behind me. There, I take a seat at my desk and open the leather folder containing my proposal, resolved to give it one last look to make sure it's in tip-top shape before presenting it to Camden.

The framework is solid; the proposal's built for an agenda to expand shifter foreign relations, creating a more cohesive international dialogue that just might save shifters when war with vampires finally reaches a boiling point, which I expect will be soon. It answers a pressing problem that not enough people have considered; what happens if the vampires team up with a species that can naturally use magic, such as the faction of dark faye? That'd leave shifters fighting tooth and claw against powers beyond their greatest comprehension.

The proposed solution is very simple: shifters create a magical alliance with witches, or at least attempt to, first. If it works, it'll serve as a deterrent to dark faye because, from what Wyatt tells me, even *they'd* think twice before making an enemy of witches. It would also open a door to much better foreign relations on a global scale. If such a historic interspecies connection and alliance is created, it'll make room for other connections and alliances that currently seem outlandish and impossible.

The implementation is a bit trickier; although the wording is careful, the proposal basically outlines using me—a particularly rare kind of witch, from what I'm told—to bring a species to the negotiating table. To dangle a queen in front of a species that is by no means friendly with shifters will be difficult to push through on all fronts. I trust Wyatt to take care of the high court, but selling this to Cam is an entirely different story.

Camden doesn't seem to have any great amount of logic or reason when it comes to me; he works primarily off of instinct, though I have seen him make a pointed effort in curbing that recently in favor of being level-headed. Hopefully, that'll work to my benefit tonight.

Deciding that it's best to get the difficult part out of the way now, I stand, close the file, and make my way through the maze of a castle I'm only just starting to familiarize myself with towards Camden's quarters. Once there, I only have to knock once before the door opens.

Like this morning, he looks surprised to see me, eyebrows rising as he gives me a long up and down look, taking in every nuance of my posture, clothing, and expression.

"I hear you and Wyatt have been plotting together all day," he says. "Something about foreign policy?"

I frown. "Where did you hear that from?"

Other than a few servants who came in and out to deliver food, books, and documents, we've been alone all day.

Camden smiles. "Very little goes on in this castle that I don't know about." His eyes drop to the leather binder I'm clutching. "I assume that's whatever you two came up with?"

I nod, holding the folder out to him. "If you want a chance against the vampires in the case that they make themselves some powerful allies, this is your only way."

Camden accepts the folder, before stepping aside. "Come on in. I'll pour you a glass of wine while I go over it."

I hesitate for a moment because being alone with Camden never goes the way I intend it to. Then, deciding it's best I'm here when he reads the contents of the folder so I can influence his decision, I nod and follow him inside.

Chapter Thirty-Five

As promised, Camden gets me a glass of white wine before seating himself beside me on the couch in front of the fireplace and flipping open the file. His eyes scan the pages quickly, and as he does so, I can feel his demeanor shift from interested to wary to closed-off entirely. His body language progressively stiffens, and his eyes shutter with distaste the further he reads.

Once he's done, Camden gives me a look that could have a lesser woman six feet under. "You want me to parlay with a coven of witches?" he asks, his tone biting. "Did my younger brother neglect to mention that they're fucking *insane*?"

I give him a censuring look. "Careful how you say that, Cam. You're talking to a witch."

"You don't count!" he growls.

Looks like we're skipping the pleasantries and getting straight to business.

I give a cold laugh, setting my glass on the table in front of us. "In what world? I'm a witch more than I'm anything else, including human and especially shifter. We already know that I share some of their qualities; I've had to ask the castle servants to cover up the gemstones on display so I don't get sidetracked when I walk by them. Other than some odd quirks, I don't think I'd call myself insane."

Camden holds the folder in front of my face and snaps, "This proposal shows you are! You intend to dangle yourself as bait to get them to negotiate? *Really,* Sierra? Do I need to point out the many times in human history where diplomacy went *disastrously* wrong?"

"Only if you want me to hit you with each time it went fantastically *right,* saving millions of lives in the process!" My volume continues to rise. "Your elitist closed-off mindset *will be the death of your kind.* A month ago, that wouldn't have bothered me—in fact, I'd have cheered the vampires and dark faye on. Thanks to *you,* my sister has already been put in the line of fire in the course of your conflicts, which means this is now my fucking problem! Since it's been made my problem, you cannot pretend to be surprised that I'm taking action, especially when nobody else seems to."

"I *am* taking action!" he explodes. "Our military has been training and preparing overtime! I've mobilized packs worldwide for when the time for battle comes! Do you know how difficult it is to keep dozens of *warrior* packs in line? Especially when I won't leave you to go speak with them in person? Coordinating our military, defensive and offensive options, takes up the vast majority of my time."

"Your military won't mean *shit* if there's magic on the other side!" I shout back.

Done with this argument and needing to show Camden the reality of the situation in terms that cannot be misunderstood, I push off the couch, walk over to the dining table, and call to my fire. My entire body warms for a moment before heat breaks out over my hand, bringing with it a black flame that bursts to life on my palm. I raise my flame covered hand in Camden's direction, assuring it has his attention before using my index finger to tap the wood of one of the dining chairs. My fire instantly transfers to it, eating through the wood at a blurring speed until the chair is entirely gone, leaving behind only the faintest dusting of black ash on the carpet.

Camden watches me do so with an expression that's half-wary, half-angry from our argument.

I enunciate every syllable as I say, "That is a fraction of magic, in the hands of a witch with no training. What do you think the entire faction of dark faye could do if they side with the vampires?" Before he can respond, I add, "Granted, I've been told black fire is an exceedingly rare power, but magic is magic, and I'm sure Claude can tell you shifters don't stand a fucking chance against it in war unless they also have magic on their side."

Camden inhales several deep breaths and then says through gritted teeth, "I see your point, but I do *not* like the idea of working with witches. They're only out for themselves."

"From everything I've read and heard, they are *extremely* protective of their own. I am one of their own, a witch living in a castle of shifters," I counter. "Don't you think that protectiveness would innately extend to me?"

Camden falls silent before standing to pace across the room. He appears to be in a battle with himself—the insular nature of shifters warring with the fact that he *must* know I'm right. We cannot win the war with vampires alone, and the war will brew over into battles any day now. I killed a member of their royal family, and I suspect the vampire royals had a hand in the death of Camden's mother. I imagine that's more than enough instigation for their conflicts to finally reach a fever pitch and turn into swift, decisive, and deadly action on both parts.

After a while of pacing a hole into the floor, Camden stops abruptly and turns to me, his eyes having taken on a strange gleam that makes me nervous. He gestures for me to sit on the couch before walking over and seating himself on it. I do so hesitantly, unsure of what his decision on the proposal will be but willing to fight for his agreement.

In a carefully measured voice, Camden tells me, "I will agree to your proposal, as long as you agree to my conditions."

Figures. I should know by now that nothing in this castle will come free; there's always a catch when working with wolves. They're cunning that way.

Camden reaches out to finger a piece of my hair, rubbing the long strands between his fingers with a contemplative expression. "Tomorrow night, you share my bed. If you agree, I'll send a liaison to reach out to the nearest coven with the proposal first thing in the morning."

"And if I don't?" I ask warily.

Camden gives me a wolfish smile, dropping my hair. "I take my chances with just my packs as defense and offense."

He's being ridiculous; at this point, especially after my demonstration, he must realize that I'm working in his and his kingdom's best interests, but being a crafty wolf he won't give any concession without also receiving concessions. I don't love the idea of sleeping in the same bed as him, but I have to admit...our most recent interactions haven't been disastrous. He's hot-headed, sure, but I'm learning how to navigate his moods.

If sharing his bed for a night is all I need to do to ensure training and protection for my sister and me, as well as a better likelihood of victory for shifter kind in the upcoming war, then that is what I'll do.

Still, I ask, "Exactly what will sleeping in your bed entail?"

He gives me a sultry smile. "The pleasure of having you near me, of course. We won't do anything you don't want to do. If that means we just sleep, then we just sleep. I give you my word, I won't touch you without your verbal consent."

The problem with that is...my verbal consent seems to be pulled out of me every time we're alone together recently, whether or not my brain actually consents. The bond between us is getting frighteningly strong, to the point where I have very little control over myself when it comes to Camden. Just sitting here with him now, the heat of his stare is already prompting a response from me. My nipples hardened the moment I entered the room, and since then, even during our argument, I've felt myself growing more and more aroused. There's no way Camden doesn't know—he has the scent of a wolf—but he also doesn't comment or push for anything, which makes me a *little* bit more comfortable at the prospect of sharing a bed tomorrow. Not excited but I think I can get through it.

On a sigh I concede. "Fine."

Camden says, "One more thing, a condition I'll collect on tonight."

"The condition being?" I ask warily.

Camden's smile is so seductive, so heated, my arousal multiplies tenfold and I feel my panties grow uncomfortably damp, to the point where I fear I might leave a wet spot on the couch.

"I get to make you come again," he purrs.

While my body kicks into overdrive, priming itself for him, I force myself to actually *think* rather than *feel*. Getting an orgasm from him strengthens our bond—I know that perfectly well at this point. I also know that...well, this'll happen eventually. I knew it last night when I held him at bay; putting him off is only a temporary solution. Eventually, he'll mark me and we'll consummate the bond entirely.

In some ways, I should probably be grateful that he's not insisting on that being a condition. I know he wants to; it's a primal instinct for him. Instead, he's taking baby steps with me, holding himself on a leash. That, I can work with. Besides, I already know he's capable of delivering *mind-blowing* pleasure, and as much as I don't *want* to want it, I do.

I swallow down what feels like a handful of gravel, my nerves making my throat tighten. Camden watches my indecision with a sharp predatory gaze, lying silently in wait for my answer. If it were my body talking, it would have screamed *oh the fuck yes* the moment he laid his eyes, heated with carnal desire, on me. My brain, however, has a few more reservations. Ultimately, though, my own desire and the need to see my proposal through wins out.

I give Camden a single anxious nod, and that's all it takes. Before I can blink or even comprehend his speed, he has me laid flat on the couch, hovering above me with a predatory, deeply excited glimmer in his eyes. My breathing speeds up, then stutters as he sits me up long enough to pull my shirt over my head. My bra is unclipped with a single, smooth flick of his hands, and they run down my spine as he leans forward to kiss me. Well, perhaps *kiss* is the wrong word—he dominates my mouth, thrusting his tongue inside, learning every crevice, groaning with satisfaction when I don't fight him.

I might not be *totally* on board with this, but the heat of his body over mine combined with his delicious taste and skilled hands roaming my flesh toss my inhibitions out of the window. I kiss him back with just as much passion and vigor, though try as I might, I'm unable to match his intensity.

He pulls his mouth away from mine, and I'm embarrassed at the whimper that's drawn from my lips, as if regretting the loss. His lips tick up into a smug smirk, and he leans back for just enough time to unbutton and unzip my pants, hooking his fingers under the waistband of my panties to peel both them and my pants off my legs at the same time. He tosses the clothing articles over his shoulders before sitting back on his haunches and simply staring at me for what feels like an eternity. Uncomfortable being naked while he's fully clothed, I demand, "Take off your shirt."

His smirk turns into a full-blown smile. "Little witch, did you like touching me last night as much as I love touching you?"

I *did* like having the opportunity to learn his body without the hovering threat of sexual acts looming over my head, but I won't admit out loud just how attractive I find him. He already has a big enough ego, there's no need for me to inflate it more.

Instead of responding, I sit up and finger the hem of his shirt, tugging it up to expose his hard taut stomach. He lifts his arms to let me pull it off entirely, then watches as I splay my hands on his six-pack appreciatively. The strength and power in his form just on its own is an aphrodisiac to me.

Camden only lets my hands roam his upper body for a few seconds before pushing me flat on the couch again. He fills his hands with my breasts, squeezing the mounds with an appreciative groan and running his fingers over my nipples, back and forth, before pinching them between two fingers, drawing a whine from me. Just his hands on my breasts and fingers on my nipples are causing molten heat to pool in my core, driving me wild with need. He leans down to kiss me again, tongues twining and teeth clashing before kissing a wet path across my jaw, down the column of my neck to my breasts. He takes one of my nipples into his mouth, applying a delicious suction that makes me afraid I'll leave a wet spot on the couch. At the same time, the hand that isn't plumping my other breast travels further south, settling between my legs. He runs his fingers up and down my slit, leisurely, groaning when he finds how wet I already am.

He pulls his mouth away from my breast to tell me, "You drive me fucking *insane*, Sierra. I can't get enough of you."

The verbal praise only adds to the heat between my thighs, and one of his big fingers slides into me, drawing a moan from deep in my throat. Another finger joins the first in my channel, and they curve upwards, hitting a spot that forces another longer moan from me. His thumb moves upward to cover my clit as he takes my other nipple in his mouth, and the overload of pleasure and stimulation becomes almost too much to bear. That thumb rubs smooth, gliding circles over the sensitive bundle of nerves, finding a spot right under my clit that makes my toes curl. I clutch his shoulders for purchase, digging my nails into his skin so hard the moisture of his blood wells up.

He kisses his way back up until his mouth is hovering by my ear, while his fingers continue their work down below, winding me tighter and tighter until I can't stand it anymore.

Cam growls in my ear, "Come for your mate."

That's all it takes to push me off the edge of a cliff and send me freefalling into a powerful orgasm that culminates in an embarrassingly loud scream. My pussy convulses around his fingers as my head falls back on the couch and my back arches. Camden continues rubbing those precise circles until I'm writhing underneath him, telling him I can't take anymore. Only once he's wrung the last drops of pleasure from my body does he ease up, taking his hand between my thighs only to pop the two fingers that were just inside me into his mouth. I watch through hooded lids, feeling arousal stir once more as his eyes blaze with satisfaction,

"I've wanted to do that since the first moment I saw you," he rumbles.

Trying to catch my breath, I manage to pant, "Mission accomplished."

His lips curl into a smile of satisfaction as he gathers me into his arms and sits up, cradling me against his chest like I'm a child. I don't protest or try to wriggle away, too spent and tired from my orgasm. I let him hold me, feeling strangely treasured and cherished as his hands rub soothing circles over my skin.

After a while, my scattered thoughts start to reform. Despite the fact that my mind is fogged up with pleasure, I mumble lethargically, "I held my end of the deal, so you better hold up yours, wolf."

"You held up the first part of our deal," he responds. "The second part extends to tomorrow night. Still, since everything I know about you tells me you're a woman of your word, I'll coordinate reaching out to the witches first thing in the morning."

Another point to the earth witch, underscored by an orgasm. Perhaps being fated to him won't be so terrible, after all—if his conditions for working with me continue being along these lines, I don't think I'll mind them at all.

Chapter Thirty-Six

T he castle was unusually quiet the following day with few servants hurrying around, a change from the usual hustle and bustle of staff. Wyatt was also nowhere to be found all day, though he did send me a written note this morning informing me that a shifter liaison was on its way to bring our potential treaty to the witches and invite them to Kinrith for negotiations, which means he got the high court on board *very* quickly. I didn't mind the quiet, workless day; I spent the entirety of it with Leisel, trying to make up for all the time we've spent apart recently.

In the morning, a tutor came not only for Leisel but for me as well—Camden stuck to his promise of getting me a proper education. While my inclination to literature has allowed me to teach myself a great deal, I'm not omniscient. During Leisel's morning lessons with her tutor, mine gave me a series of tests to better understand what areas I need improvement in. I was rather proud when he informed me that the only lessons he saw need to offer were shifter and mythic history, geography, separate worlds, and the general laws of nature all mythics abide by. In terms of most other educational skill sets, he informed me I was better than most. I suppose I have my parents to thank for that, as they drilled me rather pitilessly with studies when I was growing up and taught me the value of knowledge.

After a morning of studies, I took Leisel to the stables so we could ride our horses for the first time in too long, which both of us delighted in. Pack warriors followed us from a distance, of course, but this time I didn't mind so much—I reveled in galloping across fields and spending time with my favorite small person.

It's late in the evening, after I've read her to sleep—much to Greta's protest, as "royals shouldn't concern themselves with such trivial matters"—that I finally arrive in front of Camden's chambers.

I don't have to knock this time; the door swings open as soon as I step in front of it, revealing a disgruntled-looking Camden. I feel my eyebrows furrow as I look him over—he has dark circles under his eyes, and his face has a sunken, almost gaunt expression that makes me uneasy. Every time I've come to Camden's chambers, it appears to elate him; this time, however, he looks haunted.

Without beckoning me to come in, he retreats back into the room, leaving the door open. I take the silent invitation, growing steadily more and more anxious as I close the door behind me and examine him where he stands in the corner of the room, appearing lost in thought.

Camden is not his usual self tonight at *all*. His expression is drawn, his posture is hunched, and he looks...miserable. This has an interesting effect on me; every morsel of my being pushes me to go to Camden, hug him, and offer him comfort from whatever makes him look so miserable. *Fucking bond.* As I'm not a slave to my instincts, I manage to stay in place in the entryway, but only just.

"What's wrong?" I ask him.

Cam blinks before turning his gaze to me, looking a little surprised, as if he forgot I was here. Considering the fact that every time we've shared a room before now his complete attention was on me, I understand that whatever's going on must be *very* bad.

Camden swallows, the gesture looking like it pains him, before telling me, "My father died late last night." The words come out gravelly and so full of pain, I can't hold myself back from offering comfort.

I might not be a fan of shifters, but I do have a nurturing streak that came out when I essentially became Leisel's mother; it's hard for me to ignore people's pain, even if they might deserve it. Before now, I was angry enough at Camden to forgo any kindness, but with how our relationship has developed recently, I can't stop myself from crossing the room and snaking my arms around his shoulders, offering physical comfort I can sense he is in *desperate* need of. Camden's arms come around my waist, clutching me tightly, his hands trembling from the force of his grief.

"I'm so sorry," I murmur in his ear.

He pulls away and says gruffly, "I don't want your pity."

"Good, because I have none when it comes to shifters. What I do have is *empathy* and *compassion* for this specific situation. You may have forgotten this, but my father died when I was thirteen. He was my closest friend, he taught me everything I know, and I never recovered from the loss. I don't know what your relationship with yours was like, but I do know that no loss is easy."

That deflates Camden's ire. He takes my hand and leads me to the sofa, dropping down on the soft cushion before pulling me onto his lap. For once, I don't fight, because I can sense how deeply he needs contact from me right now, and I just don't have the heart to deny him.

When my dad died, my mom and I held each other through our grief—the contact helped me know I wasn't alone. Until she died, too, and I was entirely alone. Nobody to hold me, nobody to reassure me…I know from experience that is a very, *very* dark place to be, and I wouldn't wish that on anyone.

I let Camden position me on his lap facing him with my legs on either side of his waist. I drape my arms around his shoulders and let him hold me, feeling the depth of his pain tug on my heart. I would've *killed* to be held like this after Mom passed, so I really can't fault him from taking comfort or clinging to me.

He buries his head in my neck, holding me so close that our chests are pressed together. I don't squirm or try to move, I simply let him take what he needs. After a few minutes, I reach my hands up to run them through his hair, my gestures soft and intended to be soothing.

"Why are you being so kind?" Camden asks against my skin. "You hated my father, and with good reason. He let humans die out, wouldn't even reprimand rogue packs that targeted them."

I sigh. "I won't pretend to like your father, just like I won't pretend to be grateful we never ended up in a room together, but *you* cared about him, I can see that, and I can't ignore your pain. Nobody deserves to grieve alone, not even you."

His head still buried in my neck, Camden says, "I don't—didn't—*like* my father, per se, but I did respect him. He was not the fatherly type, but he was a very strong shifter and an even stronger ruler. He created the pyramid structure of packs that protects those on the lowest ranks—something nobody else had cared to do before. He was smart, a quick thinker, and very strategically inclined. I learned a great deal from him."

I stay quiet, sensing that Camden just needs to be heard right now. Sometimes, that's the best thing when stuck in grief, a listening ear. Not someone who offers unwanted advice, but someone who's just willing to sit in your misery with you and offer company.

He goes on, "He was a shitty father, if I'm being honest. Wyatt and I were raised by our mother, and when she passed, the castle staff took over. I don't know if he ever loved us." He pauses. "But he did love my mother. She was his sun and moon. Her death nearly destroyed him—most shifters die if their mates do, but he held on. He knew shifters still needed him, so he did the impossible and survived. He's the strongest, toughest man I've ever known. I don't think shifters will see his like again anytime soon."

"Sounds like he was an incredible ruler," I say sincerely.

While I don't think I would've liked Camden's father as a person, if what he's saying is true, he had the strength that few others do. A mate dying to *any* mythic being is usually a death sentence; just about all literature agrees on that. One would have to have a phenomenally strong soul to get through it. I also don't love that the deceased King wasn't anything resembling a father to his sons, but then again...monarchy tends to be hard on families. I've read countless recounts of how human monarchies tore families apart; why would shifters be any different?

Camden pulls back to stare into my eyes. The intensity of his gaze feels like a physical force weighing me down. He says, "I don't deserve you, Sierra, but I'm fucking keeping you."

I smile, a little sadly. "You don't deserve me, but fate has her tricks. Lucky you, I guess."

He nods slowly. "Yes. I am lucky. I hope you know there's no reality that exists in which I'll ever let you go, *especially* not now."

"Careful, Cam, that sounds like a threat."

"A promise," he corrects.

No use in arguing the point now. "What do you need?" I ask.

"You," he responds. "I'm still collecting on my condition tonight. You *will* be sharing my bed."

I wasn't going to argue before, since I'd already given my word, and I certainly won't argue now. Camden stands, keeping me in his arms. My legs wrap tightly around his waist and my hands clutch his shoulders to steady myself. His hands move to blatantly cup my ass as he carries me out of the main room, into the hallway past it, and to the very last door which is already ajar.

I only have a moment to glimpse his room before he drops me on his bed. It's rustic, decorated with dark wooden tones. The right wall of the room is made up entirely of windows, giving off a picturesque view of the land beyond the castle. It's a bit cloudy tonight, so the sky is moonless, and the only light outside comes from the occasional orb of floating light, illuminating the gardens and polished lawns. On the left wall of the room lies a collection of book cases, all of them filled, and on the back wall there's a fireplace with a chaise lounge in front of it. Camden's bed is humongous, carved from wood with masterful designs that appear to depict a garden of vines. The mattress is soft, with plenty of give, and I bounce a few times after Cam drops me before stilling.

Camden wastes no time coming down on top of me, straddling my waist and pressing delicious, wet kisses to my neck. Even while the heat of his mouth tries to lull me into a trance, I manage to say, "Wait, Cam, is now really the best time to—"

He cuts me off with a searing kiss on my lips, infusing so much passion and desire into it my body goes limp and pliable beneath him.

When he pulls back, it's to say, "Yes, now is the best time. I need you, Sierra. Don't deny me."

It feels faintly like he's using my compassion against me, which he might be, but...his grief is very real. That much I'm sure of. If what he really needs is to blow off some steam right now, I guess I'm not *entirely* opposed to the idea. Still, trapped beneath him is not a good negotiating point, so I hook a leg over his waist and use a sparring move I learned when I was a kid to flip us over, ending with me on top, straddling his waist.

Camden looks surprised at this turn of events, blinking up at me. His eyes are no longer filled with grief—now, they're brimming with lust and intrigue. I have to admit, I breathe a little easier seeing some of his sorrow alleviated, even if it is in favor of lust.

I'm about to tell him that we can fool around, but I'm not ready for sex yet, when my gaze is inexplicably pulled to the window, in time to see the clouds part just enough for the moon to become visible. Its beams spill onto the grounds below, bathing the gardens with an ethereal light. I blink to see that those moonbeams are *red* instead of silver. I'm staring at a total lunar eclipse—a blood moon. As soon as those red-tinged moon beams pass through the glass of the window and hit my skin, something very strange happens; my body *lights up* with lust.

Chapter Thirty-Seven

A soul-deep change overcomes me, sparking a craving deep within that *demands* to be satiated; a craving to have Camden inside of me. It's so intense my muscles actually start to spasm and cramp, sending bursts of pain through me at multiple points in my body. My stomach, my shoulders, my back, my womb *especially*. The discomfort and pain are so intense that I hunch over, falling flat on top of Camden's chest.

Surprisingly, the contact alleviates the worst of the cramps, but not all of them; in place of the pain is once again the insatiable, untamed need to have him fully. I don't think; I'm no longer capable of rational thought. Instead, I'm a wild creature desperate for its mate, fisting Camden's shirt and tearing it straight down the middle with a strength I didn't know I had.

I don't pause to question what's happening to me—how I suddenly went from wary of going too far to *desperate* to have Camden, right now, without any barriers. I have *zero* control over myself, and that doesn't bother me in the least. Camden's hands close around my waist and our mouths meet in a barbaric, violent kiss. It's a frenzy of passion and lust, and it doesn't take long for the taste of blood to hit my mouth, telling me that one of us bit the other hard enough to bleed. Who, I'm not sure, but what I am sure of is I don't care—nothing has *ever* felt this good, this fulfilling, this satisfying.

I pull my mouth away only long enough to strip off my shirt and bra, *desperate* to have his hands on every part of me. Then, compelled by an unseen force to leave my marks on him, I lean down and sink my teeth into his neck—not hard enough to draw blood, but hard enough that even with shifter healing he'll have a mark for at least a day. At the same time, my nails scratch down his arms, leaving a trail of wetness in their wake.

"*Fuck*," Camden murmurs before abruptly flipping me over and actually *tearing* my pants and panties off of me with a single sharp yank.

Not wasting any time, he shoves my thighs apart my thighs and buries his head between my legs, setting off fireworks in my brain and across my body. The heat and skill of his delicious mouth is at once too much and not *nearly* enough—I need more. I need *everything* from him, and I need it now. I grab handfuls of his hair and yank him up none too gently, too impatient to let him bring me to orgasm that way. What I crave in this moment, more than I've craved anything in my entire life, is to have his cock inside me, filling me, stretching me.

"So eager," Camden says, a hint of amusement in his tone.

I, on the other hand, am not amused whatsoever that he's still partially clothed. Before I can rip his pants off with my teeth, he strips them off himself, leaving him entirely, gloriously naked, kneeling before me like some kind of erotic god. His cock is long and thick, swollen and an angry reddish purple, with veins running along its length. It's big enough that the briefest flicker of concern passes through my thoughts, but they're wiped away when he fills his hands with my breasts and sucks a nipple into his mouth, drawing a long moan from me.

Dimly, I hear myself mutter, "What's happening to me?" I've never felt lust like this for Camden. Have I been turned on by him? Yes, too many times to count, but never with such soul-rending need. While the majority of my mind is stuck in a haze of unbearable desire, the small, nearly dormant part of it wonders just where this came from. To say that this is unlike me would be quite an understatement.

Camden doesn't respond to my question though, and the strong suction of his lips wipes away any lingering confusion, replacing it with unbearable need. I once again yank his hair to bring his face to mine and fuse our lips in another animalistic kiss before telling him, "I need you inside me."

His eyes turn a brighter blue than I've ever seen them, and he lets out a groan at my words. "You have no idea how long I've been waiting to hear that."

He settles his hips firmly between my thighs, and I feel his long, throbbing length pressed against my center. My eyes roll to the back of my head as he grinds his cock against me, sliding it over my sensitive, swollen flesh, hitting my clit repeatedly, and setting off a mini-orgasm with nothing more than a few thrusts that don't even penetrate me.

"Did you just come?" he asks in disbelief.

I'm no longer capable of stringing together a coherent sentence, so in response, I hook my legs around his waist and pull him tighter into the cradle of my thighs, trying to get him to quit stalling and start fucking.

He takes the hint. Staring deep into my eyes, he reaches down with one hand and places the broad head of his cock at my entrance, setting off a shiver of delight shuddering down my spine. There's no trepidation or apprehension left within me, just a sea of hunger that only he can satisfy.

"It's going to hurt a bit at first. Breathe through it," Camden tells me.

I nod, not caring for whatever pain's to come because the pain of not having him already is much, *much* worse. Once again my muscles start to cramp and clench, and I understand the only way I'll get relief is with him inside me.

He starts pushing his length into me and instantly the cramps subside, replaced with a deeply uncomfortable pressure in my nether regions that borders on pain. When he pushes in an inch further I feel the resistance inside me give way, and then, it's *all* pain, blooming from within but spreading upwards to my belly and even down to my thighs. I cry out, the noise not one of ecstasy but one of agony, and Camden goes still above me and within me. He blinks several times, appearing to try to get control of himself, while I pant harshly and shut my eyes tightly, trying to even my breathing and wait for the horrible pain to subside. He reaches a hand down, between our bodies, and slides his hand over my clit, using my wetness to tease the sensitive bundle of nerves, causing my eyes to snap open and widen. After a moment, the pleasure from his gestures expands once more, chasing away most of the pain from his invasion, though it does still have a bit of a bite.

"You good?" he asks through gritted teeth.

Feeling like I'm a puppet and my strings are being yanked by something I can't see or comprehend, I nod. Camden leans down to kiss my neck, his fingers still working their magic below, as he continues sliding himself further and further into me. It feels like my body's tearing and stretching to accommodate him, but with his fingers on my clit and lips on my neck, the sensation isn't entirely *un*pleasant. Foreign, yes, but no longer terribly painful—just a really *really* tight fit topped off with a burn.

By the time he's seated all the way inside me, our bodies fully connected, I feel like he's rearranged my internal organs to make room for his entire length. He pulls away from my neck to look down at me and take in my reaction. The sensation of fullness is overwhelming, making it difficult to breathe, but what supersedes even that is the strange, almost religious sense of connection from staring into his eyes. His gaze is completely open and unguarded, possibly for the first time since I've met him.

Being raised here, in this palace, Camden probably had to master his emotions and expressions—I can glean his moods from his non-verbal cues and mannerisms, but only if I look *really* close and analyze everything. Right now, everything is laid bare for me to see, and it's more than I can handle.

In his gaze, I see endless affection, a surplus of desire, and a great deal of uncertainty. Uncertainty of this, of us, of our circumstances and everything it means, but also the desire for more. More than physical pleasure, more than being able to stand being in a room with each other—I can both see and *feel* Camden's yearning for everything I have to give.

Unexpectedly, I feel tears well up in my eyes at the rawness of his stare. It's touching, humbling even, because I don't know that Cam has ever allowed anyone to see him this way; raw, vulnerable, a person rather than an Alpha and monarch. Right now he appears to be a man, with all the imperfections thereof, instead of the hardened leader he presents himself as to the rest of the world.

Ever so slowly, he reaches his hands up to plant both on either side of my head and slides his length out of me, pulling a small whine from me. Then, just as leisurely, he sinks back in. He repeats the smooth, prolonged gesture again and again until my body starts to become accustomed to him, allowing him to slide in even deeper and with less resistance. I arch my back, lifting my hips in offering and in an attempt to get him to go *faster*.

Though the initial frenzy of lust that had me literally tearing off his clothes has subsided, in its place remains a sense of connection—almost frightening in its depth—and the need for the pain that it took to get here to culminate in pleasure. Slow isn't going to achieve that.

Camden's lips tick up as he quickens his thrusts. His cock slides over places in me I didn't even know existed until now, sending starbursts of pleasure across my nerve endings, and causing a knot of tension to form low in my belly. The faster his pace, the further that knot expands, holding the promise of mind-melting pleasure on the other end. Cam's breathing stutters as his pace accelerates until it's brutal and painful, but I wouldn't stop it for anything.

He reaches down to twist my nipple between two fingers as his mouth crashes onto mine once more, and that's all it takes—my orgasm *erupts* from within me. Camden swallows my scream as I clench and convulse around him, out of control and desperate for this feeling to *never* end. My skin feels like it catches fire with the heat radiating off of us, every nerve ending tingling and pulsing as hormones flood my mind, turning my vision hazy and making me feel like I'm seeing everything through rose-tinted glasses.

Camden only manages two more thrusts before he stills above me, the veins bulging on his neck as he rips his mouth from mine and lowers it to my neck, shocking me by sinking teeth that aren't blunt human ones but sharp like a canine's into my skin. Dimly, I realize he's actually *marking* me—breaking my skin and embedding his saliva to permanently scent-mark me *and permanently bind us together.*

What should have me absolutely *livid* and what I thought would be painful beyond comprehension instead sets off another *stronger* orgasm—one that nearly causes me to choke on my own cries, my body thrashing under the onslaught of pleasure that's too much to handle. I rake my nails down his arms deep enough to leave gouges, then do the same to his back—trying to get a grip, to find purchase while a torrent of pleasure threatens to sweep me away. His teeth withdraw from my neck at the same time that I feel his cock pulsing inside me, followed by a warmth that spills from him, bathing my channel.

As my orgasm ebbs, a full-body feeling of weakness sweeps over me, blurring my vision and making me feel like I'm experiencing the world from within a dark fog that pulls me deeper and deeper. I barely feel Camden pull out of me and roll onto his back, I'm too depleted to say anything or even fidget as he pulls me into the circle of his arms. My eyes feel like they're lead weights, impossible to keep open. Unable to do anything else, I let the darkness pull me into a deep sleep.

Chapter Thirty-Eight

Camden

I awake at around the same time the sun starts to rise, early in the morning, feeling more satisfied and complete than I ever have. On the tail of the horrific day I experienced yesterday—filled with the pain of losing my father, though his deterioration had made our relationship a lost cause for some time—came the greatest blessing of all; I finally got to have Sierra entirely. I can feel that the bond that connects us has strengthened significantly, though it's not yet complete. Completion would require complete intimacy on both sides, not just physical or emotional, and I understand that will take quite a bit more work.

I've been watching her the last several hours as she sleeps, comfortably nestled in my arms, admiring her skin as the early morning sun bathes her in a golden glow, studying the steady rise and fall of her chest, and marveling at the new depth of the connection between us. She's mine now, completely and irrevocably. More than knowing she's mine, I also *feel* it; I feel a new strength of the connection between us, one that's soul-deep. I feel slivers of her emotions passing through our bond—faint feelings of contentment and restfulness, ones I somehow know come from her, tickle my chest.

I knew that a blood moon had a lustful effect on witches—there's a reason I insisted on her staying with me last night—but I didn't know just the extent of that lust. I didn't expect her to tear my clothes off or claw at me like a woman possessed, but I'll admit her actions and reactions delighted me. Every one of them.

The sheer, raw force of her passion was unveiled for the first time, and the result was nothing short of enlightening and addictive. Previously, a mere few touches or feeling her come undone around my tongue and fingers felt close to a religious experience, but last night was nothing short of an epiphany. Being inside her, with her moans in my ear and demands for more, felt like coming home after years away at battle.

I didn't *intend* to mark her, per se, but I'm glad I did—with a mark and consummation, our bond is now irreversible. Of course, reversing it before would have required the sort of black magic she has no access to, but the small possibility is now gone. She can't run from me; the need to return to her mate will now be too strong, too consuming. The weight this knowledge lifts off my shoulders is profound, as I hadn't realized just how much I continued to worry about her leaving me, even as she's started to settle into her role in the castle.

Recalling the way she held and soothed me last night, I can't stop my eyes from dropping to her flat stomach. With our bond marked and physically consummated, she'll now be able to bear my children—add in the fact that blood moons are hyper-fertile times for witches, and I do believe there may be a new addition to the castle quite soon. I've seen her with Leisel, seen her maternal streak front and center, so there's no doubt in my mind she'll be the best mother to the children we have.

Sierra blinks her eyes open sleepily, appearing hazy and discombobulated for a moment. She looks up into my face, and upon realizing she's half-on top of me with my arms around her, she stiffens slightly before shooting up into a sitting position. She looks around the bedroom and I hear her heartbeat speed up when she reaches a hand up to touch the red skin where I marked her, and then turns eyes laced with confusion and fear on me. Then, realizing she's still naked and my eyes are drawn down to her breasts, she yanks a blanket up to cover herself.

I feel faint echoes of her fear and panic radiating through the bond, and both prickle at my instinct to soothe and calm her. Since I know that touching her right now might only stress her more, I manage to keep myself in place and try to keep my expression calm.

"You..." She trails off, staring at me, more and more fear creeping into her body language and expression. Her hand continues rubbing at her mark, with increasing harshness, until her nails start digging into her skin.

I lean forward to lightly clasp her wrist and lower it from her neck. "Don't scratch at it, it'll probably be tender for a while."

"Camden...what the fuck?" she says, jerking her wrist away from me. "How could you...how could you do that without asking me? I wasn't—*still am not*—ready for that!"

As she speaks, she gathers the blanket before standing from the bed and looking around with growing alarm. Right now, she appears like a cornered animal—or witch—and I know I have to approach with caution or risk her incinerating my bedroom.

"I got carried away. Full moons have that effect on wolves," I tell her with some truth. Sure, I was swept up in the moment, but marking her was, at least in the back of my mind, a goal of last night. We were both swept away by lust, it was an ideal time, and now I have the defense of being in the thrall of the moon to shield myself from her anger.

I don't think Sierra's yet caught on that there is literally no length to which I won't go to keep her. Nothing I won't do, no line I won't cross—she is essential to me, and if some light manipulation combined with the moon's thrall is what it takes to further bind us, that's what I'll do. I'm surprised I hadn't gone to more drastic measures sooner.

Sierra deflates a little. "But...this means permanence."

This point I can argue. "There was always permanence here, Sierra, from minute one. Marking you was a matter of when, not if, as you damn well know. What's the issue with it happening sooner rather than later? Besides, you left plenty of your own marks on me."

Another point to my defense; she clawed and bit and scratched me like a wild little thing, so in a sense, it's only fair I bit her back.

She winces at my comment, her eyes running over the scratches on my chest and arms, along with the bite marks on my neck. Marks given from one mate to another are typically called brands among shifters, and brands do not heal with usual shifter speed, for which I'm grateful—I'll be feeling her claws and bites for at least the next few days, every time I move.

"I didn't have any control over myself," she says, frowning a little.

"Neither did I. What happened is set in stone, but it changes nothing." *It changes everything.* "You're mine with or without the claiming mark; now others will know you're mine from miles away, which will serve as a nice deterrent and garner you even more respect."

That seems to piss her off more than anything I've said so far. Her back snaps ramrod straight. "I want respect on my merits, not on a plan of fate. I don't want to be revered because I'm your mate. I want to earn my place. This doesn't exactly help with that."

"You are earning your place," I tell her, happy to switch topics and steer away from more dangerous territory. "The proposal you brought to me was masterfully constructed. Wyatt had the entire high court in complete agreement it was the right course of action in the span of a single evening, and the credit for it went to you. Speaking of, I have news from the liaison we sent to the witches."

That perks her up a little. "Being?"

"We sent a wolf to the coven in charge of witch territories on this side of the globe, The Nightshade Coven, yesterday morning. I got news later in the day that the witches agreed to a tentative negotiation, as long as it includes a welfare check on you and Leisel."

Sierra blinks. "Welfare check?"

I nod. "You were right in your assumption that witches protect their own; they've had to in order to survive. As the strongest magical species, they've faced more persecution than even humans."

Sierra looks to the window, her gaze far away. "People fear what they cannot understand."

"Precisely. They've also had growing concerns about the buildup of vampire clans and their recent attempts of invasions to nearby territories, so your proposal came at a most opportune time. They'll be here next week for discussions." As further enticement, I add, "I truly think we have a shot at an alliance and treaty. Considering you were the one to pull it all together, I figured that you, with the assistance of Wyatt, should be in charge of arrangements for negotiations. Write up an official treaty, perfect it, discuss negotiation tactics—everything that happens with them will be your triumph."

At that, Sierra looks skeptical. "You'd let me take the credit?"

"I *want* you to take the credit," I say sincerely. "You deserve it, and shifters deserve to know they have a capable queen looking out for their interests. I don't need to beat you down so that I can shine; I want you to shine alongside me, if not brighter than me. I'd be happy to bask in your glow."

I can tell that works. It softens her. She reaches up a hand, again, to rub it over her mark, but this time it's a softer touch, almost a caress. Then she points a finger at me. "If you think this gets you off the hook, you're wrong. I'll still roast your ass over an open flame for your gall, even if you got carried away."

I smile at that indulgently. "I'll take your word on it. For now, I believe we both have a great deal of work to do."

She looks down at herself, and her eyebrows furrow. I feel echoes of her panic return through our bond as she stares at her stomach. "You came inside me last night. Am I at risk for pregnancy?"

I bite my lip, considering my response. If I tell her that there's a damn near guarantee she's gotten pregnant, it'll probably send her running. So, I tell her truthfully, "Not at risk, no." *No risk, only near-certainty that you're already pregnant.* She'll find that out for herself soon enough.

* * *

An hour or two after Sierra leaves, Wyatt strolls into my chambers. I'm in the main area, seated on the couch before the fireplace—a spot that's fast becoming my favorite, second only to my bed. It's here that I've shared some of my best moments with Sierra, so I'm drawn back to it repeatedly.

I glance up at Wyatt's appearance and use a hand to motion to the dining table where there's the usual breakfast spread laid out. He doesn't appear to have shared my grief over our father's death—if anything, I can imagine he probably spent the day yesterday celebrating. When my father still lived in the castle, they butted heads *constantly* and never quite learned to tolerate each other.

"Care to explain why I saw a mark on Sierra's neck?" he asks me as he seats himself beside me.

"I took advantage of the blood moon last night. We consummated. I marked her. Odds are, she'll have conceived. Anything else you'd like to question me on?"

"I'm assuming you told her the repercussions of a mark and sex during a blood moon?" Wyatt asks.

I shake my head. "And have her refuse me? No. I didn't even tell her of my intent to mark her. I saw an opportunity to bind her to me and took it."

Wyatt's face drains of all color as he takes in the information, which is not the most appropriate reaction from someone who should be my greatest supporter. I'd expect him, of all people, to be ecstatic that I've fully consummated my bond and at a time when Sierra's most fertile too. He shouldn't suddenly appear as pale as marble.

Wyatt's wide eyes meet mine, and he breathes, "Camden, what have you done? You didn't tell her that she could get pregnant once she's marked and mated?"

"No, I didn't tell her and risk rejection." Though I doubt she would have rejected me in the state she was in last night, regardless of what I'd said. "We lost a royal, now the odds are that we'll gain one," I snap with irritation. "An heir who will guarantee more power and stability to the crown, not to mention assure Sierra never even contemplates leaving."

I could've told Sierra when she asked this morning, but I didn't want to ruin her mood just yet. She'll figure it out soon and I can deal with repercussions when she does.

Wyatt shakes his head slowly, reaching one hand up to stab his fingers through his hair, looking as distraught as I've ever seen him. "This is why grieving shifters shouldn't be allowed to make decisions."

"I'm hardly grieving," I retort, "We both knew it was only a matter of time before Father died; he's been too weak to leave his home for the better part of a year. I was distraught last night, the news came as a shock to my system, but I grieved a man who's been dead for some time—who died when Mother did. Being with Sierra helped wipe much of my sorrow away."

Growing more irate, Wyatt snaps, "You let your emotions take the wheel, and now, you've very possibly permanently fucked yourself over with your mate!"

That statement does not sit well with me at all. The idea that I've done something wrong when every morsel of my being is screaming that I've taken the exact right steps to secure a future, shakes me—especially coming from my brother, whose judgment I trust.

"What the fuck are you talking about?" I snarl.

"The fact that this is something she'll *rightfully* see as a blatant betrayal!" Wyatt snaps. "You marked and mated her during a blood moon, without informing her of the risks. What do you think will happen when she finds out she's pregnant, hmm? You think she'll just accept it?"

"I think that she has the strongest maternal instincts I've ever seen," I growl.

"Fucking *exactly!*" Wyatt shouts. "How could you think she'd bring a child into the world after being manipulated into it, *especially* while we're about to enter an all-out war with the vampires? You want to know what I think she'll do? Everything in her power to *abort* it! Then she'll take her sister and get away from shifters because you tried to *entrap* her! Any trust built between you, gone. Any progress I've made with Leisel, gone. We just lost our father, which I imagine was a blow for you, and now you've set us on a path to lose our mates too! So, I repeat, *what the fuck have you done?*"

My blood runs cold as I process Wyatt's words, forced to come to terms with the very grim truth of them. He's right, not telling Sierra the full scope of the situation last night and lying this morning will most likely come around to bite me in the ass. I don't *think* she'd ever try to end a life of a child, but then...I can't say that with certainty. What I do know is she has a vengeful streak a mile wide and could respond to her situation on principle. If she finds out I tried to trap her permanently, she'll try to escape. The smart thing to do would be to get rid of anything that could inhibit that escape, such as a life that binds us together.

Fuck.

My thoughts race at a million miles a second as I try to think through my next steps. My grief and sorrow got the best of me, causing me to act rashly. There's no going back now; all I can do is plan contingencies for the future.

I lock gazes with Wyatt, and tell him, "Nobody breathes a word of this to Sierra. She will not find out she's pregnant until the child is formed enough that she wouldn't have the heart to get rid of it. Anyone in the castle who dares tell her the truth will be executed for treason."

If possible, my brother's eyes bulge even more. His mouth falls agape, and he looks lost for words. Finally, he demands, *"Are you fucking insane?"*

"It's the only way to ensure my heir is carried to term!" I yell.

Wyatt shakes his head. "No. No, I won't be part of deceiving my Alpha female and our *queen*. She deserves the truth."

"You tell her, and I'll lock you in the dungeons to keep you away from Leisel for the next fucking year," I tell my brother clearly. "Don't test me, Wyatt. You know I will."

Wyatt deflates and fear replaces the anger in his expression. His posture slumps, and he gives me a look of such pain and betrayal that it tugs on my chest. I've always been my brother's protector; outside of play-fighting, sparring, and the occasional healthy duel between siblings, I've never threatened him. I don't think either of us can believe it in this scenario, but I can't be rational now. Not with what's at stake.

Wyatt stands slowly from the couch, trembling with a mixture of rage and pain. He says, "Maybe Sierra was right about us, Camden. At least there's no fucking doubt that you're a monster."

With that, he turns and walks out of the room, slamming the door behind him.

Chapter Thirty-Nine

Sierra

In the days that follow, I'm too swept up with duties and tasks and preparations for the upcoming negotiations to do much thinking about the bite mark that now permanently graces my neck or the fact that I still can't fathom how what was meant to be a night sharing a bed devolved into what it did. Honestly, keeping my mind off of it is a relief—being buried in work, I don't even have to see Camden, which means I don't have to confront the reality of my new situation quite yet. He has his own tasks to tend to, both related to his father's funeral in the coming weeks and to the war that's fast approaching, so we don't see much of each other.

I do, however, spend a great deal of time with Wyatt, who seems unusually subdued and quiet, staying task-oriented with minimal conversation. I assume that it's grief from his father's death that has him down, though I got the impression from Camden that there was little love lost between his brother and father.

The evening before the negotiation day, when the witches will enter Kinrith and come to the palace for discussions, I'm quarantined in the war room with Wyatt, putting in yet another *very* late night of work to make sure everything is ready. After a week of hearing only minimalistic answers from him, his usual sociopolitical rants absent, I'm starting to get a tad worried. I can't have him acting like a living corpse when the witches show up.

I don't think he'll respond to me straight up asking what crawled up his ass and died—he might consider it a tad too forward—so I decide to be a little bit more covert with my inquiry.

As we're going over pages upon pages of framework for the treaty we intend to propose, papers and books scattered in front of us on the table holding the world map, I ask Wyatt, "Were you close with your father?"

He glances up from the book he's reading, appearing a little startled at my question. Considering our conversations the last few days have been kept strictly to negotiations and everything surrounding them, I can't fault his surprise.

After a second, he snorts and shakes his head. "My father was an absolute prick with few morals and even fewer ethics. He refused to look outside the scope of shifters' lives, and he punished anyone who tried to tell him he was wrong. I was not close with him at all."

I nod slowly, taking in the new information. "So...you didn't have a good relationship with him like Camden?"

Wyatt makes a face of faint disgust. "No, I did not hold the position in his eyes and heart as the golden heir—I was the spare, and one he considered too opinionated. I was always too loud with too many ideas and too sharp a mind—something he saw as a potential threat to the crown." He pauses, a sad smile creeping onto his face. "Father actually intended to send me across the world to live and train with the warrior pack when I was fourteen. That's how much he wanted me gone."

Well, shit. Deeply interested in this peek into the not-so-great aspects of royal life, I ask, "What happened?"

"Camden found out," he tells me, "and told our father that if he sent me away, Cam would refuse the throne and abdicate the first chance he got as king. They got into a fight, a physical one, and that was the day it became clear that Camden was an even stronger Alpha with a far more dominant wolf than our father. After that, Dad quit trying to shut me down and instead decided to ignore me. A few years later the severing of the mate bond between him and Mom *really* started to take its toll, so he slowly started shifting his duties to Camden, effectively making my brother the Alpha and King. When Dad's...*problems* became too dangerous for him to be at court, he moved away to a home he shared with my mother when she was still alive on the far west side of the royal property, a few miles away. I didn't have to see him much after that."

I stare at him wide-eyed, a little stunned. I could sense from the beginning that the brotherly bond between Camden and Wyatt was strong, but I didn't expect any of this. To hear that Camden effectively put himself and the crown itself at risk to protect Wyatt is certainly unexpected—I didn't think Camden was capable of doing anything that could jeopardize the crown and, by extension, shifter kind around the globe. Evidently, his loyalty to his own runs *deep*. I have to say...that's comforting in its own way.

I'm still not okay *at all* with him abruptly marking me, but at the same time...didn't I bite and scratch and claw at him too? Besides, if he shows the loyalty to me that he's apparently capable of showing to Wyatt, I suppose there are worse fates than to be tied to him. It wouldn't hurt to have someone with his power and reach on my side, protecting both me and my sister.

Still interested to hear more, I ask Wyatt, "What problems are you referring to with your father? Does the severing of a mate bond cause chronic illness if a mythic happens to survive it?"

Wyatt sighs, pushing away the book in front of him. He stands, wanders over to the bar cart in the corner of the room, and pours himself a glass of whiskey before returning to his seat.

"Shifters who are unfortunate enough to survive the severing of the mate bond will *never* be the same person they were before. When your mate dies, they take a good chunk of you with them, forever changing the rare survivor. That change is soul-deep, affecting personality, thinking, emotions...*everything* that makes a person who they are. Eventually, the severing of a mate bond can drive shifters to a state of madness, where they border on rogue. On top of that, it also impairs a shifter's usually pristine health; they become susceptible to diseases that would otherwise never touch them." He pauses to take a sip. "For the first month after my mother died, Dad didn't come out of his room. He had the high court deputize and carry out duties in his stead. The month after that, he started showing his face, but he was...stricter. Less patient. Crueler, some might say. This didn't affect his reign—he'd never allow that—but it did affect people in the castle. In the years that followed, his decision making became impaired. He was perfectly conscientious of this; I overheard him telling Cam that he couldn't in good conscience continue to act as King of shifters, Alpha of Alphas. When his mood swings became too erratic, and he became prone to rages, he left of his own volition. By then, he'd trained my brother up pretty well. Not long after, he started getting sick physically. Colds, at first, but then more serious afflictions followed. His internal organs weakened and his skeletomuscular structure became frail. Last week, he died of cardiac arrest—a heart attack."

"What do you mean by rages?" I ask. "The usual, as in a person being angry, or is it something more?"

Wyatt lets out a dark laugh. "A wolf in a rage is a very, *very* dangerous thing. The best way to describe it is a state where their mind fogs over with fury clouding any rationale or reasonable thought. I've seen shifters in rages tear rooms apart, hurt loved ones, even kill their best friend...things they'd never otherwise do. At the end of his stay in the castle, my father got into rages a great deal, and in the unlucky times I was around I'd bear the brunt of his aggression."

I look Wyatt up and down, contemplating his words. He doesn't seem like a grieving son as he talks. Instead, one could assume we're discussing the weather. It's not that he's numb, exactly, more so that he just doesn't seem to care all that much about his father, or lack thereof. Maybe that's because the deceased King never really treated Wyatt like a son.

My father was my closest friend, most trusted confidant, and the most revered figure in my life. I adored him. When Leisel asks about him, I still get choked up while going over my most precious memories. It pains me that she never got to know our father, never got to feel his love the way I did for thirteen years, so I try to channel the teachings of both our parents with her.

I can see plainly that Wyatt holds no reverence for his father like I did, and little respect for him, at that. I'm getting the feeling more and more that Camden was Wyatt's prime father figure in life, on top of being an Alpha and premature ruler.

"So, it wouldn't be appropriate to tell you I'm sorry for your loss?" I question, trying for a light tone.

Wyatt grins. "Nope. When I heard the news, I celebrated."

I wince. "He was that bad to you?"

Wyatt shrugs, going for nonchalant, but I notice the tense set of his shoulders. "He was never good to me, Sierra. That's for damn sure." After a pause, he goes on, "Since we're getting nice and personal here, would you mind if I ask you a question?"

I try to keep myself from visibly tensing at that. I'm not a fan of being open—that probably comes from spending my life shielding my family's secret from my village, only for that secret to be exposed and then openly *accepted* by most of my fellow villagers, which shocked me. Since Wyatt and I are technically family now that my bond's consummated with Camden, though that thought brings me deep discomfort, I reply, "Go for it."

Wyatt drops his eyes to my neck, where the mark from Camden is still a bit sore, and says, "You and Cam completed your mating fairly out of the blue. I can sense that the bond within you isn't totally stable or at full capacity, which means there are still some barriers you need to overcome, but it's marked and consummated. Are you okay with that?"

What a strange question. Wyatt is the first person in this castle who has posed it; I've received nothing but congratulations and exhilaration from everyone else I cross paths with, save for Leisel. My little sister was as startled by this development as I was, but calmed when I told her it isn't the end of the world, and that she can view it as an extra layer of protection for us.

"I...I'm not sure. I haven't actually spoken to or even seen Camden since the morning after the blood moon. He's been busy with realm and military things, and I've been swept up in all this," I say, nodding at the tomes and scrolls covering the table.

Wyatt nods. "You don't seem *not* okay with it, which is good by my estimation. If you want to hear it, could I offer a piece of advice?"

"I'd appreciate it," I say.

Wyatt meets my eyes and tells me bluntly, "My brother adores you. He's possibly already in love with you. There's little he wouldn't do to keep you, but there's also little he wouldn't do for your happiness. When you inevitably clash, keep that in mind. He's an idiot, which is surprising for a ruler of such intelligence, but he isn't cruel or malicious to people who don't earn his wrath. If I were you, I'd use the way he felt about me to my advantage and gain concessions." He pauses as a half-smile forms on his lips. "Now, let's finish up here and get some rest. It's a big day tomorrow for all shifters."

Chapter Forty

I barely sleep that night, excitement and worry warring within me and filling my veins with adrenaline that makes it impossible to calm down enough to rest. In the morning, I'm awake, washed, dressed, and ready to go before Leisel even wakes up. Once my little sister awakens, I eat breakfast with her before heading down to the library where I agreed with Wyatt I'd meet him and Camden. The witches are due here within the hour, and the closer it gets to their arrival, the more amped up I feel.

As expected, Camden and Wyatt are both waiting for us outside the library. They appear to be in a tense, not altogether friendly conversation, whispering to each other in harsh tones. *Perhaps they're more concerned about the witches' visit than they've let on.* As soon as Camden glimpses my approach with Leisel, he straightens, slaps Wyatt on the back a little *too* harshly, and gives me a smile.

I haven't seen him since the morning after we had sex, and I'll admit, I've been keen on avoiding him because I don't know how to approach him after how I acted. I'm embarrassed by how I literally tore at his clothes like an animal. I suspect the full moon had some sort of mythical effect on both of us—something that Camden probably knew in advance and neglected to tell me. At this point, I'm growing used to his clever way of navigating our situation, so while I should be mad...I realize it truly was only a matter of time before we had sex and he marked me.

The strengthening of our bond becomes patently clear when the simple act of making eye contact with him lights up my body. Strangely, I'm not lit up with lust this time—more so an eagerness to be near him, to be touching him even if it's not in a sexual way. There's a strange force within me that's yearning to simply be close to him which startles me. I expected that my lust would be on overdrive around him since we consummated. Instead, it seems that consummation settled the part of me that was constantly wanting Camden *that* way and has opened up another side that simply wants him.

"Good morning," Camden tells me as I approach, his smile brightening. "Are you ready for the meeting?"

I inhale a deep breath and nod. "Wyatt and I spent last night perfecting the treaty we'll present them with."

The proposal we sent via liaison was meant to dangle certain incentives that would bring witches to the table; the goal today is to actually get into the nitty-gritty of negotiations and get all of our signatures on a piece of paper that will bind shifters and witches together. Not only as allies for upcoming wars but as two species that will start to intermix and intermingle, creating a cohesive continent and showing the rest of the world that such things are possible; different species *can* work together.

"I read over it before coming down here—it looks great. Mutually beneficial, articulately worded, and something you should be proud of," Camden says.

I feel a flush of pride as he praises me, more so than I have in the past. Partially because of our strengthened bond, but also because I put my heart and soul into the treaty. Not only will it bind the wolf-shifter nation with witches, I also wrote in aspects that are guaranteed to help humans—amendments that prioritize giving aid to human villages scattered around this continent, aid that will be the first step in making it possible for humans to lead lives that aren't drowned in poverty and difficulties.

"Thank you," I murmur.

I'm surprised when Leisel releases my hand and wanders over to Wyatt, telling him, "You were right about Grimm's Fairytales, they're *awesome*."

Wyatt blinks down at my little sister, also looking surprised at her initiating conversation without prompting or first checking with me.

A small grin forms on his lips. "Don't tell me you've made your way through all the books you've borrowed already?"

Leisel rolls her eyes. "Of course I have. I got those books *ages* ago."

Wyatt's eyebrows rise as he squats down to eye level with Leisel. "You got those books a week ago. You're a fast reader, huh?"

Leisel nods. "Mm-hmm. I get it from Sierra, I think. She reads, like, a million books a week."

Camden steps closer to me as our siblings continue to chat, murmuring, "They seem to be getting on well, and you no longer look pale as a sheet every time they interact."

I lift a shoulder. "I've gotten to know Wyatt a bit better, and he's surprised me. He's very intelligent and forward-thinking, definitely an asset to shifters."

Camden lets out a soft snort. "He'll be the first to agree with you."

A guard rounds the end of the hallway, bowing his head before saying, "Three witches have arrived on the property, Your Majesties. They're being escorted into the entrance hall as we speak."

Leisel bounces on her toes with eagerness—she's been brimming with excitement ever since I told her we'll be meeting with fellow witches earlier in the week. Wyatt stands to his full height, rolling his head to crack his neck.

Camden says to me, "This treaty will be your triumph if it goes through, so I'm leaving you in charge of negotiations. You've already proven to be a far more capable diplomat than me; I'll just be there for support."

That warms my heart. The trust he's showing in not only me but my capabilities, makes my defenses against him crumble a little more. He could take credit for my hard work—nobody would stop him—instead, he's choosing to push me into the spotlight.

"Thank you. I won't let you down," I respond quietly.

"I know you won't," he responds easily.

I take Leisel's hand, following the guard down several halls, three sets of staircases, and into the entrance hall of the castle. It's a grand hall decorated with light marble boasting a high ceiling with a glass dome top, letting in rays of morning sunlight. Stationed at the entrances of the room and on either side of the grand staircase are pack warriors, dressed in formal blue clothing indicating that they're members of the King's personal guard—a tidbit I learned from Wyatt a few days ago.

Three figures stand in the center of the entrance hall. A striking image with the sun haloing them, they appear almost ethereal in both beauty and power.

At the front stands a woman who appears to be in her late twenties, with long loosely curled raven-black hair, steel gray eyes, and golden skin. I can *feel* the magic coming off her; it's startlingly powerful, almost worryingly so. She's a similar height to me, and while nothing about her physical appearance is intimidating, sensing the strength of her magic is all I need to know I would *not* want to be on the opposite side of a battlefield from her.

Slightly behind her and to the right stands a taller, more imposing witch, with almost as much magic radiating off her as the one in front. Somewhere in the vicinity of five-seven, this witch has long platinum-blonde hair, and vivid hazel eyes that, on second glance, are made up of green and yellow with flecks of mocha and gray. She looks like she's sizing every shifter in the room up, as if preparing to take them down in case things go sideways.

To the left of her is a woman who looks like a pixie—she can't be much more than five feet tall, and she has the stereotypical red hair and vivid green eyes that old books associate with witches. The magic coming off *her* is particularly interesting because it feels like heat of some sort, calling to me in a way I've never experienced.

"My name is Camden Kent," Camden says, "I'm Alpha of the Rockwell Pack and acting monarch overseeing all shifters. On behalf of my kind, I'd like to welcome you to Kinrith. We're honored by your presence here."

The witches all give him brief, dismissive glances, before turning their gazes on Leisel and me. The tall blonde gives me a long look up and down once she's done staring at the wolves surrounding me like they're her next kill and says, "I thought you'd be taller."

The one in front shushes her. "Please excuse Reyna, she skipped the manual on manners in childhood. I'm assuming you're the famous Sierra?"

Famous? "I'm not sure about famous, but I am the only Sierra I know." I draw Leisel closer to me as she watches the other witches with wide-eyed wonder like they're mythical unicorns. "This is my younger sister, Leisel."

The dark-haired witch smiles, showcasing a perfect set of pearly-white teeth. "It's very nice to meet you both, and good to see you've been kept in good health. My name is Odelia, I'm the high priestess of the Nightshade Coven." She uses a hand to motion to the blonde witch. "This is Reyna, first Elder, and to my left is Claire, second Elder of the coven. We thank you for extending an invite."

Reyna gives her a startled glance. "We do?"

Claire, tone coated in exasperation, mutters, "Can you try to be polite for thirty seconds?"

Reyna blinks at Claire, looking genuinely confused. "But why would we be thankful for being invited to shifter land? I still maintain we should've made them come to us. Those two witches look fine, and the Alpha and Beta are keeping their expressions blank, but every other wolf we've passed looked like they wanted to either bite us or burn us at the stake."

Interesting. I haven't asked anyone in the palace what the popular opinion is among shifters regarding allying with witches, whom they historically avoid, but if it's more negative than positive, that means there will need to be some serious PR work to avoid protests and riots.

Odelia goes on as if Reyna hadn't spoken, directing her words to me. "I assume you were the one who drew up the proposal brought to us? I sensed strong magic from the writing itself."

I straighten my back. *Time to stand behind my politics.* With a nod, I say, "I was. The Beta, Wyatt, was of great help."

Wyatt *has* been surprisingly helpful throughout our project. His insight has been nothing short of integral, and his perspective and knowledge of mythic history combined with my perspective and knowledge of human history is what made our proposal so solid and worthy of the witches' attention.

Odelia nods. "Well, then, why don't we get to it? Your proposal outlined a potential alliance and treaty that would benefit both sides greatly. I'm eager to discuss."

"Please, follow us," Camden responds.

Greta steps out of a corridor where she must've been waiting, and says, "I can take the young Princess back to her chambers."

I look down at Leisel to gauge her reaction. The conversations with the witches will probably be graphic since we'll need to discuss the war with vampires that is set to break out at any moment, and I don't want to draw her into the darker part of the world we live in any more than I already have.

"I have to go do my morning lessons," she tells me. "Will you read to me before bed tonight?"

I lean down to kiss the crown of her head, telling her, "Of course, sweet girl. Go on, now, and try not to give your tutor too much trouble." Apparently, my little sister has a tendency to correct the castle tutors and get into arguments with them over particular things—a combative trait she probably got from me.

I watch as Greta whisks Leisel away, then join Camden as he leads the witches up the staircase toward the room where we'll be holding official negotiations. The space is situated in a wing of the castle I haven't explored yet, with dark wooden walls and polished stone flooring. A rectangular table is set up in the center of the room, large enough to seat ten people, with ten accompanying cushioned chairs. On the table is a tray with a water jug and several crystal glasses, along with a stack of papers—the official treaty I hope to get signed today.

Camden takes a seat at the head of the table, I stand behind my chair to his right, and Wyatt sits to his left. Odelia seats herself at the other end of the table, with Claire on her left and Reyna slouching in the seat to her right. It doesn't take a genius to tell that Reyna is the least excited about their visit here, but it seems that Odelia has the final say, so she's the person I'll have to appeal to most.

I pick up the treaty with all the terms and amendments outlined from the center of the table and toss two copies in front of Camden and Wyatt. I then walk over to the other end of the table, setting copies in front of Odelia, Reyna, and Claire.

I return to my seat, smooth down my blouse, and say, "Let's get started, shall we?"

Chapter Forty-One

A tense silence stretches out as everyone takes in the treaty I've laid out in front of them. Camden, Wyatt, and I have all read it, but we all read it over again in silence. The witches seem engrossed in the words, leaning over the pages and whispering amongst each other periodically.

I read and reread the finely scripted words, searching for any errors there might be even though I've spent the last week pouring over these contents. I wasn't the person to physically write out the pages that are being read now; Wyatt took our final draft to the royal scribe, Oscar—the same shifter who delivered an invitation for dinner to me and Leisel back in Aesara—who then made several copies. The scribe's writing is much more elegant than mine, which is a plus, but it also makes me nervous that some final errors and edits may have been made while I wasn't overseeing.

I don't think people in this castle would undermine me, but then again, the only people in this castle I truly know are Wyatt, Camden, Leisel, Greta, and Cara. That makes me nervous. In fact, everything about this situation makes me nervous, even though I try not to show it; I've never been in a position of power like this before, with so many fates and lives depending on my actions.

I have no training in diplomacy, no formal education, really—I'm trying to learn as I go, which is intimidating. The many, *many* history books and textbooks I've read over the years are my only guide, but even so, that makes me feel ridiculously under qualified for the position I've put myself in. The fact that shifters don't deal with foreign relations outside of other shifter factions is even more frightening because I understand I'm the first of my kind, and any mistake I might make could be the end of any attempts at diplomacy and interspecies integration. The work I'm doing is *integral* for the future; I can't afford to screw it up.

After twenty minutes, Odelia clears her throat. She glances at Camden, then Wyatt, before settling her gaze on me. "I'm assuming this is your work?"

I motion at Wyatt with a hand. "I took advice, but yes, I did most of the drafting."

"Obviously," Reyna says. "Only a witch would be this decent to other witches. If the Beta here had done this on his own, I'm willing to bet there would be a quarter of the provisions and offers for witches and none for humans."

"If I'd been doing this on my own," Wyatt says with a toothy smile, "I wouldn't have gotten past the first draft. I certainly wouldn't have received authorization to parlay with you. Having a witch in the palace has lent us a great deal of perspective, which is why we've finally reached out to you."

I cast Wyatt a look of surprise. I knew Camden was behind this treaty being my triumph, but also hearing Wyatt admit so frankly that without me, my work, and my perspective we wouldn't be here is warming. We've been growing closer, so I knew we were on better terms than when I first arrived, but I didn't expect him to acknowledge my part in this so wholly—wolves are proud creatures by nature, so I assumed he'd want to take as much credit for himself as possible.

"After decades of hunting our kind for sport, yes, you've decided to try for an alliance," Claire remarks in the most pleasant yet icily tipped tone. "I'm sure it has nothing to do with the fact that the dark faye are in similar negotiations with the vampires regarding their own alliance, one that would put you at a massive disadvantage when they formally declare war."

I'm startled by the news that the faye have already started talks with the vampires—I hadn't heard anything of the sort. I look to Camden, trying to gauge his reaction, only to find that he appears completely unsurprised. This isn't new information to him. The fact that he withheld it from me sends a foreign pang of pain through my chest. I frown, annoyed at my own reaction; he had no reason or even means to tell me, as we haven't seen each other or spoken in the last week. Besides, this is a war-related issue, and outside of the diplomacy I'm heading, war is his department, not mine.

And yet, the knowledge that he didn't tell me something that pertains to me and my work still hurts, which means our bond is now on steroids. In the past, I would've been irritated at a development like this—annoyed *at* him, not hurt *by* him. That fact alone frustrates me.

As if he can sense my pain, which at this point he very well could, Camden turns to me. "I just received reports this morning, unconfirmed."

That's enough to settle the pain in my chest, which on its own is concerning. Now, after he marked me and we had sex, I seem to be far more susceptible to him than I ever was before. I don't like that one bit, but it looks like this is something I'll have to get used to.

"Consider this the confirmation," Odelia says calmly. "It's only a matter of time before the dark faye and vampires settle on an agreement."

"The noble faye will contest it—they still have all the power when it comes to the faye factions," Wyatt says.

Odelia shakes her head. "Not anymore. The dark faction has been pushing against their monarchy and nobles for quite some time, and joining with the vampires will be a straightforward way to distance themselves from the nobles."

I took the liberty of reading up on faye history and power structure in the last week, withdrawing several books from the library to help me. As far as I know, like shifters, faye live in a pyramid hierarchy structure that favors power. Noble faye are deemed noble both because their lineages are prone to greater magical power and because their families have been the ruling class for centuries in their own realms. The light faye and dark faye, however, are generally said to be matched with magical power, yet the light faye sit on top of the dark faye in the pyramid structure, mainly because the dark faye are prone to unpredictability and violence.

"Some members of our coven have had...run-ins with dark faye in the past," Odelia says. "We are by no means on good terms, and they've threatened wide-scale war with us before. The only thing holding them back from making good on their threats was the noble faye. If their alliance with the vampires liberates them from allegiance to the rulers, then there's little to stop them from coming after witches in tandem with shifters."

Ah. So *that's* why the witches were so quick to take this meeting—not only due to my proposal and incentives but because they're also on the edge of war. If the witches have to fight both vampires and dark faye alone, I imagine they'll sustain heavy losses. If they team up with us, those losses will likely be fewer for both our kinds. We'll also have a fighting chance against our opponents.

"What sort of run-ins?" Camden asks.

Odelia and Reyna share a look, communicating silently, before Reyna shrugs and says, "It's your call if you want to tell them. I'm for the alliance—much as I hate it, we need the wolves. And if that one truly has the black flame," she nods her head at me, "We all need her if we hope to survive. Plus, wolf shifters have the fealty of dragon and feline shifters—that's serious manpower we could use."

I listen to her speak with deepening interest as well as a healthy dose of apprehension. I already knew I'd be desirable for my power with black fire alone, untrained though it is, but hearing Reyna say it's their hope of survival tells me that there's some disturbingly powerful magic on the other side. As far as I know, there's nothing and no one that could withstand my black fire, aside from Camden due to our bond, but it's quite possible there are powers of equal measure among the dark faye—just ones I don't know about.

Odelia looks back at us. "Certain members of the dark faye have been breeding with vampires for the last two or three decades. The offspring are hybrids, formidable and *extremely* powerful. The dual nature of their species increases both their magical and vampiric abilities. Aside from that threat, the dark faye have taken to raiding outlying villages of witches and warlocks." She pauses to look at me and explains, "Warlocks are the male counterparts of witches, as a whole we're referred to as sorcerers." Then looking between Camden, Wyatt, and me. "We've lost an entire coven to the hybrids and dark faye, and sustained major losses in other covens. Four members of the Nightshade Coven have also been killed while on missions in foreign territories. They're a growing threat, and I'm quite sick of losing my witches to their heinous crimes. They kill for sport, and for *fun*, and they do not give quick or pleasant deaths."

Shit. I knew hybrids were possible—after all, Claude is one—but I didn't even think that other species could create them. The way Odelia describes the crossbreeds of vampires and dark faye...I imagine they'd have some magical abilities that *could* rival my fire. It's no wonder the witches are seeking alliances and further protection.

Odelia inhales a deep breath. "We will agree to your treaty if you're willing to add a few amendments."

I can't make that call on my own. I look to Camden, who inclines his head in agreement.

I say to Odelia, "Name them."

Staring at Camden, she replies, "First of all, send pack warriors to our territories. We have magical provisions in place to keep out invaders, but manpower from shifters will present a united front and work as a deterrent. In return, I'll send some of my girls to ward your territories." She looks at me. "The wards you constructed around the castle are excellent, very beautiful work, but they could use some improvements to make them entirely foolproof." Back to Camden, "Next, you will send the two witches in your care to my coven so I can personally help teach and train them."

Wyatt growls, "No."

Camden snaps, "Abso*lutely* not."

Claire gives Wyatt a narrowed-eyed look. "Why do *you* care so much?"

"Because aside from Sierra being my queen, Leisel happens to be my mate. We're not just sending either of them off," Wyatt responds shortly.

The three witches exchange a long, contemplative glance, processing the new tidbit of information.

Finally, Reyna gives a snort. "Wolves and their goddamn possessiveness. My high priestess isn't saying to give up your mates for long stretches of time, just to send them to us periodically for lessons. They've been deprived of their own kind for their entire lives. That will have left their education in the magical arts dismal. Witches should stick with witches—that's the best way to grow power. Besides, don't you want them to have a place where they're accepted entirely for who they are?"

Her words spark a full-body wave of excitement. I've been wanting to ask if I can learn from witches, but prioritized these negotiations; hearing that Odelia, who's obviously an *extraordinarily* powerful high priestess, wishes to train me is electrifying. I know my magical education is sorely lacking, as is Leisel's, mainly because we only had a limited number of books to learn from and nobody to properly teach us. My mother could only teach me so much as her magic was latent; Leisel only had me.

Camden inhales a deep, calming breath, then says in a more steady tone, "Your territories are far from the capital—at least a week's ride by horseback if one rides all day and all night. I'm not comfortable sending my mate away for such long stretches of time."

Claire waves a dismissive hand. "We'll open up a portal so transport is instantaneous, the same way we did for your liaison. Take the deal, wolf. Can't you see your mate's excitement at the prospect?"

Camden looks at me, eyes running over my expression. I let him see my hope and excitement, and surprisingly, that seems to soften him. I think back to Wyatt's words in our conversation last night, the tidbit of advice he gave me regarding his older brother; *there's little he won't do for your happiness.*

"Fine," Camden says to Odelia, "I'll agree to allow you to train my mate and her sister, as long as you agree to assure their protection above all, and understand that if *any* harm befalls them, you will be answering to two very strong, very pissed-off wolves."

"Was that a threat?" Reyna questions with a toothy smile, and she actually sounds *excited* at the prospect, which makes me speculate more and more that this one's slaughter-happy when it comes to conflict.

"A fact," Camden clarifies. "You should know there's no end to the protective instincts we wolves have toward our mates."

Odelia nods, unconcerned. "I'll personally see to their protection. Will you send us warriors?"

Camden inclines his head. "Yes. I'll arrange the particulars today."

Looking satisfied, Odelia says, "One more amendment; I want shifters and witches to travel to human villages together and start with humanitarian work. Humans are the most susceptible to attacks, and the dark faye and vampires may end up wiping them all out simply for fun. They've suffered enough under the reign of mythics; it's time we return some of their dignity."

"Agreed," I say.

The reason I didn't ask for more aid for humans in the treaty is because I didn't think anyone would care enough to go for it; it's refreshing that the witches seem to care about *all* life deeply, not just the lives of their own.

"I'll forewarn you," Claire adds in, "if the wolves you send us step a toe out of line or get aggressive towards our witches, I'll drown them in lava."

There's a long pause, then Wyatt says in a stunned voice, "Hold on a fucking second, *you're* the volcano witch?"

Volcano witch? And what's that flicker of nervous recognition in Wyatt's expression as he stares at the redheaded witch? I look at Claire, who's a tiny harmless-looking thing despite the magical power radiating off of her like a furnace.

I clear my throat. "Can someone fill me in on whatever it is I seem to be missing?"

"If Wyatt's suspicion is true, Claire once erupted a volcano on a pack of shifters, killing every one of them," Camden tells me.

"A pack of *rogue* shifters who pillaged and raped the village where I grew up, killing my parents along with every other witch and warlock there," Claire says with an icy smile. "I was the sole survivor. Naturally, I saw fit to return the destructive favor. It's not *my* fault I'm better at setting homes on fire than they were."

"You call *erupting* a *volcano* that was previously dormant for *thousands of years* setting a fire?" Wyatt asks.

Claire gives a delicate shrug. "Fire, lava, either way, the result is the same: burning to death. I'm a strong advocate of an eye for an eye. At least the way I did it ensured quick deaths; the rogue shifters took pleasure in the suffering they wrought in my village."

"I heard of the conflict from my father," Camden interjects. "It was several decades back, if I recall correctly. The rogue pack was in conflict with the crown, but the Rockwell Pack was fighting rebellions on multiple fronts at the time, so we didn't have the resources to track a small group of outliers." He pauses, turning his gaze on Claire. "It's good you took care of them, less good that they didn't suffer. Any person who commits crimes of that caliber against *any* being deserves a lengthy bout of torture before death."

The conviction with which Camden speaks surprises me. Part of me expected him to defend shifters, regardless of their crimes; apparently, he has a stronger moral compass than I expected. I have to admit, I like that fact a *lot*. I'm also in complete agreement with him and find myself admiring Claire. I don't know the entirety of that particular story, as I don't know Claire's whole story, but if her response to losing her family and home was to return the favor on her enemies in a truly *spectacular* magical fashion...well, that's fucking awesome.

To hear that there are witches with powers such as making a dormant volcano erupt...it's slightly disconcerting, but mainly, it gives more fuel to the fact that shifters should be allied with them rather than hold them at a distance out of fear.

"Would you have done differently to a group of people who killed everyone you loved and left you for dead?" Reyna asks Wyatt in a dangerous purr.

"If I had that ability, I'd have used it," Wyatt instantly responds. "As is, I would track the perpetrators, spend a few months enjoying their screams of pain, and *then* kill them. Please don't mistake my surprise for condemnation; I agree with my brother that Claire gave them the easy way out."

Claire shrugs again. "I was weak, half-starved, and didn't have very good control over my powers. It was vengeance that kept me alive long enough to do what I did."

"Good thing, too," Reyna chips in. "That shockwave of magic you let out led us straight to you."

"Back to the matter at hand," Odelia interjects. She snaps her fingers, and I feel a small wave of some sort of magic travel over the room, latching onto the papers of the treaty in front of each person.

Curious, I flip through the pages, and find that the amendments and terms we just discussed were added with nothing more than a snap of Odelia's fingers and a thought. No spoken spell, no ritual...while editing words onto a page seems pretty small in the abstract sense, in reality, there's a lot of intricacy to it. Creating ink where there was none, matching the script to the writing already on the page...her little trick serves the dual purpose of adding in what we discussed, and showing off how casually she can use magic.

Wyatt and Camden also look surprised as they flip through their papers, reading the new additions. Once we're done, I say, "Everything appears to be in order. Are we ready to sign?"

Chapter Forty-Two

The treaty requires two signatures of the leaders of each nation—witches and shifter wolves—as well as a witness on both sides as a second.

"I believe we are ready," Odelia says. "If I might, I'd like to suggest forgoing the traditional signatures in ink, and instead using signatures that are magically binding so that neither side can break the treaty."

Camden arches an eyebrow. "You don't trust us?"

"I trust Sierra—she's one of ours and has proven her loyalty just through the wording of this treaty," Odelia says. "You, however, I do not trust entirely, and I hope you can understand why. I've lost hundreds—*thousands*—of my witches to the mercy of shifters."

Camden seems irritated by the doubt of his integrity—typical wolf pride. Still, instead of being combative, I choose to use persuasion. I place a hand on his shoulder and say softly, "The humans had an old saying; Rome wasn't built in a day. Likewise, trust will not be built in a day. You can't fault them for wariness."

Camden inhales deeply, takes my hand in his, and places it on his lap, then gives the witches a nod. "Fine. What will the magical signature entail?"

"You need to sign your names in blood—we have a quill that draws blood from the wielder's body without inflicting wounds," Odelia responds. "Then I'll do a simple spell that'll bind your signatures and blood to the treaty. Should it be broken by any of the signers, the blood in your body will boil and your veins and arteries will split until you hemorrhage to death."

"A good deterrent to keep you wolves honest," Reyna adds.

"Does it really need to be that...deadly?" Wyatt asks.

"Do you intend to break your word?" Claire volleys back. "If not, then this shouldn't be a problem. Blood bindings on contracts are very standard among sorcerers."

It'll probably be best if I take the initiative here. If I sign, Cam might feel more inclined to sign as well. "Sounds like a good way to hold everyone accountable. I'm on board. Where's the quilt?"

Reyna does a series of hand gestures above the table, and with them, I feel a dose of magic radiate from her, like an invisible blanket that settles over the room. That magical energy then condenses and contracts until a feathered quill appears in the palm of her hand. "Which copy will we all be signing?"

"Mine," I say since my copy is considered the official one.

Reyna slides the quill across the table to me, and I let go of Camden's hand under the table to pick it up, examining the shimmery quality of the blue feather. I flip to the last page of my contract where my signature will be next to my printed full name, position the quill over the page, before pressing it to the paper, and feel a small pressure on my arm as I glide the quill across the page—not pain, just a strange tugging sensation—and watch with no small sense of wonder as red ink, *blood*, appears on the page. As soon as I'm done, the blood dries. Odelia murmurs a few words in a language I'm unfamiliar with, and my signature on the page takes on a shimmery, shiny quality.

"The first signature has been bound," she says.

I slide the stack of papers and pen over to Camden, who repeats my actions, a slight frown marring his features. Once his signature has been bound, Odelia and Reyna add theirs.

A flush of pride and pleasure travels through me that my objective for today has been completed, and for the first time in known history, witches and shifters will work alongside each other for the greater good.

"Excellent," Odelia says. "Now, if you wolves wouldn't mind, I'd like a moment alone with Sierra to discuss her forthcoming training."

Camden looks like he's going to object, but I murmur to him, "Please, let us. They're no threat to me or any of us; the treaty guarantees it."

Camden's nostrils flare as he inhales, but then, he gives me a single, tense nod. "Fine. We'll be waiting outside."

Camden and Wyatt clear out of the war room, leaving me alone with the three witches, all of whom stare at me with varying levels of interest. I imagine my interest in them matches, if not supersedes, their interest in me; I might be one of a kind with the ability to wield black flames, but they've lived with witches their whole lives, and this is my first time meeting one outside of my family.

"Now that the wolves are out of the way, I'd like to get to know you a little bit," Odelia says. "I was very excited to hear of your existence, and saddened to know you grew up without support from your own kind. Can I ask you a few questions?"

"Of course," I reply. "As long as you're okay shouldering the copious amounts of questions I'll have for you."

Odelia smiles indulgently. "I imagine there's much you're eager to learn. I'll try to answer as many questions as I can. You grew up in Aesara?"

I incline my head. "Yes. I raised my little sister, Leisel, there on a farm."

Odelia nods pensively. "We visited Aesara a few times over the years, going around local clinics to help with healing. The destructiveness shifters wreaked with their changes was felt most heavily by humans."

"The few who survived," Reyna adds in grimly.

That sends my mood plummeting. I don't like the reminder that shifters are at fault for most of the horror that was brought upon humanity, especially when I'm desperately trying to change my views of them for the sake of Leisel's and my survival in this culture.

"My mother died giving birth to Leisel because there wasn't any proper medical care available," I admit. "My father died from cancer a year before that. I'd have killed to have your coven around to help save them."

Reyna's eyes soften. "If we'd have known there were witches in Aesara, *especially* earthly ones, we'd have been there to help."

Odelia says, "I thought I felt faint traces of magic when we passed through in the last few decades, but I couldn't be sure. You did very well hiding yourself away."

"I was afraid of the persecution that accompanied being a person with magic in a village of humans that despised magical beings," I say. "Each time I heard you were passing through, I'd hide with Leisel on our farm." Then, more quietly, "I wish I hadn't."

"That's in the past," Odelia responds firmly. "Right now, we look to the future. Now that we know of your existence, we can protect you. Especially with your condition, I expect you'll need more magical aid the farther along you get—interspecies pregnancies are very rare and by all accounts exceedingly difficult."

I fall entirely still as her words wash over me, unable to process them entirely. My condition? *Interspecies pregnancies?* I'm not...I couldn't be—

I think back to a week ago when I succumbed to my desires and slept with Camden. Reaching my hand up to the juncture where my neck meets my shoulder, I run my fingers over the scar of Camden's bite that permanently sits on my skin. He didn't warn me before marking me, and I was in the throes of so much pleasure I didn't have the presence of mind to stop or even be mad at him. The next morning, he was so smooth, so articulate, I didn't feel it was worth it to hold onto my anger.

I assumed that, because my bond with Camden wasn't fully complete yet, there was no chance of pregnancy, and I didn't bother to double-check because he told me I wasn't at risk when I asked him about it the morning after we slept together.

Shit.

I force myself to recall the few texts I've managed to get my hands on about mate bonds. There was nothing available in the library that spoke on negatively impacting them, but there were two books that helped explain them.

In one book, there was a chapter describing the necessities between mates for pregnancy to become possible. I squeeze my eyes shut and try to remember the specific passage that talked about pregnancy with shifter mates; after an intense moment of concentration, I recall the exact words, scrawled on an old, yellowed page: *for a seed to take root, the pair must be bound by marks with a consummated, if not complete, bond connecting them.*

It was also said that full moons are hyper-fertile times for wolves.

That night was a full moon. Camden marked me. He came inside me. I've been so distracted preparing for our meeting with the witches,

I didn't have time to dwell on the horrific possibility of pregnancy; it didn't even cross my mind, especially since he *told me I wasn't at risk.*

Reyna makes a faint sound in the back of her throat. "Oh, fuck. That bastard Alpha didn't even *tell* you, did he?" She turns to Claire who's staring at me with wide-eyed shock and barks, "Make a sound barrier, *now!*"

Claire shoots out of her seat and walks the perimeter of the room, murmuring quiet chants that cause a faint shimmering shield to form in front of the walls and doors. Meanwhile, my mind spirals further and further into despair.

"How do you know? How can you be sure?" I whisper.

"I can sense the presence of life," Odelia responds. "That includes pregnancies, even in their earliest stages." She pauses. "Sierra, did he...force this on you?"

Tears well in my eyes as the full weight of the situation washes over me. I'm pregnant, with Camden's child, after one night of stupid sex. A royal heir. Something that will permanently bind me to the Alpha King. He didn't force *himself* on me, but in a sense...he did force this pregnancy on me. He had to have known the possibility and he didn't fucking tell me. In fact, he outright lied to me about it. *Gods,* that hurts. I thought we were past the lies, deceit, and trickery in our relationship; evidently, I was dead wrong.

I should've trusted my mothers' words, telling me that all shifters are fucking monsters. She was right. I allowed myself to forget that for a moment, in favor of trying to better the lives of humans and work with shifters, and here's where it landed me.

"He...he didn't force the sex, but he didn't tell me the possible outcomes," I manage through numb lips. "When I asked if I was at risk for pregnancy, he said no. He lied to me."

Odelia exchanges a grim glance with Reyna.

"When did you have intercourse?" Reyna asks me. "Wait, let me guess...on the blood moon that occurred a week ago?"

I nod stiffly, feeling like there's ice coursing through my veins. An awful sensation takes up residence in my chest, feeling like a lead weight that constricts my breathing. I stand from my seat abruptly and start pacing back and forth in front of the table, my thoughts a scrambled mess of, *Oh gods oh fuck oh gods what have I gotten myself into?*

"*Fucking shifters,*" Reyna shakes her head. "And we just pledged our resources to them in the upcoming war. Un-*fucking*-believable." She turns to Odelia. "How do we get out of the treaty?"

Odelia thinks for several moments, eyes fixed on me, while I retreat further into a shell of terror that feels like it swallows me whole. My hands move down to clutch my stomach, which will soon swell with the presence of a life I did not ask for or even know I was at risk of carrying. I may have been a de facto mother since I was fourteen, but that was by choice. I fell in love with Leisel the moment I saw her, I wanted—*needed*—to raise and nurture and care for her. This thing inside of me...it was conceived in a bout of trickery.

"Blood moons are hyper-fertile times for witches," Odelia tells me. "They often send witches into our equivalent of heat—a time when we're *very* sexually active. With you marked and your bond consummated, it was just about guaranteed you'd get pregnant."

"Which Camden knew," I say monotonously.

She nods. "There's no way he didn't." After a pause, she says to Reyna, "We won't break the treaty. Besides it being magically binding to both parties, it's also too beneficial. But we also won't leave a sister witch in need." Her eyes move back to me, and she says, "Have a seat, Sierra. There's a way out of this. A difficult way, but...you won't have to give birth to a mutt you didn't expect or ask for."

Feeling shaken to my very core, I drop into the nearest chair and run my hands through my hair, feeling like I'm on the verge of losing my mind. This is all just too much to take in.

"What do you mean?" I ask.

Odelia vacates her seat, pulls up a chair beside me, and tells me, "Witches hold all life as sacred. It's why we help humans in need, even if we're not particular fans of the way they nearly destroyed this planet. What's growing inside you right now, though, isn't yet classed a life—it's just a cluster of cells. I can only sense it because I'm especially gifted in this area."

Reyna drops into another chair, adding in, "It'll only be considered a life once there's a heartbeat, which usually happens at the end of the fourth week of pregnancy. That's also when a soul starts to form. For witches who are careless with birth control and need to end unwanted pregnancies before they really start to develop...there is an elixir that'll cleanse your womb. It'll be very painful, but it'll take care of your problem."

Those words wash over me, offering an escape from my predicament, from the madness that was the cause of it; offering me a way out where I won't be trapped. For a moment, I consider it. I consider taking care of the problem before it actually becomes a fully formed problem. I consider Reyna's words, indicating that a lack of soul is equivalent to a lack of life.

A wave of disgust washes over me, poignant and pungent and nearly suffocating. *No, I can't do something like that.* Whether or not I *asked* for this pregnancy, it is indeed a pregnancy; it requires intervention to be rid of. If I take the elixir, I'll still be preventing a life, which in my mind is equivalent to killing an innocent. I've learned recently that I have no compunction with killing to protect, but that extends to people who threaten me or my sister and therefore *deserve* death.

This thing inside me that will soon become a child does not deserve to be destroyed, no matter my sentiments on how I got pregnant.

I shake my head slowly, from side to side. "I can't do that—I *won't* do that."

Odelia and Reyna exchange a look.

Claire, dropping into a seat across from me, says, "It's your funeral."

"Fucking probably," I snap, "but I can't terminate something that has potential for a life and soul. This child has my absolute protection."

Odelia holds up a hand, giving Claire a censuring look over her shoulder. She turns back to me and says, "That's your choice, and our coven always respects the choices of its individual members. If you plan to keep it, you need to understand the implications and complexities attached. Witches and shifters have different timelines for pregnancies; shifters are generally pregnant for six months before giving birth, while witches are usually pregnant for ten. That might be different with earthly witches, which I'll look into. There have only been a handful of interspecies pregnancies between shifters and witches *ever*, so I'll need to find and read up on those cases before I can properly educate you as to what to expect."

"You should come with us," Reyna adds in. "We can protect and care for you in a way that the wolves won't be equipped to."

I tug at my hair, feeling like my sanity's slowly slipping away from me. I don't know what to do right now or where to turn to, and frankly, I can see that I'm not in the right mindset to make any decisions. Before deciding my next steps, I need to *calm down*, and calming down requires getting away from this castle and into nature. Forests and mountains are a second home to me; they ground me and have always helped me calm even in the most difficult circumstances.

"Not right now," I mumble. "I can't *think straight* right now. I need...time. Time to figure out what to do."

Odelia reaches out and places a hand on my arm. "That's perfectly understandable; you've just gotten quite the shock. How about this: we'll leave you with a sigil and spell that, when drawn in blood on a mirror, turns the mirror into a portal directly to our coven house. Take whatever time you need, and if you decide to leave this place, know that you have a safe haven with us. We'd never leave one of our own without the proper support."

Even though I feel like I'm spinning out, I still have the presence of mind to ask, "Will the spell work with the wards I've put up around the castle?"

Odelia nods. "Yes. As long as you're the one to draw the sigil and say the spell, yes. Should you feel you need to get away from here, use it. You and your sister will be safe with us."

Struck with a new thought, I ask, "Who else could've known about my pregnancy?"

"Every person in this castle," Reyna replies. "Shifters have an excellent sense of smell; they'd have known you conceived within two days."

Which means the betrayals are on all fronts, and the blows just keep coming. I thought Wyatt was better than his brother; clearly, I was dead fucking wrong about that too. Any sentiment of kindness I might have been feeling for him, any acceptance of him in Leisel's life, simply evaporates. Once again, my mother's words haunt me: *all shifters are monsters.* How right she was, only I was too swept up in royal life and the possibility of making a better world to see it.

I give my head a shake. I need to get out of here and into nature so I can *think* and figure out exactly what I'm going to do. Right now, rational thought eludes me; I feel like I'm being pulled in a million different directions, and my heart feels like it's breaking.

I force myself to say, "Thank you for your visit and offer of help. While I think about what to do, is there anything else I should know about this...pregnancy?"

"The biggest issue witches generally experience is fluctuation in magical abilities," Claire says. "Dips and surges in power are very common—at times you might find it impossible to call on your magic, but at other times you'll have surges that can make your powers burst forward without being summoned. The best way to avoid that is to keep yourself calm; stress and anxiety are triggers to both surges and reductions."

Considering I'm in a place that has already proven to be stressful, and will probably grow even more so, it seems likely I'll struggle especially with the magical aspect of pregnancy. Yet another thing I'll need to consider.

Odelia, sensing that I need my space, nods. "Of course, if you need us, you know how to get to us. Until then...I look forward to the next time we meet, Sierra. It's truly been a pleasure."

Chapter Forty-Three

By some miracle, I manage to act semi-normal as I join Camden and Wyatt to escort the witches out of the castle, exchanging final pleasantries before watching them open a magical portal and disappear. I just might do the same…but not yet, not before I've thought everything through properly. We gave the witches a brief tour of the palace before seeing them off and I used the opportunity to stash the spell Odelia wrote down for me in my room, so I have a way out should I choose to use it.

Standing in the courtyard under the bright sun, I stare at the castle grounds stretching in front of me. On the far left, I see a tree line that leads into the forest surrounding the castle, which is where I need to be right now.

Camden curves an arm around my waist, pulling me close to him. I barely manage to hide my flinch, and it's a struggle not to shove him away and yell at him, but I'm not ready to talk about the information I just received yet. I can't hash this out now. I'm not in the right frame of mind. Camden has earned himself quite the shouting match, but I need to be in peak mental condition for that, not discombobulated and frazzled to the extreme.

I force a smile onto my lips as I look up at him, my eyes locking with his icy ones. I gave this man a certain amount of trust along with my *body*, and he used it to all but destroy me. How can I live with that, with *him*, knowing his deceit?

Camden's brows furrow as he looks over me. "What's wrong? I can feel your turmoil through the bond. I have been for the last little while but didn't want to say anything in front of the witches."

Fuck. I hadn't considered that the bond is a two-way street; we both get slivers of each other's emotions. I don't want him to get a whiff of something being off or put together the fact that I found out about his sordid plan prematurely—not until I've decided whether I'm staying here or taking asylum with the witches. *What to say that'll throw him off my trail?*

Thinking on the spot, I tell him, "I'm okay. We just...ended up talking about my parents a bit, which tends to put me in a bad mood. I think I'm going to take a walk, enjoy the fresh air, and clear my mind."

Camden reaches out to tuck a few strands of hair behind my ear. "I'll come with you."

No. No, that'll defeat the entire point of getting away from him and into my natural element so I can do some serious thinking about my future.

"I'd like to be alone for a while," I say.

Camden looks like he'll protest further, but Wyatt interrupts. "Come on, Cam. Let your mate have her space. She's safe here, no harm can befall her."

Yes, I am safe within the confines of the wards I put up—safe from any outsiders, but not safe from those who live in the castle. Presently, the inhabitants within the shield are the greatest threat to me, which is why I need to get out of it, at least for a little while. The wards don't extend to the forest, but it's broad daylight, and I know castle guards are patrolling the woods; I doubt any harm can come to me there.

Camden's hand flexes on my waist, and he stares at me for several long moments with furrowed brows. Finally, he releases me. "Night-fall's in about two hours—be back before then and stay in the pro-tected land within the shield."

"Of course," I say simply, with no intention of actually following his instructions. Considering the magnitude of his deceit, I don't feel bad whatsoever having some lies of my own.

Looking reluctant, Camden gives me a single nod and releases me. Wyatt claps his brother on the shoulder and says, "Come on, we should get the ball rolling to uphold our end of the treaty."

I watch as they disappear inside, then start my trek across the grounds, feeling like I'm in a haze. A haze of fear, anger, but most of all, pain. So much pain it feels like it tightens my throat and suffo-cates me slowly. I feel any seeds of affection that had been forming for them—for Camden in a romantic way and for Wyatt almost as a sibling—start to evaporate. They lied to me in an unforgivable, irrefutable way; literally tried and succeeded in *entrapping me*.

In my anger, for a brief moment, I consider finding a way to sabo-tage them; to sabotage the treaty. Odelia said it was magically binding to both parties, but surely there must be *some* way to get out of it. I immediately berate myself for my line of thinking—no matter how enraged I am with Camden, the treaty was the right thing, especially with the conflicts that I found out have been occurring between the witches and dark faye for quite some time now. They deserve the aid they'll be getting. And despite my current vitriol towards the royal family, my time here has gone to show that not all shifters are monsters. The ones who kept the truth from me are monstrous, but I can't fault the many for the actions of the few. Shifter children, along with other innocents, don't deserve to suffer and die in the upcoming war.

I'm about to quite possibly ruin my life in protection of an innocent hybrid life—I can't very well do that while withdrawing needed protection from other innocents.

As I approach the edge of the warding shield I created with the help of Claude not too long ago, I cast a quick glance around to see if there's anyone who might stop me. I see guards patrolling the land in the distance, but none of them appear to be coming in my direction or following me. Releasing a sigh of relief, I step over the boundary, feeling a small wave of magic wash over me as I do. Then, quickening my stride, I walk the remaining distance until I break through the tree line of the forest.

Lush trees tower over me, the sounds of birds chirping along with insects buzzing surround me, and the bright sun is dimmed through the thick leaves. Instantly, a sense of calm washes over me, easing my sporadic thoughts and racing heart. Slowing down to a leisurely pace, I navigate around bushes, shrubs, and trunks, heading deeper into the forest. Although turmoil still weighs heavily on me, the simple act of being in nature serves as a huge relief, and I allow myself to think about what I should do next.

Staying in the castle with Camden after his betrayal feels fundamentally wrong, but so does leaving while I'm pregnant with his child. That would be robbing him of something precious. Then again...hasn't he just robbed *me* of something precious? A sense of generalized safety and the trust that I'd slowly started to build in him has disappeared. If I stay, how can I ever trust him again? How can I keep rational while knowing he's lied to me and hurt me?

I let out a long sigh. In the distance, I hear rushing water, probably coming from a river or creek. I follow the noise until I emerge on the bank of a riverbed, showcasing a lovely view of a small, rushing creek. Sunlight filters through the openings in the trees above, glinting off the crystalline water. The riverbed is covered in grains of sand, stones, and larger boulders. I spot a deer not far away, lazily lapping at the water—the deer looks up, notices me emerging onto the bank, and trots off back into the forest.

I climb one of the larger boulders bordering the water, perch on top of it cross-legged, and drop my head into my hands with a small groan. I'm exhausted from the events of today; on the heels of my rage at Camden, Wyatt, and every person in the castle who kept a very important truth from me comes a feeling of bone-deep tiredness.

I lift my head and allow my hands to roam down to my stomach. It's flat now, but it'll soon swell with the presence of a life. A life that I did not ask for, granted, but one I'm already feeling protective of. No matter what I decide to do, my priority is to protect the child growing within me.

Quietly, I murmur, "I'll protect you, I promise. You might not have been expected, but you *will* be loved. Dearly." I feel faintly like I'm losing my mind talking to a fetus so young it's not yet classed as a life by witches, but at the same time, the words give me a strength and conviction that's been absent. I rub my palm back and forth over my abdomen. "You'll have the best big sister in the world too. Leisel loves babies; she'll be thrilled to have you." At least I'm no stranger to caring for infants; if I could raise Leisel at fourteen, there's no reason I wouldn't be able to care for my own child at twenty-three.

I think back to Odelia's words on the complexity of interspecies pregnancies. Because of that alone, I'm feeling inclined to accept her offer of safe haven and go to her. That's not to mention the depth of betrayal I've just experienced at Camden's hands; I don't *want* to be near him right now. In fact, I can barely stand the thought of it.

The complication there is the fact that our bond is now mostly complete—I've been marked and our bond has been consummated, which means distance from him isn't a long-term solution, but it could be an effective short-term one. I'll need to talk to Leisel and find out if she's okay with leaving, but I think it's safe to assume she will be. Besides, with our own kind, we'll have access to a wealth of information, knowledge, and education we previously couldn't have fathomed.

I give a nod, feeling resolved in my course of action. I'll head back to the castle, and then later tonight I'll open a portal to get away from here, even if only for a little while. Right now, anything sounds preferable to staying near Camden. I slowly climb off the boulder, then squat in front of the creek and splash my face with fresh water.

The sounds of several pairs of footsteps draw my attention to the tree line, and I stand and spin around to face it. My heart speeds up when I see three males emerge. They're dressed in tattered clothing that hints at homelessness. Their faces are unkempt and dirt-streaked, with overgrown shaggy beards. The energy emanating from them tells me they're shifters, but there's something erratic about that energy that makes me uneasy.

All three regard me with expressions ranging from lust to menace, and I immediately understand that they are not people whose company it's safe to be in.

"What do we have here?" one of them, a blond with shoulder-length, greasy hair asks with a lascivious grin that makes me uncomfortable. His eyes roam my body head to toe, raising the hairs on my arms.

The one beside him, with a bald head and the longest beard of the three, says, "Feels like a human." In a taunting tone, he goes on,

"Whatcha doin' in these parts, girly? Don't you know it ain't safe to wander the woods alone?"

Trying to keep the nerves out of my voice, I straighten and say, "I'm passing through, just like you. Not looking for any trouble."

The man in front of the three, a male with black hair and equally black eyes, says, "This isn't just a human, boys. Flaming red hair and golden eyes—that's the fuckin' *Queen*. The Earth witch—the one who just invited *witches* into Kinrith, endangering our entire kind."

Shit.

Chapter Forty-Four

I freeze, knowing I am in very precarious waters right now and any move I make has the potential to not only harm me but the life growing within me. *Gods, why was I stupid enough to leave the safety of the wards around the castle?* Especially at a time like this? I know the answer; I was so disgruntled I needed to get into nature, and now that might cost me greatly.

These men clearly haven't accosted me for any wholesome reasons. From the way they're looking at me, especially after the black-haired one told them who I actually am, it appears they want to tear me to shreds or worse.

The bald one, eyes glittering with menace, says, "Her being the King's mate is enough of a danger, then she had to go and invite even more of those vermin like her here. You wanna get all shifters killed, girl?"

Looks like not everyone's on board with the alliance between witches and shifters. That's something I can unpack at another time, once I've gotten myself out of this situation.

Dark Hair takes a few steps forward, followed by the other two. I can't step back or I'll fall into the slippery creek, so I stay in place and summon my flame to the surface, preparing for the worst-case scenario; one in which I destroy them with the help of my fire to protect myself, then sprint back to warded grounds.

I hold a hand out in front of me and say, "Stay right there. If you've heard of me, you've heard what I can do. Don't make me hurt you." If I *can* get out of this without taking life, I'd prefer to. I'm not a particularly kill-happy person—to me, killing is a last resort.

Dark Hair scoffs, saying, "The royals like to exaggerate to protect themselves from rogues like us. See, I don't think you've got half the power they say you do."

Rogues like us. His casual use of that phrase makes me realize exactly what the strange, erratic energy I sensed from them is: the mark of a rogue. My thoughts flick back to Claire who was a victim of a rogue attack that destroyed her home and killed the inhabitants of her village. I can't let such a fate befall me; I won't. There's too much at stake, *especially* now. Now, I don't just have Leisel to protect, I also have the baby inside me.

If these rogues don't believe me, then they'll feel free to do whatever they wish with me. I draw forward my flame, ready to put an end to this before it can even begin. To my shock, nothing happens. I feel my fire rising within me until it's right below the surface of my skin, but for some reason, it's unable to break that surface and come forward.

Oh, fuck. Odelia warned me that my magic would be erratic; I just didn't expect that to happen so soon. After all, I'm currently a week pregnant—I haven't felt any other symptoms of pregnancy, so I hadn't assumed I would run into magical problems just yet. *Shit, shit, shit.*

There aren't any patrolling guards in sight, which means it's up to me to figure a way out of this. My eyes flick to the forest, towards the direction of the castle. Though I can't see it, I know where it lies. Even in my frazzled state earlier, I didn't allow myself to lose my sense of direction—growing up in and around forests has given me a good internal compass. *Maybe if I make a break for it, I can outrun them?*

It's worth a shot, and my only option without the cooperation of my magic. I launch into a sprint to the left of where the rogues stand, going as fast as I possibly can. I hear the rogues giving chase behind me as I *literally* run for my life, fueled by fear and determination like I've never felt before. I only manage a couple of steps into the forest before a pair of thick, dirty arms close around my waist and slam me face-first against the trunk of the nearest tree, dazing me.

Despite that, I struggle with all of my might, trying to dislodge whoever grabbed me, kicking and elbowing, even throwing my head back to try to head-butt whichever one of them grabbed me. None of it works, and no matter how many times I call upon my fire, it doesn't come.

The shifter holding me spins me around and slams me against the trunk of the tree again. My head bounces off the wood, and a wave of terrible dizziness washes over me, blurring my vision. I blink several times to clear it, identifying my assailant as Dark Hair, who strikes me as the most dangerous of the three. He grins down at me, baring a row of yellow teeth.

"What should I do with you now?" he asks, wrapping a filthy hand around my throat to pin me in place.

I glimpse the two others standing behind him, exchanging looks of excitement. I don't want to find out what these rogues will do to me because if Claire's story is indicative of anything, it'll go something along the lines of rape and then murder. Especially if they already view me hostilely for my connection with the witches, and for being a witch myself.

"Let me go," I manage to say, clutching at the hand holding my throat. "If you release me, you'll be rich men until the end of your days." That much is probably true—I imagine I could fetch a very handsome price. There's little Camden wouldn't do to ensure my safety, especially now that I carry his heir.

The shifter shakes his head. "I don't think so. I don't care about money but what I *do* care about is some earthly witch inviting the enemy to us. You know how hard it is to survive on our own? It'll only get worse if there are witches around and witches like *you* in the castle."

He inhales deeply, nostrils flaring, and then goes still. Ice-cold fear washes over me as his eyes slowly travel down to my stomach, and I realize he just scented my pregnancy. The new gleam of excitement in his eyes confirms it.

"Well, now, looks like we've got ourselves *two* royals here," he sneers, bringing his free hand down to rest on top of my stomach. His expression morphs into one drenched with anger, teeth bared as his hand digs into the flesh of my torso. "You think you can bring *another* abomination into this world? A fuckin' *hybrid?*"

I kick out, trying to dislodge him, desperation to get out of here overwhelming me. The only effect that has is for the shifter to shift his stance forward, using his entire body to pin me tightly to the wood at my back. Again, I call to my fire, and again, nothing happens. Tears spark in my eyes as I wriggle and struggle to no avail.

"I don't think so," Dark Hair says, just as I feel the nails digging into my stomach lengthen into claws.

My eyes widen with terror and I let out a scream as those claws puncture my flesh, digging deep inside of me, sending stabs of agonizing, burning pain all throughout my midsection. He twists his hand, and I *feel* his claws slicing through my internal organs like they're butter. The agony spreads through my entire body, robbing me of breath and making me panic like I never have before. *He's trying to cut the fetus right out of me.*

Black fires *bursts* from me, breaking the barrier of my skin and traveling to Dark Hair with lightning speed, but I fear it's too little too late. In a matter of seconds, it consumes him entirely, leaving nothing in his wake. I drop to my knees with another cry of agony, my vision swimming as blood pours from my stomach, creating a dark puddle in front of me.

The two remaining shifters exchange looks of absolute shock, before taking off running away from me in opposite directions. The bald one disappears through a thick collection of greenery, but blondie isn't quite so fast. Fueled by pain and *so much* rage, anger like I've never felt before, I use the last of my remaining strength to hold out my hand and direct my fire to the blonde before he can make it out of my line of sight. My black flame scorches a path along the forest ground, traveling much faster than the rogue can. It creates a deafening racket, crackling and hissing and popping as it rages.

He lets out a yell of pain as the fire reaches him, licking at his heels before climbing up his legs, circling around his waist, and then enveloping him fully in a golden-black shroud. When my fire subsides, he's gone.

Overwhelming weakness washes over me, either a result of my substantial wound or the amount of power I exerted. I slump to my side, my breathing shallow, and watch as black dots start to float around my vision. Those dots grow in size, as does my dizziness. Dimly, I hear yells in the distance but don't have the presence of mind to call out or even move. I don't know who's approaching, and at this point, I don't care. There's no way the life inside of me survived that mauling. I *failed* to protect it.

That's my last thought before the black dots take over entirely, pulling me into a sea of darkness.

Chapter Forty-Five

Whén I awaken again, it's to a foggy mind and full-body ache, along with a horrible sensation of nausea crawling up my throat. There's a cramp low in my stomach, pulsing and insistent. I swallow down the bile several times before attempting to crack open my eyes. The process is a struggle; it feels like thirty-pound weights have been attached to my eyelids. When I finally manage to open them, light blinds me, forcing me to blink repeatedly while I adjust.

I feel worse than I have...ever. The witches, the treaty, finding out I'm *pregnant,* and running into rogues *right after resolving to protect the pregnancy* flash through my mind.

Once my vision adjusts and the worst of the blurriness has abated, I let my eyes travel over my surroundings. I'm in Camden's room. With great effort, I force myself into a sitting position, feeling like all the energy has been siphoned from me. Tears gather in my eyes as I move an arm—it feels made of rubber—down to my stomach. I lift the nightshirt I'm wearing and see that the only evidence of the dissection I got via shifter claws are faint pink scratch marks. A deep sadness grips me, an abysmal depression that feels like it drags me down with every breath. That sadness is replaced by anxiety when the door to the room opens and Camden steps inside. He has dark circles under his eyes and his hair is disheveled.

"You're awake," he looks at me, eyebrows creased.

"I am," I croak out and then, because there's only one thing on my mind, I ask, "The baby...did it survive the attack?" I suspect the answer, but I need confirmation.

Camden's eyes widen as he stares at me, making me recall that I hadn't yet told him I knew about the pregnancy, about his successful scheme to entrap me.

"You *knew*?" His voice is laced with shock.

That doesn't seem like the greatest concern at the moment; it certainly isn't the most pressing in my mind. Irritation renews within me, but it's overshadowed by a need to have my question answered. "Yes, the witches sensed the pregnancy and informed me. Something neither you nor anyone in this godsforsaken castle had the grace to do. *Did my baby survive?*"

"No," he snaps, his voice dripping with anger. "Claude expended half his power healing you, but no, the wounds were too severe and the child was lost." His eyes bore into me, filled with an anger I've never seen before. "You knew about the pregnancy, and you *left the warded grounds?* Was that your plan all along, to get rid of *our child?*"

I gape at him, shock filling me. He thinks...he thinks I *wanted* to get rid of it? I was given the opportunity and I chose to *protect* it! Following my shock comes a rage so consuming that my vision goes red and my body starts to tremble.

"Are you fucking kidding me?" I hiss, my voice rising in pitch. "You think I *wanted* to lose the baby? Even though you practically *forced* the pregnancy on me and *lied when I asked you if I was at risk,* I was going to keep it! Raise the child, love it, *protect* it! What the *fuck* is wrong with you?"

Camden works his jaw for several moments, looking to the wall. "So you're attempting to convince me that, after finding out about an unwanted pregnancy, you planned to go through with it? *Really,* Sierra?"

"Yes, Camden, fucking really!" I yell. "Your deceit and trickery do not justify putting a stop to the growth of an innocent life. I left warded grounds and went into the forest so I could think after receiving the shock of my life, not to do myself harm. That you could think otherwise means you don't know me at all!"

His eyes cut a path back to me, feeling like they slice through my skin with the ire swirling in them. Not just ire but distrust. Dear gods, he thinks that I wanted to get attacked? That I wandered off the property with the intent of...of aborting my child?

"You *knew* you were pregnant, and yet you left the warded grounds without telling anyone, without properly protecting yourself. You left yourself open to attack, and that attack *cost us our child.*"

I'm stunned that Camden is actually going as far as to blame *me* for what happened. I didn't ask to be targeted by a group of witch-hating shifters; I was half out of my mind with confusion, anger, and *fear*! How could he think this is in any way on me? I chose to keep the life inside me even though I didn't *ask* for it.

Feeling tears well up in my eyes, I ask, "How can you *say* that? *You* were the one who tricked me into this!"

"I gave you freedom, and *this* is what you did with it!" Camden shouts, more enraged than I've ever seen him.

I'm also more enraged than he's ever seen me. "I gave you a chance and you *used it to betray me!*" I yell back.

"Don't act like the damn victim here, Sierra. You wanted me just as much as I wanted you—you tore my clothes off in your haste to fuck me."

That makes me *seething* mad. How *dare* he use that against me? I am *not* the one who knew it would be a blood moon that night, nor was I told the effects that a blood moon would have on me. Nobody in this fucking palace had the goddamn *decency* to inform me of the risks of sleeping with him on a blood moon, especially after he marked me without even asking for my consent; namely, that it was a near-guarantee I'd end up pregnant.

"I trusted you with my body, Camden, and what you did was use it to meet your own ends. Sure, I was under the effects of a blood moon, so yeah, I ripped your clothes because I was *in the moon's thrall.* Something you would've warned me about if you had even an iota of respect for me. Instead, you put me in a situation like that blind, *knowing* the outcome. I may have wanted to fuck you in that moment, but I sure as *shit* did not want you to *bite* me."

"Is *that* why you nearly strangled my cock with the force of your orgasm when I marked you?" he asks snarkily.

The low blows just keep coming. I don't think Camden's yet grasped that his anger can't hold a candle to the force of my rage. Rage that stems from the fact that I was *just* starting to trust him, which he turned around and used against me. On top of that, I just had a *miscarriage!* Instead of supporting me, he has the gall to try to *blame* me. That, even more than his deception, is unforgivable.

"You *motherfucker,*" I seethe, throwing the blankets off and pushing myself out of bed.

Instantly, a wave of overpowering weakness washes over me and my head spins, but I don't let that pull me down; I clutch one of the posts of the bed to stay upright, glaring at Camden.

"You knew what you were doing while I didn't. That means you took advantage of me and of my compassion in the worst *possible* way. Then you swore everyone in this godforsaken castle to silence to meet your own ends. You think *you* have the right to be angry, Camden? We *both* just lost a child, but what you took from me is *much* worse; you stole any possibility of safety or a future for me here with you. You twisted my trust and used it against me. You *used* me." I let out a low, dark laugh, scratchy and filled with hate. "You know, the witches gave me an option to put an end to the pregnancy. I said *no*—"

In a blur of movement so fast I don't even see it coming, Camden lunges at me, taking us both down to the mattress. I let out a shriek and a loud cracking noise precedes the windows in Camden's room all breaking at once, causing glass to shatter to the floor, but Camden doesn't even seem to notice—I barely do either. He straddles my waist, pinning my hips to the bed. He gathers my hands in one of his and pins them above my head before bringing his other hand around my throat, squeezing until my airflow isn't entirely cut off, but my breathing is constricted. I struggle, trying to buck him off and free myself from his grip, but it has no measurable impact; Camden's too strong and too angry for me to dislodge him.

He says in a voice so soft it raises the hairs on my arms, "You committed treason, Sierra. You killed a royal. That's a crime punishable by death regardless of your fucking station."

I gape at him. "I did no such thing! I wanted to keep the baby—"

His hand around my throat tightens as his eyes blaze, and for the first time since I met him, I fear for my life. He's furious enough in this moment that I think he just might kill me. If he does see my actions as killing a royal—which I absolutely did not do, though he seems convinced otherwise—then I am in very dangerous and uncharted territory.

A wolf in a rage is a deadly thing to all around them. Right now, I'm the only person around, and this wolf's rage is directed solely at me. Camden's hand around my throat squeezes so tightly I fear he'll crush my windpipe. Pain blooms from my neck to my chest, and my head starts to pound with a horrible headache that feels like a knife twisting in my skull.

"Be careful," he whispers. "Be very, very careful, Sierra. Right now, I have very little reason to let you live. You're a traitor living under my roof, *and I have no use for traitors.*"

My vision starts to blur as black dots take over, the lack of oxygen starting to take its toll. I struggle, trying to free myself, but Camden doesn't budge, if anything he squeezes harder, and I realize this is a punishment. I'm not sure he knows if he'll kill me, just as I don't know if he'll kill me, and that terror makes me desperate. Unfortunately, that desperation still isn't enough for me to free myself; I'm too weak right now, too depleted. He said Claude had healed me, not Leisel, so I'm probably not *entirely* healed yet, which is why I lack the strength to dislodge him to try to make him *see reason.*

Just when I'm positive Camden is about to end my life, belying everything ever said about a wolf's devotion to his mate, he lets go of my throat. I suck in deep lungful's of air, feeling my throat and chest burn with pain as my eyes water. I cough several times, each one feeling like hot needles scraping across my raw throat and diaphragm.

Camden seems entirely unconcerned as he climbs off of me and stands from the bed, glaring at me. "Get the fuck out," he barks. "You're quarantined to your room until I figure out what to do with you. There'll be guards posted outside, so don't even *think* about escape. You're in deep enough shit with your treason as it is."

Chapter Forty-Six

E ven though I have very little strength left in my body, the rush of fear-fueled adrenaline gives me just enough energy to roll off the bed, clutching my quickly swelling throat, and stumble out of his room. It's clear he won't listen right now; more, it becomes glaringly clear that he doesn't deserve an explanation—he nearly choked me to death when I tried to give him one.

I follow his instructions, forcing one foot in front of another as I pass through the castle corridors, each one seeming exponentially long. The farther I go, the more my throat constricts until it's almost like Camden's hand is still around it, still choking the life out of me. I persevere through the agony, tilting my head to the ceiling to try to clear my airway at least a little, get myself just enough oxygen to get to my room, grab Leisel, and get us away from here. The spell and sigil the witches left me are hidden in my room; I have no option but to use them because I now understand there's no safety for me in this castle and there never was.

After a while, I'm no longer able to stand upright on my own; the dizziness becomes too much, as does the pain, and I resolve to cling to the walls in order to keep going. It doesn't help that the cramps in my stomach are getting worse, making nausea rise in my throat. *Almost there.*

When I'm just one hallway away from my room, I have the extraordinary misfortune of running into Wyatt. Well, perhaps it is a *bit* fortunate because I'm weak enough that even clinging to the walls is barely enough to keep me upright.

Wyatt's striding down the end of the hall opposite me, but when he sees me, he breaks out into a run, alarm overcoming his expression. He reaches my side at the same time that a terrible coughing fit overcomes me, sending me crashing to the carpeted floor. Each cough feels like a knife scraping down my throat and burying itself in my lungs.

Tears stream down my cheeks as I cough and hack, gasping for air, *desperate* to get the fuck away from this monstrous place. That I ever saw a future for myself and Leisel here is *incomprehensible.* Faintly, I feel Wyatt's hand on my shoulder, as well as hear him telling me to breathe, that it'll pass. When a particularly brutal cough ends with warm liquid splattering my hands, I open my eyes, horrified to see blood on my skin and on the carpet beneath me. With great effort, I force myself to swallow several times, wincing at the metallic taste in my mouth, before taking long, deep breaths, each more agonizing than the last. If I have to crawl to my room, I will.

"What happened?" Wyatt says faintly.

I turn my head to the side, taking in his horrified expression and shirt that's splattered with the blood I coughed up because of his *psychotic* older brother.

"Camden," I manage to whisper raggedly.

Wyatt's expression falls, and all the blood drains from his face as his eyes move to my neck, which I imagine is now bruised with the shape of the Alpha's hand. His eyes flick down to my stomach and understanding seems to dawn on him as he deflates. "You lost the baby in the rogue attack." It's not a question but a statement.

My voice thick with both the swelling in my throat and clog of emotions, I say, "Before it could even form into a baby." I'm only capable of whispering, but I'm furious enough with Wyatt for keeping a *very fucking important* piece of knowledge from me to not try to soften the blow. Everything right now makes me furious, but most of all, I am *crushed* at my failure to protect the life that was inside me.

"Why would Cam do this?" Wyatt asks.

"He thought I found a couple of rogues and had them dissect me for *fun*," I whisper-hiss back. The idea of that is so boggling and hurtful, I don't want to even consider it. So I pull on my rage and manage to force out, "You knew about the pregnancy and didn't tell me." Blood drips from my mouth and onto my hands with the words, but I'm beyond caring.

Wyatt lets out a long breath and shakes his head. "Camden is in a rage from the double loss of his father and now his child; he won't be reasonable until he's calmed." After a pause, he goes on, "That fucking asshole threatened to lock me in the dungeons, away from Leisel, if I said anything. He threatened everyone else in the castle with death if they breathed a word."

Good to know that, despite the small technicality of my *being their Alpha female and Queen*, nobody had the balls to oppose Camden for my benefit. Further fuel for my leaving this wretched place, as if his reaction to my miscarriage wasn't enough.

Now that my coughing has stopped and my breathing is as calm as it's going to be until I get healed, I once again try to push myself to a standing position, only to fail and end up tumbling face-first back to the ground. Another coughing fit overcomes me, followed by even more blood and what appears to be cartilage. It feels like my chest and throat are both on fire, slowly swelling more and more until I can barely see. Wyatt puts his hands on my shoulders, wordlessly scooping me into his arms and effortlessly standing.

"Don't try to move. You don't have the strength. I'll carry you." Wyatt's tone brooks no argument, so I don't argue, because he's right; I don't have the strength. I can barely breathe and my head is spinning so much I think I'll pass out at any second. I let him carry me down this hall and the next. I let him open the door to my room and lay me on a bed like I'm a helpless child.

The door to the adjoining room creaks open, and I crane my neck in time to see Leisel slip through the doorway. She takes one look at me and lets out a sound of distress, running across the room to hop on my bed and climbing up next to me.

"What happened?" she cries, her tiny hands hovering above me as if afraid to touch. Tears of horror spill over her eyes and down onto her cheeks, and I can't stop myself from reaching up to wipe them away, grimacing when I leave a smudge of my blood on her cheek.

I know I probably look like I've seen better days, but this reaction from my sister, who's used to seeing me covered in scrapes, bruises, blood, and sweat from my time in the fields, means that Camden must've *really* done a number on me. I'm almost glad there are no mirrors in my room to look into.

"Can you heal her, Leisel?" Wyatt asks. "I think there might be some damage to her windpipe."

Although she's trembling and practically sobbing, Leisel wastes no time putting her hands on my chest. Even that small bit of contact causes a fresh burst of pain, but I force myself to hide it. I won't alarm Leisel or scare her anymore—I feel terrible for letting her see me this way in the first place. I should be able to protect her from sights like this.

A golden glow sparks from her and travels into me, bringing with it a wave of healing warmth that shoots to my throat, chest, and stomach. After a moment, the glow subsides, and for the first time since Camden lost his mind, I draw in a breath that *doesn't* hurt.

At this point, Leisel's more worked up than I am, so I sit up and gather her in my arms, rocking her gently and stroking my hand down her back, no longer caring that I'm leaving blood on her clothes. For a moment, when Camden was strangling me, I thought I might not see her again, so the relief of holding her is overwhelming.

While I feel much better physically, there's a strange feeling in my chest; like a chasm right in the center of it, dark and infectious. After a moment, I realize just what's causing the uncomfortable, prickly sensation; *the bond*. Something's wrong with it—I'm not sure how or why, but it feels different. Darker, weaker somehow. I try to ignore the feeling, focusing instead on the small human curled in my arms, her tears dampening my shirt. I murmur quiet reassurances to her, kissing her head every so often while holding her tight.

After several minutes, Leisel calms, although she remains latched onto me like she never intends to let go. I don't think I'll be ready to let go of her any time soon either.

"It's okay," I whisper in her ear soothingly. Though the pain is gone, the memory of it makes each word feel like sand scraping across my throat. "Everything's okay now. You did so well healing me, sweet girl. Thank you."

Wyatt, from his position standing at the base of the bed, says, "I'm going to go beat the shit out of my brother, hopefully knock some sense into him. Sierra, stay here for now. Once he comes out of his rage and back to himself, Cam should feel terrible, but until then…"

He trails off with a shake of his head before turning and exiting the room, closing the door behind him. I hear his unspoken words hang in the air: *until then, it isn't safe.* What Wyatt doesn't seem to understand is that there is no reality in which I'll ever feel safe here again. I'm ready to crucify myself for giving in to any false sense of security before.

After kissing Leisel on her head, I switch from nurture mode to game mode. I almost hope Wyatt isn't successful in calming Camden down because if the Beta is right in that once Cam calms he'll realize the errors of his ways, that gives me a very small timeframe before he might come looking for me. He's already shown he has no sense of common decency when it comes to me, which means I doubt he'll be smart enough to give me space.

I believe the side I saw of Camden earlier was one of pure rage. I don't think that was *really* him because I felt just how *off* he was in the moment, but...that side exists. Now that its existence has been revealed to me, I can't in good conscience keep myself or my sister around. What happens the next time I do something he sees as treason? I might not live to tell the tale.

I set Leisel aside on the mattress, and tell her, "Go lock your door. Then pack a change of clothes into a bag."

Leisel blinks, wiping the last of her tears away. "We're leaving this place?" She sounds so hopeful; it further cements my decision.

I nod, keeping my voice low in the unlikely case that someone's at the door listening in when I say, "We're going to stay with the witch coven."

Surprisingly, that perks her up a little. With a sniffle, she asks, "With Reyna?" Quietly, she adds, "I like her."

I nod, tucking her hair behind her ear. "Yes, my love, with Reyna and Odelia. They've offered us sanctuary away from here; offered to train us and protect us."

Leisel nods slowly. "They're telling the truth."

She says the statement with such conviction, it gives me pause. "How do you know?"

She shrugs. "I just do. When people lie, they *feel* a little wrong. Reyna wasn't lying when she told me she'd love to have us with her coven and that she'd protect us."

Looks like healing might not be Leisel's only magical ability. She might not be able to articulate it properly, but what she's describing—someone feeling wrong—is a burst of intuitive clarity. One that just might make my little sister a living lie detector.

I nod. "So we'll go, but we need to go now."

Leisel's eyes drop to my neck, and her eyes fill with tears again, even though there's no longer any injury—just the remembrance of one.

She asks tremulously, "Did Camden do this to you?"

"He wasn't himself," I respond.

My response surprises both of us, but me most of all because even after he nearly fucking *killed* me, I'm still defending him. That causes an unprecedented level of self-disgust to well up within me and also tells me that our bond is now a dangerous thing, even in it's oddly damaged state. If it can get me to make verbal excuses for Camden after what he did...

Granted, I know he wasn't himself, I pushed him when he was already grieving, but he absolutely deserved it. There are no excuses to be made for his behavior.

"Get your things, sweet girl," I tell Leisel. "We need to go now before anyone comes looking for us."

Chapter Forty-Seven

Camden

When Wyatt bursts into my room, going as far as to kick down the door to my chambers, I don't bother to acknowledge his presence. Seated in front of the fireplace where I've spent several intimate moments with Sierra—where I can almost still feel her beside me—I continue staring into the guttering embers of the fireplace. Rage clouds my mind, fogging and twisting and warping my thoughts. The half-bottle of liquor I've consumed since she stumbled out of my room isn't helping calm the noise in my head.

I'm groggy and disoriented enough from the potent mix of anger and liquor that I don't even see it coming when Wyatt stops in front of me, pulls me to my feet by my shirt, and punches me in the face so hard I feel my nose splinter before I fall right back down on the couch.

"What the *fuck*—" I snap.

Another blow cuts me off, this time to my cheekbone, the hit hard enough that it causes my head to spin. Wyatt might be the younger one, but he's no less of a warrior than I am—his hits are phenomenally strong, and the effects cause blood to well up in my mouth.

I catch his hand before he can punch me a third time, using it to wrench him on the couch beside me. "What's your godsdamned problem?" I growl.

Wyatt stands and, again, pulls me to my feet by my shirt, apparently not interested in talking. I dodge his next punch but then comes a kick to my chest that sends me hurtling to the ground, gasping in pain as two of my ribs snap under the force.

He circles me, his eyes glaring holes into my skull. Before I can get to my feet or formulate any sort of defense, his boot comes down on my throat with such force I can no longer draw in a proper breath. I roll to my side, coughing and wheezing, thinking of a thousand ways to rip him apart in response to this.

"Hurts, doesn't it?" Wyatt says conversationally, though his tone is infused with the sort of vitriol I've never heard from him "You're a fucking shifter, Camden, and a few good hits have you gasping on the floor like a little bitch. Ask yourself, what would a half-crushed windpipe do to a witch, who doesn't have our strength or healing?"

That gets my attention more than any of his hits. My accelerated healing means it only takes a moment for my ribs, nose, and throat to right themselves, and when they do, I push myself to my feet, demanding, "What are you talking about?"

"The fact that I just had to *carry* a *half-dead* Sierra to get healed by her sister," Wyatt bellows as he grabs me by the hair, directing my line of vision to his chest. I feel myself pale when I see it's covered with splatters of blood and what looks like little bits of cartilage. One sniff tells me that the blood isn't his or mine. It's Sierra's.

Oh, *fuck*. That's when it hits me: I lost it earlier. I let my anger get the best of me until all I could see was a red haze. I already knew I scared Sierra, wrapped my hand around her throat and squeezed, but I didn't even use a quarter of my strength while doing it. I wanted to *scare* her, not do something that resulted in *this.*

When I looked at her, all I could see was the loss of our child, and all I could think was that she might've intentionally put a stop to the pregnancy. If not by doing it herself, then by making reckless moves that caused it to happen.

Now, though, fear takes me by the throat, chasing away any lingering bits of anger at what Sierra did. In this moment, I couldn't care less about my anger; in fact, I can't even remember what I was angry about. Right now, all I can remember is the sheer terror on Sierra's face when I had my hand around her throat. I was too furious to pay it any notice before, but now I understand her pallid pale features weren't just sheet-white from fear, they were sheet-white because I was actually *truly* hurting her.

"You goddamn *idiot,*" Wyatt seethes, shoving me so hard I fall onto the couch again. "I told you this would happen. When you brought me in here, smug as shit after having sex with her during a blood moon, I told you what your actions would result in, but *you didn't believe me.* And then, when things took course *exactly* as I predicted, you responded by *trying to kill your own mate.*"

I stand back up with a growl. "You're the one who put the thought of her aborting the child in my head!"

"And I was obviously wrong!" Wyatt bellows. "Claude told me the state she was found in by castle guards, wounded and bleeding heavily. He also spoke of a rogue the guards detained, who was all too happy to spew information on what exactly occurred. Namely, one of his friends cut her open. How does that sound *anything* like her deciding to end the pregnancy?"

Now that the rage has cleared from my head, I can see how wrong I was to think Sierra could've subjected herself or a potential child to such treatment. Before, however, I wasn't exactly in a rational mindset, and now I understand I must've truly hurt her.

Wyatt lets out a low, angry laugh. "You know, Cam, I never thought I would have the reason to say this, but you are even *worse* than our father. At least he'd have never lain a cruel hand on Mom. You, on the other hand...you don't even have that sliver of honor."

His taunts hurt more than the physical blows, but they're not my focal point right now. At this moment, all I need to know is, "Is she okay?"

Wyatt lets out more of that awful laugh, sounding like he wants to strangle me himself. "Yes, Camden, she's fine now, no thanks to you or me. In fact, I can say with confidence that the *only* reason she's not breathing out of a tube or *dead* is her sister's phenomenal healing capabilities."

That only diffuses the worst of my fear because in this moment I understand the full weight of my actions. I may not have intended to hurt Sierra—I *never* would—but my pain and rage literally blinded me to the point that I almost hurt her *fatally*. If I had held on a moment longer...I don't want to think of what the result could've been.

The fact that she's healed now in no way takes away my alarm because even if she's *physically* okay, the mental strain of being injured by one's mate isn't something that goes away.

One of the few things that can cause a bond between mates to reverse itself and become dormant is just that; serious, potentially deadly harm done from one mate to another. Even *that* isn't my main point of concern because regardless of whether the bond survived, any progress I've made with Sierra will have been undone by that one act.

I realize with no small amount of fear that I haven't felt a single wisp of emotion emanating from Sierra through our bond since I sent her away. I've become so accustomed to getting whispers of her emotions transmitted through our bond that they're background noise most times; now that they're gone, however, I feel like I've been stripped of something integral.

She held me on this very couch when I was sick with grief just a week ago, murmured reassurances to me, and stroked her hands through my hair, and I repaid that by almost killing her—crushing her windpipe if Wyatt's to be believed. While I don't *want* to believe him, her blood staining his shirt is evidence I can't ignore or disregard.

The images of her face beneath me not too long ago, eyes bulging, lips straining, strength waning assault me until it feels like my mind's going to split open under the force of them.

My wolf, who's been dormant under the onslaught of my emotional turmoil these last hours, lays down with one prolonged whine, radiating shame.

"It's hitting you now, isn't it?" Wyatt asks, his tone still so harsh an outsider would be forgiven for thinking we're mortal enemies, not brothers. "The fact that you've fucked both of us over in the most spectacular way possible is finally worming itself into that thick skull of yours. Good. You deserve to rot, Camden. Anyone who could do *that* to the person our moon goddess *entrusted* to them deserves a spot in the worst bowels of the underworld."

Through turmoil that takes up every inch of my being, I manage to gasp, "I need to see her."

Wyatt might have *told* me she's fine, but I need to *see* for myself that she's healed. I stand, only to be shoved back down by Wyatt.

"Abso*lutely* not," he growls. "She sees you right now, she could very well assume you're there to finish what you started. Considering she plays host to a fire that could turn this whole castle to rubble, and the fact that I have no inclination to stop her from taking revenge, you stay the fuck down. You had a chance to handle things your way; it ended up in a clusterfuck of cosmic proportion that probably just cost us our future."

That ignites my anger, although this time, it's not aimed at Sierra; it's aimed at the person who's trying to keep me from her. "You want to try to get between me and my mate?" I snarl.

Wyatt gives me a cruel smile. "I don't have to do that, Cam. You went into a rage and put a chasm the size of a universe between you and her all on your own."

Those words hit their intended mark, causing me to wince. He's right. There's no denying I've done a whole lot of *serious* harm. My anger doesn't give me an excuse to lose control of myself to the point where I would not only blame but *hurt* my own mate. Now, I understand the distance between us is even worse than when we first met, and all Sierra had for me was disdain.

My head whips to the doorway when I hear three sets of footsteps running down my hall, preceding three castle guards, all of whom look red-faced and breathless, stopping in front of my kicked-in door.

In no mood for bullshit, I bark, "What is it?"

The two in front exchange nervous glances, as if afraid to speak. I growl in my most authoritative voice, "Tell me *now*!" My tone has the desired effect as the guards bow their heads in submission.

One of them mumbles, "The Queen and Princess, Your Majesty. We found their rooms empty."

I feel the hair at the back of my neck stand on end as my entire body stiffens. "So where are they?"

Another guard says, "We don't know, sir. We followed the scent of blood to a mirror in the Queen's bathroom where…" He trails off, shifting from foot to foot nervously.

Worst case scenarios flash through my mind and I demand, "Where *what?*"

"Where there was a symbol drawn on the glass in blood. It would appear the Queen used witchcraft, a spell of some sort, to escape," the third finishes.

My blood freezes to ice in my veins as one thought bounces around my skull on repeat: *Sierra's gone.*

End of Book 1

Afterword

Thank you so much for reading A Court of Wolves and Witches. If you enjoyed it, please leave a review. Your support will help me grow as an author, reach new readers, and will mean the world to me.

If you'd like to connect with other readers and me, please join my Facebook group, Rose Gravestone's Readers: https://www.faceboo k.com/groups/397068176443890/

Next up will be the conclusion to Sierra and Camden's duet, title and cover coming soon on my website: https://rosegravestone.com

About the author

Rose likes to write about complex, oftentimes twisted main characters who grow stronger together on whichever journey they take. Watch out for sexy morally grey heroes and sharp, intelligent heroines within settings ranging from fantasy to academia to the underworld of organized crime.

Find Rose Below:

Website: https://rosegravestone.com

Facebook Group: https://www.facebook.com/groups/397068176443890/